Collier's *Junior* Classics

Series Editor
Margaret E. Martignoni

Series Titles	*Volume Editors*
A, B, C: GO!	**Rosemary E. Livsey**
ONCE UPON A TIME	**Elizabeth H. Gross**
MAGIC IN THE AIR	**Mary V. Gaver**
JUST AROUND THE CORNER	**Alice Brooks McGuire**
IN YOUR OWN BACKYARD	**Marian C. Young**
HARVEST OF HOLIDAYS	**Ruth Weeden Stewart**
LEGENDS OF LONG AGO	**Jane Darrah**
ROADS TO GREATNESS	**Louise Galloway**
CALL OF ADVENTURE	**Charlemae Rollins**
GIFTS FROM THE PAST	**Elenora Alexander**

MAgIC
in the air

A completely new selection of outstanding children's stories and poems compiled for enrichment reading by a distinguished editorial board of children's librarians.

Series Editor
MARGARET E. MARTIGNONI
Former Superintendent
Work with Children
Brooklyn Public Library

Editor-in-Chief
DR. LOUIS SHORES
Dean, Library School
Florida State University

Managing Editor
HARRY R. SNOWDEN, JR.

Volume Editor
MARY V. GAVER
Professor
Graduate School of Library Service
Rutgers University

Collier's *Junior* Classics Series

THE CROWELL-COLLIER PUBLISHING COMPANY • NEW YORK

Magic in the Air

Copyright © 1962 by The Crowell-Collier Publishing Company
Library of Congress Catalog Card Number 61-17993
Printed in the United States of America
Thirteenth Printing

Introduction

Collier's Junior Classics Series

We are children only once, and then only for a few brief years. But these are the most impressionable years of a lifetime. Never again will the world and everything in it be so eternally new, so filled with wonder. Never again will physical, mental, spiritual growth be so natural and unavoidable. During these years, habits become ingrained, tastes are developed, personality takes form. The child's whole being is geared toward learning. He instinctively reaches out for truth and, having no prejudices, seizes upon that which is good, just, beautiful. For these reasons, a child deserves what Walter de la Mare has called "only the rarest kind of best."

What do we mean by "best" in a book for children? Best books reflect universal truths with clarity and artistry. Such books reveal that man is essentially good and that life is infinitely worth living. They do not deny the existence of evil, but rather emphasize man's thrilling struggle against evil through faith, courage, and perseverance. They awaken the young reader's imagination, call forth his laughter as well as his tears, help him to understand and to love his fellow man. The reading of such books constitutes a rich heritage of experience which is every child's birthright.

The librarian-editors of *Collier's Junior Classics* have combed the best children's books of the past and present to assemble in a single series a sampling of the finest literature for boys and girls. High standards have been maintained for the art work also, which in most instances has been taken from the original book. No attempt has been made to cover all fields of knowledge or to include factual material for its own sake. The emphasis here is on good literature, chiefly fiction and biography, folk lore and legend, and some poetry. Special attention is given to the American scene and American democratic ideals, but many selections cover other cultures, geographical areas, and historical periods.

The purpose of *Collier's Junior Classics* is to introduce boys and girls to some of the best books ever written for children, to stimulate young readers to seek for themselves the books from which the selections have been drawn as well as other good books of similar appeal, and to encourage children to become discriminating, thoughtful, life-time readers. Author, title, and publisher are given at the foot of the page on which each selection opens. This enables readers to ask for the complete book at a library or bookstore. When necessary, brief introductions set the scene for the selection, while follow-up recommendations, complete with publishers' names, appear at the end of most stories.

Collier's Junior Classics is a series of ten individually indexed volumes. A, B, C: GO! has been lovingly compiled for the youngest, and consists of nursery rhymes, favorite folk tales, best-loved poems, and stories for reading aloud. Four volumes have been assembled for the intermediate group: ONCE UPON A TIME, a wonderous collection of fables, world folk tales, and modern fairy tales; MAGIC IN THE AIR, selections from great masterpieces of fantasy; JUST AROUND THE CORNER, excerpts from warm-hearted stories of other lands; and IN YOUR OWN BACKYARD, selections from stirring books about our own country. Four additional volumes cater to the interests of more mature boys and girls: GIFTS FROM THE PAST, memorable selections from world classics; LEGENDS OF LONG AGO, selections from great myths, epics, and American tall tales; ROADS TO GREATNESS, excerpts from biographies of some of the greatest men and women of the world; and CALL OF ADVENTURE, selections from action and suspense stories of today and yesterday. Finally, and most unusual of all, is the volume entitled HARVEST OF HOLIDAYS, a feast of stories, poems, documents, and factual material about twenty-two American national and religious holidays. Although perhaps of greatest interest to the intermediate group, HARVEST OF HOLIDAYS will intrigue and delight all ages.

The tables of contents for the ten volumes read like an all-time Who's Who of distinguished writers. A brief mention of only a few of these authors would include such names as Lewis Carroll, Kenneth Grahame, Charles Dickens, Mark Twain, Louisa May Alcott, Pearl Buck, Laura Ingalls Wilder, Eleanor Estes, Genevieve Foster, Robert Louis Stevenson, Robert McCloskey, Valenti Angelo, Carl Sandburg, A. A. Milne, Eleanor Farjeon, Elizabeth Enright, and Margaret Wise Brown. Among the illustrators, many of whom are also authors, are to be found the Petershams, the d'Aulaires, Wanda Gág, Louis Slobodkin, Helen Sewell, Lois Lenski, Roger Duvoisin, Maurice Sendak, Kurt Wiese, Marguerite de Angeli, Steele Savage, Howard Pyle, Lynd Ward, James Daugherty, Arthur Rackham, Fritz Kredel, and Gustave Dore.

Collier's Junior Classics is intended primarily for the home, although libraries will find the series valuable for browsing as well as for introducing children to many different books. Because each book is an individual volume, complete with its own index, it can be shelved where the librarian believes it will be most useful to the children.

No pains have been spared to make the individual volumes a series of stepping stones to all that is best in the magic world of children's books.

Margaret E. Martignoni
SERIES EDITOR

Contents

Magic in the Air

There is nothing quite so much fun as wandering through the land of dreams, hobnobbing with Borrowers and genies, stopping now and then for a bite of magic with Alice, motoring with Toad on the open road, or chatting with Winnie-the-Pooh.

In this rare, wonderful world, magic is matter-of-fact, the fantastic is real, and the impossible is easy. The things you do you'll remember forever, and the friends you meet will be with you for life.

"One *can't* believe impossible things," said Alice in *Through the Looking Glass*. If you agree with her, we beg you to consider carefully the White Queen's answer, "I daresay you haven't had much practice. When I was your age, I always did it for half-an-hour a day. Why sometimes I've believed as many as six impossible things before breakfast."

But most of us don't have to practice. We can just stroll casually into the land of dreams where far is near and near is far, where up is down and down is up, where big and small are all the same, and anything you wish is real. So let's set off on a journey to this wonderful land where animals talk, people fly, and all around there's MAGIC IN THE AIR.

MARY V. GAVER
Professor,
Graduate School of Library Service,
Rutgers University

The Adventures of Pinocchio

BY CARLO COLLODI

Illustrations by Anne Heyneman

> *Pinocchio the marionette was a naughty, impudent boy from the moment old Gepetto finished carving him from a block of wood. Vain and boastful, given to telling lies, the little puppet is constantly in trouble. But he really loves his old father very much.*

CAT and Fox and Marionette walked and walked and walked. At last, toward evening, dead tired, they came to the Inn of the Red Lobster.

"Let us stop here for a while," said the Fox, "to eat a bite and rest for a few hours. At midnight we'll start out again, for at dawn to-morrow we must be at the Field of Wonders."

They went into the Inn and all three sat down at the same table. However, not one of them was very hungry.

The poor Cat felt very weak, and he was able to eat only thirty-five mullets with tomato sauce and four portions of tripe with cheese. Moreover, as he was so in need of strength, he had to have four more helpings of butter and cheese.

The Fox, after a great deal of coaxing, tried his best to eat a little. The doctor had put him on a diet, and he had to be satisfied with a small hare dressed with a dozen young and tender spring chickens. After the hare, he ordered some partridges, a few pheasants, a couple of rabbits, and a dozen frogs and lizards. That was all. He felt ill, he said, and could not eat another bite.

From *The Adventures of Pinocchio*, by Carlo Collodi. Illustrations by Anne Heyneman, copyright 1945 by J. B. Lippincott Company.

Pinocchio ate least of all. He asked for a bite of bread and a few nuts and then hardly touched them. The poor fellow, with his mind on the Field of Wonders, was suffering from a gold-piece indigestion.

Supper over, the Fox said to the Innkeeper:

"Give us two good rooms, one for Mr. Pinocchio and the other for me and my friend. Before starting out, we'll take a little nap. Remember to call us at midnight sharp, for we must continue on our journey."

"Yes, sir," answered the Innkeeper, winking in a knowing way at the Fox and the Cat, as if to say, "I understand."

As soon as Pinocchio was in bed, he fell fast asleep and began to dream. He dreamed he was in the middle of a field. The field was full of vines heavy with grapes. The grapes were no other than gold coins which tinkled merrily as they swayed in the wind. They seemed to say, "Let him who wants us take us!"

Just as Pinocchio stretched out his hand to take a handful of them, he was awakened by three loud knocks at the door. It was the Innkeeper who had come to tell him that midnight had struck.

"Are my friends ready?" the Marionette asked him.

"Indeed, yes! They went two hours ago."

"Why in such a hurry?"

"Unfortunately the Cat received a telegram which said that his first-born was suffering from chilblains and was on the point of death. He could not even wait to say good-by to you."

"Did they pay for the supper?"

"How could they do such a thing? Being people of great refinement, they did not want to offend you so deeply as not to allow you the honor of paying the bill."

"Too bad! That offense would have been more than pleasing to me," said Pinocchio, scratching his head.

"Where did my good friends say they would wait for me?" he added.

"At the Field of Wonders, at sunrise to-morrow morning."

Pinocchio paid a gold piece for the three suppers and started on his way toward the field that was to make him a rich man.

He walked on, not knowing where he was going, for it was dark, so dark that not a thing was visible. Round about him, not a leaf stirred. A few bats skimmed his nose now and again and scared him half to death. Once or twice he shouted, "Who goes there?" and the far-away hills echoed back to him, "Who goes there? Who goes there? Who goes. . . ?"

As he walked, Pinocchio noticed a tiny insect glimmering on the trunk of a tree, a small being that glowed with a pale, soft light.

"Who are you?" he asked.

"I am the ghost of the Talking Cricket," answered the

little being in a faint voice that sounded as if it came
from a far-away world.

"What do you want?" asked the Marionette.

"I want to give you a few words of good advice. Return home and give the four gold pieces you have left
to your poor old Father who is weeping because he has
not seen you for many a day."

"To-morrow my Father will be a rich man, for these
four gold pieces will become two thousand."

"Don't listen to those who promise you wealth over-
night, my boy. As a rule they are either fools or swin-
dlers! Listen to me and go home."

"But I want to go on!"

"The hour is late!"

"I want to go on."

"The night is very dark."

"I want to go on."

"The road is dangerous."

"I want to go on."

"Remember that boys who insist on having their own
way, sooner or later come to grief."

"The same nonsense. Good-by, Cricket."

"Good night, Pinocchio, and may Heaven preserve you
from the Assassins."

There was silence for a minute and the light of the Talking Cricket disappeared suddenly, just as if someone had snuffed it out. Once again the road was plunged in darkness.

"Dear, oh, dear! When I come to think of it," said the Marionette to himself, as he once more set out on his journey, "we boys are really very unlucky. Everybody scolds us, everybody gives us advice, everybody warns us. If we were to allow it, everyone would try to be father and mother to us; everyone, even the Talking Cricket. Take me, for example. Just because I would not listen to that bothersome Cricket, who knows how many misfortunes may be awaiting me! Assassins indeed! At least I have never believed in them, nor ever will. To speak sensibly, I think assassins have been invented by fathers and mothers to frighten children who want to run away at night. And then, even if I were to meet them on the road, what matter? I'll just run up to them, and say, 'Well, signori, what do you want? Remember that you can't fool with me! Run along and mind your business.' At such a speech, I can almost see those poor fellows running like the wind. But in case they don't run away, I can always run myself. . ."

Pinocchio was not given time to argue any longer, for he thought he heard a slight rustle among the leaves behind him.

He turned to look and behold, there in the darkness stood two big black shadows, wrapped from head to foot in black sacks. The two figures leaped toward him as softly as if they were ghosts.

"Here they come!" Pinocchio said to himself, and, not knowing where to hide the gold pieces, he stuck all four of them under his tongue.

He tried to run away, but hardly had he taken a step, when he felt his arms grasped and heard two horrible, deep voices say to him: "Your money or your life!"

On account of the gold pieces in his mouth, Pinocchio could not say a word, so he tried with head and hands and body to show, as best he could, that he was only a poor Marionette without a penny in his pocket.

"Come, come, less nonsense, and out with your money!" cried the two thieves in threatening voices.

Once more, Pinocchio's head and hands said, "I haven't a penny."

"Out with that money or you're a dead man," said the taller of the two Assassins.

"Dead man," repeated the other.

"And after having killed you, we will kill your Father also."

"Your Father also!"

"No, no, no, not my Father!" cried Pinocchio, wild with terror; but as he screamed, the gold pieces tinkled together in his mouth.

"Ah, you rascal! So that's the game! You have the money hidden under your tongue. Out with it!"

But Pinocchio was as stubborn as ever.

"Are you deaf? Wait, young man, we'll get it from you in a twinkling!"

One of them grabbed the Marionette by the nose and the other by the chin, and they pulled him unmercifully from side to side in order to make him open his mouth.

All was of no use. The Marionette's lips might have been nailed together. They would not open.

In desperation the smaller of the two Assassins pulled out a long knife from his pocket, and tried to pry Pinocchio's mouth open with it.

Quick as a flash, the Marionette sank his teeth deep into the Assassin's hand, bit it off and spat it out. Fancy his surprise when he saw that it was not a hand, but a cat's paw.

Encouraged by this first victory, he freed himself from the claws of his assailers and, leaping over the bushes along the road, ran swiftly across the fields. His pursuers were after him at once, like two dogs chasing a hare.

After running seven miles or so, Pinocchio was well-nigh exhausted. Seeing himself lost, he climbed up a giant pine tree and sat there to see what he could see. The Assassins tried to climb also, but they slipped and fell.

Far from giving up the chase, this only spurred them on. They gathered a bundle of wood, piled it up at the foot of the pine, and set fire to it. In a twinkling the tree began to sputter and burn like a candle blown by the wind. Pinocchio saw the flames climb higher and higher. Not wishing to end his days as a roasted Marionette, he jumped quickly to the ground and off he went, the Assassins close to him, as before.

Dawn was breaking when, without any warning whatsoever, Pinocchio found his path barred by a deep pool full of water the color of muddy coffee.

What was there to do? With a "One, two, three!" he jumped clear across it. The Assassins jumped also, but not having measured their distance well—splash!!!—they fell right into the middle of the pool. Pinocchio who heard the splash and felt it, too, cried out, laughing, but never stopping in his race:

"A pleasant bath to you, signori!"

He thought they must surely be drowned and turned his head to see. But there were the two somber figures still following him, though their black sacks were drenched and dripping with water.

As he ran, the Marionette felt more and more certain that he would have to give himself up into the hands of his pursuers. Suddenly he saw a little cottage gleaming white as the snow among the trees of the forest.

"If I have enough breath left with which to reach that little house, I may be saved," he said to himself.

Not waiting another moment, he darted swiftly through the woods, the Assassins still after him.

After a hard race of almost an hour, tired and out of breath, Pinocchio finally reached the door of the cottage and knocked. No one answered.

He knocked again, harder than before, for behind him he heard the steps and the labored breathing of his persecutors.

The same silence followed.

As knocking was of no use, Pinocchio, in despair, began to kick and bang against the door, as if he wanted to break it. At the noise, a window opened and a lovely maiden looked out. She had azure hair and a face white as wax. Her eyes were closed and her hands crossed on her breast. With a voice so weak that it hardly could be heard, she whispered:

"No one lives in this house. Everyone is dead."

"Won't you, at least, open the door for me?" cried Pinocchio in a beseeching voice.

"I also am dead."

"Dead? What are you doing at the window, then?"

"I am waiting for the coffin to take me away."

After these words, the little girl disappeared and the window closed without a sound.

"Oh, Lovely Maiden with Azure Hair," cried Pinocchio, "open, I beg of you. Take pity on a poor boy who is being chased by two Assass—"

He did not finish, for two powerful hands grasped him by the neck and the same two horrible voices growled threateningly: "Now we have you!"

The Marionette, seeing death dancing before him, trembled so hard that the joints of his legs rattled and the coins tinkled under his tongue.

"Well," the Assassins asked, "will you open your mouth now or not? Ah! You do not answer? Very well, this time you shall open it."

Taking out two long, sharp knives, they struck two heavy blows on the Marionette's back.

Happily for him, Pinocchio was made of very hard wood and the knives broke into a thousand pieces. The Assassins looked at each other in dismay, holding the handles of the knives in their hands.

"I understand," said one of them to the other, "there is nothing left to do now but to hang him."

"To hang him," repeated the other.

They tied Pinocchio's hands behind his shoulders and slipped the noose around his neck. Throwing the rope over the high limb of a giant oak tree, they pulled till the poor Marionette hung far up in space.

Satisfied with their work, they sat on the grass waiting for Pinocchio to give his last gasp. But after three hours the Marionette's eyes were still open, his mouth still shut, and his legs kicked harder than ever.

Tired of waiting, the Assassins called to him mockingly:

"Good-by till to-morrow. When we return in the morning, we hope you'll be polite enough to let us find you dead and gone and with your mouth wide open." With these words they went.

A few minutes went by and then a wild wind started to blow. As it shrieked and moaned, the poor little sufferer was blown to and fro like the hammer of a bell. The rocking made him seasick and the noose, becoming tighter and tighter, choked him. Little by little a film covered his eyes.

Death was creeping nearer and nearer, and the Marionette still hoped for some good soul to come to his rescue, but no one appeared. As he was about to die, he thought of his poor old Father, and hardly conscious of what he was saying, murmured to himself:

"Oh, Father, dear Father! If you were only here!"

These were his last words. He closed his eyes, opened his mouth, stretched out his legs, and hung there, as if he were dead.

If the poor Marionette had dangled there much longer, all hope would have been lost. Luckily for him, the Lovely Maiden with Azure Hair once again looked out of her window. Filled with pity at the sight of the poor little fellow being knocked helplessly about by the wind, she clapped her hands sharply together three times.

At the signal, a loud whirr of wings in quick flight was heard and a large Falcon came and settled itself on the window ledge.

"What do you command, my charming Fairy?" asked the Falcon, bending his beak in deep reverence (for it must be known that, after all, the Lovely Maiden with Azure Hair was none other than a very kind Fairy who had lived, for more than a thousand years, in the vicinity of the forest).

"Do you see that Marionette hanging from the limb of that giant oak tree?"

"I see him."

"Very well. Fly immediately to him. With your strong beak, break the knot which holds him tied, take him down, and lay him softly on the grass at the foot of the oak."

The Falcon flew away and after two minutes returned, saying:

"I have done what you have commanded."

"How did you find him? Alive or dead?"

"At first glance, I thought he was dead. But I found I was wrong, for as soon as I loosened the knot around his neck, he gave a long sigh and mumbled with a faint voice, 'Now I feel better!' "

The Fairy clapped her hands twice. A magnificent Poodle appeared, walking on his hind legs just like a man. He was dressed in court livery. A tricorn trimmed with gold lace was set at a rakish angle over a wig of white curls that dropped down to his waist. He wore a jaunty coat of chocolate-colored velvet, with diamond buttons, and with two huge pockets which were always filled with bones, dropped there at dinner by his loving mistress. Breeches of crimson velvet, silk stockings, and low, silver-buckled slippers completed his costume. His tail was encased in a blue silk covering, which was to protect it from the rain.

"Come, Medoro," said the Fairy to him. "Get my best coach ready and set out toward the forest. On reaching the oak tree, you will find a poor, half-dead Marionette stretched out on the grass. Lift him up tenderly, place him on the silken cushions of the coach, and bring him here to me."

The Poodle, to show that he understood, wagged his silk-covered tail two or three times and set off at a quick pace.

In a few minutes, a lovely little coach, made of glass, with lining as soft as whipped cream and chocolate pudding, and stuffed with canary feathers, pulled out of the stable. It was drawn by one hundred pairs of white mice, and the Poodle sat on the coachman's seat and snapped his whip gayly in the air, as if he were a real coachman in a hurry to get to his destination.

In a quarter of an hour the coach was back. The Fairy, who was waiting at the door of the house, lifted the poor little Marionette in her arms, took him to a dainty room with mother-of-pearl walls, put him to bed, and sent immediately for the most famous doctors of the neighborhood to come to her.

One after another the doctors came, a Crow, an Owl, and a Talking Cricket.

"I should like to know, signori," said the Fairy, turning to the three doctors gathered about Pinocchio's bed, "I should like to know if this poor Marionette is dead or alive."

At this invitation, the Crow stepped out and felt Pinocchio's pulse, his nose, his little toe. Then he solemnly pronounced the following words:

"To my mind this Marionette is dead and gone; but if, by any evil chance, he were not, then that would be a sure sign that he is still alive!"

"I am sorry," said the Owl, "to have to contradict the Crow, my famous friend and colleague. To my mind this Marionette is alive; but if, by any evil chance, he were not, then that would be a sure sign that he is wholly dead!"

"And do you hold any opinion?" the Fairy asked the Talking Cricket.

"I say that a wise doctor, when he does not know what he is talking about, should know enough to keep his mouth shut. However, that Marionette is not a stranger to me. I have known him a long time!"

Pinocchio, who until then had been very quiet, shuddered so hard that the bed shook.

"That Marionette," continued the Talking Cricket, "is a rascal of the worst kind."

Pinocchio opened his eyes and closed them again.

"He is rude, lazy, a runaway."

Pinocchio hid his face under the sheets.

"That Marionette is a disobedient son who is breaking his Father's heart!"

Long shuddering sobs were heard, cries, and deep sighs. Think how surprised everyone was when, on raising the sheets, they discovered Pinocchio half melted in tears!

"When the dead weep, they are beginning to recover," said the Crow solemnly.

"I am sorry to contradict my famous friend and colleague," said the Owl, "but as far as I'm concerned, I think that when the dead weep, it means they do not want to die."

As soon as the three doctors had left the room, the Fairy went to Pinocchio's bed and, touching him on the forehead, noticed that he was burning with fever.

She took a glass of water, put a white powder into it, and, handing it to the Marionette, said lovingly to him:

"Drink this, and in a few days you'll be up and well."

Pinocchio looked at the glass, made a wry face, and asked in a whining voice: "Is it sweet or bitter?"

"It is bitter, but it is good for you."

"If it is bitter, I don't want it."

"Drink it!"

"I don't like anything bitter."

"Drink it and I'll give you a lump of sugar to take the bitter taste from your mouth."

"Where's the sugar?"

"Here it is," said the Fairy, taking a lump from a golden sugar bowl.

"I want the sugar first, then I'll drink the bitter water."

"Do you promise?"

"Yes."

The Fairy gave him the sugar and Pinocchio, after chewing and swallowing it in a twinkling, said, smacking his lips:

"If only sugar were medicine! I should take it every day."

"Now keep your promise and drink these few drops of water. They'll be good for you."

Pinocchio took the glass in both hands and stuck his nose into it. He lifted it to his mouth and once more stuck his nose into it.

"It is too bitter, much too bitter! I can't drink it."

"How do you know, when you haven't even tasted it?"

"I can imagine it. I smell it. I want another lump of sugar, then I'll drink it."

The Fairy, with all the patience of a good mother, gave him more sugar and again handed him the glass.

"I can't drink it like that," the Marionette said, making more wry faces.

"Why?"

"Because that feather pillow on my feet bothers me."

The Fairy took away the pillow.

"It's no use. I can't drink it even now."

"What's the matter now?"

"I don't like the way that door looks. It's half open."

The Fairy closed the door.

"I won't drink it," cried Pinocchio, bursting out crying. "I won't drink this awful water. I won't. I won't! No, no, no, no!"

"My boy, you'll be sorry."

"I don't care."

"You are very sick."

"I don't care."

"In a few hours the fever will take you far away to another world."

"I don't care."

"Aren't you afraid of death?"

"Not a bit. I'd rather die than drink that awful medicine."

At that moment, the door of the room flew open and in came four Rabbits as black as ink, carrying a small black coffin on their shoulders.

"What do you want from me?" asked Pinocchio.

"We have come for you," said the largest Rabbit.

"For me? But I'm not dead yet!"

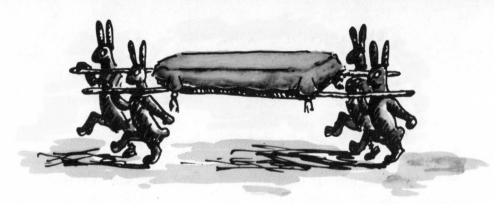

"No, not dead yet; but you will be in a few moments since you have refused to take the medicine which would have made you well."

"Oh, Fairy, my Fairy," the Marionette cried out, "give me that glass! Quick, please! I do not want to die! No, no, not yet—not yet!"

And holding the glass with his two hands, he swallowed the medicine at one gulp.

"Well," said the four Rabbits, "this time we have made the trip for nothing."

And turning on their heels, they marched solemnly out of the room, carrying their little black coffin and muttering and grumbling between their teeth.

In a twinkling, Pinocchio felt fine. With one leap he was out of bed and into his clothes.

The Fairy, seeing him run and jump around the room gay as a bird on wing, said to him:

"My medicine was good for you, after all, wasn't it?"

"Good indeed! It has given me new life."

"Why, then, did I have to beg you so hard to make you drink it?"

"I'm a boy, you see, and all boys hate medicine more than they do sickness."

"What a shame! Boys ought to know, after all, that medicine, taken in time, can save them from much pain and even from death."

"Next time I won't have to be begged so hard. I'll remember those black Rabbits with the black coffin on their shoulders and I'll take the glass and pouf!—down it will go!"

"Come here now and tell me how it came about that you found yourself in the hands of the Assassins."

"It happened that Fire Eater gave me five gold pieces to give to my Father, but on the way, I met a Fox and a Cat, who asked me, 'Do you want the five pieces to become two thousand?' And I said, 'Yes.' And they said, 'Come with us to the Field of Wonders.' And I said, 'Let's go.' Then they said, 'Let us stop at the Inn of the Red Lobster for dinner and after midnight we'll set out again.' We ate and went to sleep. When I awoke they were gone and I started out in the darkness all alone. On the road I met two Assassins dressed in black coal sacks, who said to me, 'Your money or your life!' and I said, 'I haven't any money'; for, you see, I had put the money under my tongue. One of them tried to put his hand in my mouth and I bit it off and spat it out; but it wasn't a hand; it was a cat's paw. And they ran after me and I ran and ran, till at last they caught me and tied my neck with a rope and hanged me to a tree, saying, 'To-morrow we'll come back for you and you'll be dead and your mouth will be open, and then we'll take the gold pieces that you have hidden under your tongue.' "

"Where are the gold pieces now?" the Fairy asked.

"I lost them," answered Pinocchio, but he told a lie, for he had them in his pocket.

As he spoke, his nose, long though it was, became at least two inches longer.

"And where did you lose them?"

"In the wood near by."

At this second lie, his nose grew a few more inches.

"If you lost them in the near-by wood," said the Fairy, "we'll look for them and find them, for everything that is lost there is always found."

"Ah, now I remember," replied the Marionette, becom-

ing more and more confused. "I did not lose the gold pieces, but I swallowed them when I drank the medicine."

At this third lie, his nose became longer than ever, so long that he could not even turn around. If he turned to the right, he knocked it against the bed or into the windowpanes; if he turned to the left, he struck the walls or the door; if he raised it a bit, he almost put the Fairy's eyes out.

The Fairy sat looking at him and laughing.

"Why do you laugh?" the Marionette asked her, worried now at the sight of his growing nose.

"I am laughing at your lies."

"How do you know I am lying?"

"Lies, my boy, are known in a moment. There are two kinds of lies, lies with short legs and lies with long noses. Yours, just now, happen to have long noses."

Pinocchio, not knowing where to hide his shame, tried to escape from the room, but his nose had become so long that he could not get it out of the door.

Crying as if his heart would break, the Marionette mourned for hours over the length of his nose. No matter how he tried, it would not go through the door. The Fairy showed no pity toward him, as she was trying to teach him a good lesson, so that he would stop telling lies, the worst habit any boy may acquire. But when she saw him, pale with fright and with his eyes half out of his head from terror, she began to feel sorry for him and clapped her hands together. A thousand woodpeckers flew in through the window and settled themselves on Pinocchio's nose. They pecked and pecked so hard at that enormous nose that in a few moments, it was the same size as before.

"How good you are, my Fairy," said Pinocchio, drying his eyes, "and how much I love you!"

The Adventures of Pinocchio, by Carlo Collodi (whose real name was Carlo Lorenzini), was first published in 1881. Attractive editions are now issued by Macmillan (New Children's Classics), with illustrations after Attilio Mussino; by Grosset (Illustrated Junior Library), illustrated by Fritz Kredel; and by Lippincott (the Lippincott Classics), illustrated by Anne Heyneman.

Alice's Adventures In Wonderland

BY LEWIS CARROLL

Illustrations by Sir John Tenniel

It seems something of a miracle that the serious Oxford mathematics lecturer, Charles Lutwidge Dodgson, could have written the exquisite fantasy Alice's Adventures in Wonderland, even though he did try to protect his anonymity with the pseudonym "Lewis Carroll." Most readers today know that the story was invented for a little girl named Alice Liddell, and that it was told to her out loud one summer's day before it was written down on paper.

1: Down the Rabbit-Hole

ALICE was beginning to get very tired of sitting by her sister on the bank, and of having nothing to do: once or twice she had peeped into the book her sister was reading, but it had no pictures or conversations in it, "and what is the use of a book," thought Alice, "without pictures or conversations?"

So she was considering, in her own mind (as well as she could, for the hot day made her feel very sleepy and stupid), whether the pleasure of making a daisy-chain would be worth the trouble of getting up and picking the daisies, when suddenly a white rabbit with pink eyes ran close by her.

There was nothing so *very* remarkable in that; nor did Alice think it so *very* much out of the way to hear the Rabbit say to itself, "Oh dear! Oh dear! I shall be too late!" (when she thought it over afterwards, it occurred to her that she ought to have wondered at this, but at the time it all seemed quite natural); but when the Rabbit actually *took a watch out of its waistcoat-pocket*, and looked at it, and then hurried on, Alice started to her feet, for it flashed across her mind that she had never before seen a rabbit with either a waistcoat-pocket, or a watch to take out of it, and, burning with curiosity, she ran across the field after it, and was just in time to see it pop down a large rabbit-hole under the hedge.

In another moment down went Alice after it, never once considering how in the world she was to get out again.

The rabbit-hole went straight on like a tunnel for some way, and then dipped suddenly down, so suddenly that Alice had not a moment to think about stopping herself before she found herself falling down what seemed to be a very deep well.

Either the well was very deep, or she fell very slowly, for she had plenty of time as she went down to look about her, and to wonder what was going to happen next. First, she tried to look down and make out what she was coming to, but it was too dark to see anything: then she looked at the sides of the well, and noticed that they were filled with cupboards and bookshelves: here and there she saw maps and pictures hung upon pegs. She took down a jar from one of the shelves as she passed: it was labeled "ORANGE MARMALADE," but to her great disappointment it was empty: she did not like to drop the jar, for fear of killing somebody underneath, so managed to put it into one of the cupboards as she fell past it.

"Well!" thought Alice to herself, "after such a fall as
this, I shall think nothing of tumbling downstairs! How
brave they'll all think me at home! Why, I wouldn't say
anything about it, even if I fell off the top of the house!"
(Which was very likely true.)

Down, down, down. Would the fall *never* come to an
end? "I wonder how many miles I've fallen by this time?"
she said aloud. "I must be getting somewhere near the
centre of the earth. Let me see: that would be four thousand miles down, I think—" (for, you see, Alice had learnt
several things of this sort in her lessons in the schoolroom, and though this was not a *very* good opportunity
for showing off her knowledge, as there was no one to
listen to her, still it was good practice to say it over)
"—yes, that's about the right distance—but then I wonder
what Latitude or Longitude I've got to?" (Alice had not
the slightest idea what Latitude was, or Longitude either,
but she thought they were nice grand words to say.)

Presently she began again. "I wonder if I shall fall
right *through* the earth! How funny it'll seem to come
out among the people that walk with their heads downwards! The Antipathies, I think—" (she was rather glad
there *was* no one listening, this time, as it didn't sound at
all the right word) "—but I shall have to ask them what
the name of the country is, you know. Please, Ma'am, is
this New Zealand or Australia?" (and she tried to curt-
sey as she spoke—fancy *curtseying* as you're falling
through the air! Do you think you could manage it?)
"And what an ignorant little girl she'll think me for asking! No, it'll never do to ask: perhaps I shall see it written
up somewhere."

Down, down, down. There was nothing else to do, so
Alice soon began talking again. "Dinah'll miss me very
much to-night, I should think!" (Dinah was the cat.) "I
hope they'll remember her saucer of milk at tea-time.
Dinah, my dear! I wish you were down here with me!

There are no mice in the air, I'm afraid, but you might catch a bat, and that's very like a mouse, you know. But do cats eat bats, I wonder?" And here Alice began to get rather sleepy, and went on saying to herself, in a dreamy sort of way, "Do cats eat bats? Do cats eat bats?" and sometimes, "Do bats eat cats?" for, you see, as she couldn't answer either question, it didn't much matter which way she put it. She felt that she was dozing off, and had just begun to dream that she was walking hand in hand with Dinah, and was saying to her, very earnestly, "Now, Dinah, tell me the truth: did you ever eat a bat?" when suddenly, thump! thump! down she came upon a heap of sticks and dry leaves, and the fall was over.

Alice was not a bit hurt, and she jumped up on to her feet in a moment: she looked up, but it was all dark overhead; before her was another long passage, and the White Rabbit was still in sight, hurrying down it. There was not a moment to be lost: away went Alice like the wind, and was just in time to hear it say, as it turned a corner, "Oh my ears and whiskers, how late it's getting!" She was close behind it when she turned the corner, but the Rabbit was no longer to be seen: she found herself in a long, low hall, which was lit up by a row of lamps hanging from the roof.

There were doors all round the hall, but they were all locked; and when Alice had been all the way down one side and up the other, trying every door, she walked sadly down the middle, wondering how she was ever to get out again.

Suddenly she came upon a little three-legged

table, all made of solid glass: there was nothing on it but
a tiny golden key, and Alice's first idea was that this might
belong to one of the doors of the hall; but, alas! either the
locks were too large, or the key was too small, but at any
rate it would not open any of them. However, on the
second time round, she came upon a low curtain she had
not noticed before, and behind it was a little door about
fifteen inches high: she tried the little golden key in the
lock, and to her great delight it fitted!

Alice opened the door and found that it led into a small
passage, not much larger than a rat-hole: she knelt down
and looked along the passage into the loveliest garden
you ever saw. How she longed to get out of that dark hall,
and wander about among those beds of bright flowers
and those cool fountains, but she could not even get her
head through the doorway; "and even if my head *would*
go through," thought poor Alice, "it would be of very
little use without my shoulders. Oh, how I wish I could
shut up like a telescope! I think I could, if I only knew
how to begin." For, you see, so many out-of-the-way
things had happened lately that Alice had begun to think
that very few things indeed were really impossible.

There seemed to be no use in
waiting by the little door, so she
went back to the table, half hoping she might find another key
on it, or at any rate a book of
rules for shutting people up like
telescopes: this time she found
a little bottle on it ("which certainly was not here before," said
Alice), and tied round the neck
of the bottle was a paper label
with the words "DRINK ME"
beautifully printed on it in
large letters.

It was all very well to say "Drink me," but the wise little Alice was not going to do *that* in a hurry. "No, I'll look first," she said, "and see whether it's marked *'poison'* or not;" for she had read several nice little stories about children who had got burnt, and eaten up by wild beasts, and other unpleasant things, all because they *would* not remember the simple rules their friends had taught them: such as, that a red-hot poker will burn you if you hold it too long; and that, if you cut your finger *very* deeply with a knife, it usually bleeds; and she had never forgotten that, if you drink much from a bottle marked "poison," it is almost certain to disagree with you, sooner or later.

However, this bottle was *not* marked "poison," so Alice ventured to taste it, and, finding it very nice (it had, in fact, a sort of mixed flavour of cherry-tart, custard, pine-apple, roast turkey, toffy, and hot buttered toast), she very soon finished it off.

"What a curious feeling!" said Alice. "I must be shutting up like a telescope!"

And so it was indeed: she was now only ten inches high, and her face brightened up at the thought that she was now the right size for going through the little door into that lovely garden. First, however, she waited for a few minutes to see if she was going to shrink any further: she felt a little nervous about this; "for it might end, you know," said Alice to herself, "in my going out altogether, like a candle. I wonder what I should be like then?" And she tried to fancy what the flame of a candle looks like after the candle is blown out, for she could not remember ever having seen such a thing.

After a while, finding that nothing more happened, she decided on going into the garden at once; but, alas for poor Alice! when she got to the door, she found she had forgotten the little golden key, and when she went back to the table for it, she found she could not possibly reach it: she could see it quite plainly through the glass, and she tried her best to climb up one of the legs of the table, but it was too slippery; and when she had tired herself out with trying, the poor little thing sat down and cried.

"Come, there's no use in crying like that!" said Alice to herself, rather sharply. "I advise you to leave off this minute!" She generally gave herself very good advice (though she very seldom followed it), and sometimes she scolded herself so severely as to bring tears into her eyes; and once she remembered trying to box her own ears for having cheated herself in a game of croquet she was playing against herself, for this curious child was very fond of pretending to be two people. "But it's no use now," thought poor Alice, "to pretend to be two people! Why, there's hardly enough of me left to make *one* respectable person!"

Soon her eye fell on a little glass box that was lying under the table: she opened it, and found in it a very small cake, on which the words "EAT ME" were beautifully marked in currants. "Well, I'll eat it," said Alice, "and if it makes me grow larger, I can reach the key; and if it makes me grow smaller, I can creep under the door: so either way I'll get into the garden, and I don't care which happens!"

She ate a little bit, and said anxiously to herself, "Which way? Which way?" holding her hand on the top of her head to feel which way it was growing, and she was quite surprised to find that she remained the same size. To be sure, this is what generally happens when one eats cake; but Alice had got so much into the way of expecting nothing but out-of-the-way things to happen, that it seemed quite dull and stupid for life to go on in the common way.

So she set to work, and very soon finished off the cake.

2: The Pool of Tears

"Curiouser and curiouser!" cried Alice (she was so much surprised, that for the moment she quite forgot how to speak good English). "Now I'm opening out like the largest telescope that ever was! Good-bye, feet!" (for when she looked down at her feet, they seemed to be almost out of sight, they were getting so far off). "Oh, my poor little feet, I wonder who will put on your shoes and stockings for you now, dears? I'm sure *I* shan't be able! I shall be a great deal too far off to trouble myself about you: you must manage the best way you can—but I must be kind to them," thought Alice, "or perhaps they won't walk the way I want to go! Let me see: I'll give them a new pair of boots every Christmas."

And she went on planning to herself how she would manage it. "They must go by the carrier," she thought; "and how funny it'll seem, sending presents to one's own feet! And how odd the directions will look!

Alice's Right Foot, Esq.
Hearthrug,
near the Fender,
(with Alice's love).

Oh dear, what nonsense I'm talking!"

Just at this moment her head struck against the roof of the hall: in fact she was now rather more than nine feet high, and she at once took up the little golden key and hurried off to the garden door.

Poor Alice! It was as much as she could do, lying down on one side, to look through into the garden with one eye;

but to get through was more hopeless than ever: she sat down and began to cry again.

"You ought to be ashamed of yourself," said Alice, "a great girl like you," (she might well say this), "to go on crying in this way! Stop this moment, I tell you!" But she went on all the same, shedding gallons of tears, until

there was a large pool all round her, about four inches deep and reaching half down the hall.

After a time she heard a little pattering of feet in the distance, and she hastily dried her eyes to see what was coming. It was the White Rabbit returning, splendidly dressed, with a pair of white kid gloves in one hand and a large fan in the other: he came trotting along in a great hurry, muttering to himself as he came, "Oh! The Duchess, the Duchess! Oh! Won't she be savage if I've kept her waiting!" Alice felt so desperate that she was ready to ask help of anyone: so, when the Rabbit came near her she began, in a low, timid voice, "If you please, Sir—" The Rabbit started violently, dropped the white kid gloves and the fan, and skurried away into the darkness as hard as he could go.

Alice took up the fan and gloves, and, as the hall was very hot, she kept fanning herself all the time she went on talking. "Dear, dear! How queer everything is to-day! And yesterday things went on just as usual. I wonder if I've been changed in the night? Let me think: *was* I the same when I got up this morning? I almost think I can remember feeling a little different. But if I'm not the same, the next question is, 'Who in the world am I?' Ah, *that's* the great puzzle!" And she began thinking over all the children she knew that were of the same age as herself, to see if she could have been changed for any of them.

"I'm sure I'm not Ada," she said, "for her hair goes in such long ringlets, and mine doesn't go in ringlets at all; and I'm sure I can't be Mabel, for I know all sorts of things, and she, oh! she knows such a very little! Besides, *she's* she, and *I'm* I, and—oh dear, how puzzling it all is! I'll try if I know all the things I used to know. Let me see: four times five is twelve, and four times six is thirteen, and four times seven is—oh dear! I shall never get to twenty at that rate! However, the Multiplication Table doesn't signify: let's try Geography. London is the capital of Paris, and Paris is the capital of Rome, and Rome—no, *that's* all wrong, I'm certain! I must have been changed for Mabel! I'll try and say *'How doth the little—',*" and she crossed her hands on her lap, as if she were saying lessons, and began to repeat it, but her voice sounded hoarse and strange, and the words did not come the same as they used to do:—

> *"How doth the little crocodile*
> *Improve his shining tail,*
> *And pour the waters of the Nile*
> *On every golden scale!*
>
> *"How cheerfully he seems to grin,*
> *How neatly spreads his claws,*
> *And welcomes little fishes in*
> *With gently smiling jaws!"*

"I'm sure those are not the right words," said poor Alice, and her eyes filled with tears again as she went on, "I must be Mabel after all, and I shall have to go and live in that poky little house, and have next to no toys to play with, and oh! ever so many lessons to learn! No, I've made up my mind about it: if I'm Mabel, I'll stay down here! It'll be no use their putting their heads down and saying, 'Come up again, dear!' I shall only look up and say, 'Who am I, then? Tell me that first, and then, if I like being that person, I'll come up: if not, I'll stay down here till I'm somebody else'—but, oh dear!" cried Alice, with a sudden burst of tears, "I do wish they *would* put their heads down! I am so *very* tired of being all alone here!"

As she said this, she looked down at her hands, and was surprised to see that she had put on one of the Rabbit's little white kid gloves while she was talking. "How *can* I have done that?" she thought. "I must be growing small again." She got up and went to the table to measure herself by it, and found that, as nearly as she could guess, she was now about two feet high, and was going on shrinking rapidly: she soon found out that the cause of this was the fan she was holding, and she dropped it hastily, just in time to save herself from shrinking away altogether.

"That *was* a narrow escape!" said Alice, a good deal frightened at the sudden change, but very glad to find herself still in existence. "And now for the garden!" And she ran with all speed back to the little door; but, alas!

the little door was shut again, and the little golden key was lying on the glass table as before, "and things are worse than ever," thought the poor child, "for I never was so small as this before, never! And I declare it's too bad, that it is!"

As she said these words her foot slipped, and in another moment, splash! she was up to her chin in salt water. Her first idea was that she had somehow fallen into the sea, "and in that case I can go back by railway," she said to herself. (Alice had been to the seaside once in her life, and had come to the general conclusion that, wherever you go to on the English coast, you find a number of bathing machines in the sea, some children digging in the sand with wooden spades, then a row of lodging-houses, and behind them a railway station.) However, she soon made out that she was in the pool of tears which she had wept when she was nine feet high.

"I wish I hadn't cried so much!" said Alice, as she swam about, trying to find her way out. "I shall be punished for it now, I suppose, by being drowned in my own tears! That *will* be a queer thing, to be sure! However, everything is queer to-day."

Just then she heard something splashing about in the pool a little way off, and she swam nearer to make out what it was: at first she thought it must be a walrus or hippopotamus, but then she remembered how small she was now, and she soon made out that it was only a mouse, that had slipped in like herself.

"Would it be of any use, now," thought Alice, "to speak to this mouse? Everything is so out-of-the-way down here, that I should think very likely it can talk: at any rate, there's no harm in trying." So she began: "O Mouse, do you know the way out of this pool? I am very tired of swimming about here, O Mouse!" (Alice thought this must be the right way of speaking to a mouse: she had never done such a thing before, but she remembered having seen, in her brother's Latin Grammar, "A mouse —of a mouse—to a mouse—a mouse—O mouse!" The mouse looked at her rather inquisitively, and seemed to her to wink with one of its little eyes, but it said nothing.

"Perhaps it doesn't understand English," thought Alice. "I daresay it's a French mouse, come over with William the Conqueror." (For, with all her knowledge of history, Alice had no very clear notion how long ago anything had happened.) So she began again: "Où est ma chatte?" which was the first sentence in her French lesson-book. The Mouse gave a sudden leap out of the water, and seemed to quiver all over with fright. "Oh, I beg your pardon!" cried Alice hastily, afraid she had hurt the poor animal's feelings. "I quite forgot you didn't like cats."

"Not like cats!" cried the Mouse in a shrill, passionate voice. "Would *you* like cats, if you were me?"

"Well, perhaps not," said Alice in a soothing tone: "don't be angry about it. And yet I wish I could show you our cat Dinah. I think you'd take a fancy to cats, if you could only see her. She is such a dear quiet thing," Alice went on, half to herself, as she swam lazily about in the pool, "and she sits purring so nicely by the fire, licking her paws and washing her face—and she is such a nice soft thing to nurse—and she's such a capital one for catching mice—oh, I beg your pardon!" cried Alice again, for this time the Mouse was bristling all over, and she felt certain it must be really offended. "We won't talk about her any more, if you'd rather not."

"We, indeed!" cried the Mouse, who was trembling down to the end of his tail. "As if *I* would talk on such a subject! Our family always *hated* cats: nasty, low, vulgar things! Don't let me hear the name again!"

"I won't indeed!" said Alice, in a great hurry to change
the subject of conversation. "Are you—are you fond—
of—of dogs?" The Mouse did not answer, so Alice went
on eagerly: "There is such a nice little dog near our
house I should like to show you! A little bright-eyed

terrier, you know, with oh, such long curly brown hair!
And it'll fetch things when you throw them, and it'll sit
up and beg for its dinner, and all sorts of things—I can't
remember half of them—and it belongs to a farmer, you
know, and he says it's so useful, it's worth a hundred
pounds! He says it kills all the rats and—oh dear!" cried
Alice in a sorrowful tone. "I'm afraid I've offended it
again!" For the Mouse was swimming away from her as
hard as it could go, and making quite a commotion in the
pool as it went.

So she called softly after it, "Mouse dear! Do come
back again, and we won't talk about cats, or dogs either,
if you don't like them!" When the Mouse heard this, it
turned round and swam slowly back to her: its face was
quite pale (with passion, Alice thought), and it said, in a
low, trembling voice, "Let us get to the shore, and then
I'll tell you my history, and you'll understand why it is I
hate cats and dogs."

It was high time to go, for the pool was getting quite

crowded with the birds and animals that had fallen into it: there was a Duck and a Dodo, a Lory and an Eaglet, and several other curious creatures. Alice led the way, and the whole party swam to the shore.

3: A Caucus-Race and a Long Tale

They were indeed a queer-looking party that assembled on the bank—the birds with draggled feathers, the animals with their fur clinging close to them, and all dripping wet, cross, and uncomfortable.

The first question of course was, how to get dry again: they had a consultation about this, and after a few minutes it seemed quite natural to Alice to find herself talking familiarly with them, as if she had known them all her life. Indeed, she had quite a long argument with the Lory, who at last turned sulky, and would only say, "I am older than you, and must know better." And this Alice would not allow, without knowing how old it was, and, as the Lory positively refused to tell its age, there was no more to be said.

At last the Mouse, who seemed to be a person of some authority among them, called out, "Sit down, all of you, and listen to me! *I'll* soon make you dry enough!" They all sat down at once, in a large ring, with the Mouse in the middle. Alice kept her eyes anxiously fixed on it, for she felt sure she would catch a bad cold if she did not get dry very soon.

"Ahem!" said the Mouse with an important air. "Are you all ready? This is the driest thing I know. Silence all round, if you please! 'William the Conqueror, whose cause was favoured by the pope, was soon submitted to by the English, who wanted leaders, and had been of late much accustomed to usurpation and conquest. Edwin and Morcar, the earls of Mercia and Northumbria—'"

"Ugh!" said the Lory, with a shiver.

"I beg your pardon!" said the Mouse, frowning, but very politely. "Did you speak?"

"Not I!" said the Lory, hastily.

"I thought you did," said the Mouse. "I proceed. 'Edwin and Morcar, the earls of Mercia and Northumbria, declared for him; and even Stigand, the patriotic archbishop of Canterbury, found it advisable—'"

"Found *what?*" said the Duck.

"Found *it,*" the Mouse replied rather crossly: "of course you know what 'it' means."

"I know what 'it' means well enough, when *I* find a thing," said the Duck: "it's generally a frog, or a worm. The question is, what did the archbishop find?"

The Mouse did not notice this question, but hurriedly went on, " '—found it advisable to go with Edgar Atheling to meet William and offer him the crown. William's conduct at first was moderate. But the insolence of his Normans—' How are you getting on now, my dear?" it continued, turning to Alice as it spoke.

"As wet as ever," said Alice in a melancholy tone: "it doesn't seem to dry me at all."

"In that case," said the Dodo solemnly, rising to its feet, "I move that the meeting adjourn, for the immediate adoption of more energetic remedies—"

"Speak English!" said the Eaglet. "I don't know the meaning of half those long words, and, what's more, I don't believe you do either!" And the Eaglet bent down its head to hide a smile: some of the other birds tittered audibly.

"What I was going to say," said the Dodo in an offended tone, "was, that the best thing to get us dry would be a Caucus-race."

"What *is* a Caucus-race?" said Alice; not that she much wanted to know, but the Dodo had paused as if it thought that *somebody* ought to speak, and no one else seemed inclined to say anything.

"Why," said the Dodo, "the best way to explain it is to do it." (And, as you might like to try the thing yourself, some winter day, I will tell you how the Dodo managed it.)

First it marked out a race-course, in a sort of circle, ("the exact shape doesn't matter," it said) and then all the party were placed along the course, here and there. There was no "One, two, three, and away!" but they began running when they liked, and left off when they liked, so that it was not easy to know when the race was over. However, when they had been running half an hour or so, and were quite dry again, the Dodo suddenly called out, "The race is over!" and they all crowded round it, panting, and asking, "But who has won?"

This question the Dodo could not answer without a great deal of thought, and it stood for a long time with one finger pressed upon its forehead (the position in which you usually see Shakespeare, in the pictures of him), while the rest waited in silence. At last the Dodo said, "*Everybody* has won, and *all* must have prizes."

"But who is to give the prizes?" quite a chorus of voices asked.

"Why, *she*, of course," said the Dodo, pointing to Alice with one finger; and the whole party at once crowded round her, calling out in a confused way, "Prizes! Prizes!"

Alice had no idea what to do, and in despair she put her hand into her pocket, and pulled out a box of comfits (luckily the salt water had not got into it), and handed them round as prizes. There was exactly one a-piece, all round.

"But she must have a prize herself, you know," said the Mouse.

"Of course," the Dodo replied very gravely. "What else

have you got in your pocket?" he went on, turning to Alice.

"Only a thimble," said Alice sadly.

"Hand it over here," said the Dodo.

Then they all crowded round her once more while the Dodo solemnly presented the thimble, saying, "We beg your acceptance of this elegant thimble;" and, when it had finished this short speech, they all cheered.

Alice thought the whole thing very absurd, but they all looked so grave that she did not dare to laugh; and, as she could not think of anything to say, she simply bowed, and took the thimble, looking as solemn as she could.

The next thing was to eat the comfits: this caused some noise and confusion, as the large birds complained that they could not taste theirs, and the small ones choked and had to be patted on the back. However, it was over at last, and they sat down again in a ring, and begged the Mouse to tell them something more.

"You promised to tell me your history, you know," said Alice, "and why it is you hate—C and D," she added in a whisper, half afraid that it would be offended again.

"Mine is a long and a sad tale!" said the Mouse, turning
to Alice, and sighing.

"It *is* a long tail, certainly," said Alice, looking down with
wonder at the Mouse's tail; "but why do you call it sad?"
And she kept on puzzling about it while the Mouse was
speaking, so that her idea of the tale was something like
this:—

<pre>
        "Fury said to
           a mouse, That
              he met in the
                 house, 'Let
                    us both go
                       to law: I
                        will prose-
                         cute you.—
                         Come, I'll
                         take no de-
                         nial; We
                       must have
                     a trial:
                   For really
                  this morn-
                 ing I've
                nothing
               to do.'
               Said the
                mouse to
                  the cur,
                    'Such a
                      trial, dear
                        sir. With
                          no jury
                            or judge,
                               would
                              be wast-
                              ing our
                             breath.'
                           'I'll be
                          judge,
                         I'll be
                        jury,'
                       said
                      cun-
                      ning
                      old
                      Fury;
                       'I'll
                        try
                         the
                          whole
                           cause,
                            and
                           con-
                          demn
                         you to
                    death.' "
</pre>

"You are not attending!" said the Mouse to Alice, severely. "What are you thinking of?"

"I beg your pardon," said Alice very humbly: "you had got to the fifth bend, I think?"

"I had *not!*" cried the Mouse, sharply and very angrily.

"A knot!" said Alice, always ready to make herself useful, and looking anxiously about her. "Oh, do let me help to undo it!"

"I shall do nothing of the sort," said the Mouse, getting up and walking away. "You insult me by talking such nonsense!"

"I didn't mean it!" pleaded poor Alice. "But you're so easily offended, you know!"

The Mouse only growled in reply.

"Please come back, and finish your story!" Alice called after it. And the others all joined in chorus, "Yes, please do!" But the Mouse only shook its head impatiently, and walked a little quicker.

"What a pity it wouldn't stay!" sighed the Lory, as soon as it was quite out of sight. And an old Crab took the opportunity of saying to her daughter, "Ah, my dear! Let this be a lesson to you never to lose *your* temper!"

"Hold your tongue, Ma!" said the young Crab, a little snappishly. "You're enough to try the patience of an oyster."

"I wish I had our Dinah here, I know I do!" said Alice aloud, addressing nobody in particular. "*She'd* soon fetch it back!"

"And who is Dinah, if I might venture to ask the question?" said the Lory.

Alice replied eagerly, for she was always ready to talk about her pet: "Dinah's our cat. And she's such a capital one for catching mice, you can't think! And oh, I wish you could see her after the birds! Why, she'll eat a little bird as soon as look at it!"

This speech caused a remarkable sensation among the

party. Some of the birds hurried off at once: one old
Magpie began wrapping itself up very carefully, remarking, "I really must be getting home: the night-air doesn't
suit my throat!" And a Canary called out in a trembling
voice to its children, "Come away, my dears! It's high
time you were all in bed!" On various pretexts they all
moved off, and Alice was soon left alone.

"I wish I hadn't mentioned Dinah!" she said to herself
in a melancholy tone. "Nobody seems to like her, down
here, and I'm sure she's the best cat in the world! Oh,
my dear Dinah! I wonder if I shall ever see you any
more!" And here poor Alice began to cry again, for she
felt very lonely and low-spirited. In a little while, however, she again heard a little pattering of footsteps in the
distance, and she looked up eagerly, half hoping that the
Mouse had changed his mind, and was coming back to
finish his story.

4: *The Rabbit Sends in a Little Bill*

It was the White Rabbit, trotting slowly back again,
and looking anxiously about as it went, as if it had lost
something; and she heard it muttering to itself, "The
Duchess! The Duchess! Oh my dear paws! Oh my fur
and whiskers! She'll get me executed, as sure as ferrets
are ferrets! Where *can* I have dropped them, I wonder?"
Alice guessed in a moment that it was looking for the fan
and the pair of white kid gloves, and she very good-
naturedly began hunting about for them, but they were
nowhere to be seen—everything seemed to have changed
since her swim in the pool; and the great hall, with the
glass table and the little door, had vanished completely.

Very soon the Rabbit noticed Alice, as she went hunting about, and called out to her, in an angry tone, "Why,
Mary Ann, what *are* you doing out here? Run home this

moment, and fetch me a pair of gloves and a fan! Quick, now!" And Alice was so much frightened that she ran off at once in the direction it pointed to, without trying to explain the mistake that it had made.

"He took me for his housemaid," she said to herself as she ran. "How surprised he'll be when he finds out who I am! But I'd better take him his fan and gloves—that is, if I can find them." As she said this, she came upon a neat little house, on the door of which was a bright brass plate with the name "W. RABBIT" engraved upon it. She went in without knocking, and hurried upstairs, in great fear lest she should meet the real Mary Ann, and be turned out of the house before she had found the fan and gloves.

"How queer it seems," Alice said to herself, "to be going messages for a rabbit! I suppose Dinah'll be sending me on messages next!" And she began fancying the sort of thing that would happen: " 'Miss Alice! Come here directly, and get ready for your walk!' 'Coming in a minute, Nurse! But I've got to watch this mouse hole till Dinah comes back, and see that the mouse doesn't get out.' Only I don't think," Alice went on, "that they'd let Dinah stop in the house if it began ordering people about like that!"

By this time she had found her way into a tidy little room with a table in the window, and on it (as she had hoped) a fan and two or three pairs of tiny white kid gloves: she took up the fan and a pair of the gloves, and was just going to leave the room, when her eye fell upon a little bottle that stood near the looking-glass. There was no label this time with the words "DRINK ME," but nevertheless she uncorked it and put it to her lips. "I know *something* interesting is sure to happen," she said to herself, "whenever I eat or drink anything; so I'll just see what this bottle does. I do hope it'll make me grow large again, for really I'm quite tired of being such a tiny little thing!"

It did so indeed, and much sooner than she had expected: before she had drunk half the bottle, she found her head pressing against the ceiling, and had to stoop to save her neck from being broken. She hastily put down the bottle, saying to herself, "That's quite enough—I hope I shan't grow any more—As it is, I can't get out at the door—I do wish I hadn't drunk quite so much!"

Alas! It was too late to wish that! She went on growing, and growing, and very soon had to kneel down on the floor: in another minute there was not even room for this, and she tried the effect of lying down with one elbow

against the door, and the other arm curled round her head. Still she went on growing, and, as a last resource, she put one arm out of the window and one foot up the chimney, and said to herself, "Now I can do no more, whatever happens. What *will* become of me?"

Luckily for Alice, the little magic bottle had now had its full effect, and she grew no larger: still it was very uncomfortable, and, as there seemed to be no sort of chance of her ever getting out of the room again, no wonder she felt unhappy.

"It was much pleasanter at home," thought poor Alice, "when one wasn't always growing larger and smaller, and being ordered about by mice and rabbits. I almost wish I hadn't gone down that rabbit-hole—and yet—and yet—it's rather curious, you know, this sort of life! I do wonder what *can* have happened to me! When I used to read fairy tales, I fancied that kind of thing never happened, and now here I am in the middle of one! There ought to be a book written about me, that there ought! And when I grow up, I'll write one—but I'm grown up now," she added in a sorrowful tone: "at least there's no room to grow up any more *here*."

"But then," thought Alice, "shall I *never* get any older than I am now? That'll be a comfort, one way—never to be an old woman—but then—always to have lessons to learn! Oh, I shouldn't like *that*!"

"Oh, you foolish Alice!" she answered herself. "How can you learn lessons in here? Why, there's hardly room for *you*, and no room at all for any lesson-books!"

And so she went on, taking first one side and then the other, and making quite a conversation of it altogether; but after a few minutes she heard a voice outside, and stopped to listen.

"Mary Ann! Mary Ann!" said the voice, "fetch me my gloves this moment!" Then came a little pattering of feet on the stairs. Alice knew it was the Rabbit coming to look for her, and she trembled till she shook the house, quite forgetting that she was now about a thousand times as large as the Rabbit, and had no reason to be afraid of it.

Presently the Rabbit came up to the door, and tried to open it; but, as the door opened inwards, and Alice's elbow was pressed hard against it, that attempt proved a failure. Alice heard it say to itself, "Then I'll go round and get in at the window."

"*That* you won't!" thought Alice, and, after waiting till she fancied she heard the Rabbit just under the window, she suddenly spread out her hand, and made a snatch in the air. She did not get hold of anything, but she heard a little shriek and a fall, and a crash of broken glass, from which she concluded that it was just possible it had fallen into a cucumber-frame, or something of the sort.

Next came an angry voice —the Rabbit's—"Pat! Pat! Where are you?" And then a voice she had never heard before, "Sure then I'm here! Digging for apples, yer honour!"

"Digging for apples, indeed!" said the Rabbit angrily. "Here! Come and help me out of *this!*" (Sounds of more broken glass.)

"Now tell me, Pat, what's that in the window?"

"Sure, it's an arm, yer honour!" (He pronounced it "arrum.")

"An arm, you goose! Who ever saw one that size? Why, it fills the whole window!"

"Sure, it does, yer honour: but it's an arm for all that."

"Well, it's got no business there, at any rate: go and take it away!"

There was a long silence after this, and Alice could only hear whispers now and then, such as, "Sure, I don't like it, yer honour, at all, at all!" "Do as I tell you, you coward!" and at last she spread out her hand again, and made another snatch in the air. This time there were *two* little shrieks, and more sounds of broken glass. "What a number of cucumber-frames there must be!" thought Alice. "I wonder what they'll do next! As for pulling me out of the window, I only wish they *could!* I'm sure *I* don't want to stay in here any longer!"

She waited for some time without hearing anything

more: at last came a rumbling of little cart-wheels, and the sound of a good many voices all talking together: she made out the words: "Where's the other ladder?—Why, I hadn't to bring but one. Bill's got the other—Bill! Fetch it here, lad!—Here, put 'em up at this corner—No, tie 'em together first—they don't reach half high enough yet—Oh, they'll do well enough. Don't be particular—Here, Bill! Catch hold of this rope—Will the roof bear?—Mind that loose slate—Oh, it's coming down! Heads below!" (a loud crash) "Now, who did that?—It was Bill, I fancy—Who's to go down the chimney?—Nay, *I* shan't! *You* do it!—*That* I won't then!—Bill's got to go down—Here, Bill! The master says you've got to go down the chimney!"

"Oh, so Bill's got to come down the chimney, has he?" said Alice to herself. "Why, they seem to put everything upon Bill! I wouldn't be in Bill's place for a good deal, this fireplace is narrow, to be sure; but I *think* I can kick a little!"

She drew her foot as far down the chimney as she could, and waited till she heard a little animal (she couldn't guess of what sort it was) scratching and scrambling about in the chimney close above her: then, saying to herself, "This is Bill," she gave one sharp kick, and waited to see what would happen next.

The first thing she heard was a general chorus of "There goes Bill!" then the Rabbit's voice alone—"Catch him, you by the hedge!" then silence, and then another confusion of voices: "Hold up his head—Brandy now—Don't choke him—How was it, old fellow? What happened to you? Tell us all about it!"

Last came a little feeble, squeaking voice ("That's Bill," thought Alice), "Well, I hardly know—No more, thank ye; I'm better now—but I'm a deal too flustered to tell you—all I know is, something comes at me like a Jack-in-the-box, and up I goes like a sky-rocket!"

"So you did, old fellow!" said the others.

"We must burn the house down!" said the Rabbit's voice. And Alice called out, as loud as she could, "If you do, I'll set Dinah at you!"

There was a dead silence instantly, and Alice thought to herself, "I wonder what they *will* do next! If they had any sense, they'd take the roof off." After a minute or two, they began moving about again, and Alice heard the Rabbit say, "A barrowful will do, to begin with."

"A barrowful of *what?*" thought Alice. But she had not long to doubt, for the next moment a shower of little pebbles came rattling in at the window, and some of them hit her in the face. "I'll put a stop to this," she said to herself, and shouted out, "You'd better not do that again!" which produced another dead silence.

Alice noticed, with some surprise, that the pebbles were all turning into little cakes as they lay on the floor, and a bright idea came into her head. "If I eat one of these cakes," she thought, "it's sure to make *some* change in my size; and, as it can't possibly make me larger, it must make me smaller, I suppose."

So she swallowed one of the cakes, and was delighted to find that she began shrinking directly. As soon as she was small enough to get through the door, she ran out of the house, and found quite a crowd of little animals and birds waiting outside. The poor little Lizard, Bill, was in the middle, being held up by two guinea-pigs, who were giving it something out of a bottle. They all made a rush at Alice the moment she appeared; but she ran off as hard as she could, and soon found herself safe in a thick wood.

"The first thing I've got to do," said Alice to herself, as she wandered about in the wood, "is to grow to my right size again; and the second thing is to find my way into that lovely garden. I think that will be the best plan."

It sounded an excellent plan, no doubt, and very neatly and simply arranged: the only difficulty was, that she had not the smallest idea how to set about it; and, while she was peering about anxiously among the trees, a little sharp bark just over her head made her look up in a great hurry.

An enormous puppy was looking down at her with large round eyes, and feebly stretching out one paw, trying to touch her. "Poor little thing!" said Alice, in a coaxing tone, and she tried hard to whistle to it; but she was terribly frightened all the time at the thought that it

might be hungry, in which case it would be very likely
to eat her up in spite of all her coaxing.

Hardly knowing what she did, she picked up a little
bit of stick, and held it out to the puppy: whereupon the
puppy jumped into the air off all its feet at once, with a
yelp of delight, and rushed at the stick, and made believe
to worry it: then Alice dodged behind a great thistle, to
keep herself from being run over; and, the moment she
appeared on the other side, the puppy made another rush
at the stick, and tumbled head over heels in its hurry to
get hold of it: then Alice, thinking it was very like having
a game of play with a cart-horse, and expecting every
moment to be trampled under its feet, ran round the
thistle again: then the puppy began a series of short
charges at the stick, running a very little way forwards
each time and a long way back, and barking hoarsely all
the while, till at last it sat down a good way off, panting,
with its tongue hanging out of its mouth, and its great
eyes half shut.

This seemed to Alice a good opportunity for making
her escape: so she set off at once, and ran till she was
quite tired and out of breath, and till the puppy's bark
sounded quite faint in the distance.

"And yet what a dear little puppy it was!" said Alice,
as she leant against a buttercup to rest herself, and
fanned herself with one of the leaves. "I should have
liked teaching it tricks very much, if—if I'd only been the
right size to do it! Oh dear! I'd nearly forgotten that I've
got to grow up again! Let me see—how *is* it to be managed? I suppose I ought to eat or drink something or
other; but the great question is 'What?'"

The great question certainly was "What?" Alice looked
all round her at the flowers and the blades of grass, but
she could not see anything that looked like the right
thing to eat or drink under the circumstances. There was
a large mushroom growing near her, about the same

height as herself; and when she had looked under it, and on both sides of it, and behind it, it occurred to her that she might as well look and see what was on top of it.

She stretched herself up on tiptoe, and peeped over the edge of the mushroom, and her eyes immediately met those of a large blue caterpillar, that was sitting on the top, with its arms folded, quietly smoking a long hookah, and taking not the smallest notice of her or of anything else.

5. *Advice from a Caterpillar*

The Caterpillar and Alice looked at each other for some time in silence: at last the Caterpillar took the hookah out of its mouth, and addressed her in a languid, sleepy voice.

"Who are *you?*" said the Caterpillar.

This was not an encouraging opening for a conversation. Alice replied, rather shyly, "I—I hardly know, Sir, just at present—at least I know who I *was* when I got up this morning, but I think I must have changed several times since then."

"What do you mean by that?" said the Caterpillar, sternly. "Explain yourself!"

"I can't explain *myself*, I'm afraid, sir," said Alice, "because I'm not myself, you see."

"I don't see," said the Caterpillar.

"I'm afraid I can't put it more clearly," Alice replied, very politely, "for I can't understand it myself to begin with; and being so many different sizes in a day is very confusing."

"It isn't," said the Caterpillar.

"Well, perhaps you haven't found it so yet," said Alice; "but when you have to turn into a chrysalis—you will some day, you know—and then after that into a butterfly,

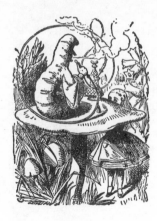

I should think you'll feel it a little queer, won't you?"

"Not a bit," said the Caterpillar.

"Well, perhaps *your* feelings may be different," said Alice: "all I know is, it would feel very queer to *me*."

"You!" said the Caterpillar contemptuously. "Who are *you?*"

Which brought them back again to the beginning of the conversation. Alice felt a little irritated at the Caterpillar's making such *very* short remarks, and she drew herself up and said, very gravely, "I think you ought to tell me who *you* are, first."

"Why?" said the Caterpillar.

Here was another puzzling question; and, as Alice could not think of any good reason, and the Caterpillar seemed to be in a *very* unpleasant state of mind, she turned away.

"Come back!" the Caterpillar called after her. "I've something important to say!"

This sounded promising, certainly. Alice turned and came back again.

"Keep your temper," said the Caterpillar.

"Is that all?" said Alice, swallowing down her anger as well as she could.

"No," said the Caterpillar.

Alice thought she might as well wait, as she had nothing else to do, and perhaps after all it might tell her something worth hearing. For some minutes it puffed away without speaking; but at last it unfolded its arms, took the hookah out of its mouth again, and said, "So you think you're changed, do you?"

"I'm afraid I am, Sir," said Alice. "I can't remember things as I used—and I don't keep the same size for ten minutes together!"

"Can't remember *what* things?" said the Caterpillar.

"Well, I've tried to say '*How doth the little busy bee,*' but it all came different!" Alice replied in a very melancholy voice.

"Repeat '*You are old, Father William,*'" said the Caterpillar.

Alice folded her hands, and began:—

"You are old, Father William," the young man said,
    "And your hair has become very white;
And yet you incessantly stand on your head—
    Do you think, at your age, it is right?"

"In my youth," Father William replied to his son,
    "I feared it might injure the brain;
But, now that I'm perfectly sure I have none,
    Why, I do it again and again."

"You are old," said the youth, "as I mentioned before,
    And have grown most uncommonly fat;
Yet you turned a back-somersault in at the door—
    Pray, what is the reason of that?"

"In my youth," said the sage, as he shook his grey locks,
    "I kept all my limbs very supple
By the use of this ointment—one shilling the box—
    Allow me to sell you a couple."

"You are old," said the youth, "and your jaws are too weak
    For anything tougher than suet;
Yet you finished the goose, with the bones and the beak—
    Pray, how did you manage to do it?"

"In my youth," said his father, "I took to the law,
*   And argued each case with my wife;*
And the muscular strength, which it gave to my jaw
*   Has lasted the rest of my life."*

"You are old," said the youth, "one would hardly suppose
*   That your eye was as steady as ever;*
Yet you balanced an eel on the end of your nose—
*   What made you so awfully clever?"*

"I have answered three questions, and that is enough,"
*   Said his father. "Don't give yourself airs!*
Do you think I can listen all day to such stuff?
*   Be off, or I'll kick you down-stairs!"*

"That is not said right," said the Caterpillar.

"Not *quite* right, I'm afraid," said Alice, timidly: "some of the words have got altered."

"It is wrong from beginning to end," said the Caterpillar, decidedly; and there was silence for some minutes.

The Caterpillar was the first to speak.

"What size do you want to be?" it asked.

"Oh, I'm not particular as to size," Alice hastily replied;
"only one doesn't like changing so often, you know."

"I *don't* know," said the Caterpillar.

Alice said nothing: she had never been so much con-
tradicted in all her life before, and she felt that she was
losing her temper.

"Are you content now?" said the Caterpillar.

"Well, I should like to be a *little* larger, Sir, if you
wouldn't mind," said Alice: "three inches is such a
wretched height to be."

"It is a very good height indeed!" said the Caterpillar
angrily, rearing itself upright as it spoke (it was exactly
three inches high).

"But I'm not used to it!" pleaded poor Alice in a piteous
tone. And she thought to herself, "I wish the creatures
wouldn't be so easily offended!"

"You'll get used to it in time," said the Caterpillar; and
it put the hookah into its mouth, and began smoking
again.

This time Alice waited patiently until it chose to speak
again. In a minute or two the Caterpillar took the hookah
out of its mouth, and yawned once or twice, and shook
itself. Then it got down off the mushroom, and crawled
away into the grass, merely remarking as it went, "One
side will make you grow taller, and the other side will
make you grow shorter."

"One side of *what*? The other side of *what*?" thought
Alice to herself.

"Of the mushroom," said the Caterpillar, just as if she
had asked it aloud; and in another moment it was out of
sight.

Alice remained looking thoughtfully at the mushroom
for a minute, trying to make out which were the two sides
of it; and, as it was perfectly round, she found this a very
difficult question. However, at last she stretched her arms

round it as far as they would go, and broke off a bit of the edge with each hand.

"And now which is which?" she said to herself, and nibbled a little of the right-hand bit to try the effect. The next moment she felt a violent blow underneath her chin: it had struck her foot!

She was a good deal frightened by this very sudden change, but she felt that there was no time to be lost, as she was shrinking rapidly: so she set to work at once to eat some of the other bit. Her chin was pressed so closely against her foot, that there was hardly room to open her mouth; but she did it at last, and managed to swallow a morsel of the left-hand bit.

"Come, my head's free at last!" said Alice in a tone of delight, which changed into alarm in another moment, when she found that her shoulders were nowhere to be found: all she could see, when she looked down, was an immense length of neck, which seemed to rise like a stalk out of a sea of green leaves that lay far below her.

"What *can* all that green stuff be?" said Alice. "And where *have* my shoulders got to? And oh, my poor hands, how is it I can't see you?" She was moving them about as she spoke, but no result seemed to follow, except a little shaking among the distant green leaves.

As there seemed to be no chance of getting her hands up to her head, she tried to get her head down to *them,* and was delighted to find that her neck would bend about easily in any direction, like a serpent. She had just succeeded in curving it down into a graceful zigzag, and was going to dive in among the leaves, which she found to be nothing but the tops of the trees under which she had been wandering, when a sharp hiss made her draw back in a hurry: a large pigeon had flown into her face, and was beating her violently with its wings.

"Serpent!" screamed the Pigeon.

"I'm *not* a serpent!" said Alice indignantly. "Let me alone!"

"Serpent, I say again!" repeated the Pigeon, but in a more subdued tone, and added, with a kind of sob, "I've tried every way, but nothing seems to suit them!"

"I haven't the least idea what you're talking about," said Alice.

"I've tried the roots of trees, and I've tried banks, and I've tried hedges," the Pigeon went on, without attending to her; "but those serpents! There's no pleasing them!"

Alice was more and more puzzled, but she thought there was no use in saying anything more till the Pigeon had finished.

"As if it wasn't trouble enough hatching the eggs," said the Pigeon; "but I must be on the look-out for serpents, night and day! Why, I haven't had a wink of sleep these three weeks!"

"I'm very sorry you've been annoyed," said Alice, who was beginning to see its meaning.

"And just as I'd taken the highest tree in the wood," continued the Pigeon, raising its voice to a shriek, "and just as I was thinking I should be free of them at last, they must needs come wriggling down from the sky! Ugh! Serpent!"

"But I'm *not* a serpent, I tell you!" said Alice. "I'm a— I'm a—"

"Well! *What* are you?" said the Pigeon. "I can see you're trying to invent something!"

"I—I'm a little girl," said Alice, rather doubtfully, as she remembered the number of changes she had gone through that day.

"A likely story indeed!" said the Pigeon, in a tone of the deepest contempt. "I've seen a good many little girls

in my time, but never *one* with such a neck as that!
No, no! You're a serpent; and there's no use denying it.
I suppose·you'll be telling me next that you never tasted
an egg!"

"I *have* tasted eggs, certainly," said Alice, who was a
very truthful child; "but little girls eat eggs quite as
much as serpents do, you know."

"I don't believe it," said the Pigeon; "but if they do,
why then they're a kind of serpent, that's all I can say."

This was such a new idea to Alice, that she was quite
silent for a minute or two, which gave the Pigeon the
opportunity of adding, "You're looking for my eggs, I
know *that* well enough; and what does it matter to me
whether you're a little girl or a serpent?"

"It matters a good deal to *me*," said Alice hastily; "but
I'm not looking for eggs, as it happens; and, if I was, I
shouldn't want *yours*: I don't like them raw."

"Well, be off, then!" said the Pigeon in a sulky tone, as
it settled down again into its nest. Alice crouched down
among the trees as well as she could, for her neck kept
getting entangled among the branches, and every now
and then she had to stop and untwist it. After a while she
remembered that she still held the pieces of mushroom
in her hands, and she set to work very carefully, nibbling
first at one and then at the other, and growing sometimes
taller, and sometimes shorter, until she had succeeded in
bringing herself down to her usual height.

It was so long since she had been anything near the
right size, that it felt quite strange at first; but she got
used to it in a few minutes, and began talking to herself,
as usual, "Come, there's half my plan done now! How
puzzling all these changes are! I'm never sure what I'm
going to be, from one minute to another! However, I've
got back to my right size: the next thing is, to get into
that beautiful garden—how *is* that to be done, I wonder?"
As she said this, she came suddenly upon an open place,

with a little house in it about four feet high. "Whoever lives there," thought Alice, "it'll never do to come upon them *this* size: why, I should frighten them out of their wits!" So she began nibbling at the right-hand bit again, and did not venture to go near the house till she had brought herself down to nine inches high.

6: *Pig and Pepper*

For a minute or two she stood looking at the house, and wondering what to do next, when suddenly a footman in livery came running out of the wood—(she considered him to be a footman because he was in livery: otherwise, judging by his face only, she would have called him a fish)—and rapped loudly at the door with his knuckles. It was opened by another footman in livery, with a round face, and large eyes like a frog; and both footmen, Alice noticed, had powdered hair that curled all over their heads. She felt very curious to know what it was all about, and crept a little way out of the wood to listen.

The Fish-Footman began by producing from under his arm a great letter, nearly as large as himself, and this he handed over to the other, saying, in a solemn tone, "For the Duchess. An invitation from the Queen to play croquet." The Frog-Footman repeated, in the same solemn tone, only changing the order of the words a little, "From the Queen. An invitation for the Duchess to play croquet."

Then they both bowed low, and their curls got entangled together.

Alice laughed so much at this, that she had to run back into the wood for fear of their hearing her; and, when she next peeped out, the Fish-Footman was gone, and the other was sitting on the ground near the door, staring stupidly up into the sky.

Alice went timidly up to the door, and knocked.

"There's no sort of use in knocking," said the Footman, "and that for two reasons. First, because I'm on the same side of the door as you are; secondly because they're making such a noise inside, no one could possibly hear you." And certainly there *was* a most extraordinary noise going on within—a constant howling and sneezing, and every now and then a great crash, as if a dish or kettle had been broken to pieces.

"Please, then," said Alice, "how am I to get in?"

"There might be some sense in your knocking," the Footman went on, without attending to her, "if we had the door between us. For instance, if you were *inside*, you might knock, and I could let you out, you know." He was looking up into the sky all the time he was speaking, and this Alice thought decidedly uncivil. "But perhaps he can't help it," she said to herself; "his eyes are so *very* nearly at the top of his head. But at any rate he might answer questions—How am I to get in?" she repeated, aloud.

"I shall sit here," the Footman remarked, "till tomorrow—"

At this moment the door of the house opened, and a large plate came skimming out, straight at the Footman's head: it just grazed his nose, and broke to pieces against one of the trees behind him.

"—or next day, maybe," the Footman continued in the same tone, exactly as if nothing had happened.

"How am I to get in?" asked Alice again, in a louder tone.

"*Are* you to get in at all?" said the Footman. "That's the first question, you know."

It was, no doubt: only Alice did not like to be told so. "It's really dreadful," she muttered to herself, "the way all the creatures argue. It's enough to drive one crazy!"

The Footman seemed to think this a good opportunity for repeating his remark, with variations. "I shall sit here," he said, "on and off, for days and days."

"But what am *I* to do?" said Alice.

"Anything you like," said the Footman, and began whistling.

"Oh, there's no use in talking to him," said Alice desperately: "he's perfectly idiotic!" And she opened the door and went in.

The door led right into a large kitchen, which was full of smoke from one end to the other: the Duchess was sitting on a three-legged stool in the middle, nursing a baby; the cook was leaning over the fire, stirring a large cauldron which seemed to be full of soup.

"There's certainly too much pepper in that soup!" Alice said to herself, as well as she could for sneezing.

There was certainly too much of it in the *air*. Even the Duchess sneezed occasionally; and as for the baby, it was sneezing and howling alternately without a moment's pause. The only two creatures in the kitchen that did not sneeze were the cook, and a large cat which was lying on the hearth and grinning from ear to ear.

"Please, would you tell me," said Alice, a little timidly,

for she was not quite sure whether it was good manners
for her to speak first, "why your cat grins like that?"

"It's a Cheshire Cat," said the Duchess, "and that's
why. Pig!"

She said the last word with such sudden violence that
Alice quite jumped; but she saw in another moment that
it was addressed to the baby, and not to her, so she took
courage, and went on again:—

"I didn't know that Cheshire Cats always grinned; in
fact, I didn't know that cats *could* grin."

"They all can," said the Duchess; "and most of 'em do."

"I don't know of any that do," Alice said very politely,
feeling quite pleased to have got into a conversation.

"You don't know much," said the Duchess; "and that's
a fact."

Alice did not at all like the tone of this remark, and
thought it would be as well to introduce some other subject of conversation. While she was trying to fix on one,
the cook took the cauldron of soup off the fire, and at
once set to work throwing everything within her reach
at the Duchess and the baby—the fire-irons came first;

then followed a shower of saucepans, plates, and dishes.
The Duchess took no notice of them even when they hit
her; and the baby was howling so much already, that it
was quite impossible to say whether the blows hurt it or
not.

"Oh, *please* mind what you're doing!" cried Alice, jumping up and down in an agony of terror. "Oh, there goes
his *precious* nose!" as an unusually large saucepan flew
close by it, and very nearly carried it off.

"If everybody minded their own business," the Duchess
said, in a hoarse growl, "the world would go round a deal
faster than it does."

"Which would *not* be an advantage," said Alice, who
felt very glad to get an opportunity of showing off a little
of her knowledge. "Just think what work it would make
with the day and night! You see the earth takes twenty-
four hours to turn round on its axis—"

"Talking of axes," said the Duchess, "chop off her head!"

Alice glanced rather anxiously at the cook, to see if she
meant to take the hint; but the cook was busily stirring
the soup, and seemed not to be listening, so she went on
again: "Twenty-four hours, I *think*; or is it twelve? I—"

"Oh, don't bother *me*!" said the Duchess. "I never could
abide figures!" And with that she began nursing her
child again, singing a sort of lullaby to it as she did so,
and giving it a violent shake at the end of every line:—

> "Speak roughly to your little boy,
>   And beat him when he sneezes;
> He only does it to annoy,
>   Because he knows it teases."

CHORUS

(in which the cook and the baby joined)
"Wow! wow! wow!"

While the Duchess sang the second verse of the song,
she kept tossing the baby violently up and down, and the

poor little thing howled so, that Alice could hardly hear the words:—

"I speak severely to my boy,
I beat him when he sneezes;
For he can thoroughly enjoy
The pepper when he pleases!"

CHORUS
"Wow! wow! wow!"

"Here! You may nurse it a bit, if you like!" the Duchess said to Alice, flinging the baby at her as she spoke. "I must go and get ready to play croquet with the Queen," and she hurried out of the room. The cook threw a frying-pan after her as she went, but it just missed her.

Alice caught the baby with some difficulty, as it was a queer-shaped little creature, and held out its arms and legs in all directions, "just like a star-fish," thought Alice. The poor little thing was snorting like a steam-engine when she caught it, and kept doubling itself up and straightening itself out again, so that altogether, for the first minute or two, it was as much as she could do to hold it.

As soon as she had made out the proper way of nursing it (which was to twist it up into a sort of knot, and then keep tight hold of its right ear and left foot, so as to prevent its undoing itself), she carried it out into the open air. "If I don't take this child away with me," thought Alice, "they're sure to kill it in a day or two. Wouldn't it be murder to leave it behind?" She said the last words out loud, and the little thing grunted in reply (it had left off sneezing by this time). "Don't grunt," said Alice; "that's not at all a proper way of expressing yourself."

The baby grunted again, and Alice looked very anxiously into its face to see what was the matter with it.

There could be no doubt that it had a *very* turn-up nose, much more like a snout than a real nose: also its eyes were getting extremely small for a baby: altogether Alice did not like the look of the thing at all. "But perhaps it was only sobbing," she thought, and looked into its eyes again, to see if there were any tears.

No, there were no tears. "If you're going to turn into a pig, my dear," said Alice, seriously, "I'll have nothing more to do with you. Mind now!" The poor little thing sobbed again (or grunted, it was impossible to say which), and they went on for some while in silence.

Alice was just beginning to think to herself, "Now, what am I going to do with this creature, when I get it home?" when it grunted again, so violently, that she looked down into its face in some alarm. This time there could be *no* mistake about it: it was neither more nor less than a pig, and she felt that it would be quite absurd for her to carry it any further.

So she set the little creature down, and felt quite relieved to see it trot away quietly into the wood. "If it had grown up," she said to herself, "it would have made a dreadfully ugly child: but it makes rather a handsome pig, I think." And she began thinking over other children she knew, who might do very well as pigs, and was just saying to herself, "if one only knew the right way to change them—" when she was a little startled by seeing the Cheshire Cat sitting on a bough of a tree a few yards off.

The Cat only grinned when it saw Alice. It looked good-natured, she thought: still it had *very* long claws and a great many teeth, so she felt that it ought to be treated with respect.

"Cheshire Puss," she began, rather timidly, as she did not at all know whether it would like the name: however, it only grinned a little wider. "Come, it's pleased so far," thought Alice, and she went on. "Would you tell me, please, which way I ought to walk from here?"

"That depends a good deal on where you want to get to," said the Cat.

"I don't much care where—" said Alice.

"Then it doesn't matter which way you walk," said the Cat.

"—so long as I get *somewhere*," Alice added as an explanation.

"Oh, you're sure to do that," said the Cat, "if you only walk long enough."

Alice felt that this could not be denied, so she tried another question. "What sort of people live about here?"

"In *that* direction," the Cat said, waving its right paw round, "lives a Hatter: and in *that* direction," waving the other paw, "lives a March Hare. Visit either you like: they're both mad."

"But I don't want to go among mad people," Alice remarked.

"Oh, you can't help that," said the Cat: "we're all mad here. I'm mad. You're mad."

"How do you know I'm mad?" said Alice.

"You must be," said the Cat, "or you wouldn't have come here."

Alice didn't think that proved it at all: however, she went on: "And how do you know that you're mad?"

"To begin with," said the Cat, "a dog's not mad. You grant that?"

"I suppose so," said Alice.

"Well, then," the Cat went on, "you see a dog growls when it's angry, and wags its tail when it's pleased. Now *I* growl when I'm pleased, and wag my tail when I'm angry. Therefore I'm mad."

"*I* call it purring, not growling," said Alice.

"Call it what you like," said the Cat. "Do you play croquet with the Queen to-day?"

"I should like it very much," said Alice, "but I haven't been invited yet."

"You'll see me there," said the Cat, and vanished.

Alice was not much surprised at this, she was getting so well used to queer things happening. While she was still looking at the place where it had been, it suddenly appeared again.

"By-the-bye, what became of the baby?" said the Cat. "I'd nearly forgotten to ask."

"It turned into a pig," Alice answered very quietly, just as if the Cat had come back in a natural way.

"I thought it would," said the Cat, and vanished again.

Alice waited a little, half expecting to see it again, but it did not appear, and after a minute or two she walked on in the direction in which the March Hare was said to live. "I've seen hatters before," she said to herself: "the March Hare will be much the most interesting, and perhaps, as this is May, it won't be raving mad—at least not so mad as it was in March." As she said this, she looked up, and there was the Cat again, sitting on a branch of a tree.

"Did you say 'pig' or 'fig'?" said the Cat.

"I said 'pig'," replied Alice; "and I wish you wouldn't keep appearing and vanishing so suddenly: you make one quite giddy!"

"All right," said the Cat; and this time it vanished quite slowly, beginning with the end of the tail, and ending with the grin, which remained some time after the rest of it had gone.

"Well! I've often seen a cat without a grin," thought Alice; "but a grin without a cat! It's the most curious thing I ever saw in all my life!"

She had not gone much farther before she came in sight of the house of the March Hare: she thought it must be the right house, because the chimneys were shaped like ears and the roof was thatched with fur. It was so large a house, that she did not like to go nearer till she had nibbled some more of the left-hand bit of mushroom, and raised herself to about two feet high: even then she walked up towards it rather timidly, saying to herself, "Suppose it should be raving mad after all! I almost wish I'd gone to see the Hatter instead!"

7: A Mad Tea-Party

There was a table set out under a tree in front of the house, and the March Hare and the Hatter were having tea at it: a Dormouse was sitting between them, fast asleep, and the other two were using it as a cushion, resting their elbows on it, and talking over its head. "Very uncomfortable for the Dormouse," thought Alice; "only as it's asleep, I suppose it doesn't mind."

The table was a large one, but the three were all crowded together at one corner of it. "No room! No room!" they cried out when they saw Alice coming. "There's *plenty* of room!" said Alice indignantly, and she sat down in a large arm-chair at one end of the table.

"Have some wine," the March Hare said in an encouraging tone.

Alice looked all round the table, but there was nothing on it but tea. "I don't see any wine," she remarked.

"There isn't any," said the March Hare.

"Then it wasn't very civil of you to offer it," said Alice angrily.

"It wasn't very civil of you to sit down without being invited," said the March Hare.

"I didn't know it was *your* table," said Alice; "it's laid for a great many more than three."

"Your hair wants cutting," said the Hatter. He had been looking at Alice for some time with great curiosity, and this was his first speech.

"You should learn not to make personal remarks," Alice said with some severity: "it's very rude."

The Hatter opened his eyes very wide on hearing this; but all he *said* was, "Why is a raven like a writing-desk?"

"Come, we shall have some fun now!" thought Alice. "I'm glad they've begun asking riddles—I believe I can guess that," she added aloud.

"Do you mean that you think you can find out the answer to it?" said the March Hare.

"Exactly so," said Alice.

"Then you should say what you mean," the March Hare went on.

"I do," Alice hastily replied; "at least—at least I mean what I say—that's the same thing, you know."

"Not the same thing a bit!" said the Hatter. "Why, you might just as well say that 'I see what I eat' is the same thing as 'I eat what I see'!"

"You might just as well say," added the March Hare, "that 'I like what I get' is the same thing as 'I get what I like'!"

"You might just as well say," added the Dormouse, which seemed to be talking in its sleep, "that 'I breathe when I sleep' is the same thing as 'I sleep when I breathe'!"

"It *is* the same thing with you," said the Hatter, and here the conversation dropped, and the party sat silent for a minute, while Alice thought over all she could remember about ravens and writing-desks, which wasn't much.

The Hatter was the first to break the silence. "What day of the month is it?" he said, turning to Alice: he had taken his watch out of his pocket, and was looking at it uneasily, shaking it every now and then, and holding it to his ear.

Alice considered a little, and then said, "The fourth."

"Two days wrong!" sighed the Hatter. "I told you butter wouldn't suit the works!" he added, looking angrily at the March Hare.

"It was the *best* butter," the March Hare meekly replied.

"Yes, but some crumbs must have got in as well," the Hatter grumbled: "you shouldn't have put it in with the bread-knife."

The March Hare took the watch and looked at it gloomily: then he dipped it into his cup of tea, and looked at it again: but he could think of nothing better to say than his first remark, "It was the *best* butter, you know."

Alice had been looking over his shoulder with some curiosity. "What a funny watch!" she remarked. "It tells the day of the month, and doesn't tell what o'clock it is!"

"Why should it?" muttered the Hatter. "Does *your* watch tell you what year it is?"

"Of course not," Alice replied very readily: "but that's because it stays the same year for such a long time together."

"Which is just the case with *mine*," said the Hatter.

Alice felt dreadfully puzzled. The Hatter's remark seemed to her to have no sort of meaning in it, and yet it was certainly English. "I don't quite understand you," she said, as politely as she could.

The Dormouse shook its head impatiently, and said, he poured a little hot tea on to its nose.

The Dormouse shook its head impatiently, and said, without opening its eyes, "Of course, of course: just what I was going to remark myself."

"Have you guessed the riddle yet?" the Hatter said, turning to Alice again.

"No, I give it up," Alice replied. "What's the answer?"

"I haven't the slightest idea," said the Hatter.

"Nor I," said the March Hare.

Alice sighed wearily. "I think you might do something

better with the time," she said, "than wasting it in asking riddles that have no answers."

"If you knew Time as well as I do," said the Hatter, "you wouldn't talk about wasting *it*. It's *him*."

"I don't know what you mean," said Alice.

"Of course you don't!" the Hatter said, tossing his head contemptuously. "I dare say you never even spoke to Time!"

"Perhaps not," Alice cautiously replied; "but I know I have to beat time when I learn music."

"Ah! That accounts for it," said the Hatter. "He won't stand beating. Now, if you only kept on good terms with him, he'd do almost anything you liked with the clock. For instance, suppose it were nine o'clock in the morning, just time to begin lessons: you'd only have to whisper a hint to Time, and round goes the clock in a twinkling! Half-past one, time for dinner!"

("I only wish it was," the March Hare said to itself in a whisper.)

"That would be grand, certainly," said Alice thoughtfully; "but then—I shouldn't be hungry for it, you know."

"Not at first, perhaps," said the Hatter: "but you could keep it to half-past one as long as you liked."

"Is that the way *you* manage?" Alice asked.

The Hatter shook his head mournfully. "Not I!" he replied. "We quarreled last March—just before *he* went mad, you know—" (pointing with his teaspoon at the March Hare) "—it was at the great concert given by the Queen of Hearts, and I had to sing

'*Twinkle, twinkle, little bat!*
How I wonder what you're at!'

You know the song, perhaps?"

"I've heard something like it," said Alice.

"It goes on, you know," the Hatter continued, "in this way:—

> *'Up above the world you fly,*
> *Like a tea-tray in the sky.*
>   *Twinkle, twinkle—' "*

Here the Dormouse shook itself, and began singing in its sleep, *"Twinkle, twinkle, twinkle, twinkle—"* and went on so long that they had to pinch it to make it stop.

"Well, I'd hardly finished the first verse," said the Hatter, "when the Queen bawled out, 'He's murdering the time! Off with his head!' "

"How dreadfully savage!" exclaimed Alice.

"And ever since that," the Hatter went on in a mournful tone, "he won't do a thing I ask! It's always six o-clock now."

A bright idea came into Alice's head. "Is that the reason so many tea-things are put out here?" she asked.

"Yes, that's it," said the Hatter with a sigh: "it's always tea-time, and we've no time to wash the things between whiles."

"Then you keep moving round, I suppose?" said Alice.

"Exactly so," said the Hatter: "as the things get used up."

"But what happens when you come to the beginning again?" Alice ventured to ask.

"Suppose we change the subject," the March Hare interrupted, yawning. "I'm getting tired of this. I vote the young lady tells us a story."

"I'm afraid I don't know one," said Alice, rather alarmed at the proposal.

"Then the Dormouse shall!" they both cried. "Wake up, Dormouse!" And they pinched it on both sides at once.

The Dormouse slowly opened its eyes. "I wasn't asleep," it said in a hoarse, feeble voice, "I heard every word you fellows were saying."

"Tell us a story!" said the March Hare.

"Yes, please do!" pleaded Alice.

"And be quick about it," added the Hatter, "or you'll be asleep again before it's done."

"Once upon a time there were three little sisters," the Dormouse began in a great hurry; "and their names were Elsie, Lacie, and Tillie; and they lived at the bottom of a well—"

"What did they live on?" said Alice, who always took a great interest in questions of eating and drinking.

"They lived on treacle," said the Dormouse, after thinking a minute or two.

"They couldn't have done that, you know," Alice gently remarked. "They'd have been ill."

"So they were," said the Dormouse; "*very* ill."

Alice tried a little to fancy to herself what such an extraordinary way of living would be like, but it puzzled her too much: so she went on: "But why did they live at the bottom of a well?"

"Take some more tea," the March Hare said to Alice, very earnestly.

"I've had nothing yet," Alice replied in an offended tone: "so I can't take more."

"You mean you can't take *less*," said the Hatter: "it's very easy to take *more* than nothing."

"Nobody asked *your* opinion," said Alice.

"Who's making personal remarks now?" the Hatter asked triumphantly.

Alice did not quite know what to say to this: so she helped herself to some tea and bread-and-butter, and then turned to the Dormouse, and repeated her question. "Why did they live at the bottom of a well?"

The Dormouse again took a minute or two to think about it, and then said, "It was a treacle-well."

"There's no such thing!" Alice was beginning very angrily, but the Hatter and the March Hare went "Sh! Sh!" and the Dormouse sulkily remarked, "If you can't be civil, you'd better finish the story for yourself."

"No, please go on!" Alice said very humbly. "I won't interrupt you again. I dare say there may be *one*."

"One, indeed!" said the Dormouse indignantly. However, he consented to go on. "And so these three little sisters—they were learning to draw, you know—"

"What did they draw?" said Alice, quite forgetting her promise.

"Treacle," said the Dormouse, without considering at all, this time.

"I want a clean cup," interrupted the Hatter: "let's all move one place on."

He moved on as he spoke, and the Dormouse followed him: the March Hare moved into the Dormouse's place, and Alice rather unwillingly took the place of the March Hare. The Hatter was the only one who got any advantage from the change; and Alice was a good deal worse off than before, as the March Hare had just upset the milk-jug into his plate.

Alice did not wish to offend the Dormouse again, so she began very cautiously: "But I don't understand. Where did they draw the treacle from?"

"You can draw water out of a water-well," said the Hatter; "so I should think you could draw treacle out of a treacle-well—eh, stupid?"

"But they were *in* the well," Alice said to the Dormouse, not choosing to notice this last remark.

"Of course they were," said the Dormouse: "well in."

This answer so confused poor Alice, that she let the Dormouse go on for some time without interrupting it.

"They were learning to draw," the Dormouse went on, yawning and rubbing its eyes, for it was getting very sleepy: "and they drew all manner of things—everything that begins with an M—"

"Why with an M?" said Alice.

"Why not?" said the March Hare.

Alice was silent.

The Dormouse had closed its eyes by this time, and was going off into a doze; but, on being pinched by the Hatter, it woke up again with a little shriek, and went on: "—that begins with an M, such as mouse-traps, and the moon, and memory, and muchness—you know you say things are 'much of a muchness'—did you ever see such a thing as a drawing of a muchness?"

"Really, now you ask me," said Alice, very much confused, "I don't think—"

"Then you shouldn't talk," said the Hatter.

This piece of rudeness was more than Alice could bear: she got up in great disgust, and walked off: the Dor-

mouse fell asleep instantly, and neither of the others took the least notice of her going, though she looked back once or twice, half hoping that they would call after her: the last time she saw them they were trying to put the Dormouse into the teapot.

"At any rate I'll never go *there* again!" said Alice, as she picked her way through the wood. "It's the stupidest tea-party I ever was at in all my life!"

Just as she said this, she noticed that one of the trees had a door leading right into it. "That's very curious!" she thought. "But everything's curious to-day. I think I may as well go in at once." And in she went.

Once more she found herself in the long hall, and close to the little glass table. "Now, I'll manage better this time," she said to herself, and began by taking the little golden key, and unlocking the door that led into the garden. Then she set to work nibbling at the mushroom (she had kept a piece of it in her pocket) till she was about a foot high: then she walked down the little passage: and *then*—she found herself at last in the beautiful garden, among the bright flower-beds and the cool fountains.

8: *The Queen's Croquet-Ground*

A large rose-tree stood near the entrance of the garden: the roses growing on it were white, but there were three gardeners at it, busily painting them red. Alice thought this a very curious thing, and she went nearer to watch them, and, just as she came up to them, she heard one of them say, "Look out now, Five! Don't go splashing paint over me like that!"

"I couldn't help it," said Five, in a sulky tone. "Seven jogged my elbow."

On which Seven looked up and said, "That's right, Five! Always lay the blame on others!"

"*You'd* better not talk!" said Five. "I heard the Queen say only yesterday you deserved to be beheaded."

"What for?" said the one who had spoken first.

"That's none of *your* business, Two!" said Seven.

"Yes, it *is* his business!" said Five. "And I'll tell him— it was for bringing the cook tulip-roots instead of onions."

Seven flung down his brush, and had just begun, "Well, of all the unjust things—" when his eye chanced to fall upon Alice, as she stood watching them, and he checked himself suddenly: the others looked round also, and all of them bowed low.

"Would you tell me, please," said Alice, a little timidly, "why you are painting those roses?"

Five and Seven said nothing, but looked at Two. Two began, in a low voice, "Why, the fact is, you see, Miss, this here ought to have been a *red* rose-tree, and we put a white one in by mistake; and if the Queen was to find it out, we should all have our heads cut off, you know. So you see, Miss, we're doing our best, afore she comes, to—" At this moment Five, who had been anxiously looking across the garden, called out, "The Queen! The Queen!" and the three gardeners instantly threw themselves flat upon their faces. There was a sound of many footsteps, and Alice looked round, eager to see the Queen.

First came ten soldiers carrying clubs: these were all shaped like the three bardeners, oblong and flat, with their hands and feet at the corners: next the ten courtiers: these were ornamented all over with diamonds, and walked two and two, as the soldiers did. After these came the royal children: there were ten of them, and the little dears came jumping merrily along, hand in hand, in couples: they were all ornamented with hearts. Next came the guests, mostly Kings and Queens, and among them Alice recognized the White Rabbitt: it was talking in a hurried nervous manner, smiling at everything that was said, and went by without noticing her. Then followed the Knave of Hearts, carrying the King's crown on a crimson velvet cushion: and, last of all this grand procession came THE KING AND THE QUEEN OF HEARTS.

Alice was rather doubtful whether she ought not to lie down on her face like the three gardeners, but she could not remember ever having heard of such a rule at processions; "and besides, what would be the use of a procession," thought she, "if people had all to lie down on their faces, so that they couldn't see it?" So she stood where she was, and waited.

When the procession came opposite to Alice, they all

stopped and looked at her, and the Queen said, severely,
"Who is this?" She said it to the Knave of Hearts, who
only bowed and smiled in reply.

"Idiot!" said the Queen, tossing her head impatiently;
and, turning to Alice, she went on: "What's your name,
child?"

"My name is Alice, so
please your Majesty," said
Alice very politely; but she
added, to herself, "Why,
they're only a pack of
cards, after all. I needn't
be afraid of them!"

"And who are *these*?" said
the Queen, pointing to the
three gardeners who were
lying round the rose-tree;
for, you see, as they were
lying on their faces, and the pattern on their backs was
the same as the rest of the pack, she could not tell
whether they were gardeners, or soldiers, or courtiers,
or three of her own children.

"How should *I* know?" said Alice, surprised at her own
courage. "It's no business of *mine*."

The Queen turned crimson with fury, and, after glaring at her for a moment like a wild beast, began screaming, "Off with her head! Off—"

"Nonsense!" said Alice, very loudly and decidedly, and
the Queen was silent.

The King laid his hand upon her arm, and timidly said,
"Consider, my dear: she is only a child!"

The Queen turned angrily away from him, and said to
the Knave, "Turn them over!"

The Knave did so, very carefully, with one foot.

"Get up!" said the Queen in a shrill, loud voice, and
the three gardeners instantly jumped up, and began bow-

ing to the King, the Queen, the royal children, and everybody else.

"Leave off that!" screamed the Queen. "You make me
giddy." And then, turning to the rose-tree, she went on,
"What *have* you been doing here?"

"May it please your Majesty," said Two, in a very
humble tone, going down on one knee as he spoke, "we
were trying—"

"*I* see!" said the Queen, who had meanwhile been examining the roses. "Off with their heads!" and the procession moved on, three of the soldiers remaining behind
to execute the unfortunate gardeners, who ran to Alice
for protection.

"You shan't be beheaded!" said Alice, and she put them
into a large flower-pot that stood near. The three soldiers
wandered about for a minute or two, looking for them,
and then quietly marched off after the others.

"Are their heads off?" shouted the Queen.

"Their heads are gone, if it please your Majesty!" the
soldiers shouted in reply.

"That's right!" shouted the Queen. "Can you play
croquet?"

The soldiers were silent, and looked at Alice, as the
question was evidently meant for her.

"Yes!" shouted Alice.

"Come on, then!" roared the Queen, and Alice joined
the procession, wondering very much what would happen next.

"It's—it's a very fine day!" said a timid voice at her side.
She was walking by the White Rabbit, who was peeping
anxiously into her face.

"Very," said Alice. "Where's the Duchess?"

"Hush! Hush!" said the Rabbit in a low, hurried tone. He
looked anxiously over his shoulder as he spoke, and then
raised himself upon tiptoe, put his mouth close to her ear,
and whispered, "She's under sentence of execution."

"What for?" said Alice.

"Did you say 'What a pity!'?" the Rabbit asked.

"No, I didn't," said Alice. "I don't think it's at all a pity. I said 'What for?'"

"She boxed the Queen's ears—" the Rabbit began. Alice gave a little scream of laughter. "Oh, hush!" the Rabbit whispered in a frightened tone. "The Queen will hear you! You see she came rather late, and the Queen said—"

"Get to your places!" shouted the Queen in a voice of thunder, and people began running about in all directions, tumbling up against each other: however, they got settled down in a minute or two, and the game began.

Alice thought she had never seen such a curious croquet-ground in her life: it was all ridges and furrows: the croquet balls were live hedgehogs, and the mallets live flamingoes, and the soldiers had to double themselves up and stand on their hands and feet, to make the arches.

The chief difficulty Alice found at first was in managing her flamingo: she succeeded in getting its body tucked away, comfortably enough, under her arm, with its legs hanging down, but generally, just as she had got its neck nicely straightened out, and was going to give the hedgehog a blow with its head, it *would* twist itself round and look up in her face, with such a puzzled expression that she could not help bursting out laughing; and, when she had got its head down, and was going to begin again, it was very provoking to find that the hedgehog had unrolled itself, and was in the act of crawling away: besides all this, there was generally a ridge or a furrow in the way

wherever she wanted to send the hedgehog to, and, as the doubled-up soldiers were always getting up and walking off to other parts of the ground, Alice soon came to the conclusion that it was a very difficult game indeed.

The players all played at once, without waiting for turns, quarreling all the while, and fighting for the hedgehogs; and in a very short time the Queen was in a furious passion, and went stamping about, and shouting "Off with his head!" or "Off with her head!" about once in a minute.

Alice began to feel very uneasy: to be sure, she had not as yet had any dispute with the Queen, but she knew that it might happen any minute, "and then," thought she, "what would become of me? They're dreadfully fond of beheading people here: the great wonder is, that there's anyone left alive!"

She was looking about for some way of escape, and wondering whether she could get away without being seen, when she noticed a curious appearance in the air: it puzzled her very much at first, but after watching it a minute or two she made it out to be a grin, and she said to herself, "It's the Cheshire Cat: now I shall have somebody to talk to."

"How are you getting on?" said the Cat, as soon as there was mouth enough for it to speak with.

Alice waited till the eyes appeared, and then nodded. "It's no use speaking to it," she thought, "till its ears have come, or at least one of them." In another minute the whole head appeared, and then Alice put down her flamingo, and began an account of the game, feeling very glad she had someone to listen to her. The Cat seemed to think that there was enough of it now in sight, and no more of it appeared.

"I don't think they play at all fairly," Alice began, in rather a complaining tone, "and they all quarrel so dreadfully one can't hear oneself speak—and they don't seem to have any rules in particular: at least, if there are, no-body attends to them—and you've no idea how confusing it is all the things being alive: for instance, there's the arch I've got to go through next walking about at the other end of the ground—and I should have croqueted the Queen's hedgehog just now, only it ran away when it saw mine coming!"

"How do you like the Queen?" said the Cat in a low voice.

"Not at all," said Alice: "she's so extremely—" Just then she noticed that the Queen was close behind her, listen-ing: so she went on "—likely to win, that it's hardly worth while finishing the game."

The Queen smiled and passed on.

"Who *are* you talking to?" said the King, coming up to Alice, and looking at the Cat's head with great curiosity.

"It's a friend of mine—a Cheshire Cat," said Alice: "allow me to introduce it."

"I don't like the look of it at all," said the King: "how-ever, it may kiss my hand, if it likes."

"I'd rather not," the Cat remarked.

"Don't be impertinent," said the King, "and don't look at me like that!" He got behind Alice as he spoke.

"A cat may look at a king," said Alice. "I've read that in some book, but I don't remember where."

"Well, it must be removed," said the King very de-cidedly; and he called to the Queen, who was passing at the moment, "My dear! I wish you would have this cat removed!"

The Queen had only one way of settling all difficulties, great or small. "Off with his head!" she said without even looking round.

"I'll fetch the executioner myself," said the King eager-ly, and he hurried off.

Alice thought she might as well go back and see how

the game was going on, as she heard the Queen's voice in the distance, screaming with passion. She had already heard her sentence three of the players to be executed for having missed their turns, and she did not like the look of things at all, as the game was in such confusion that she never knew whether it was her turn or not. So she went off in search of her hedgehog.

The hedgehog was engaged in a fight with another hedgehog, which seemed to Alice an excellent opportunity for croqueting one of them with the other: the only

difficulty was, that her flamingo was gone across to the other side of the garden, where Alice could see it trying in a helpless sort of way to fly up into a tree.

By the time she had caught the flamingo and brought it back, the fight was over, and both the hedgehogs were out of sight: "but it doesn't matter much," thought Alice,

"as all the arches are gone from this side of the ground."
So she tucked it away under her arm, that it might not
escape again, and went back to have a little more conversation with her friend.

When she got back to the Cheshire Cat, she was surprised to find quite a large crowd collected round it:
there was a dispute going on between the executioner,
the King, and the Queen, who were all talking at once,
while all the rest were quite silent, and looked very uncomfortable.

The moment Alice appeared, she was appealed to by
all three to settle the question, and they repeated their
arguments to her, though, as they all spoke at once, she
found it very hard to make out exactly what they said.

The executioner's argument was, that you couldn't
cut off a head unless there was a body to cut it off from:
that he had never had to do such a thing before, and he
wasn't going to begin at *his* time of life.

The King's argument was that anything that had a
head could be beheaded, and that you weren't to talk
nonsense.

The Queen's argument was that, if something wasn't
done about it in less than no time, she'd have everybody
executed, all round. (It was this last remark that had
made the whole party look so grave and anxious.)

Alice could think of nothing else to say but, "It belongs
to the Duchess: you'd better ask *her* about it."

"She's in prison," the Queen said to the executioner:
"fetch her here." And the executioner went off like an
arrow.

The Cat's head began fading away the moment he was
gone, and, by the time he had come back with the Duchess, it had entirely disappeared: so the King and the
executioner ran wildly up and down, looking for it, while
the rest of the party went back to the game.

9: *The Mock Turtle's Story*

"You can't think how glad I am to see you again, you dear old thing!" said the Duchess, as she tucked her arm affectionately into Alice's, and they walked off together.

Alice was very glad to find her in such a pleasant temper, and thought to herself that perhaps it was only the pepper that had made her so savage when they met in the kitchen.

"When *I'm* a Duchess," she said to herself (not in a very hopeful tone, though), "I won't have any pepper in my kitchen *at all*. Soup does very well without—Maybe it's always pepper that makes people hot-tempered," she went on, very much pleased at having found out a new kind of rule, "and vinegar that makes them sour—and camomile that makes them bitter—and—and barley-sugar and such things that make children sweet-tempered. I only wish people knew *that*: then they wouldn't be so stingy about it, you know—"

She had quite forgotten the Duchess by this time, and was a little startled when she heard her voice close to her ear. "You're thinking about something, my dear, and that makes you forget to talk. I can't tell you just now what the moral of that is, but I shall remember it in a bit."

"Perhaps it hasn't one," Alice ventured to remark.

"Tut, tut, child!" said the Duchess. "Everything's got a moral, if only you can find it." And she squeezed herself up closer to Alice's side as she spoke.

Alice did not much like her keeping so close to her: first, because the Duchess was *very* ugly; and secondly, because she was exactly the right height to rest her chin on Alice's shoulder, and it was an uncomfortably sharp chin. However, she did not like to be rude: so she bore it as well as she could.

"The game's going on rather better now," she said, by way of keeping up the conversation a little.

"'Tis so," said the Duchess: "and the moral of that is— 'Oh, 'tis love, 'tis love, that makes the world go round!'"

"Somebody said," Alice whispered, "that it's done by everybody minding their own business!"

"Ah, well! It means much the same thing," said the Duchess, digging her sharp little chin into Alice's shoulder as she added, "and the moral of *that* is—'Take care of the sense, and the sounds will take care of themselves.'"

"How fond she is of finding morals in things!" Alice thought to herself.

"I dare say you're wondering why I don't put my arm round your waist," the Duchess said, after a pause: "the reason is, that I'm doubtful about the temper of your flamingo. Shall I try the experiment?"

"He might bite," Alice cautiously replied, not feeling at all anxious to have the experiment tried.

"Very true," said the Duchess: "flamingoes and mustard both bite. And the moral of that is—'Birds of a feather flock together.'"

"Only mustard isn't a bird," Alice remarked.

"Right, as usual," said the Duchess: "what a clear way you have of putting things!"

"It's a mineral, I *think*," said Alice.

"Of course it is," said the Duchess, who seemed ready to agree to everything that Alice said: "there's a large mustard-mine near here. And the moral of that is—'The more there is of mine, the less there is of yours.'"

"Oh, I know!" exclaimed Alice, who had not attended

to this last remark. "It's a vegetable. It doesn't look like one, but it is."

"I quite agree with you," said the Duchess; "and the moral of that is—'Be what you would seem to be'—or, if you'd like it put more simply—'Never imagine yourself not to be otherwise than what it might appear to others that what you were or might have been was not otherwise than what you had been would have appeared to them to be otherwise.'"

"I think I should understand that better," Alice said very politely, "if I had it written down: but I can't quite follow it as you say it."

"That's nothing to what I could say if I chose," the Duchess replied, in a pleased tone.

"Pray don't trouble yourself to say it any longer than that," said Alice.

"Oh, don't talk about trouble!" said the Duchess. "I make you a present of everything I've said as yet."

"A cheap sort of present!" thought Alice. "I'm glad people don't give birthday-presents like that!" But she did not venture to say it out loud.

"Thinking again?" the Duchess asked, with another dig of her sharp little chin.

"I've a right to think," said Alice sharply, for she was beginning to feel a little worried.

"Just about as much right," said the Duchess, "as pigs have to fly; and the m—"

But here, to Alice's great surprise, the Duchess' voice died away, even in the middle of her favourite word 'moral,' and the arm that was linked into hers began to tremble. Alice looked up, and there stood the Queen in front of them, with her arms folded, frowning like a thunderstorm.

"A fine day, your Majesty!" the Duchess began in a low, weak voice.

"Now, I give you fair warning," shouted the Queen,

stamping on the ground as she spoke; "either you or your head must be off, and that in about half no time! Take your choice!"

The Duchess took her choice and was gone in a moment.

"Let's go on with the game," the Queen said to Alice; and Alice was too much frightened to say a word, but slowly followed her back to the croquet-ground.

The other guests had taken advantage of the Queen's absence, and were resting in the shade: however, the moment they saw her, they hurried back to the game, the Queen merely remarking that a moment's delay would cost them their lives.

All the time they were playing the Queen never left off quarreling with the other players, and shouting "Off with his head!" or "Off with her head!" Those whom she sentenced were taken into custody by the soldiers, who of course had to leave off being arches to do this, so that by the end of half an hour or so there were no arches left, and all the players, except the King, the Queen, and Alice, were in custody and under sentence of execution.

Then the Queen left off, quite out of breath, and said to Alice, "Have you seen the Mock Turtle yet?"

"No," said Alice. "I don't even know what a Mock Turtle is."

"It's the thing Mock Turtle Soup is made from," said the Queen.

"I never saw one, or heard of one," said Alice.

"Come on, then," said the Queen, "and he shall tell you his history."

As they walked off together, Alice heard the King say in a low voice, to the company generally, "You are all pardoned." "Come, *that's* a good thing!" she said to herself, for she had felt quite unhappy at the number of executions the Queen had ordered.

They very soon came upon a Gryphon, lying fast asleep

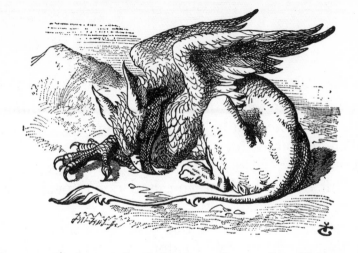

in the sun. (If you don't know what a Gryphon is, look at the picture.)

"Up, lazy thing!" said the Queen, "and take this young lady to see the Mock Turtle, and to hear his history. I must go back and see after some executions I have ordered;" and she walked off, leaving Alice alone with the Gryphon. Alice did not quite like the look of the creature, but on the whole she thought it would be quite as safe to stay with it as to go after that savage Queen: so she waited.

The Gryphon sat up and rubbed its eyes: then it watched the Queen till she was out of sight: then it chuckled. "What fun!" said the Gryphon, half to itself, half to Alice.

"What *is* the fun?" said Alice.

"Why, *she*," said the Gryphon. "It's all her fancy, that: they never executes nobody, you know. Come on!"

"Everybody says 'come on!' here," thought Alice, as she went slowly after it: "I never was so ordered about before in all my life, never!"

They had not gone far before they saw the Mock Turtle in the distance, sitting sad and lonely on a little ledge of rock, and, as they came nearer, Alice could hear him sighing as if his heart would break. She pitied him deeply. "What is his sorrow?" she asked the Gryphon. And the Gryphon answered, very nearly in the same words as before, "It's all his fancy, that: he hasn't got no sorrow, you know. Come on!"

So they went up to the Mock Turtle, who looked at them with large eyes full of tears, but said nothing.

"This here young lady," said the Gryphon, "she wants for to know your history, she do."

"I'll tell it her," said the Mock Turtle in a deep, hollow tone. "Sit down, both of you, and don't speak a word till I've finished."

So they sat down, and nobody spoke for some minutes. Alice thought to herself, "I don't see how he can *ever* finish, if he doesn't begin." But she waited patiently.

"Once," said the Mock Turtle at last, with a deep sigh, "I was a real Turtle."

These words were followed by a very long silence, broken only by an occasional exclamation of "Hjckrrh!" from the Gryphon, and the constant heavy sobbing of the Mock Turtle. Alice was very nearly getting up and say-

ing, "Thank you, Sir, for your interesting story," but she could not help thinking there *must* be more to come, so she sat still and said nothing.

"When we were little," the Mock Turtle went on at last, more calmly, though still sobbing a little now and then, "we went to school in the sea. The master was an old Turtle—we used to call him Tortoise—"

"Why did you call him Tortoise, if he wasn't one?" Alice asked.

"We called him Tortoise because he taught us," said the Mock Turtle angrily. "Really you are very dull!"

"You ought to be ashamed of yourself for asking such a simple question," added the Gryphon; and then they both sat silent and looked at poor Alice, who felt ready to sink into the earth. At last the Gryphon said to the Mock Turtle, "Drive on, old fellow! Don't be all day about it!" and he went on in these words:—

"Yes, we went to school in the sea, though you mayn't believe it—"

"I never said I didn't!" interrupted Alice.

"You did," said the Mock Turtle.

"Hold your tongue!" added the Gryphon, before Alice could speak again. The Mock Turtle went on.

"We had the best of educations—in fact, we went to school every day—"

"*I've* been to a day-school, too," said Alice. "You needn't be so proud as all that."

"With extras?" asked the Mock Turtle, a little anxiously.

"Yes," said Alice: "we learned French and music."

"And washing?" said the Mock Turtle.

"Certainly not!" said Alice indignantly.

"Ah! Then yours wasn't a really good school," said the Mock Turtle in a tone of great relief. "Now, at *ours* they had at the end of the bill, 'French, music, *and wash-ing*—extra.'"

"You couldn't have wanted it much," said Alice; "living at the bottom of the sea."

"I couldn't afford to learn it," said the Mock Turtle
with a sigh. "I only took the regular course."

"What was that?" inquired Alice.

"Reeling and Writhing, of course, to begin with," the
Mock Turtle replied; "and then the different branches
of Arithmetic—Ambition, Distraction, Uglification, and
Derision."

"I never heard of 'Uglification,'" Alice ventured to
say. "What is it?"

The Gryphon lifted up both its paws in surprise.
"Never heard of uglifying!" it exclaimed. "You know
what to beautify is, I suppose?"

"Yes," said Alice doubtfully: "it means—to—make—
anything—prettier."

"Well, then," the Gryphon went on, "if you don't know
what to uglify is, you *are* a simpleton."

Alice did not feel encouraged to ask any more questions about it: so she turned to the Mock Turtle, and
said, "What else had you to learn?"

"Well, there was Mystery," the Mock Turtle replied,
counting off the subjects on his flappers,—"Mystery, ancient and modern, with Seaography: then Drawling—the
Drawling-master was an old conger-eel, that used to
come once a week: *he* taught us Drawling, Stretching,
and Fainting in Coils."

"What was *that* like?" said Alice.

"Well, I can't show it you, myself," the Mock Turtle
said. "I'm too stiff. And the Gryphon never learnt it."

"Hadn't time," said the Gryphon: "I went to the Classi-
cal master, though. He was an old crab, *he* was."

"I never went to him," the Mock Turtle said with a
sigh. "He taught Laughing and Grief, they used to say."

"So he did, so he did," said the Gryphon, sighing in his
turn; and both creatures hid their faces in their paws.

"And how many hours a day did you do lessons?" said
Alice, in a hurry to change the subject.

"Ten hours the first day," said the Mock Turtle: "nine the next, and so on."

"What a curious plan!" exclaimed Alice.

"That's the reason they're called lessons," the Gryphon remarked: "because they lessen from day to day."

This was quite a new idea to Alice, and she thought it over a little before she made her next remark. "Then the eleventh day must have been a holiday?"

"Of course it was," said the Mock Turtle.

"And how did you manage on the twelfth?" Alice went on eagerly.

"That's enough about lessons," the Gryphon interrupted in a very decided tone. "Tell her something about the games now."

10: The Lobster-Quadrille

The Mock Turtle sighed deeply, and drew the back of one flapper across his eyes. He looked at Alice and tried to speak, but for a minute or two sobs choked his voice. "Same as if he had a bone in his throat," said the Gryphon; and it set to work shaking him and punching him in the back. At last the Mock Turtle recovered his voice, and, with tears running down his cheeks, he went on again:—

"You may not have lived much under the sea—" ("I haven't," said Alice)—"and perhaps you were never even introduced to a lobster—" (Alice began to say, "I once tasted—" but checked herself hastily, and said, "No, never.") "—so you can have no idea what a delightful thing a Lobster-Quadrille is!"

"No, indeed," said Alice. "What sort of a dance is it?"

"Why," said the Gryphon, "you first form into a line along the sea-shore—"

"Two lines!" cried the Mock Turtle. "Seals, turtles, salmon, and so on: then, when you've cleared all the jelly-fish out of the way—"

"*That* generally takes some time," interrupted the Gryphon.

"—you advance twice—"

"Each with a lobster as a partner!" cried the Gryphon.

"Of course," the Mock Turtle said: "advance twice, set to partners—"

"—change lobsters, and retire in same order," continued the Gryphon.

"Then, you know," the Mock Turtle went on, "you throw the—"

"The lobsters!" shouted the Gryphon, with a bound into the air.

"—as far out to sea as you can—"

"Swim after them!" screamed the Gryphon.

"Turn a somersault in the sea!" cried the Mock Turtle, capering wildly about.

"Change lobsters again!" yelled the Gryphon at the top of its voice.

"Back to land again, and—that's all the first figure," said the Mock Turtle, suddenly dropping his voice; and the two creatures, who had been jumping about like mad things all this time, sat down again very sadly and quietly and looked at Alice.

"It must be a very pretty dance," said Alice timidly.

"Would you like to see a little of it?" said the Mock Turtle.

"Very much indeed," said Alice.

"Come, let's try the first figure!" said the Mock Turtle to the Gryphon. "We can do it without lobsters, you know. Which shall sing?"

"Oh, *you* sing," said the Gryphon. "I've forgotten the words."

So they began solemnly dancing round and round Alice, every now and then treading on her toes when they passed too close, and waving their fore-paws to mark the time, while the Mock Turtle sang this, very slowly and sadly:—

"Will you walk a little faster?" said a whiting to a snail,
"There's a porpoise close behind us, and he's treading on my
*   tail.*
See how eagerly the lobsters and the turtles all advance!
They are waiting on the shingle—will you come and join the
*   dance?*
*   Will you, won't you, will you, won't you, will you join the*
*   dance?*
*   Will you, won't you, will you, won't you, won't you join*
*   the dance?*

"You can really have no notion how delightful it will be
When they take us up and throw us, with the lobsters, out to
*   sea!"*
But the snail replied, "Too far, too far!" and gave a look
*   askance—*
Said he thanked the whiting kindly, but he would not join the
*   dance.*
*   Would not, could not, would not, could not, would not join*
*   the dance.*
*   Would not, could not, would not, could not, could not join*
*   the dance.*

"What matters it how far we go?" his scaly friend replied.
"There is another shore, you know, upon the other side.
The further off from England the nearer is to France—
Then turn not pale, beloved snail, but come and join the dance.
*   Will you, won't you, will you, won't you, will you join the*
*   dance?*
*   Will you, won't you, will you, won't you, won't you join the*
*   dance?*

"Thank you, it's a very interesting dance to watch," said Alice, feeling very glad that it was over at last: "and I do so like that curious song about the whiting!"

"Oh, as to the whiting," said the Mock Turtle, "they —you've seen them, of course?"

"Yes," said Alice, "I've often seen them at dinn—" she checked herself hastily.

"I don't know where Dinn may be," said the Mock Turtle; "but, if you've seen them so often, of course you know what they're like?"

"I believe so," Alice replied thoughtfully. "They have their tails in their mouths—and they're all over crumbs."

"You're wrong about the crumbs," said the Mock Turtle: "crumbs would all wash off in the sea. But they *have* their tails in their mouths; and the reason is—" here the Mock Turtle yawned and shut his eyes—"Tell her about the reason and all that," he said to the Gryphon.

"The reason is," said the Gryphon, "that they *would* go with the lobsters to the dance. So they got thrown out to sea. So they had to fall a long way. So they got their tails fast in their mouths. So they couldn't get them out again. That's all."

"Thank you," said Alice, "it's very interesting. I never knew so much about a whiting before."

"I can tell you more than that, if you like," said the Gryphon. "Do you know why it's called a whiting?"

"I never thought about it," said Alice. "Why?"

"*It does the boots and shoes,*" the Gryphon replied very solemnly.

Alice was thoroughly puzzled. "Does the boots and shoes!" she repeated in a wondering tone.

"Why, what are *your* shoes done with?" said the Gryphon. "I mean, what makes them so shiny?"

Alice looked down at them, and considered a little before she gave her answer. "They're done with blacking, I believe."

"Boots and shoes under the sea," the Gryphon went on in a deep voice, "are done with whiting. Now you know."

"And what are they made of?" Alice asked in a tone of great curiosity.

"Soles and eels, of course," the Gryphon replied rather impatiently: "any shrimp could have told you that."

"If I'd been the whiting," said Alice, whose thoughts were still running on the song, "I'd have said to the porpoise 'Keep back, please! We don't want *you* with us!'"

"They were obliged to have him with them," the Mock Turtle said. "No wise fish would go anywhere without a porpoise."

"Wouldn't it, really?" said Alice, in a tone of great surprise.

"Of course not," said the Mock Turtle. "Why, if a fish came to *me*, and told me he was going a journey, I should say 'With what porpoise?'"

"Don't you mean 'purpose'?" said Alice.

"I mean what I say," the Mock Turtle replied, in an offended tone. And the Gryphon added, "Come, let's hear some of *your* adventures."

"I could tell you my adventures—beginning from this morning," said Alice a little timidly; "but it's no use going back to yesterday, because I was a different person then."

"Explain all that," said the Mock Turtle.

"No, no! The adventures first," said the Gryphon in an impatient tone: "explanations take such a dreadful time."

So Alice began telling them her adventures from the time when she first saw the White Rabbit. She was a little nervous about it just at first, the two creatures got so close to her, one on each side, and opened their eyes and mouths so *very* wide; but she gained courage as she went on. Her listeners were perfectly quiet till she got to the part about her repeating "*You are old, Father William*," to the Caterpillar, and the words all coming different, and then the Mock Turtle drew a long breath, and said, "That's very curious!"

"It's all about as curious as it can be," said the Gryphon.

"It all came different!" the Mock Turtle repeated thoughtfully. "I should like to hear her try and repeat something now. Tell her to begin." He looked at the Gryphon as if he thought it had some kind of authority over Alice.

"Stand up and repeat *'Tis the voice of the sluggard,'*" said the Gryphon.

"How the creatures order one about, and make one repeat lessons!" thought Alice. "I might just as well be at school at once." However, she got up, and began to repeat it, but her head was so full of the Lobster-Quadrille, that she hardly knew what she was saying; and the words came very queer indeed:—

> " 'Tis the voice of the Lobster: I heard him declare,
> 'You have baked me too brown, I must sugar my hair.'
> As a duck with its eyelids, so he with his nose
> Trims his belt and his buttons, and turns out his toes.
> When the sands are all dry, he is gay as a lark,
> And will talk in contemptuous tones of the Shark:
> But, when the tide rises and sharks are around,
> His voice has a timid and tremulous sound."

"That's different from what *I* used to say when I was a child," said the Gryphon.

"Well, *I* never heard it before," said the Mock Turtle; "but it sounds uncommon nonsense."

Alice said nothing: she had sat down with her face in her hands, wondering if anything would *ever* happen in a natural way again.

"I should like to have it explained," said the Mock Turtle.

"She can't explain it," said the Gryphon hastily. "Go on with the next verse."

"But about his toes?" the Mock Turtle persisted. "How *could* he turn them out with his nose, you know?"

"It's the first position in dancing," Alice said; but she was dreadfully puzzled by the whole thing, and longed to change the subject.

"Go on with the next verse," the Gryphon repeated: "it begins '*I passed by his garden.*'"

Alice did not dare to disobey, though she felt sure it would all come wrong, and she went on in a trembling voice:—

"I passed by his garden, and marked, with one eye,
How the Owl and the Panther were sharing a pie:
The Panther took pie-crust, and gravy, and meat,
While the Owl had the dish as its share of the treat.
When the pie was all finished, the Owl, as a boon,
Was kindly permitted to pocket the spoon:
While the Panther received knife and fork with a growl,
And concluded the banquet by—"

"What *is* the use of repeating all that stuff?" the Mock Turtle interrupted, "if you don't explain it as you go on? It's by far the most confusing thing *I* ever heard!"

"Yes, I think you'd better leave off," said the Gryphon, and Alice was only too glad to do so.

"Shall we try another figure of the Lobster-Quadrille?"

the Gryphon went on. "Or would you like the Mock
Turtle to sing you a song?"

"Oh, a song, please, if the Mock Turtle would be so
kind," Alice replied, so eagerly that the Gryphon said, in
a rather offended tone, "Hm! No accounting for tastes!
Sing her *Turtle Soup,*' will you, old fellow?"

The Mock Turtle sighed deeply, and began, in a voice
choked with sobs, to sing this:—

> *"Beautiful Soup, so rich and green,*
> *Waiting in a hot tureen!*
> *Who for such dainties would not stoop?*
> *Soup of the evening, beautiful Soup!*
> *Soup of the evening, beautiful Soup!*
> *Beau—ootiful Soo—oop!*
> *Beau—ootiful Soo—oop!*
> *Soo—oop of the e—e—evening,*
> *Beautiful, beautiful Soup!*

> *"Beautiful Soup! Who cares for fish,*
> *Game, or any other dish?*
> *Who would not give all else for two p*
> *ennyworth only of beautiful Soup?*
> *Pennyworth only of beautiful soup?*
> *Beau—ootiful Soo—oop!*
> *Beau—ootiful Soo—oop!*
> *Soo—oop of the e—e—evening,*
> *Beautiful, beauti—FUL SOUP!"*

Chorus again!" cried the Gryphon, and the Mock
Turtle had just begun to repeat it, when a cry of "The
trial's beginning!" was heard in the distance.

"Come on!" cried the Gryphon, and, taking Alice by
the hand, it hurried off, without waiting for the end of
the song.

"What trial is it?" Alice panted as she ran; but the
Gryphon only answered "Come on!" and ran the faster,

while more and more faintly came, carried on the breeze
that followed them, the melancholy words:—

> "Soo—oop of the e—e—evening,
> Beautiful, beautiful Soup!"

11: Who Stole the Tarts?

The King and Queen of Hearts were seated on their
throne when they arrived, with a great crowd assembled
about them—all sorts of little birds and beasts, as well as
the whole pack of cards: the Knave was standing before
them, in chains, with a soldier on each side to guard him;
and near the King was the White Rabbit, with a trumpet
in one hand, and a scroll of parchment in the other. In the
very middle of the court was a table, with a large dish
of tarts upon it: they looked so good, that it made Alice
quite hungry to look at them—"I wish they'd get the trial
done," she thought, "and hand round the refreshments!"
But there seemed to be no chance of this; so she began
looking at everything about her to pass away the time.

Alice had never been in a court of justice before, but
she had read about them in books, and she was quite
pleased to find that she knew the name of nearly everything there. "That's the judge," she said to herself, "because of his great wig."

The judge, by the way, was the King; and, as he wore
his crown over the wig (look at the picture on the next
page if you want to see how he did it), he did not look
at all comfortable, and it was certainly not becoming.

"And that's the jury-box," thought Alice; "and those
twelve creatures," (she was obliged to say "creatures,"
you see, because some of them were animals, and some
were birds), "I suppose they are the jurors." She said
this last word two or three times over to herself, being

rather proud of it: for she thought, and rightly too, that very few little girls of her age knew the meaning of it at all. However, "jurymen" would have done just as well.

The twelve jurors were all writing very busily on slates. "What are they doing?" Alice whispered to the Gryphon. "They can't have anything to put down yet, before the trial's begun."

"They're putting down their names," the Gryphon whispered in reply, "for fear they should forget them before the end of the trial."

"Stupid things!" Alice began in a loud indignant voice; but she stopped herself hastily, for the White Rabbit cried out, "Silence in the court!" and the King put on his spectacles and looked anxiously round, to make out who was talking.

Alice could see, as well as if she were looking over their shoulders, that all the jurors were writing down "Stupid things!" on their slates, and she could even make out that one of them didn't know how to spell "stupid," and that he had to ask his neighbour to tell him. "A nice muddle their slates'll be in, before the trial's over!" thought Alice.

One of the jurors had a pencil that squeaked. This, of course, Alice could *not* stand, and she went round the court and got behind him, and very soon found an opportunity of taking it away. She did it so quickly that the poor little juror (it was Bill, the Lizard) could not make out at all what had become of it; so, after hunting all about for it, he was obliged to write with one finger for the rest of the day;  and this was of little use, as it left no mark on the slate.

"Herald, read the accusation!" said the King.

On this the White Rabbit blew three blasts on the trumpet, and then unrolled the parchment-scroll, and read as follows:—

> "The Queen of Hearts, she made some tarts,
>   All on a summer day:
> The Knave of Hearts, he stole those tarts
>   And took them quite away!"

"Consider your verdict," the King said to the jury.

"Not yet, not yet!" the Rabbit hastily interrupted. "There's a great deal to come before that!"

"Call the first witness," said the King; and the White Rabbit blew three blasts on the trumpet, and called out, "First witness!"

The first witness was the Hatter. He came in with a teacup in one hand and a piece of bread-and-butter in the other. "I beg pardon, you Majesty," he began, "for bringing these in; but I hadn't quite finished my tea when I was sent for."

"You ought to have finished," said the King. "When did you begin?"

The Hatter looked at the March Hare, who had fol- 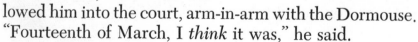 lowed him into the court, arm-in-arm with the Dormouse. "Fourteenth of March, I *think* it was," he said.

"Fifteenth," said the March Hare.

"Sixteenth," said the Dormouse.

"Write that down," the King said to the jury; and the jury eagerly wrote down all three dates on their slates, and then added them up, and reduced the answer to shillings and pence.

"Take off your hat," the King said to the Hatter.

"It isn't mine," said the Hatter.

"*Stolen!*" the King exclaimed, turning to the jury, who instantly made a memorandum of the fact.

"I keep them to sell," the Hatter added as an explanation. "I've none of my own. I'm a hatter."

Here the Queen put on her spectacles, and began staring hard at the Hatter, who turned pale and fidgeted.

"Give your evidence," said the King; "and don't be
nervous, or I'll have you executed on the spot."

This did not seem to encourage the witness at all: he
kept shifting from one foot to the other, looking uneasily
at the Queen, and in his confusion he bit a large piece
out of his teacup instead of the bread-and-butter.

Just at this moment Alice felt a very curious sensation,
which puzzled her a good deal until she made out what it
was: she was beginning to grow larger again, and she
thought at first she would get up and leave the court; but
on second thoughts she decided to remain where she was
as long as there was room for her.

"I wish you wouldn't squeeze so," said the Dormouse,
who was sitting next to her. "I can hardly breathe."

"I can't help it," said Alice very meekly: "I'm growing."

"You've no right to grow *here*," said the Dormouse.

"Don't talk nonsense," said Alice more boldly: "you
know you're growing too."

"Yes, but *I* grow at a reasonable pace," said the Dormouse: "not in that ridiculous fashion." And he got up
very sulkily and crossed over to the other side of the
court.

All this time the Queen had never left off staring at the
Hatter, and, just as the Dormouse crossed the court, she
said, to one of the officers of the court, "Bring me the list
of the singers in the last concert!" on which the wretched
Hatter trembled so, that he shook off both his shoes.

"Give your evidence," the King repeated angrily, "or
I'll have you executed, whether you're nervous or not."

"I'm a poor man, your Majesty," the Hatter began in a
trembling voice, "and I hadn't but just begun my tea—
not above a week or so—and what with the bread-and-
butter getting so thin—and the twinkling of the tea—"

"The twinkling of *what?*" said the King.

"It *began* with the tea," the Hatter replied.

"Of course twinkling *begins* with a T!" said the King sharply. "Do you take me for a dunce? Go on!"

"I'm a poor man," the Hatter went on, "and most things twinkled after that—only the March Hare said—"

"I didn't!" the March Hare interrupted in a great hurry.

"You did!" said the Hatter.

"I deny it!" said the March Hare.

"He denies it," said the King: "leave out that part."

"Well, at any rate, the Dormouse said—" the Hatter went on, looking anxiously round to see if he would deny it too; but the Dormouse denied nothing, being fast asleep.

"After that," continued the Hatter, "I cut some more bread-and-butter—"

"But what did the Dormouse say?" one of the jury asked.

"That I can't remember," said the Hatter.

"You *must* remember," remarked the King, "or I'll have you executed."

The miserable Hatter dropped his teacup and bread-and-butter, and went down on one knee. "I'm a poor man, your Majesty," he began.

"You're a *very* poor *speaker*," said the King.

Here one of the guinea-pigs cheered, and was immediately suppressed by the officers of the court. (As that is rather a hard word, I will just explain to you how it was done. They had a large canvas bag, which tied up at the mouth with strings: into this they slipped the guinea-pig, head first, and then sat upon it.)

"I'm glad I've seen that done," thought Alice. "I've so often read in the newspapers, at the end of trials, 'There was some attempt at applause, which was immediately suppressed by the officers of the court,' and I never understood what it meant till now."

"If that's all you know about it, you may stand down," continued the King.

"I can't go no lower," said the Hatter: "I'm on the floor, as it is."

"Then you may *sit* down," the King replied.

Here the other guinea-pig cheered, and was suppressed.

"Come, that finishes the guinea-pigs!" thought Alice. "Now we shall get on better."

"I'd rather finish my tea," said the Hatter, with an anxious look at the Queen, who was reading the list of singers.

"You may go," said the King, and the Hatter hurriedly left the court, without even waiting to put his shoes on.

"—and just take his head off outside," the Queen added to one of the officers; but the Hatter was out of sight before the officer could get to the door.

"Call the next witness!" said the King.

The next witness was the Duchess' cook. She carried the pepper-box in her hand, and Alice guessed who it was, even before she got into the court, by the way the people near the door began sneezing all at once.

"Give your evidence," said the King.

"Shan't," said the cook.

The King looked anxiously at the White Rabbit, who said, in a low voice, "Your Majesty must cross-examine *this* witness."

"Well, if I must, I must," the King said with a melancholy air, and, after folding his arms and frowning at the cook till his eyes were nearly out of sight, he said, in a deep voice, "What are tarts made of?"

"Pepper, mostly," said the cook.

"Treacle," said a sleepy voice behind her.

"Collar that Dormouse!" the Queen shrieked out. "Behead that Dormouse! Turn that Dormouse out of court! Suppress him! Pinch him! Off with his whiskers!"

For some minutes the whole court was in confusion getting the Dormouse turned out, and, by the time they had settled down again, the cook had disappeared.

"Never mind!" said the King, with an air of great relief. "Call the next witness." And, he added, in an under-tone to the Queen, "Really, my dear, *you* must cross-examine the next witness. It quite makes my forehead ache!"

Alice watched the White Rabbit as he fumbled over the list, feeling very curious to see what the next witness would be like, "—for they haven't got much evidence *yet*," she said to herself. Imagine her surprise, when the White Rabbit read out, at the top of his shrill little voice, the name "Alice!"

12: *Alice's Evidence*

"HERE!" cried Alice, quite forgetting in the flurry of the moment how large she had grown in the last few minutes, and she jumped up in such a hurry that she tipped over the jury-box with the edge of her skirt, upsetting all the jurymen onto the heads of the crowd below, and there they lay sprawling about, reminding her very much of a globe of gold-fish she had accidentally upset the week before.

"Oh, I *beg* your pardon!" she exclaimed in a tone of great dismay, and began picking them up again as quickly as she could, for the accident of the gold-fish kept running in her head, and she had a vague sort of idea that they must be collected at once and put back into the jury-box, or they would die.

"The trial cannot proceed," said the King, in a very grave voice, "until all the jurymen are back in their proper places—*all*," he repeated with great emphasis, looking hard at Alice as he said so.

Alice looked at the jury-box, and saw that, in her haste, she had put the Lizard in head downwards, and the poor little thing was waving its tail about in a melancholy way, being quite unable to move. She soon got it out again, and put it right; "not that it signifies much," she said to herself; "I should think it would be *quite* as much use in the trial one way up as the other."

As soon as the jury had a little recovered from the shock of being upset, and their slates and pencils had been found and handed back to them, they set to work very diligently to write out a history of the accident, all except the Lizard, who seemed too much overcome to do anything but sit with its mouth open, gazing up into the roof of the court.

"What do you know about this business?" the King said to Alice.

"Nothing," said Alice.

"Nothing *whatever?*" persisted the King.

"Nothing whatever," said Alice.

"That's very important," the King said, turning to the jury. They were just beginning to write this down on their slates, when the White Rabbit interrupted: "*Un*-important, your Majesty means, of course," he said, in a very respectful tone, but frowning and making faces at him as he spoke.

"*Un*important, of course, I meant," the King hastily said, and went on to himself in an undertone, "important —unimportant—unimportant—important—" as if he were trying which word sounded best.

Some of the jury wrote it down "important," and some "unimportant." Alice could see this, as she was near enough to look over their slates; "but it doesn't matter a bit," she thought to herself.

At this moment the King, who had been for some time busily writing in his notebook, called out "Silence!" and read out from his book, "Rule Forty-two. *All persons more than a mile high to leave the court.*"

Everybody looked at Alice.

"*I'm* not a mile high," said Alice.

"You are," said the King.

"Nearly two miles high," added the Queen.

"Well, I shan't go, at any rate," said Alice: "besides, that's not a regular rule: you invented it just now."

"It's the oldest rule in the book," said the King.

"Then it ought to be Number One," said Alice.

The King turned pale, and shut his notebook hastily. "Consider your verdict," he said to the jury, in a low, trembling voice.

"There's more evidence to come yet, please your Majesty," said the White Rabbit, jumping up in a great hurry: "this paper has just been picked up."

"What's in it?" said the Queen.

"I haven't opened it yet," said the White Rabbit; "but it seems to be a letter, written by the prisoner to—to somebody."

"It must have been that," said the King, "unless it was written to nobody, which isn't usual, you know."

"Who is it directed to?" said one of the jurymen.

"It isn't directed at all," said the White Rabbit: "in fact, there's nothing written on the *outside*." He unfolded the paper as he spoke, and added, "It isn't a letter, after all: it's a set of verses."

"Are they in the prisoner's handwriting?" asked another of the jurymen.

"No, they're not," said the White Rabbit, "and that's the queerest thing about it." (The jury all looked puzzled.)

"He must have imitated somebody else's hand," said the King. (The jury all brightened up again.)

"Please your Majesty," said the Knave, "I didn't write it, and they can't prove that I did: there's no name signed at the end."

"If you didn't sign it," said the King, "that only makes the matter worse. You *must* have meant some mischief, or else you'd have signed your name like an honest man."

There was a general clapping of hands at this: it was the first really clever thing the King had said that day.

"That *proves* his guilt," said the Queen.

"It proves nothing of the sort!" said Alice. "Why, you don't even know what they're about!"

"Read them," said the King.

The White Rabbit put on his spectacles. "Where shall I begin, please your Majesty?" he asked.

"Begin at the beginning," the King said, gravely, "and go on till you come to the end: then stop."

These were the verses the White Rabbit read:—

> *"They told me you had been to her,*
>   *And mentioned me to him:*
> *She gave me a good character,*
>   *But said I could not swim.*
>
> *He sent them word I had not gone*
>   *(We know it to be true):*
> *If she should push the matter on,*
>   *What would become of you?*
>
> *I gave her one, they gave him two,*
>   *You gave us three or more;*
> *They all returned from him to you,*
>   *Though they were mine before.*

If I or she should chance to be
  Involved in this affair,
He trusts to you to set them free,
  Exactly as we were.

My notion was that you had been
  (Before she had this fit)
An obstacle that came between
  Him, and ourselves, and it.

Don't let him know she liked them best,
  For this must ever be
A secret, kept from all the rest,
  Between yourself and me."

"That's the most important piece of evidence we've heard yet," said the King, rubbing his hands; "so now let the jury—"

"If any one of them can explain it," said Alice (she had grown so large in the last few minutes that she wasn't a bit afraid of interrupting him), "I'll give him sixpence. *I* don't believe there's an atom of meaning in it."

The jury all wrote down on their slates, "*She* doesn't believe there's an atom of meaning in it," but none of them attempted to explain the paper.

"If there's no meaning in it," said the King, "that saves a world of trouble, you know, as we needn't try to find any. And yet I don't know," he went on, spreading out the verses on his knee, and looking at them with one eye; "I seem to see some meaning in them, after all. '—*said I could not swim*—' you can't swim, can you?" he added, turning to the Knave.

The Knave shook his head sadly. "Do I look like it?" he said. (Which he certainly did *not*, being made entirely of cardboard.)

"All right, so far," said the King; and he went on muttering over the verses to himself: " '*We know it to be true*'

—that's the jury, of course—'*If she should push the matter on*'—that must be the Queen—'*What would become of you?*'—What, indeed!—'*I gave her one, they gave him two*'—why, that must be what he did with the tarts, you know—"

"But it goes on '*they all returned from him to you,*'" said Alice.

"Why, there they are!" said the King triumphantly, pointing to the tarts on the table. "Nothing can be clearer than *that*. Then again—'*before she had this fit*'—you never had fits, my dear, I think?" he said to the Queen.

"Never!" said the Queen furiously, throwing an inkstand at the Lizard as she spoke. (The unfortunate little Bill had left off writing on his slate with one finger, as he found it made no mark; but he now hastily began again, using the ink, that was trickling down his face, as long as it lasted.)

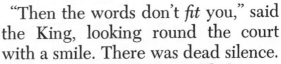

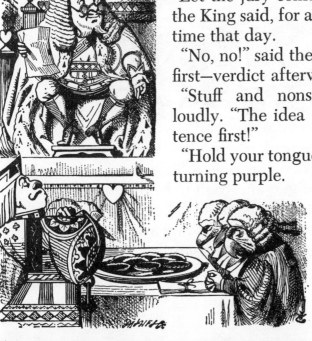

"Then the words don't *fit* you," said the King, looking round the court with a smile. There was dead silence.

"It's a pun!" the King added in an angry tone, and everybody laughed. "Let the jury consider their verdict," the King said, for about the twentieth time that day.

"No, no!" said the Queen. "Sentence first—verdict afterwards."

"Stuff and nonsense!" said Alice loudly. "The idea of having the sentence first!"

"Hold your tongue!" said the Queen, turning purple.

"I won't" said Alice.

"Off with her head!" the Queen shouted at the top of her voice. Nobody moved.

"Who cares for you?" said Alice (she had grown to her full size by this time). "You're nothing but a pack of cards!"

At this the whole pack rose up into the air and came flying down upon her; she gave a little scream, half of fright and half of anger, and tried to beat them off, and found herself lying on the bank, with her head in the lap of her sister, who was gently brushing away some dead leaves that had fluttered down from the trees onto her face.

"Wake up, Alice dear!" said her sister. "Why, what a long sleep you've had!"

"Oh, I've had such a curious dream!" said Alice. And she told her sister, as well as she could remember them, all these strange Adventures of hers that you have just been reading about; and, when she had finished, her sister kissed her, and said, "It *was* a curious dream, dear, certainly; but now run in to your tea: it's getting late." So Alice got up and ran off, thinking while she ran, as well she might, what a wonderful dream it had been.

But her sister sat still just as she left her, leaning her head on her hand, watching the setting sun, and thinking of little Alice and all her wonderful Adventures, till she too began dreaming after a fashion, and this was her dream:

First, she dreamed of little Alice herself: once again the tiny hands were clasped upon her knee, and the bright eager eyes were looking up into hers—she could hear the very tones of her voice, and see that queer little toss of her head, to keep back the wandering hair that *would* always get into her eyes—and still as she listened, or seemed to listen, the whole place around her became alive with the strange creatures of her little sister's dream.

The long grass rustled at her feet as the White Rabbit hurried by—the frightened Mouse splashed his way through the neighbouring pool—she could hear the rattle of the teacups as the March Hare and his friends shared their never-ending meal, and the shrill voice of the Queen ordering off her unfortunate guests to execution —once more the pig-baby was sneezing on the Duchess' knee, while plates and dishes crashed around it—once more the shriek of the Gryphon, the squeaking of the

Lizard's slate-pencil, and the choking of the suppressed guinea-pigs, filled the air, mixed up with the distant sob of the miserable Mock Turtle.

So she sat on, with closed eyes, and half believed herself in Wonderland, though she knew she had but to open them again and all would change to dull reality—the grass would be only rustling in the wind, and the pool rippling to the waving of the reeds—the rattling teacups would change to tinkling sheep-bells, and the Queen's shrill cries to the voice of the shepherd boy—and the sneeze of the baby, the shriek of the Gryphon, and all the other queer noises, would change (she knew) to the confused clamour of the busy farmyard—while the lowing of the cattle in the distance would take the place of the Mock Turtle's heavy sobs.

Lastly, she pictured to herself how this same little sister of hers would, in the after-time, be herself a grown woman; and how she would keep, through all her riper years, the simple and loving heart of her childhood: and how she would gather about her other little children, and make *their* eyes bright and eager with many a strange tale, perhaps even with the dream of Wonderland of long ago: and how she would feel with all their simple sorrows, and find a pleasure in all their simple joys, remembering her own child-life, and the happy summer days.

Lewis Carroll's Alice's Adventures in Wonderland *was first published in 1865. Attractive editions are now published by Macmillan (New Children's Classics), with forty-two illustrations by Sir John Tenniel; and by Grosset (Illustrated Junior Library), illustrated by Sir John Tenniel. The sequel,* Through the Looking-glass, *is included in both of the above editions.*

The Borrowers

BY MARY NORTON

Illustrations by Beth and Joe Krush

Pod and Homily and their daughter Arrietty
are a tiny family who live under the floor-
boards in an English country house. They
"borrow" their supplies from the human
family that lives in the house. But acquiring
these treasures has its dangers. For to be
"seen" by the humans is the worst tragedy
that can befall a Borrower.

IT was an eye. Or it looked like an eye. Clear and
bright like the color of the sky. An eye like her own but
enormous. A glaring eye. Breathless with fear, she sat
up. And the eye blinked. A great fringe of lashes came
curving down and flew up again out of sight. Cautiously,
Arrietty moved her legs: she would slide noiselessly in
among the grass stems and slither away down the bank.

"Don't move!" said a voice, and the voice, like the eye,
was enormous but, somehow, hushed—and hoarse like
a surge of wind through the grating on a stormy night
in March.

Arrietty froze. "So this is it," she thought, "the worst
and most terrible thing of all: I have been 'seen'! Whatever happened to Eggletina will now, almost certainly,
happen to me!"

There was a pause and Arrietty, her heart pounding
in her ears, heard the breath again drawn swiftly into
the vast lungs. "Or," said the voice, whispering still, "I
shall hit you with my ash stick."

Suddenly Arrietty became calm. "Why?" she asked. How strange her own voice sounded! Crystal thin and harebell clear, it tinkled in the air.

"In case," came the surprised whisper at last, "you ran toward me, quickly, through the grass . . . in case," it went on, trembling a little, "you came and scrabbled at me with your nasty little hands."

Arrietty stared at the eye; she held herself quite still. "Why?" she asked again, and again the word tinkled— icy cold it sounded this time, and needle sharp.

"Things do," said the voice. "I've seen them. In India."

Arrietty thought of her Gazetteer of the World. "You're not in India now," she pointed out.

"Did you come out of the house?"

"Yes," said Arrietty.

"From whereabouts in the house?"

Arrietty stared at the eye. "I'm not going to tell you," she said at last bravely.

"Then I'll hit you with my ash stick!"

"All right," said Arrietty, "hit me!"

"I'll pick you up and break you in half!"

Arrietty stood up. "All right," she said and took two paces forward.

There was a sharp gasp and an earthquake in the grass: he spun away from her and sat up, a great mountain in a green jersey. He had fair, straight hair and golden eyelashes. "Stay where you are!" he cried.

Arrietty stared up at him. So this was "the boy"! Breathless, she felt, and light with fear. "I guessed you were about nine," she gasped after a moment.

He flushed. "Well, you're wrong, I'm ten." He looked down at her, breathing deeply. "How old are you?"

"Fourteen," said Arrietty. "Next June," she added, watching him.

There was silence while Arrietty waited, trembling a little. "Can you read?" the boy said at last.

"Of course," said Arrietty. "Can't you?"

"No," he stammered. "I mean—yes. I mean I've just come from India."

"What's that got to do with it?" asked Arrietty.

"Well, if you're born in India, you're bilingual. And if you're bilingual, you can't read. Not so well."

Arrietty stared up at him: what a monster, she thought, dark against the sky.

"Do you grow out of it?" she asked.

He moved a little and she felt the cold flick of his shadow.

"Oh, yes," he said, "it wears off. My sisters were bilingual; now they aren't a bit. They could read any of those books upstairs in the schoolroom."

"So could I," said Arrietty quickly, "if someone could hold them, and turn the pages. I'm not a bit bilingual. I can read anything."

"Could you read out loud?"

"Of course," said Arrietty.

"Would you wait here while I run upstairs and get a book now?"

"Well," said Arrietty; she was longing to show off; then a startled look came into her eyes. "Oh—" she faltered.

"What's the matter?" The boy was standing up now. He towered above her.

"How many doors are there to this house?" She squinted up at him against the bright sunlight. He dropped on one knee.

"Doors?" he said. "Outside doors?"

"Yes."

"Well, there's the front door, the back door, the gun

room door, the kitchen door, the scullery door . . . and the french windows in the drawing room."

"Well, you see," said Arrietty, "my father's in the hall, by the front door, working. He . . . he wouldn't want to be disturbed."

"Working?" said the boy. "What at?"

"Getting material," said Arrietty, "for a scrubbing brush."

"Then I'll go in the side door"; he began to move away but turned suddenly and came back to her. He stood a moment, as though embarrassed, and then he said: "Can you fly?"

"No," said Arrietty, surprised; "can you?"

His face became even redder. "Of course not," he said angrily; "I'm not a fairy!"

"Well, nor am I," said Arrietty, "nor is anybody. I don't believe in them."

He looked at her strangely. "You don't believe in them?"

"No," said Arrietty; "do you?"

"Of course not!"

Really, she thought, he is a very angry kind of boy. "My mother believes in them," she said, trying to appease him. "She thinks she saw one once. It was when she was a girl and lived with her parents behind the sand pile in the potting shed."

He squatted down on his heels and she felt his breath on her face. "What was it like?" he asked.

"About the size of a glowworm with wings like a butterfly. And it had a tiny little face, she said, all alight and moving like sparks and tiny moving hands. Its face was changing all the time, she said, smiling and sort of shimmering. It seemed to be talking, she said, very quickly— but you couldn't hear a word. . . ."

"Oh," said the boy, interested. After a moment he asked: "Where did it go?"

"It just went," said Arrietty. "When my mother saw it, it seemed to be caught in a cobweb. It was dark at the time. About five o'clock on a winter's evening. After tea."

"Oh," he said again and picked up two petals of cherry blossom which he folded together like a sandwich and ate slowly. "Supposing," he said, staring past her at the wall of the house, "you saw a little man, about as tall as a pencil, with a blue patch in his trousers, halfway up a window curtain, carrying a doll's tea cup—would you say it was a fairy?"

"No," said Arrietty, "I'd say it was my father."

"Oh," said the boy, thinking this out, "does your father have a blue patch on his trousers?"

"Not on his best trousers. He does on his borrowing ones."

"Oh," said the boy again. He seemed to find it a safe sound, as lawyers do. "Are there many people like you?"

"No," said Arrietty. "None. We're all different."

"I mean as small as you?"

Arrietty laughed. "Oh, don't be silly!" she said. "Surely you don't think there are many people in the world your size?"

"There are more my size than yours," he retorted.

"Honestly—" began Arrietty helplessly and laughed again. "Do you really think—I mean, whatever sort of a world would it be? Those great chairs . . . I've seen them. Fancy if you had to make chairs that size for everyone? And the stuff for their clothes . . . miles and miles of it . . . tents of it . . . and the sewing! And their great houses, reaching up so you can hardly see the ceilings . . . their great beds . . . the *food* they eat . . . great, smoking mountains of it, huge bogs of stew and soup and stuff."

"Don't you eat soup?" asked the boy.

"Of course we do," laughed Arrietty. "My father had an uncle who had a little boat which he rowed round in the stock-pot picking up flotsam and jetsam. He did bottom-fishing too for bits of marrow until the cook got suspicious through finding bent pins in the soup. Once he was nearly shipwrecked on a chunk of submerged shinbone. He lost his oars and the boat sprang a leak but he flung a line over the pot handle and pulled himself alongside the rim. But all that stock—fathoms of it! And the size of the stock-pot! I mean, there wouldn't be enough stuff in the world to go round after a bit! That's why my father says it's a good thing they're dying out . . . just a few, my father says, that's all we need—to keep us. Otherwise, he says, the whole thing gets"—Arrietty hesitated, trying to remember the word—"exaggerated, he says—"

"What do you mean," asked the boy, " 'to keep us'?"

So Arrietty told him about borrowing—how difficult it was and how dangerous. She told him about the store-rooms under the floor; about Pod's early exploits, the skill he had shown and the courage; she described those far-off days, before her birth, when Pod and Homily had been rich; she described the musical snuffbox of gold filigree, and the little bird which flew out of it made of kingfisher feathers, how it flapped its wings and sang its song; she described the doll's wardrobe and the tiny green glasses; the little silver teapot out of the drawing-room case; the satin bedcovers and embroidered sheets . . . "those we have still," she told him, "they're Her handkerchiefs. . . ." "She," the boy realized gradually, was his Great-Aunt Sophy upstairs, bedridden since a hunting accident some twenty years before; he heard how Pod would borrow from Her room, picking his way—in the firelight—among the trinkets on Her dressing table, even climbing Her bedcurtains and walking on Her quilt. And of how She would watch him and sometimes talk to him because, Arrietty explained, every day at six o'clock they brought Her a decanter of Fine Old Pale Madeira, and how before midnight She would

drink the lot. Nobody blamed Her, not even Homily, because, as Homily would say, She had so few pleasures, poor soul, but, Arrietty explained, after the first three glasses Great-Aunt Sophy never believed in anything she saw. "She thinks my father comes out of the decanter," said Arrietty, "and one day when I'm older he's going to take me there and She'll think I come out of the decanter too. It'll please Her, my father thinks, as She's used to him now. Once he took my mother, and She perked up like anything and kept asking after her and why didn't she come any more and saying they'd watered the Madeira because once, She says, She saw a little man *and* a little woman and now she only sees a little man. . . ."

"I wish she thought I came out of the decanter," said the boy. "She gives me dictation and teaches me to write. I only see her in the mornings when she's cross. She sends for me and looks behind my ears and asks Mrs. D. if I've learned my words."

"What does Mrs. D. look like?" asked Arrietty. (How delicious it was to say "Mrs. D." like that . . . how careless and daring!)

"She's fat and has a mustache and gives me my bath and hurts my bruise and my sore elbow and says she'll take a slipper to me one of these days. . . ." The boy pulled up a tuft of grass and stared at it angrily and Arrietty saw his lip tremble. "My mother's very nice," he said. "She lives in India. Why did you lose all your worldly riches?"

"Well," said Arrietty, "the kitchen boiler burst and hot water came pouring through the floor into our house and everything was washed away and piled up in front of the grating. My father worked night and day. First hot, then cold. Trying to salvage things. And there's a dreadful draught in March through that grating. He got ill, you see, and couldn't go borrowing. So my Uncle Hendreary had to do it and one or two others and my mother gave them things, bit by bit, for all their trouble. But the kingfisher bird was spoilt by the water; all its feathers fell off and a great twirly spring came jumping out of its side. My father used the spring to keep the door shut against draughts from the grating and my mother put the feathers in a little moleskin hat. After a while I got born and my father went borrowing again. But he gets tired now and doesn't like curtains, not when any of the bobbles are off. . . ."

"I helped him a bit," said the boy, "with the tea cup. He was shivering all over. I suppose he was frightened."

"My father frightened!" exclaimed Arrietty angrily. "Frightened of you!" she added.

"Perhaps he doesn't like heights," said the boy.

"He loves heights," said Arrietty. "The thing he doesn't like is curtains. I've told you. Curtains make him tired."

The boy sat thoughtfully on his haunches, chewing a blade of grass. "Borrowing," he said after a while. "Is that what you call it?"

"What else could you call it?" asked Arrietty.

"I'd call it stealing."

Arrietty laughed. She really laughed. "But we *are* Borrowers," she explained, "like you're a—a human bean or whatever it's called. We're part of the house. You might as well say that the fire grate steals the coal from the coal scuttle."

"Then what is stealing?"

Arrietty looked grave. "Don't you know?" she asked. "Stealing is—well, supposing my Uncle Hendreary borrowed an emerald watch from Her dressing-table and my father took it and hung it up on our wall. That's stealing."

"An emerald watch!" exclaimed the boy.

"Well, I just said that because we have one on the wall at home, but my father borrowed it himself. It needn't be a watch. It could be anything. A lump of sugar even. But Borrowers don't steal."

"Except from human beings," said the boy.

Arrietty burst out laughing; she laughed so much that she had to hide her face in the primrose. "Oh dear," she gasped with tears in her eyes, "you are funny!" She stared upward at his puzzled face. "Human beans are *for* Borrowers—like bread's for butter!"

The boy was silent awhile. A sigh of wind rustled the cherry tree and shivered among the blossoms.

"Well, I don't believe it," he said at last, watching the falling petals. "I don't believe that's what we're for at all and I don't believe we're dying out!"

"Oh, goodness!" exclaimed Arrietty impatiently, staring up at his chin. "Just use your common sense: you're the only real human bean I ever saw (although I do just know of three more—Crampfurl, Her, and Mrs. Driver). But I know lots and lots of Borrowers: the Overmantels and the Harpsichords and the Rain-Barrels and the Linen-Presses and the Boot-Racks and the Hon. John Studdingtons and—"

He looked down. "John Studdington? But he was our grand-uncle—"

"Well, this family lived behind a picture," went on Arrietty, hardly listening, "and there were the Stove-Pipes and the Bell-Pulls and the—"

"Yes," he interrupted, "but did you see them?"

"I saw the Harpsichords. And my mother was a Bell-Pull. The others were before I was born. . . ."

He leaned closer. "Then where are they now? Tell me that."

"My Uncle Hendreary has a house in the country," said Arrietty coldly, edging away from his great lowering face; it was misted over, she noticed, with hairs of palest gold. "And four children, Harpsichords and Clocks."

"But where are the others?"

"Oh," said Arrietty, "they're somewhere." But where? she wondered. And she shivered slightly in the boy's cold shadow which lay about her, slant-wise, on the grass.

He drew back again, his fair head blocking out a great piece of sky. "Well," he said deliberately after a moment, and his eyes were cold, "I've only seen two Borrowers but I've seen hundreds and hundreds and hundreds and hundreds and hundreds—"

"Oh no—" whispered Arrietty.

"Of human beings." And he sat back.

Arrietty stood very still. She did not look at him. After a while she said: "I don't believe you."

"All right," he said, "then I'll tell you—"

"I still won't believe you," murmured Arrietty.

"Listen!" he said. And he told her about railway stations and football matches and racecourses and royal processions and Albert Hall concerts. He told her about India and China and North America and the British Commonwealth. He told her about the July sales. "Not hundreds," he said, "but thousands and millions and billions and trillions of great, big, enormous people. Now do you believe me?"

Arrietty stared up at him with frightened eyes: it gave her a crick in the neck. "I don't know," she whispered.

"As for you," he went on, leaning closer again, "I don't believe that there are any more Borrowers anywhere in the world. I believe you're the last three," he said.

Arrietty dropped her face into the primrose. "We're not. There's Aunt Lupy and Uncle Hendreary and all the cousins."

"I bet they're dead," said the boy. "And what's more," he went on, "no one will ever believe I've seen *you*. And you'll be the very last because you're the youngest. One day," he told her, smiling triumphantly, "you'll be the only Borrower left in the world!"

He sat still, waiting, but she did not look up. "Now you're crying," he remarked after a moment.

"They're not dead," said Arrietty in a muffled voice; she was feeling in her little pocket for a handkerchief. "They live in a badger's set two fields away, beyond the spinney. We don't see them because it's too far. There are weasels and things and cows and foxes . . . and crows. . . ."

"Which spinney?" he asked.

"I don't KNOW!" Arrietty almost shouted. "It's along by the gas-pipe—a field called Parkin's Beck." She blew her nose. "I'm going home," she said.

"Don't go," he said, "not yet."

"Yes, I'm going," said Arrietty.

His face turned pink. "Let me just get the book," he pleaded.

"I'm not going to read to you now," said Arrietty.

"Why not?"

She looked at him with angry eyes. "Because—"

"Listen," he said, "I'll go to that field. I'll go and find Uncle Hendreary. And the cousins. And Aunt Whatever-she-is. And, if they're alive, I'll tell you. What about that? You could write them a letter and I'd put it down the hole—"

Arrietty gazed up at him. "Would you?" she breathed.

"Yes, I would. Really I would. Now can I go and get the book? I'll go in by the side door."

"All right," said Arrietty absently. Her eyes were shining. "When can I give you the letter?"

"Any time," he said, standing above her. "Where in the house do you live?"

"Well—" began Arrietty and stopped. Why once again did she feel this chill? Could it only be his shadow . . . towering above her, blotting out the sun? "I'll put it somewhere," she said hurriedly, "I'll put it under the hall mat."

"Which one? The one by the front door?"

"Yes, that one."

He was gone. And she stood there alone in the sunshine, shoulder deep in grass. What had happened seemed too big for thought; she felt unable to believe it really had happened: not only had she been "seen" but she had been talked to; not only had she been talked to but she had—

"Arrietty!" said a voice.

She stood up startled and spun round: there was Pod, moon-faced, on the path looking up at her. "Come on down!" he whispered.

She stared at him for a moment as though she did not recognize him; how round his face was, how kind, how familiar!

"Come on!" he said again, more urgently; and obediently because he sounded worried, she slithered quickly toward him off the bank, balancing her primrose. "Put that thing down," he said sharply, when she stood at last beside him on the path. "You can't lug great flowers about—you got to carry a bag. What you want to go up there for?" he grumbled as they moved off across the stones. "I might never have seen you. Hurry up now. Your mother'll have tea waiting!"

This book was awarded the Carnegie Medal in 1952. Pod, Homily, and Arrietty continue their adventures in two sequels: The Borrowers Afield *and* The Borrowers Afloat, *both published by Harcourt, Brace.*

Miss Hickory

BY CAROLYN SHERWIN BAILEY

Illustrations by Ruth Gannett

Miss Hickory had a body made of apple-wood twig and a hickory nut for a head. She spent her summers in a corncob house beneath the lilac bush and her winters on Great-granny Brown's windowsill. And then Great-granny Brown went away.

MISS Hickory heard heavy footsteps, clump, clumping along the stones of the pasture, then approaching her lilac bush. Out of the corner of one sharp little black eye she could see a pair of large yellow feet but she did not turn her head. As a matter of fact Miss Hickory had difficulty in turning her head. It was a hickory nut that had grown with an especially sharp and pointed nose. Her eyes and mouth were inked on. Her body was an apple-wood twig formed like a body with two arms and two legs, hands and feet, as twigs sometimes grow. To this body Miss Hickory's nut head was glued. She wore a blue-and-white checked gingham dress. A white cap with ruffles was tied in a smart bow beneath her chin. Many persons, looking first at Miss Hickory, would have said that she was a country doll, made by Miss Keturah who kept the notions store in Hillsborough, and given to Ann. But not you or I. The tilt of her sharp little nose, her pursed mouth and her keen eyes were not those of a doll. You and I would have known Miss Hickory as the real person that she was.

A black shadow passed the doorsill of Miss Hickory's house. A coarse *caw* seemed intended to catch her attention, but she continued sweeping with her broom that was made of pine needles. She had just finished her tea and her acorn cup and saucer, neatly washed, stood on a shelf above the stove. A bed of discarded pullets' feathers covered with a bright quilt of patched sumac leaves was ready for pleasant dreams. Miss Hickory's house was made of corncobs, notched, neatly fitted together and glued. It stood beneath the lilac bush that was so sweet and purple when in bloom, so thickly green and cheerful with birds all summer long. If one had to live in town, Miss Hickory had always said, take a house under a lilac bush.

Soon, through her front door, the sunset would toss a few colored pieces from the orchard sky. Soon, too, the sun would drop like the biggest apple in the world, red and round, behind Temple Mountain that guarded the orchard spring, summer, autumn and winter, world without end. The sun set earlier now, for it was late September. Miss Hickory swept more briskly to warm herself. Thinking of cold weather made her shiver. But a large dark head with beady eyes and a long bill, thrust in through the window, stopped her.

"Are you at home, Miss Hickory?" Crow asked in his hoarse voice.

"Well, what do you think, if you ever do think?" she asked. "I heard your big yellow clodhoppers, and I saw you pass by. If you think there is one kernel of corn left in my house walls that you can peck out you are mistaken. You have eaten them all."

"Dear lady!" said Crow, stooping, entering and making himself at home. "Always so polite, so generous!"

A small smile seemed to move the wrinkles of Miss Hickory's face. "Here." She took from her pocket a few hard yellow kernels and held them out. Crow gobbled, choked, bowed low.

"Don't try to thank me," she urged. "You'll get the hiccoughs. What is the news? If there is any, you have heard it."

"Precisely why I am here, as they put it over the radio," he said. "News indeed, and it concerns you."

Miss Hickory sat down on her toadstool, spreading her skirts neatly to cover her ankles. Crow rested his wings comfortably, eased his toes and leaned against the wall. These two might spat and tiff, but they had fellow feelings. Crow made no pretensions; he was a country man. The earth owed him a living and so he helped himself to cherries and corn. Summer boarders, the bluebirds, thrushes, and larks, could fend for themselves, Crow felt, paying high prices for any berries and seeds that they got from his feeding ground. But he knew what was going on throughout the entire countryside. He was tough and weatherwise. He set the date for Old Crow Week in Hillsborough every spring, and so started the season with noisy promise. He could walk as well as fly, which meant that he got around more than most birds. He knew that Miss Hickory had once been part of a tree and he respected her for that ancestry. In certain ways they were alike. He waited for her to speak.

"Well," she said at last.

Crow folded his wings over his stomach and pointed his beak at Miss Hickory.

"Great-granny Brown is closing this house for the winter. She plans to live in the Women's City Club on Beacon Hill, Boston, until spring." The house was full of stillness for a while, thick with thoughts that could not break it. His words stunned Miss Hickory. She could not speak.

"I know," Crow said at last, "that you expected to live another winter, house and all, on Great-granny Brown's kitchen windowsill. You expected Ann to drop in almost every day and bring you something useful, a little iron stove, a pot or a tin teakettle. But the entire family is going to Boston. Ann is to be put into school there." Crow rolled his eyes toward the ceiling, pretending to be shocked. Truly, however, he was enjoying himself. A love of gossip is hatched from every crow's egg.

Miss Hickory arose. She came close to him, her sharp little nose almost touching his face.

"They could not! They would not!"

"Ah, yes, Miss Hickory," he assured her. "Two-leggers who have been to Boston long for wings. Only we country people who can fly never feel the need of a city. Now, I once knew a starling who went to the Public Gardens in Boston for a visit, but—"

"Stop! Don't gabble." Miss Hickory twisted her hands in distress. "Come to the point."

"The point is yours, dear lady." Crow tapped her shoulder playfully with one wing-tip. "You have seen through Great-granny Brown's kitchen window how deep the snowdrifts are in New Hampshire. I'll wager that there were days when you could not see through the windows. The winters are long and hard here, Miss Hickory."

"What could one do?" she begged. She would not believe him yet.

"Don't feel too badly, as if they had forgotten you," he said kindly, "Ann has other matters than dolls to fill her mind now. Great-granny Brown was born and bred in New Hampshire. She expects you to be equal to any weather. You'll have to move, Miss Hickory."

"Where?" She went over to the window and looked west. There each year the forest, wild and deep, marched closer to the Old Place. They had both forgotten to admire the sunset. The afterglow, like a blanket of woven rainbows, had folded about Temple Mountain.

"Aye, that's the rub!" Crow replied hoarsely.

Miss Hickory stamped her foot. "Don't talk like a Poll-Parrot. Whatever you hear, either the radio or William Shakespeare, you repeat. You know you can't read a word."

Crow bowed his head humbly. "Right you are, but what I meant was that we shall have to make a plan, and make it speedily. You can't live under a lilac bush all winter."

"We? This isn't your home. It belongs to me. I like it here. I can't move. Where would I take my stove, my pot and my teakettle, my cup and saucer and my bed? If I lived in a crows' nest, with no nice house furnishings and no good housekeeping . . ." She could not say any more. She could only look with love and fear at her four corn-cob walls.

"You give me an idea, Miss Hickory." Crow balanced himself on one foot and scratched his head with the other.

"I will have no idea of yours."

"But a little change is good for us all," Crow said smirkingly. "You must remember, dear lady, that you weren't born with a cup and saucer in your hand."

It was more than Miss Hickory could stand. She lost her temper. "I believe that this is all a piece of gossip on your part, Crow. I shall never believe that the Old Place is empty until I ask Mr. T. Willard-Brown. He will tell me the truth. As for you, Crow—" She stood as tall and brave as she could beside her door. "Get out of my house!" she ordered.

"As you wish." Crow walked in a dignified manner toward the door. "But don't worry. Something is bound to turn up!"

"I won't move!" she repeated as he stepped across the threshold. But he tapped her head lightly with his beak.

"Hardheaded, that's what you are!" And with that Crow walked off in the direction of the pine wood, he and the falling night one, in the color of dusk.

Miss Hickory put her twig hands up to her nut head. Crow, she knew, was right. Her head was undoubtedly hard. She moved slowly about her house, lifting a stove lid to poke the red coals, turning down her bedspread. But as she comforted herself with these homely tasks, a feeling that she had never experienced before came to Miss Hickory Perhaps it was caused by the sap that was still in her twig body. Perhaps it was the essence of the sweet nut inside the hard shell of her head. Whatever caused it, Miss Hickory began to cry. Tears came out of her eyes and rolled down her wrinkled cheeks. They fell so fast that she had to staunch them with her cap ties. It was dark then, so no one saw her break down. No one heard Miss Hickory sob, "It isn't true! I won't move! Mr. T. Willard-Brown will tell me tomorrow that I only had a bad dream."

"A good day to finish my canning," Miss Hickory said to herself as she built up a wood fire and started toward the forest for berries.

It was a beautiful day, crisp but with warm sunshine that made her forget Crow's warning visit. Crow was so ready with raucous chit-chatter that she did not take him seriously. "He always has something to say and likes to hear himself say it," she reminded herself as she put a small rush basket over her arm and stepped briskly off

on her twig feet. Although the torches that the golden-
rod had lighted along the October road towered above
Miss Hickory's head, she found her way easily in and out
among them. Their brightness made her feel gay. Farther
on the purple asters made a royal canopy beneath which
she walked proudly until she came to the edge of the
woods. She left the road and was at once in the deep
green of the pines.

Miss Hickory's nose was as keen as a fox's. The smell of
pine trees never failed to go to her head. She could not
explain why, but when she was alone in the woods, sniffing rich earth, wandering through the lacy lanes of ferns,
and smelling the pines, she felt like another person. She
wished that she had time to dig up one of the tiny new
hemlock trees to set out at the front of her corncob house,
an idea that she had treasured for some time. But the
cold of the woods, now that she had left the sunny road,
made her realize that there would not be many more
berrying days. She knelt down, dug away the leaves that
already were making a thick covering on the earth.

It always surprised her to feel how warm the earth
kept under the leaves, even on a cold day. She dug them
aside, here and there, uncovering the vines that she
wanted. It was as delightful to thrust her twig arms up to
the elbows in the warm tangle as to sniff the woods. She
began to pick the bright red berries and fill her basket.
There was no time to lose, she knew. Cock-Pheasant
lived close by and was a famous berry-picker.

Checkerberries first! They stood up straight, in plain
sight on their stems, and could be picked fast. But for
preserving and storing away in her acorn jugs for the
winter, Miss Hickory knew that checkerberry preserve
needed a good deal of sweetening, more honey than she
had been able to save that season. She picked up a few
checkerberry leaves. They were tasty and crisp served
with a cup of tea.

Next, the partridgeberries that ripened close to the

ground, little crimson balls in twins, two growing side
by side secretly on their low-lying running vine. Miss
Hickory canned partridgeberries whole in their own
sweet juice. As she finished gathering berries and started
home with her filled basket she remembered something
that Cock-Pheasant had once told her.

"When the partridgeberries are ripe," Cock-Pheasant
had said, "it is only two full moons before the first snow-
fall."

When she came home, Miss Hickory saw that the
entire front of her house was covered by the fat brindled
haunches of Mr. T. Willard-Brown. He was enjoying
the sunshine that trickled down through the bare lilac
bushes and waving his long tail to and fro like a banner.
He was a wandering barn cat, a hunter of renown, but
Miss Hickory liked him. Mr. T. Willard-Brown lived a
secret life closer to the ground than did Crow. He was
a newsy man and willing to share his stories.

"You are late this morning," she told him.

"The milking was late," he explained. "I can't start the day without my regular breakfast of a dish of warm milk, right from the cow."

Miss Hickory set down her basket of berries, came close, and looked sharply into Mr. T. Willard-Brown's green eyes.

"That would have been a better story, my friend," she said, "if you had washed your face before you told it. There is a feather sticking out of your mouth." She flipped it off.

"Oh, my ears and whiskers," he explained in mock chagrin. "However did I get into feathers so early in the morning? Now, if it had been teatime here at the Old Place and I had dropped in and someone had urged me to take a nap on one of those soft feather pillows—" He purred loudly to cover his embarrassment.

"Never mind," she said. "We all know your habits, Mr. T., and I am glad to see you this morning. Crow called a few days ago."

"Don't speak of him!" Mr. T. Willard-Brown spat. "I wouldn't eat crow on a wager. The last time I saw Crow he walked right toward me and said a bad word. I spat at him."

"If you ate crow occasionally you might be a better man," she told him. "What I was about to say when you interrupted me was that Crow spoke of the family as planning to leave Hillsborough for the winter. He said that Great-granny Brown was thinking of living at the Women's City Club on Beacon Hill, Boston, and Ann was going to school there. Nothing but hearsay on his part, of course."

Mr. T. Willard-Brown arose, stretched and yawned. "Not a plan, not hearsay, my love," he told Miss Hickory, "but the truth. They have gone!"

She listened without words, her eyes full of terror. He continued:

"You ought to get about more, Miss Hickory. All summer you have stayed here under the lilacs, only going to the woods for berries, or on Sunday when Jack-in-the-Pulpit preached. If you had gone around to the front of the house lately you would have seen trunks coming down from the attic."

"Gone!" she breathed at last. Now she knew that it was true. She would not let him see her cry. Instead she stamped her twig feet.

"It's all your fault, Mr. T. They had to leave to get away from *you*, scratching on doors and purring in the kitchen for milk. You are only a cat with a cat's ways. I shall tell all Hillsborough what your given name is, *Tippy*, because you have a white tip to your tail. Willard is for the barn where you were born. Brown is pretense. The hyphen is putting on airs. You are sly, Tippy. I always suspected it."

He purred loudly, curling his claws and smiling. "I am so famous a mouser that my given name and my humble birth are always overlooked. If you doubt Crow and me, why not go around to the front of the house and look in? See for yourself." He walked, with flowing tail, toward the barn.

Miss Hickory was unable to move for a space. She watched Mr. T. Willard-Brown, swinging his sides and disappearing at last through the wide red doors of the barn. Then she walked slowly away from the lilac bush, the corncob house, her basket of berries. She skirted the garden, crossed the lawn and came to the pink rambler-rose trellis beside the front porch. Up the trellis she climbed, braving the sharp thorns, up, up, until she could peer underneath the crack of the window where the shade was not completely pulled down.

Blue Rocking Chair stood empty and still. The fireplace was boarded. The family Bible on the center-table was folded carefully in a white towel. The shining brass pendulum of the grandfather clock hung motionless and the hands pointed to eight o'clock. It must, by the shadow on the lawn sundial, be noon now. The Old Farmer's Almanac that had hung by a loop of string on the wall was gone. She had been alone, without knowing it, for some time.

She knew now that everything that Crow and Mr. T. Willard-Brown had told her was true. Her head would have whirled if it could. She felt too weak to hold on to the rose trellis, but she backed slowly down. Mr. T. Willard-Brown was waiting for her, having come softly around the corner of the house.

"Well, there you are, Miss Hickory," he purred. "Two of us in the same fix. Why not come over to the barn with me? It is to be kept open all winter and I have been offered a permanent position as head-ratter."

"I wasn't born to live in a barn," she told him desperately.

"Where then?" he asked.

"I am going home," she said. "Today I shall finish my canning."

"Home?" he smiled. "Amusing, that! I just passed your house and it was occupied. You know Chipmunk of course, who lives in the stone wall and has been so spoiled with gifts of peanuts that he expects to be supported? He has moved into your house, Miss Hickory. I should say that he is there for the winter. He was finishing his dinner when I saw him, your basket of berries."

Miss Hickory never remembered how long she sat on the ground under the rambler-rose trellis. If she had been living in her own home at the back of the house she might have cried, but that small corncob home, so cozy and familiar, was now occupied by Chipmunk.

Here, with the open road in front, she was too proud
to show her sorrow. More than sorrow, she felt despair.
She became damp with the heavy dew and then stiff
with the first frost. The wind whistling down from
Temple Mountain whipped her wet skirts around her
shivering legs. None of the few passers-by noticed her.
Mr. T. Willard-Brown, warm and busy in the barn, gave
her no thought. A light flurry of snow powdered her cap.

But one day, when Miss Hickory was sure that her
end was near, down the road from the orchard, walking
briskly, came Crow. Would he, too, pass her by? No.
Crow turned into the front path and approached. He
came close to the spot where Miss Hickory huddled
under the poor shelter of the rambler-rose trellis. He
raised one foot in salute.

"Dear lady!" Crow croaked, ignoring her bedraggled
state. He understood that she had suffered a great loss.
He was a busybody and had heard about Chipmunk.

"Don't try to explain, Miss Hickory," he said hoarsely.
"We all have our troubles. I told you that something
would turn up. It has."

"What?" She stood up and leaned against the trellis.

"First of all," he told her, "you must realize that a
change, travel, a new scene, are good for all of us.
Especially you, Miss Hickory, need a change. You have
been living for two years with those who feel that they
need a grocery store, a Ford car, a stove, and storm
windows. You have grown soft."

She held out her arms, no longer proud.

"Don't preach to me, Crow! What has turned up?"

"A new home for you." He gave a hop-jig step and
a swing for show. "Don't ask any questions, but come
along with me. There isn't any time to lose. I shall very
likely be off for good tomorrow and I want to see you
well settled in before I leave. Come with me, dear lady."

Miss Hickory stumbled weakly toward Crow, but he

caught her underneath one wide black wing. His wing was like a tent, warm and strong. His big yellow feet guided her small twig ones as the two left the Old Place behind and took to the road. He shortened his steps to suit hers, talking earnestly in his rough voice as he led her toward the orchard.

"You spoke of the untidiness of my nest. How right you are, Miss Hickory. Sticks, chaff and bark are all I ever use. But please realize that I am a man of affairs. I spend my days here and there, in the cornfield, the orchard, the vegetable garden. All I need in the way of a home is a place to hang my hat. But my nest is built high at the top of a tall pine tree as a lookout. From it I saw your new home."

They reached the orchard.

"Turn this way," he told her. "We are going to follow McIntosh Lane along the sidehill. You can't imagine how sheltered it is there, under the lee of the mountain with the pine woods up above for a windbreak. Lean on me, Miss Hickory. We are almost there."

As they found and took the stubble-grown path where the older apple trees had twisted in odd bent shapes, the better to climb the sidehill of the orchard and reach the sun, Miss Hickory felt herself floating, rather than trudging along. She was lifted off her feet every now and then as she clung to Crow's wing. She felt again the energy that the woods always gave her. The exercise of trying to keep up with Crow warmed her. Her heart pounded with excitement, for she believed that Crow was helping her to begin a great adventure. Perhaps a small log cabin with a fireplace and a chimney was waiting on beyond. When she had signed the lease she would return, evict Chipmunk and move her things up there to the sidehill on McIntosh Lane.

"Is it much farther?" she gasped.

Crow was muttering and did not answer at once. He

had never been able to count above one. One cherry; gulp it down. One plump green pea. One mouthful of corn. His father had taught him the Corn-planting Rule:

> "One for the cut-worm
> One for the crow,
> One for the farmer . . ."

"Never mind the rest of it," Crow's father had said. "It signifies nothing for us until later: *'Two to grow.'*"

So Crow was not counting the trees on the sidehill, but naming them.

"Cherry. Northern Spy. Clapp's Favorite Pear. McIntosh. McIntosh. Mc—Mc—Tosh—Tosh—." His tongue was becoming twisted. "Here we are!" he told her at last, as they were halfway or so along the sidehill and deep among the leafless gnarled shapes of the apple trees. He stopped beneath one that had not seemed worth pruning that spring. The branches touched the ground and it leaned comfortably toward the slope of the hill, away from the wind. He loosed his hold on Miss Hickory and hopped toward a low-lying bough. "Climb up!" he ordered.

"But—I don't understand." She hesitated.

Crow spread his wings and disappeared among the branches of the apple tree but his voice croaked down to her:

"He who hesitates is lost. Do you or do you not want to live until spring? Climb, I told you!"

She grasped the low bough. How homelike it felt in her strong little twig fingers!

"Swing a bit and then jump!" Crow's call came to her from higher up. This, she decided, was a game that he wanted her to learn. She pulled on the bough, swayed pleasantly a moment and then jumped to another branch farther on.

"Keep on!" Crow croaked. "Climb along up."

So she continued to swing, jump and climb, feeling

more adventurous and bold with each step. Up, up, Miss
Hickory climbed into the apple tree until the ground
was dizzying to look down upon and she could see
Temple Mountain, keeping vigil to the west.

"How much farther?" she called.

"Here you are," he answered from a perch right beside her. "Careful now. Easy does it. How's this, dear
lady, for your new home?"

She looked in astonishment at what he pointed out
to her, a large and deep nest resting securely in a crotch
of the apple tree. Crow knew that it might not suit her
at first sight so he began to argue and boast, like a real
estate agent.

"Light and heat free, whenever the sun shines. A
long lease. Although Robin built it for his own use and
planned to stay north this winter, Mr. T. Willard-Brown
drove him away. Hooks for hanging your clothes; Robin
builds carelessly and leaves twigs sticking out. Insulated
against the cold with good country mud." Crow's sales
talk went on and on, but Miss Hickory had not listened
after he had mentioned Mr. T. Willard-Brown. No cat,
she decided, would drive *her* out of her home. She balanced on a bough and inspected the empty nest. It was
indeed well placed, sheltered and strong. As she peered
inside she saw that the wind had cushioned the empty
nest deeply with milkweed down and lined it with rose-
brown oak leaves. She stepped inside and sank down
deliciously into its warm comfort.

"Not bad at all, Crow," she admitted.

"It struck me favorably," he croaked.

The nest was so well suited to her size that when she
stood up, she had to stretch a bit to pull herself out.
When she lay down, as she now did, for she was very
tired, she was snug and unseen. She was alone in a
world that had no need of the things she had left behind.

"I don't know what I shall do here all winter," she said, "without a broom in my hands."

"You'll find plenty to do," he told her. "New things to collect, new friends, new places to explore. Well, it's time I was off."

"I am greatly obliged to you, Crow." She leaned over the edge of the nest as Crow opened his wings.

"Don't give it a thought," he said.

"How long until spring?" she ventured to ask. "They took the Old Farmer's Almanac to Boston."

"It doesn't matter," he assured her. "Spring always comes. Remember this, though, dear lady. This is important. Get it through your head. *Keep your sap running!*"

Crow spread his wings, cawed loudly and started. Miss Hickory watched Crow cross the Old Place, the barn, the woods, then disappear as he flew toward the south.

This book was awarded the Newbery Medal in 1947. Another story which takes place in Great-granny Brown's New Hampshire farm is Mrs. Bailey's Finnegan II: His Nine Lives, *also published by The Viking Press. Other good doll stories are* Hitty—Her First Hundred Years, *by Rachel Field, published by The Macmillan Company;* Floating Island, *by Anne Parrish, published by Harper & Brothers; and* The Doll's House, *by Rumer Godden, published by The Viking Press.*

Winnie-the-Pooh

BY A. A. MILNE

Illustrations by Ernest H. Shepard

Christopher Robin was a real little boy whose father put him in books so that he might live forever. Like other small boys, Christopher Robin often pretended that his toys were alive. Out of this world of make-believe, A. A. Milne has fashioned the wonderful world of Winnie-the-Pooh.

HERE is Edward Bear, coming downstairs now, bump, bump, bump, on the back of his head, behind Christopher Robin. It is, as far as he knows, the only way of coming downstairs, but sometimes he feels that there really is another way, if only he could stop bumping for a moment and think of it. And then he feels that perhaps there isn't. Anyhow, here he is at the bottom, and ready to be introduced to you.

Winnie-the-Pooh.

When I first heard his name, I said, just as you are going to say, "But I thought he was a boy?"

"So did I," said Christopher Robin.

"Then you can't call him Winnie?"

"I don't."

"But you said——"

"He's Winnie-ther-Pooh. Don't you know what *'ther'* means?"

"Ah, yes, now I do," I said quickly; and I hope you do too, because it is all the explanation you are going to get.

Sometimes Winnie-the-Pooh likes a game of some sort when he comes downstairs, and sometimes he likes to sit quietly in front of the fire and listen to a story. This evening——

"What about a story?" asked Christopher Robin.

"*What* about a story?" I said.

"Could you very sweetly tell Winnie-the-Pooh one?"

"I suppose I could," I said. "What sort of stories does he like?"

"About himself. Because he's *that* sort of Bear."

"Oh, I see."

"So could you very sweetly?"

"I'll try," I said.

So I tried.

Once upon a time, a very long time ago now, about last Friday, Winnie-the-Pooh lived in a forest all by himself under the name of Sanders.

(*"What does 'under the name' mean?" asked Christopher Robin.*

"It means he had the name over the door in gold letters, and lived under it."

"Winnie-the-Pooh wasn't quite sure," said Christopher Robin.

"Now I am," said a growly voice.

"Then I will go on," said I.)

One day when he was out walking, he came to an open place in the middle of the forest, and in the middle of this place was a large oak-tree, and, from the top of the tree, there came a loud buzzing-noise.

Winnie-the-Pooh sat down at the foot of the tree, put his head between his paws and began to think.

First of all he said to himself: "That buzzing-noise means something. You don't get a buzzing-noise like that, just buzzing and buzzing, without its meaning something. If there's a buzzing-noise, somebody's making a buzzing-noise, and the only reason for making a buzzing-noise that I know of is because you're a bee."

Then he thought another long time, and said: "And the only reason for being a bee that I know of is making honey."

And then he got up, and said: "And the only reason for making honey is so as I can eat it." So he began to climb the tree.

He
climbed
and
he
climbed
and
he
climbed
and
as
he
climbed
he
sang
a
little
song
to
himself.
It
went
like
this:

> Isn't it funny
> How a bear likes honey?
> Buzz! Buzz! Buzz!
> I wonder why he does?

Then he climbed a little further . . . and a little further . . . and then just a little further. By that time he had thought of another song.

> It's a very funny thought that, if Bears were Bees,
> They'd build their nests at the *bottom* of trees.
> And that being so (if the Bees were Bears),
> We shouldn't have to climb up all these stairs.

He was getting rather tired by this time, so that is why he sang a Complaining Song. He was nearly there now, and if he just stood on that branch . . . *Crack!*

"Oh, help!" said Pooh, as he dropped ten feet on the branch below him.

"If only I hadn't——" he said, as he bounced twenty feet on to the next branch.

"You see, what I *meant* to do," he explained, as he turned head-over-heels, and crashed on to another branch thirty feet below, "what I *meant* to do——"

"Of course, it *was* rather——" he admitted, as he slithered very quickly through the next six branches.

"It all comes, I suppose," he decided, as he said good-bye to the last branch, spun round three times, and flew gracefully into a gorse-bush, "it all comes of *liking* honey so much. Oh, help!"

He crawled out of the gorse-bush, brushed the prickles from his nose, and began to think again. And the first person he thought of was Christopher Robin.

(*"Was that me?" said Christopher Robin in an awed voice, hardly daring to believe it.*

"That was you."

Christopher Robin said nothing, but his eyes got larger and larger, and his face got pinker and pinker.)

So Winnie-the-Pooh went round to his friend Christopher Robin, who lived behind a green door in another part of the forest.

"Good morning, Christopher Robin," he said.

"Good morning, Winnie-*ther*-Pooh," said you.

"I wonder if you've got such a thing as a balloon about you?"

"A balloon?"

"Yes, I just said to myself coming along: 'I wonder if Christopher Robin has such a thing as a balloon about him?' I just said it to myself, thinking of balloons, and wondering."

"What do you want a balloon for?" you said.

Winnie-the-Pooh looked round to see that nobody was listening, put his paw to his mouth, and said in a deep whisper: "*Honey!*"

"But you don't get honey with balloons!"

"*I* do," said Pooh.

Well, it just happened that you had been to a party the day before at the house of your friend Piglet, and you had balloons at the party. You had had a big green balloon; and one of Rabbit's relations had had a big blue one, and had left it behind, being really too young to go to a party at all; and so you had brought the green one *and* the blue one home with you.

"Which one would you like?" you asked Pooh.

He put his head between his paws and thought very carefully.

"It's like this," he said, "When you go after honey with a balloon, the great thing is not to let the bees know you're coming. Now, if you have a green balloon, they might think you were only part of the tree, and not notice you, and if you have a blue balloon, they might think you were only part of the sky, and not notice you, and the question is: Which is most likely?"

"Wouldn't they notice *you* underneath the balloon?" you asked.

"They might or they might not," said Winnie-the-Pooh. "You never can tell with bees." He thought for a moment and said: "I shall try to look like a small black cloud. That will deceive them."

"Then you had better have the blue balloon," you said; and so it was decided.

Well, you both went out with the blue balloon, and you took your gun with you, just in case, as you always did, and Winnie-the-Pooh went to a very muddy place that he knew of, and rolled and rolled until he was black all over; and then, when the balloon was blown up as big as big, and you and Pooh were both holding on to the string, you let go suddenly, and Pooh Bear floated gracefully up into the sky, and stayed there—level with the top of the tree and about twenty feet away from it.

"Hooray!" you shouted.

"Isn't that fine?" shouted Winnie-the-Pooh down to you. "What do I look like?"

"You look like a Bear holding on to a balloon," you said.

"Not," said Pooh anxiously, "—not like a small black cloud in a blue sky?"

"Not very much."

"Ah, well, perhaps from up here it looks different. And, as I say, you never can tell with bees."

There was no wind to blow him nearer to the tree, so there he stayed. He could see the honey, he could smell the honey, but he couldn't quite reach the honey.

After a little while he called down to you.

"Christopher Robin!" he said in a loud whisper.

"Hallo!"

"I think the bees *suspect* something!"

"What sort of thing?"

"I don't know. But something tells me that they're *suspicious!*"

"Perhaps they think that you're after their honey."

"It may be that. You never can tell with bees."

There was another little silence, and then he called down to you again.

"Christopher Robin!"

"Yes?"

"Have you an umbrella in your house?"

"I think so."

"I wish you would bring it out here, and walk up and down with it, and look up at me every now and then, and say 'Tut-tut, it looks like rain.' I think, if you did that, it would help the deception which we are practising on these bees."

Well, you laughed to yourself, "Silly old Bear!" but you didn't say it aloud because you were so fond of him, and you went home for your umbrella.

"Oh, there you are!" called down Winnie-the-Pooh, as soon as you got back to the tree. "I was beginning to get anxious. I have discovered that the bees are now definitely Suspicious."

"Shall I put my umbrella up?" you said.

"Yes, but wait a moment. We must be practical. The important bee to deceive is the Queen Bee. Can you see which is the Queen Bee from down there?"

"No."

"A pity. Well, now, if you walk up and down with your umbrella, saying, 'Tut-tut, it looks like rain,' I shall do what I can by singing a little Cloud Song, such as a cloud might sing. . . . Go!"

So, while you walked up and down and wondered if it would rain, Winnie-the-Pooh sang this song:

> How sweet to be a Cloud
> 　　Floating in the Blue!
> Every little cloud
> *Always* sings aloud.

"How sweet to be a Cloud
Floating in the Blue!"
It makes him very proud
To be a little cloud.

The bees were still buzzing as suspiciously as ever. Some of them, indeed, left their nest and flew all round the cloud as it began the second verse of this song, and one bee sat down on the nose of the cloud for a moment, and then got up again.

"Christopher—*ow!*—Robin," called out the cloud.

"Yes?"

"I have just been thinking, and I have come to a very important decision. *These are the wrong sort of bees.*"

"Are they?"

"Quite the wrong sort. So I should think they would make the wrong sort of honey, shouldn't you?"

"Would they?"

"Yes. So I think I shall come down."

"How?" asked you.

Winnie-the-Pooh hadn't thought about this. If he let go of the string, he would fall—*bump*—and he didn't like the idea of that. So he thought for a long time, and then he said:

"Christopher Robin, you must shoot the balloon with your gun. Have you got your gun?"

"Of course I have," you said. "But if I do that, it will spoil the balloon," you said.

"But if you *don't*," said Pooh, "I shall have to let go, and that would spoil *me*."

When he put it like this, you saw how it was, and you aimed very carefully at the balloon, and fired.

"*Ow!*" said Pooh.

"Did I miss?" you asked.

"You didn't exactly *miss*," said Pooh, "but you missed the *balloon*."

"I'm so sorry," you said, and you fired again, and this time you hit the balloon, and the air came slowly out, and Winnie-the-Pooh floated down to the ground.

But his arms were so stiff from holding on to the string of the balloon all that time that they stayed up straight

in the air for more than a week, and whenever a fly came and settled on his nose he had to blow it off. And I think—but I am not sure—that *that* is why he was always called Pooh.

"Is that the end of the story?" asked Christopher Robin.

"That's the end of that one. There are others."

"About Pooh and Me?"

"And Piglet and Rabbit and all of you. Don't you remember?"

"I do remember, and then when I try to remember, I forget."

"That day when Pooh and Piglet tried to catch the Heffalump——"

"They didn't catch it, did they?"

"No."

"Pooh couldn't, because he hasn't any brain. Did *I* catch it?"

"Well, that comes into the story."

Christopher Robin nodded.

"I do remember," he said, "only Pooh doesn't very well,

so that's why he likes having it told to him again. Because then it's a real story and not just a remembering."

"That's just how *I* feel," I said.

Christopher Robin gave a deep sigh, picked up his Bear by the leg, and walked off to the door, trailing Pooh behind him. At the door he turned and said, "Coming to see me have my bath?"

"I might," I said.

"I didn't hurt him when I shot him, did I?"

"Not a bit."

He nodded and went out, and in a moment I heard Winnie-the-Pooh—*bump, bump, bump*—going up the stairs behind him.

To find out what happened when Pooh and Piglet tried to catch the Heffalump, see the complete book, Winnie-the-Pooh. The Adventures of Christopher Robin, Pooh, and their many friends are continued in The House at Pooh Corner. You will also enjoy the poems about Christopher Robin in When We Were Very Young and Now We Are Six.

A Crime Wave
in the Barnyard

BY WALTER R. BROOKS

Illustrations by Kurt Wiese

> *Freddy the pig—who lives on Mr. Bean's farm in upstate New York—has amazing abilities as a sleuth. With so much skulduggery on the farm, Freddy and his partner, Mrs. Wiggins, the cow, have a busy detective business.*

FREDDY took Mrs. Wiggins into partnership, and it was an excellent combination, he supplying the ideas and she the common sense, neither of which is of much use without the other. They themselves handled only the more difficult cases, turning over the simpler ones to their staff, which consisted of several smaller animals who were good at shadowing and gathering information. Freddy printed a large sign and hung it on the shed which had once been the offices of Barnyard Tours, Inc. It read:

FREDERICK & WIGGINS
Detectives

Plain and fancy shadowing. Stolen articles restored. Criminals captured. Missing animals found and returned to bosoms of families. Our unexcelled record makes it worth your while to investigate. Not a loss to a client in more than a century.

Mrs. Wiggins objected at first to the last sentence. "We haven't been in business but a week," she said.

"What difference does that make?" asked Freddy. "It's true, isn't it?"

She had to admit that it was. "But, don't you see, it sounds as if we'd been detectives for a long time."

"That's just the way I want it to sound," replied the pig.

So Mrs. Wiggins didn't say any more.

Pretty soon there were eight animals in the jail. There was Ezra, and there were two rabbits who had stolen some parsnips, and there was a goat named Eric, who had come to the farm to visit his friend Bill and had eaten Mrs. Bean's filet lace table-cloth and Mr. Bean's best night-shirt right off the clothes-line. Then there were two snails who had come up on Mrs. Bean's freshly scrubbed front porch one night and left little shiny trails all over it. And there was a tramp cat who had chased Henrietta up into a tree one day when she was out calling. And finally there was a horse-fly named Zero.

The capture of this fly had been a difficult matter. The two dogs, Jock and Robert, who had been appointed policemen, could of course do nothing about it. Zero was not an ordinary fly who bit and flew away. He had attached himself to Mrs. Wogus. He lived in the cow-barn, and as soon as it was light in the morning, he started biting her. When she went down to the pasture, he followed along and bit her some more. He was very agile, and when she swished her tail at him, he only

laughed. Even when she climbed down into the duck-
pond and lay in the water with only the tip of her nose
showing, he would fly down and bite her nose. It got
so bad that she appealed to Freddy.

Now, every night Zero slept on the ceiling of the cow-
barn. He was right over Mrs. Wogus, so that as soon
as it was light enough for him to see, he could drop
down without wasting a second and begin biting.
"Perfectly simple matter, Mrs. W.," said Freddy in his
business-like way. "Just you leave it to me." And he
went into the house and borrowed a piece of fly-paper
from Mrs. Bean and put it in the cow-barn. "That'll
do the business," he said.

Early the next morning he was awakened by a great
commotion, and he ran out and saw a crowd of animals
gathered about the cow-barn. He hurried up to them
importantly. "Where's the prisoner?" he demanded.

They made way for him and he saw, struggling feebly
in the sticky paper, not Zero, but Eeny, who had gone
into the barn to see Mrs. Wiggins and, knowing nothing
about the trap, had walked straight into it.

With some difficulty, and after getting a good deal
of stickiness on his own snout, Freddy rescued the unfortunate mouse, while Zero buzzed round impudently
overhead. After listening to all the unpleasant things
that Eeny's family had to say to him, the pig went outside to think. Undoubtedly he'd have to try something
different now. And he was wondering what it would
be when he gave a sharp squeal and jumped into the
air. Something had stung him on the ear.

He looked around angrily, and there was Zero circling
above his head, and a thin, whining laughter came down
to him. "That's something for *you*, pig, in exchange
for the fly-paper," buzzed Zero. "It'll be worse next time,
so better leave me alone." And he flew off in search of
Mrs. Wogus.

But Freddy had no intention of being intimidated by a fly. He got some jam and put it on Mrs. Wogus's nose. "Now," he said, "get into the pond with just your nose showing. Then when Zero lights, duck under the water for a minute. His feet will be stuck so he can't get away and he'll be drowned and that'll be the end of *him*."

So Mrs. Wogus went into the water, and Freddy sat down on the bank to watch. Zero was not in sight for the moment, and Freddy started thinking how clever he was, and then he got to thinking how comfortable he was, and his head nodded and nodded—and he woke up suddenly with a squeal of pain, for Zero had quietly alighted on his snout and bitten him ferociously.

"There's another for you, pig," droned the fly as he swooped over the enraged Freddy's head. "Maybe now you'll let me alone. I don't eat jam. It makes me fat, and a fly can't afford to be fat and slow on his wings these days. Too many birds and wasps around. But pigs! Why, Freddy, you couldn't catch a blind fly with one wing. No, sir, you—"

But Freddy, although he was hopping mad, was too good a detective to pay much attention to empty insults. Zero's words had given him an idea. Off he went at a fast trot, stopping only now and then to rub his smarting nose in the cool grass, and presently he was talking to a family of wasps who were building a new house under the eaves of the barn.

"It's a bad time to ask our help now," said the father wasp when he had heard what Freddy wanted. "We've got this house on our hands, and the days are getting shorter all the time. Still—I might let you have George. Hey, George!"

George was a husky young wasp who was only too glad of any excuse to get away from house-building. Wasps build their houses of chewed-up leaves and things, and George had chewed until his jaws were lame. He listened to Freddy's instructions and then flew off toward the pasture. The pig trotted along after him.

When they reached the pasture, Mrs. Wogus was not in sight, and Freddy remembered uneasily that he had forgotten to tell her to come out of the pond. Good gracious, she had been sitting there for over an hour now! Sure enough, there was her black nose, smeared with jam, making a queer little island in the water. He threw pebbles at her until she came up; then he explained.

Mrs. Wogus was rather vexed. "You ought to have told me," she said. "It's no fun sitting there in the mud and the cold, with nothing to do but shiver. And the way the minnows tickle you, you wouldn't believe! I do hope I haven't caught a cold."

But she soon got warm in the hot sun, and Freddy went over with her into the pasture to watch proceedings. Pretty soon Zero came buzzing along. But this time as he dropped down to settle on Mrs. Wogus's nose, he heard the deep drone of George's wings and hastily went into a nose dive, flew right under the cow, then dashed off with the wasp in hot pursuit. It was like an airplane battle, with Zero dodging and twisting and George trying to get above him and drop on him, but it didn't last long, and presently Zero was driven down to the ground, where he took refuge in a small hole under a stone. George tried to go in after him, but the hole was too small.

"I'll dig him out," said Freddy. "You stand by to chase him again."

So Freddy turned the stone over, and up buzzed Zero into the air, and the chase was on again. But this time when the fly was driven down, he went into a crevice in the stone foundation of the barn.

"You can't turn that over," said George. "Guess you'd better give up for today. Some time when I haven't got so much to do, I'd like nothing better than to catch that insect for you, but I ought to get back now. Father won't like it."

"Wait," said Freddy; "I've got an idea. You watch till I come back."

He went into the barn, and in a few minutes came out with the two spiders, Mr. and Mrs. Webb, who were great friends of his. In no time at all they had woven a web over the entrance of the crevice, and then they had Zero safe and fast. After that there was nothing for the fly to do but surrender, so he came out and the Webbs tied his feet and wings together, and Freddy carried him off to jail.

Freddy was very much pleased when they had eight prisoners in the jail. He wasn't so much pleased when, a week after the capture of Zero, they had thirty-four. "I don't understand it," he said to Mrs. Wiggins. "I suppose it must be one of these crime waves we read about."

"We'll have to enlarge the jail, at this rate," said Mrs. Wiggins.

"There'll be more animals inside than out," said Freddy.

They were strolling down through the pasture, and a number of strange animals passed them, going toward the barnyard. At last one, a motherly-looking Jersey cow, stopped and asked the way to the jail.

Freddy pointed it out to her. "Nothing wrong, I hope?" he said. "I mean, none of your family or friends are—er—*in*, are they?"

"Oh no," said the cow. "But I've heard of those poor animals locked up in jail and I *do* feel so sorry for them, poor things! It's just *dreadful* not to be able to get out in the fresh air among their friends."

"If they'd behaved themselves, they wouldn't be there," said Freddy.

"Oh yes, I know," said the cow, "but it's so horrible

to be locked up, isn't it? It makes me quite sad to think of them." And a tear rolled down her broad cheek.

"As a matter of fact, they have a pretty easy time," put in Mrs. Wiggins. "Play games and lie round and get lots to eat. I don't think you need be so sorry for them."

"I suppose it *is* silly of me," replied the other, "but I've always been that way. Anyone in trouble just wrings my heart strings. And it's better to be too tender-hearted, I always say, than to run the risk of getting too hard. Don't you think so?"

"Oh, undoubtedly," said Freddy. "But I wouldn't get very tender-hearted about that bunch of prisoners. They're a tough lot."

"Well," said the cow, "perhaps you're right. But I thought I'd just go down and see if there wasn't anything I could do to make things easier for them. I can't bear to think of them being unhappy. It hurts me here." And she tapped her left side with her right front hoof.

When the cow had gone, Freddy said: "That's one reason—all these sentimental animals that come to visit the jail and feel sorry for the prisoners and want to do things for them. After all, they're there to be punished, not to have a good time. And we treat 'em well. There's no reason to cry over them and bring them better food than they ever get at home.—Why, what are you getting so red for?" he demanded suddenly. For a blush had overspread Mrs. Wiggins's large face.

You have probably never seen a cow blush. And indeed the sight is unusual. There are two reasons for this. One is that cows are a very simple people, who do whatever they feel like doing and never realize that sometimes they ought to be embarrassed. You might think that they lack finer feelings. And in a way they do. They are not sensitive. But they are kind and good-natured, and if sometimes they seem rude, it is only due to their rather clumsy thoughtlessness.

The other reason is that cows' faces are not built for blushing. But as Mrs. Wiggins was so talented above her sisters in other directions, it is not to be marveled at that she could blush very handsomely.

Her flush deepened as Freddy spoke. "Why, I—now that you speak of it," she stammered, "I see that you're right, but—well, Freddy—land's sakes, I might as well confess it to you—I got to feeling sorry for those prisoners myself yesterday, especially those two goats. It seemed such a pity they couldn't be jumping round on the hills instead of sweltering in that hot barn. And I went out and got them a nice bunch of thistles for their supper."

Freddy frowned. "That's it!" he exclaimed. "That's just it! Sentimentality, that's what's going to ruin our jail. I *did* think, Mrs. W., that you had more sense!"

The cow looked a little angry. "If I knew what you were talking about," she said stiffly, "perhaps I might agree with you."

"Being sentimental?" said Freddy. "I'll tell you what it is. It's going round looking for someone or something to cry over, just for the fun of crying. You knew you weren't doing those goats any good. You just wanted to have a good time feeling sorry."

The nice thing about Mrs. Wiggins was that she always admitted it when she was wrong. She did so now after she had thought about it for a few minutes. "I guess you're right, Freddy," she said. "I won't do it again.—But, good grief, what's that rabbit up to?"

Freddy had noticed the rabbit too. It had hopped out of the long grass, turned and looked straight at them, then deliberately went into the garden where

Mr. Bean grew lettuce and radishes and other vegetables and began nibbling at a head of lettuce. Now,
no animals were allowed in this garden except the head
squirrel and his gang, who did the weeding and could
be trusted not to eat the vegetables. So Freddy was
greatly shocked by such bold behavior.

"Come, come!" he shouted, hurrying up to the rabbit.
"You're a bold one, I *must* say! You just come along
with me. You're under arrest."

"Yes, sir," said the rabbit meekly. "Do we go to jail
right away?"

"Jail?" said Freddy. "I guess we do go to jail, just as
soon as the judge can sentence you."

The rabbit looked quite pleased at this and started
hopping off, his mouth still full of lettuce leaves.

"Stop!" called Freddy, hurrying after him. "No use
your trying to escape. Better come along quietly. You'll
just make matters worse for yourself if you don't."

"I wasn't trying to escape," said the rabbit. "I was
just starting for the hen-house so I could be sentenced.—
I really was, sir," he added, as Freddy stared at him
in amazement.

The pig was rather puzzled. The rabbit was evidently
telling the truth, and yet such eagerness to be punished
didn't seem reasonable. "You're a queer one," said
Freddy. "I don't believe you understand. You've been
stealing lettuce, and it's against the rules, and you're
going to be punished by being sent to jail."

"But I *do* understand, sir," replied the prisoner. "I
know I've done wrong, and—well, sir, I think I *ought*
to be punished. As a lesson to me, sir. I ought to know
better than to do such things."

"H'm," said Freddy, "you're saying all the things *I*
ought to say. Still, they're true, and I'm glad you see
it. Only if you feel that way, I can't see why you stole
the lettuce in the first place."

"I can tell you that," said the rabbit. "But—well, I'd rather wait until after I'm sentenced."

"All right," said the pig. "And I'll do my best with the judge to see that your sentence isn't a long one. I'm sure you won't do it again."

"Oh, yes I shall!" exclaimed the rabbit anxiously. "Yes, sir, I'm apt to do things like that any time. I'm quite a desperate character, sir, really I am. You'd better get me a good long sentence."

"Say, look here!" said Freddy sharply. "Are you trying to make fun of me, or what? If you're a good law-abiding rabbit, as you seem to be, I can understand your being sorry that you'd done wrong and thinking that you ought to be punished. But I don't believe that anybody, animal or human, ever thought that he ought to be punished *a lot*. Come on, now, tell me the truth!"

At this the rabbit broke down and began to cry. "Oh dear!" he sobbed. "I thought it would be so easy to get into jail! I thought all you had to do was steal something. And I wanted to go to jail—the animals there all have such a good time, and don't have to work, and they play games and sing songs all day long, and other animals are sorry for them and bring them lots of good things to eat! Oh, please, Mr. Freddy, take me to the judge and get me a good long sentence."

"I'll do nothing of the kind," said Freddy crossly. "And, what's more, I'm not going to arrest you at all. I'm going to give your ears a good boxing"—which he did while the rabbit submitted meekly—"and then you can go. Only let me tell you something. Don't go stealing any more lettuce in the hope that you'll be sent to jail. Because you won't. You'll get something you won't like at all."

"Wh—what's that?" sniveled the rabbit.

"I don't know," said Freddy. "I'll have to think up something. But you can bet it'll be something good."

Then he went back to where Mrs. Wiggins was waiting for him. "Can you beat it?" he exclaimed. "Did you hear that?"

"I certainly did," said the cow. "I tell you, Freddy, something's got to be done, and done quick. Let's go have a talk with Charles. Maybe he can suggest something."

They found the hen-house in a great state of excitement. A flock of young chickens—Henrietta's gawky, long-legged daughters—were crowding about their mother or dashing in and out on errands, and the older hens were running round distractedly, squawking and clucking, some of them bringing water in their beaks to sprinkle over one of their sisters, who had fainted, others merely hurrying aimlessly out of the door to stop and give several loud squawks and then hurry as aimlessly inside again.

At first the two detectives could get no answers to their questions in the general hubbub, but at last Freddy, losing patience, squeezed his way inside, seized Henrietta by a wing and pulled her over into a corner. "Come, now; what's the trouble here?" he demanded. "Pull yourself together, hen, and tell me what's wrong."

Henrietta glared at him for a moment without seeming to see him. Then suddenly she seemed to recognize him, and burst out wildly: "You!" she cried. "You *dare* come here, you wretched pig, with your fine airs and your lordly ways—you that's to blame for all this, you and all your smart friends that told him how fine it would be to be a judge! *You* are the one that got him into this, you imitation detective, you; you big chunk of fat pork!"

Freddy backed away a little. "Come, come, Henrietta," he said soothingly. "Let's not talk about me. I may be everything you say, but that doesn't get us anywhere, does it? I don't even know what's the matter yet."

But Henrietta's rage was quickly spent. She broke down and began to cry. "He's gone!" she sobbed. "My Charles, the finest husband a hen ever had! They've got him, my good, kind, noble Charles!"

Serious as the situation seemed, Freddy had to repress a grin. When Charles was around, Henrietta did nothing but scold him and tell him what a silly rooster he was. Outside the hen-house there was a strange whining, grumbling sound, and Freddy recognized it as Mrs. Wiggins's giggle. But fortunately the hen did not hear it and went on with her story.

There wasn't very much of it. Charles had been missing since late the previous afternoon. None of the animals on the farm had seen him.

Freddy suggested the only thing he could think of. "He may have gone visiting," he said, "and been invited to stay all night."

"He wouldn't *dare* stay out all night!" flashed the hen. "Just let him try it once!" Then she began to cry again. "No, he's gone. It's one of those animals he sentenced to jail. There were a couple of them that said they'd get even with him when they got out. And now they've gone and done it. And I shall never see him again! Oh, my poor Charles! My noble husband!" And she flopped round in a violent fit of hysterics.

Freddy shook his head dolefully and went outside. "Come on," he said to the cow. "Nothing more to be got out of her. We'd better get busy right away. Now, where in the world do you suppose he can be?"

"Off somewhere having a good time probably," replied Mrs. Wiggins. "Though it *is* funny. Henrietta would peck his eyes out if he stayed out a minute after ten o'clock."

"Yes," said Freddy, "and none of the animals he has sentenced to jail have got out yet, so it can't be that. Of course, he might have been carried off by a hawk, or had a fight with a stray cat. But, for all his bluster and boasting, Charles is too clever to be caught like that. I expect we'd better put the whole force on it to go round and find out all they can."

So they got all their helpers together and sent them out in different directions to ask questions and look for signs of the missing rooster. Both Freddy and Mrs. Wiggins went out too. But when they met again late that evening, nothing had been found. Charles had vanished without leaving so much as a feather behind.

The next morning Freddy was up and out before the dew was off the grass, for this, he felt, was a case on which his reputation as a detective rested. It wasn't just an ordinary disappearance. Charles was the judge, an important personage, and if he wasn't found, and quickly, nobody would bring any more cases to the detectives.

He was on his way down to the cow-barn to get Mrs. Wiggins when he heard a loud moo behind him and, turning, saw that animal galloping toward him as fast as she could come.

"Come with me over to the jail," she panted. "I've got something to show you. I went over there when I got up, to check over the prisoners and see that they were all there, because I thought some of them might have escaped and perhaps murdered Charles—though, goodness knows, none of 'em are mad at him for sentencing them. Quite the contrary. Just listen to them."

The sounds of shouts and laughter and songs greeted them as they approached. Hank, from his stall, turned a weary eye on them as they entered. "I do wish you would do something about this," he said. "I thought it was going to be company for me, having the jail here, but, my land! nobody wants company twenty-four hours a day! They just keep it up all night. I haven't had a wink of sleep for ten days."

Freddy nodded. "Yes, we'll have to make some other arrangements. This jail isn't a punishment any more at all. But we'll talk about that later. What was it you wanted to show me?" he asked the cow.

Without speaking she led him to the door of one of the stalls, hooked the wooden pin out of the staple, and opened the door. Inside, some twenty animals and birds were crowded together. One group was in a circle, watching two rabbits doing gymnastic stunts. Another group, with their heads together, were singing "Sweet Adeline" with a great deal of expression. Mrs. Wiggins raised one hoof and pointed dramatically at a third group. In the center of it was the missing judge, declaiming at the top of his lungs.

"On with the dance!" declaimed Charles.

"Stop! Silence!" shouted Freddy, and Mrs. Wiggins stamped on the floor to get attention.

"Let joy be unconfined!" went on Charles dramatically. Then he saw the visitors, and his voice flattened out into a whisper.

Heads turned; the song died down; the groups broke up and surrounded the detectives.

Freddy pushed his way through them and confronted Charles. "What on earth does this mean?" he demanded. "What are you doing here? Don't you know that Henrietta is half crazy with worry?"

"Why I—I'm in jail," exclaimed Charles a little hesitantly; then, gaining courage at the immediate applause which this remark drew from his fellow prisoners: "Tell Henrietta I'm very sorry," he went on, "but I'm serving a six weeks' sentence, and I can't come home until my time's up."

"A sentence!" exclaimed Mrs. Wiggins. "But how can you be serving a sentence? You're the judge. Who can sentence you?"

"The judge!" said Charles triumphantly. "I'm the judge, and I sentenced myself!"

"What for?"

"Well, I'll tell you," said Charles, now thoroughly at ease. "You see, two or three years ago I stole something. It doesn't matter what it was. Well, then, when I was elected judge, that old crime worried me. Here I am, I thought, sentencing other animals to jail for crimes no worse than the one I committed, and yet *I* never served any sentence for it. It got on my nerves after a while. It didn't seem right, somehow. What right had I to set myself up as better than these other animals and punish them for things when I was no better myself? The only fair thing, it seemed to me, the only just thing, the only honest thing, the only noble thing, was to punish myself. And so I did. I'm serving my sentence now."

The other prisoners set up a cheer, but Freddy scowled. "Nonsense!" he exclaimed. "I'll tell you why you're here. You're sick of being nagged at by Henrietta. I don't blame you there—I shouldn't like it either. And so you thought this would give you an excuse to stay away from home and have a good time. But you can't get away with it, Charles. This jail isn't a club. It—"

"But I stole something, I tell you," insisted the rooster. "I'm only getting the punishment I deserve. I can't get out."

"You can and you're going to," said Freddy. "You never stole anything in your life. And how are you going to be of any use as a judge when you're in jail yourself?"

"I don't see why I won't," protested Charles. "Bring

the prisoners down here and I can sentence 'em just the same, can't I?"

"No, you can't," put in Mrs. Wiggins. "Come along, now. Henrietta's waiting for you."

"I'm not going," said Charles.

Freddy turned and winked secretly at the cow. "Oh, all right, then," he said. "Let him stay here. We'll just have to elect another judge, that's all. We'll get Peter. There's a lot of the animals thought he would be a better judge anyway, and there'll be plenty more now, when this gets out."

But this didn't suit the rooster either. "You can't do that!" he shouted, hopping up and down in his excitement. "You can't do that! I was elected, and you can't put me out that way."

"Oh, can't we?" said Freddy. "Don't you know that a judge loses his job when he goes to jail? We don't have to put you out. You're just *out*, anyway. Unless, of course, you decide that there was some mistake about it and take back your sentence."

For a few minutes the crestfallen rooster thought this over in silence. He was having a very good time in the jail. On the other hand, in jail he was really just one of the prisoners. And outside he was a judge, looked up to and respected by the entire community. Still—there was Henrietta. He knew that no story he could fix up would go down with Henrietta. And what she'd say— he shivered to think of it.

"Come on," said Freddy. "Henrietta is taking on terribly. You don't want her to feel badly, do you? She misses you, Charles." And he repeated some of the things Henrietta had said, about how good and noble he was.

Charles looked up quickly. "She said *that*!" he exclaimed.

"She certainly did," said Mrs. Wiggins.

"Well, then, I guess—I guess I'd better go back," said the rooster. And he walked dejectedly out of the door and reluctantly took the path toward the hen-house.

That evening Freddy and Mrs. Wiggins were strolling down through the pasture, talking over the new problems that confronted them in their detective work. From the hen-house came the angry clucking and gabbling of Henrietta's voice, going on and on and punctuated occasionally with Charles's shrill squawks. They listened for a few minutes, then grinned at each other and walked on.

"It's really a swell joke on us," said Freddy. "We were looking for a missing rooster, and there he was in jail all the time—the one place nobody'd ever look for him."

"We find 'em," said Mrs. Wiggins complacently. "Wherever they are, we find 'em."

Freddy grinned more broadly as a particularly agonized shriek came from the hen-house. "We'd have no trouble finding the judge tonight," he said. "I bet that's the last time he stays out all night."

"He won't have a tail-feather left by morning," said the cow.

There are over twenty books in the hilarious "Freddy" series. Among the most popular are Freddy the Magician, Freddy the Cowboy, and Freddy and the Men from Mars, all published by Alfred A. Knopf.

Mischief in Fez

BY ELEANOR HOFFMANN

Illustrations by Fritz Eichenberg

This is a tale of the mischief and magic of djinns in the city of Fez. Although the story is entirely a fairy tale, it gives a very realistic picture of life and customs in Morocco.

1: *The Household of Muhammed Ali*

ALLAH be praised! At last the afternoon call to prayer and school over for the day! No more chanted verses from the Koran; no more alphabet hen tracks across slates; no more switching from the master's olive twig. Before the muezzin's call had died away across the roof-tops, they were filling the narrow street,—Mousa, Muhammed, Zaid, Hassan,—boys of Fez in their hooded burnouses with pigtails dangling from their shaven heads. Now the rest of the daylight was theirs to amuse themselves as they saw fit. Some of them drifted off to the Street of the Bakers to fill their pockets with almond cakes; others hurried off to the Charada barracks to watch the black Senegalese soldiers drill, while others, among them

Mischief in Fez, by Eleanor Hoffmann, copyright 1943 by Eleanor Hoffmann, is published by Holiday House, Inc.

Mousa Ben Muhammed Ali, climbed the steep streets to the market place.

"Mousa, come and watch the acrobats," urged Hassan. "There is a new one from the south. By Allah, I think his bones are made of rubber."

But Mousa shook his head. Though his friends followed Hassan to the acrobat, he himself let the sound of a tom-tom guide him through the crowd till he came to a semi-circle of men and boys squatting in the dust with eyes and ears on the story-teller.

Here Mousa, son of Muhammed Ali, the richest and most important judge in the city of Fez, squeezed in between beggars, bootblacks and village children from the hills.

While the story-teller's assistants still beat tom-tom and tambourine to attract listeners, the story-teller himself was looking slyly about to size up the prosperity and generosity of his audience. At last he stood up. The tom-toms rose to final fury, then stopped suddenly.

"One night among nights," began the story-teller, and the circle became a pool of quiet in the noisy market place. Beggars and judges' sons leaned forward with equal eagerness.

"One night among nights, a strange dream came to a youth by the name of Zama, the son of a poor ferryman in the city of Rabat. Every day from sunrise to sunset he helped his father row the rich and the poor, their mules and their sheep, across the river-mouth between Rabat and the city of Salé. Ordinarily Zama was too tired at the end of his day's work for dreaming, but on this particular night he dreamed a terrible dream,—a dream, by Allah, that was enough to frighten our Lord the Sultan himself! He dreamt he was standing on the river bank at midnight with his boat when three figures approached him in the darkness, saying in thin voices: 'O Boatman, take us across the river!' And just as he was about to push off with them, three more figures appeared, saying in piping voices: 'There is room in your boat for us; take us also across the river.' The first thing that he noticed about his six passengers—and it made his skin grow cold—was that the boat was no heavier than if he had been rowing himself alone; the second thing that he noticed—and this made his knees shake—was that the passengers seemed to speak in the high voices of demons; and the third thing—and this was the most horrible of all—that they were talking about him, speaking of him by name. They were saying. . . ."

Here the story-teller, noting the eagerness in the eyes of his listeners, stopped and waited while his assistant made the round of the circle with the tambourine inverted for the copper coins that were dropped into it.

"They were saying," he continued, "those with the thin voices: 'When Zama the Ferryman comes at midnight to dig up the treasure the pirates buried three centuries ago in the right-hand corner of the cave by the three flat stones, let us devour him. It is many months since we have tasted the flesh of man.'

"But those with the piping voices answered: 'No, O djinns, he is a poor and honest youth, let him have the treasure. Let him enjoy it. Let us devour a robber instead. There is a fine fat one in the Mamora Forest. . . .'

"And now of course Zama knew for certain that they were djinns and that the three to speak first with the thin voices were evil and that the three who spoke last with the piping voices were djinns in the service of honest men. . . ."

"Ya Allah," muttered the audience, shuddering, for there was not one among them, man or boy, who did not know and fear these dangerous spirits, these djinns who were created before Adam, who were the eighty-seven thousand bodily manifestations of Satan, who for the most part delighted in plaguing mankind with their destructive mischief.

" 'No,' said the thin, evil voices. 'Let him dig up the treasure. Let him finger the gold coins and watch them shine in the moonlight; let him delight in the sparkle of the emeralds and the rubies. Let him imagine the palaces and the fine food he will buy. Let us then pounce upon him and crunch his bones.'

" 'No,' said the piping voices again. 'We forbid it and we shall be there when he comes to defend him.'

" 'Ha,' shrieked the others. 'We are stronger than you. Our teeth are longer and we shall come in greater numbers.'

" 'We shall protect him,' answered the good ones.

" 'That remains to be seen,' countered the evil ones. And with these parting words both evil demons and honest demons flew up from the boat with a flapping of wings,— three in the form of monstrous bats, three in the form of ravens."

Again the audience uttered a "Ya Allah" of horror. Now the story-teller stopped. Again he passed the tambourine.

"O sons of notables," he began, though there were few besides Mousa, the judge's son, whom such a complimentary title fitted. "O sons of notables, thus ends the dream of Zama. Come again tomorrow at sunset if you would learn what happened when Zama went to the cave by the three flat stones."

Reluctantly the crowd unfolded their legs and began to scatter. Mousa Ben Muhammed Ali did not bother to look for his friend Hassan and the others. His mind was too full of the story-teller's tale. In imagination he followed Zama to the cave. He could see this cave clearly in his mind's eye, for last year at the feast that celebrates the birthday of the Prophet his father had taken him to Rabat. There they had been rowed across the river-mouth by just such a ferryman as Zama. The cave would be in the wild black rocks on the Rabat side. And it was easy to believe in the pirate treasure, for had his father

not told him tales of this river, first as they were being
ferried across it and again as they sat in the Oudaia Café
drinking mint-tea and looking across at white Salé, so
famous for her pirates before the Christians seized the
Mogreb?

Yes, he could see the cave where Zama would come
at midnight, but the demons, the Hidden Ones, the Unseen Ones, Those Who Shun Salt,—even in his mind he
did not dare give them their names of *djinns,*—these he
could not visualize. They melted from one monstrous
shape into another and he thanked Allah that it was
Zama and not he who had to face them. If he were Zama
would he dare encounter them for the sake of the treasure? He shuddered at the thought and began to hurry
as darkness choked the narrow streets, for it was with
the coming of darkness that the Unseen Ones left their
subterranean kingdom and roamed freely over the earth
and through the air.

At last he reached the door of his father's palace and
knocked three times with the bronze knocker.

"Who is there?" called the voice of Zaid the porter.

"I, Mousa," he answered and heard the bolts being
drawn, watched the heavy door open, and slipped quickly inside where he would be well protected, *inchallah,*
Allah willing, from demons and their like.

Now he passed through the jogged vestibule that prevented the patio from being seen from the street door.
How peaceful everything looked with the fountain gur-
gling in its marble vase, doves cooing in the orange tree
and his father's musicians playing reed-pipe and lute in
a far corner. His father himself sat in one of the long
rooms that opened into the patio, making the tea that
a serving girl had just brought. Mousa shuffled out of his
yellow slippers, arranged them neatly together and
stepped into the room. After kissing his father on the
right shoulder he dropped down beside him on the cush-

ions. This was the time of day he loved, when they were alone together.

Though Mousa's mother had died before he could remember, his life in spite of this loss had not been an unhappy one. He was the only child of a father who had adored him from babyhood. When Muhammed Ali rode his magnificent mule through the city, he held his son on his left arm. When Mousa grew too old for that, he sat behind his father's crimson velvet saddle. Here in the palace his black nurse Loualou spoiled him,—Loualou, who had crossed the Sahara by caravan from the fabulous city of Timbuctu when she was Mousa's age. Now Mousa was dearer to her than the gold earrings that hung in her ears, dearer than the sacred lion's claw that hung from her black throat. And the other servants of the palace,—the cook, the serving girl, the scribes, the musicians and Zaid the porter,—all loved Mousa. And Mousa loved them all in return but above all he loved his father Muhammed Ali. Next to him, he loved black Loualou.

Today his father seemed to listen with less interest than usual to all Mousa had to tell of school, of the market place and the tale of Zama. When Mousa had finished with his chattering, Muhammed Ali took his son's hand and his grave face seemed graver than usual.

"And now, O Mousa," he said, "I have something of importance to tell you. Tomorrow I am leaving for Meknès-of-the-Olives to bring back a bride. Her name is Fatma Bent Nor, Fatma, daughter of Nor. Everyone speaks of her beauty. It will be good for this house to have a mistress again; good for you to have a mother."

Mousa was delighted at this news.

When he went to bed that night, the thought of his new stepmother drove out all thought of the story-teller's tale of Zama and the djinns. "Everyone speaks of her beauty," his father had said. His friend Hassan boasted

of his mother's beauty and often his other friends by their
talk of their mothers made him feel sad and left out of
things. Dearly as he loved his black Loualou, beauty was
not a quality he could attribute to her. Yes, he thought, as
he went to sleep, it would be good to have a beautiful
mother.

2: *The Bride Brings a Gazelle*

No sooner had Muhammed Ali
ridden off to Meknès-of-the-Olives
to bring back his bride than the
palace was turned upside down to
make it bright and shining for the
new mistress. The maids tied up
their skirts and scrubbed every tile
of floor and wall till they shim-
mered and gleamed like water. They cleaned the marble
fountain in the middle of the court. They polished the
brass samovar for the tea, and every brass tray and every
copper tray, and covered the divans and cushions with
fresh muslin and the finest embroidery.

Mousa himself, young lord of the house in the absence
of his father, stalked gravely and imperiously about giving orders, as calm of face as if he wore his father's grey
beard, but with his heart thudding like a tom-tom in its
excitement. When would she come? What would she
be like?

On the seventh day after Muhammed Ali's departure,
there was a great commotion in the street,—a shouting of
men, a stamping of mules, a knocking at the massive
door. Imperious though it was, it was not the familiar
knock of the master. When Zaid the porter, with Mousa
all curiosity at his heels, drew the bolts, he opened the
door upon a string of mules heavily laden with long

wooden chests—the trousseau and belongings of the bride. The arrogant muleteers brushed the porter aside, even ignored Mousa, as they led their animals through the door to unload them.

"What is she like?" asked the palace servants, crowding around them. "Tell us what she is like!"

"What is she like?" they answered haughtily. "Her beauty is known from here to the Niger. She descends from the great Sultan Ahmed the Gilded. It is a crime that she is wasting herself on this fat city of merchants."

The next morning when Muhammed Ali and his heavily veiled bride arrived, three mules pawed the dust at the street door, the tall black mule of the master, the delicate brown one of his bride, and a third, smallest of the three, a cream-colored one. As the household pressed about the porter in their curiosity to see their new mistress and in their eagerness to welcome her, they looked puzzled at the strange rider of the third mule, for it was not the childhood nurse that every well-bred bride brings with her to her new home, but a cage fastened firmly to the saddle. Within the cage, looking out between the bars with twitching, disdainful nostrils, lay a gazelle.

As soon as Muhammed Ali had lifted his bride to the ground, Mousa ran forward and kissed his father's hand, then stood on tiptoe and kissed his right shoulder. Muhammed Ali took him by the hand and turned to his bride, saying, "Here is my son Mousa!"

But the attention of the bride was not on her husband or her husband's son, for she had turned to the cage and was stroking the nose of the gazelle and speaking to him in tones of endearment.

"Allak, Allak," she murmured, "my sweet one, at last the long journey is over. Come," she said to Muhammed Ali, "have your porter take down the cage of my dear one and carry it most carefully to my quarters. I will follow close behind to see that no harm comes to him."

"I will follow too," said Mousa shyly, wanting to be of help, "and see that no harm comes to him."

"No," said his new mother. "Stay. He detests children. You will only frighten him."

"But this is my son, my only son Mousa, of whom I have told you," said Muhammed Ali. "There is no animal that does not love him."

"That may be," answered the bride, "but today Allak is tired after his journey. He has had enough new faces for the time being. Come," she ordered the porter, "take down the cage."

"Wait," said Muhammed Ali, with a hand on her sleeve, as the porter unfastened the cage and lifted it to his shoulders. "Wait, my love," he said as his bride started to follow the porter. "Surely it is the custom in your Meknès as here in Fez for salt to be strewn on a threshold before a bride crosses into her new home and surely it is also the custom for the bride not to set her own feet to the threshold but to be carried across in the arms of her husband in order that no evil and unseen power may enter at the same time."

The bride tossed her head with a high tinkling laugh. "My Meknès is not a city of old-fashioned superstitions," she answered. Before Muhammed Ali could say another word she had stepped over the threshold behind the porter and the gazelle.

A gasp of disapproval could be heard among the watching servants.

"How beautiful she must be," Mousa could hear them whisper, "to dare such disobedience so soon. She has bewitched him already." And they waited with heightened curiosity for the moment when they should see the face of their new mistress without its silken veil.

Mousa felt for his father's hand and held it tightly.

"Welcome, welcome," exclaimed the servants as father and son followed her across the threshold.

"Peace be upon you," they said, crowding round to kiss their master's elbow and the hem of his burnous, for unlike most rich judges of the city, Muhammed Ali was a just and good man loved by his servants as well as by his friends.

When the procession had reached the patio, Muhammed Ali gently disengaged Mousa's hand.

"Wait here till I call you," he said. "When your stepmother is ready, I will take you to her."

Restlessly and impatiently Mousa wandered round the patio and into the rooms opening into it. In the kitchen Zara the cook had gone back to her pots stewing over the charcoal fires. The serving maids were again at their work of peeling tomatoes, blanching almonds, and seeding raisins. Zara smiled indulgently as Mousa went from dish to dish, lifting the tall, conical covers and sniffing the feast simmering in honor of his stepmother's arrival.

"Here," she said, pulling a pigeon leg from one of the many dishes and offering it to Mousa. "Taste and tell me if the cooks of Meknès can equal this stew."

Mousa gnawed the leg clean. "O Zara, how can I answer your question with such a small sample? Give me another leg and I will say how it compares with the cooking of Meknès."

Everyone laughed as Zara pulled another leg out of the stew.

"O Zara," said Mousa this time, "there is no cook in all Meknès who can produce such a stew, such a perfect blending of spices. Give me one more leg and I will tell you how it compares with the pigeon stews made in the kitchen of our Lord the Sultan—may Allah preserve him."

"Mousa!" His father was calling him from the balcony above.

Giving his fingers a final lick, he dashed out of the kitchen, across the court and up the stairs to his stepmother's apartments.

Mousa was of course used to the contrast between the sombre cocoon look of women dressed for the street and the gay butterfly appearance when they shed the outer wrapping, for he had seen the mothers and sisters of his friends. Modesty did not compel them to veil their faces or cover their jewels and rich brocades from a boy of his age.

But as his father led him from the door to the cushions where his stepmother sat, he was unprepared for the beauty of her face, the richness of her jewels, the magnificence of her velvet kaftan.

Her eyes were blacker and more enormous than the famous eyes of Zoreida, the mother of Hassan. Her skin was whiter than that of Aziza, known throughout Fez for her beauty. And her hair! Black, soft, silken! There was no woman in all Fez with such hair; no woman in all the palaces of Fez with such gold jewels sparkling with sapphires and emeralds, edged with seed pearls, cunningly inlaid with gleaming enamel. And surely the Sultana herself wore no kaftan of richer velvet, no belt more heavily encrusted with gold, no slippers more richly embroidered with threads of silk and silver.

"Peace be upon you, O Mousa," she said, holding out a slender white hand that seemed to droop under the weight of rings and bracelets.

"And upon you the peace and welcome to this house, O Mother," answered Mousa shyly.

When silence fell after this remark, Mousa, to hide his embarrassment, stretched out a hand to stroke the gazelle Allak, who lay on a cushion beside his mistress.

"No," said his stepmother sharply. "Never touch him. He is not used to being handled by strangers. He is timid and easily frightened."

This surprised and disappointed Mousa. There were pet gazelles in many of the palaces of Fez. All those he had known were tame and loving, enjoyed being patted

and scratched behind the ears, came bounding full of trust to anyone who held out a handful of tobacco, their favorite food.

"If I could feed him something he liked?" said Mousa.

"He takes food only from me." His stepmother's voice was still cold, as if he had offended her by wanting to pat her gazelle, whereas he had only been doing what he thought would please her.

"Let us have it understood," she continued, looking at both her stepson and her husband, "that no one in this household except me is to touch or feed Allak."

"It shall be as you wish," said Muhammed Ali.

In the meantime Mousa, forbidden to touch Allak, looked at him with added curiosity. In the gazelle's limpid eyes there seemed to be a vain awareness of his own beauty and grace. There was a haughty backward sweep of his horns, a contemptuous quivering of his nostrils. The longer Mousa looked at him, the less he wanted to pat him.

Moreover, it shocked Mousa to notice that his stepmother had taken one of the fine cushions from her own couch to put on the floor for Allak. This was one of the three cushions that Muhammed Ali valued most highly, for they had been embroidered by the fingers of Mousa's own mother,—such delicate work that you could cover two hundred of the tiny feathery stitches with the smallest coin. As a special honor, Muhammed Ali had ordered them to be placed on the couch of his bride. And now she in turn had thrown one to the floor for a gazelle!

As soon as the subject of Allak was dropped, her voice grew less unfriendly. For a few minutes she asked Mousa questions about his companions, his school, what he did with himself. Then she dismissed him, saying she was tired from the long ride and wished to rest.

Mousa left her proudly, trying to put into words a description of this new stepmother that would make him the envy of Hassan and his other friends.

Though she kept to her own apartments during the rest of the day and he did not see her again, one by one the servants were summoned to welcome her. Like Mousa, they too were dazzled by her appearance and could find no words to describe it. But also like Mousa, they could not understand how a gazelle, ordinarily such an affectionate pet, could wear such an aloof and malignant air.

The gazelle, however, was soon forgotten as their talk went back to their mistress. They too were proud of the beauty that was now theirs to boast of. And thanks to those among them who found excuses to go to market before the day was over, thanks to Muhammed Ali's musicians who lingered by the Mosque of Moulai Idriss after the sunset prayer, and to all those of the household who could find a listener in the streets of Fez, the rumor of the bride's beauty had not only spread by nightfall from wall to wall of the city but was already making its way on the tongues of returning farmers to the scattered villages of the hills.

Only Loualou remained strangely silent and tight-lipped concerning her new mistress and Mousa's new mother.

"Tell us what you think, O Loualou," said Zara the cook, said Zaid the porter, said the serving girls. "Is there another palace in all Fez that can boast a mistress with more beauty?"

Loualou only wrinkled her black forehead. "A gazelle that cannot be properly tamed should be sent back to the desert where it came from and not lie on the treasured cushions of a fine palace."

"We are not asking you about the gazelle, O Loualou. We are asking you about our new mistress."

When Loualou only grunted, the others laughed.

"Loualou is jealous," they said. "With her own skin as black and wrinkled as the neck of a turtle, she is jealous of the smooth whiteness of the young bride."

But before Mousa went to sleep that night he asked her again. In answer she took his hand in one of hers, while she held the other to her throat where the lion-claw amulet lay.

"O Mousa, all day Sidi Lion has been tickling my skin, trying to tell me something. When I close my eyes, I see trouble rising like a sandstorm and sifting in over everything. Who knows what evil powers crossed the threshold of this house when no salt was strewn under the feet of the bride and when the bride herself was not carried across in the arms of her husband!"

3: Was Loualou Right?

Everyone felt full of apologies to the bride the next morning at the discovery of a scourge of scorpions that had somehow found their way into the palace. Had they fallen from the orange tree or come up through the drains? No one seemed to know, but wherever one looked or stepped there was the curved tail of one of the creatures ready to inflict its poisoned sting.

Mousa found the first one when he awoke in the morning. It was advancing toward him along the coverlet. Fortunately he was able to throw it off and kill it. As he shook his babouches before stepping into them, another scorpion fell out of the left toe.

When he went down to the patio to warn the household, he found everybody already stepping gingerly as they hunted the creatures.

"What will the new bride think of this city and this house?" they kept repeating as they collected the bodies. They saved them carefully, of course, to be charred and used as an antidote in case anyone were bitten. The bride, warned of the menace by her husband, kept herself and her gazelle to her own apartments.

Fortunately the day passed with only one accident and this not to any member of the household, but to the master's mule as it stood in its dark stable by the porter's door. When they came to saddle it, they found its nose swollen and hot. A scorpion had crawled into the barley and stung the poor beast. Luckily Zara was ready with a paste of the charred bodies mixed with oil and saffron, and the mule, Muhammed Ali's favorite, was able to throw off the poison before nightfall.

All in all it was not a happy day and the next morning there was rejoicing to discover that the scorpions had left as suddenly as they had come.

Though the second day started with relief at the departure of the venomous insects, trouble of a different kind soon flared up in the patio. The fountain that sent its jet of water high into the air till it fell back tinkling and splashing into the marble vase, had become clogged in the night. Today no flight of drops sparkled in the sun, while scum and slime had already begun to collect in the fluted basin. Though this in itself threatened no such harm as the sting of scorpions, it carried with it the foreboding of evil. For if a fountain dries up and no one can discover the cause, it means, as everyone knows, that the Hidden Ones, the Masters of the Dark, have been wreaking their mischief in the night. If it is discovered that the drying up was caused not by a djinn but by a human then that person wishes harm to the house and its inmates.

At noon artisans came and pried the base of the fountain from its position in the tiled floor of the court and cut through the pipe. There at last they discovered the cause.

"Ya Allah," muttered the watching household, shocked

as seven date stones fell out of the narrow pipe. *"Bis-millah,* in the name of Allah," they repeated, casting suspicious glances to right and left. "Who has done such a wicked thing? Who among us would dare! It must be the mischief of a child." And everyone turned questioning eyes upon Mousa.

"Mousa?" The same question was in his father's voice.

"No, no! Of course I did not do it," Mousa protested.

"It is strange," everyone muttered, looking up at the orange tree by the fountain. "Since when have dates grown on orange trees that the stones could fall into our fountain?"

It was not to be wondered at that the next morning everyone awoke thinking, "What will happen today?" Zara the cook expected to lift the lids from her pots and perhaps find serpents instead of stews; Zaid the porter feared that he might open his door to an ogre or an afreet. But it seemed at last as if the palace could offer the bride Fatma a day of tranquillity. No scorpion crawled forth from the cracks; the fountain splashed as sweetly as if no date stones had ever clogged it and all day the doves cooed around the edge of the basin and among the orange blossoms. The bride and her gazelle came out of their seclusion and inspected the palace from kitchen to roof.

Mousa looked longingly from his father to the oranges that hung on the patio tree. These oranges were the finest in all Fez and were admired by every guest that came to the palace. Muhammed Ali carefully counted them himself and forbade everyone, including Mousa, to touch them. At the present there were twenty-seven on the tree, as large and heavy as the round melons that the hill people brought to market. Muhammed Ali understood Mousa's questioning look, which meant, "Let me this once pick one of our beautiful oranges in honor of the bride." But he shook his head. A rule was a rule.

Disappointed, Mousa instead picked jasmine blossoms from the vine that climbed from patio to balcony.

Toward twilight, when Muhammed Ali had unlocked the cupboard above his couch and taken down the tea canister and the sugar loaf and sat in front of his samovar pouring boiling water over the tea-leaves, the sugar and the mint, with his bride and her gazelle on cushions at his right and his son Mousa on a cushion at his left, the peace that the Faithful are always wishing upon each other seemed at last to have entered the palace.

Outside in the court by the fountain, the musicians sat playing their pipes and their lutes and singing sweetly wailing songs in praise of their master and his bride. When they stopped to drink the glasses of tea that Muhammed Ali sent out to them, the doves took up the mournful music with their gentle cooing.

Mousa had loved these doves ever since he could remember. It was their soft voices that woke him every morning. When he was younger they had sung him to sleep. And at this twilight hour when they fluttered about the fountain, clinging to the white marble with their pink feet, sipping the sparkling water and caressing each other with their bills and their murmurous voices, he never tired of watching and listening.

Today as he listened a curious thing seemed to be happening. The cooing grew fainter and fainter until little by little it died away altogether. Though every dove fluttered and walked about as usual, no more sound came from their throats.

Just as Mousa was about to call his father's attention to the silence, the musicians picked up their instruments again and began the ballad called the "Sultana of Seville." It was his father's favorite and no interruptions were ever allowed until the end of the thirty-seven verses. When they came to the nineteenth verse where the blind beggar reveals himself as the young prince in disguise, Mousa, who was watching his dear doves more attentively than he was listening to the song, suddenly saw them all spread their wings at once and fly up toward the roof and out of sight.

He gasped. This had never happened before. Never had they all flown off together, leaving the patio doveless.

"O Father, look! Look!" he exclaimed as soon as the last quavering note of the music died.

Muhammed Ali looked. Yes, the doves were gone. But he was in no mood to share his son's alarm and distress.

"That which happens, happens," he said. Though Mousa was used to this fatalistic point of view, he had never learned to accept it.

"*Inchallah*, if Allah is willing, they will return," his father added and ordered the musicians to continue with their music.

All that night Mousa kept waking up, hoping that morning would come, hoping that he would hear the voices of his doves. Morning came at last but no dove voices in the orange tree!

Downstairs around the fountain faces were grave, but not because of the missing doves. The seven largest of the twenty-seven oranges were gone from the tree and Muhammed Ali's glances were falling as sternly on his household as if they had been the criminals that stood before him waiting for their sentences. Everybody had been questioned. Everybody had pleaded innocence.

Again Mousa sensed suspicion against him. "It must have been Mousa," they were all thinking.

Fortunately for him, he had a reputation for telling the truth, so that when he too pleaded innocence his father believed him and nothing more was said about the oranges. But a feeling of suspicion and ill-will began to spread through the household.

Only the bride herself remained aloof and indifferent

to the new mischiefs that seemed to be occurring each
day. As she passed from room to room, her beauty made
all her servants forget the grave looks of the master. And
Allak the gazelle, as he frisked about the court, cheered
them with something alive and graceful to look at, for,
like Mousa, they missed the doves.

But Mousa, to his surprise, found no pleasure in
watching his stepmother's gazelle. In all his life this was
the first animal that he had not loved,—perhaps because
he had been so sharply forbidden to touch him, perhaps
because of the disdainful twitching of his nostrils, the
hostile glowering of his eyes. Was it possible, he wondered, that Allak had stolen and devoured the oranges?
They had hung well out of his reach, but how often had
he not seen goats not only standing on their hind legs
to reach some tender olive twig but actually climbing
up into the lower branches of trees? And this Allak with
his cloven hooves, his horns, his nibbling mouth, was
perhaps not so unlike a goat as to make the theft of the
oranges impossible!

When he suggested this theory to Loualou, the only
one of the household who still seemed to trust him, she
looked at him gravely and laid her arm protectingly
around his shoulder.

"Either that or. . . ." she said mysteriously.

"Or what, Loualou?"

"Nothing, Mousa, nothing," she added and quickly
changed the subject.

Muhammed Ali's temper did not improve the next day
when it was found that his favorite mule, hardly recovered from the scorpion bite, had gone lame for no
good reason, in its left hind leg. This mule, Buazza, was
Muhammed Ali's pride. All Fez knew the magnificent
head, the glossy black flanks. When men saw it standing
outside the door of the Pasha, they said: "Muhammed
Ali is inside having tea." And on this very day when

Buazza went lame, Muhammed Ali had been invited to take tea with the Pasha, who was entertaining three viziers from the Sultan's court at Rabat. It disappointed him to have to ride, instead, the brown mule Heeana, a hand's breadth shorter than Buazza and in every way less noble, from his nose to his tail.

"Ya Allah, let nothing untoward happen today," thought everyone on the sixth day after the arrival of the bride. Muhammed Ali had himself invited the Pasha and his three guests, the Sultan's viziers, to dine.

As mistress of the household for the first time, Fatma moved about supervising the preparations for the feast. Later she would only look down upon her husband and her husband's guests from a distance, hidden behind the carved lattice of the balcony. Nor would Muhammed Ali himself sit with his guests, but move about in proper host fashion supervising the servants. When the feast was over, during the tea and the music, Mousa would be invited to join them.

Evening came and with it the arrival of the distinguished visitors.

"Allah be praised, all goes smoothly," said Zara the cook. Zaid the porter and all the other servants gathered in the kitchen as the maids came back and reported that the guests were dipping their right hands enthusiastically into platter after platter.

"Praise be to Allah and to his Prophet Muhammed," they kept repeating, for the house was highly honored by the visit of the three viziers.

But while they were saying, "Our master's guests will return to Rabat and speak of this house and this feast and this music to our Lord the Sultan, to Sidna Moulai Mohand himself," the musician who had taken up his lute uttered so loud a "Ya Allah" of consternation that everyone looked up. In dismay he held out his lute. The strings had been cut and hung dangling in the air.

Mousa, as shocked as everyone else, watched a flush
of shame spread over his father's face. The snapping of
one lute string was evil omen enough and here were
all the strings severed.

"Do not let it distress you," said the eldest of the viziers.

"It is without doubt the mischief of some child," said
the second vizier, forgetting the presence of Mousa.

"The child of some servant," added the third vizier,
noticing him.

"Oh, if there were only some other child in this house,"
thought Mousa unhappily. "Is there no end to the mischief they suspect me of?"

How miserable Mousa was the next day when his
father accused him of having cut the lute strings, of
having spoiled the entertainment offered to the viziers
of Sidna Moulai Mohand; how miserable, because for
the first time in his life, he did not think his father believed that he was telling the truth.

On the day following this, to make his life even more
wretched, Zara the cook accused him of breaking the
green enameled jar that held the almond cakes and the
"gazelle horns." One of the serving maids, she said, had
seen him slip out of the kitchen early in the morning
when she came down to light the fires. Up and down
Mousa denied this. Zara only scowled at the broken
pieces of the jar and ordered him to keep out of the
kitchen.

Everybody was now against him. Even Zaid the porter,
until now his good friend, refused to open the street
door for him without his father's permission.

Only Loualou had the same loving eyes for him that
she had always had. Loualou, however, had been as-
signed to take care of her new mistress, who not only
kept her busy mending, washing and ironing her enormous trousseau, but scolded whenever Mousa approached his old nurse.

"Let Loualou alone, Mousa," she ordered. "Can't you see she is busy? She has no time for your chattering."

There was no doubt that his stepmother disliked him. Why, he had no idea, any more than he could understand why the whole household was turning against him. Was it Fatma and her gazelle who were responsible for his unhappiness?

In spite of all that had happened in the last days, the ninth morning held a climax for which he was utterly unprepared.

Muhammed Ali summoned him to the long room where he entertained his friends at feasts and at tea. From the center of the wall, over the main divan, hung a painted wooden cupboard. To this cupboard Muhammed Ali kept the key and in it, among other things, were the tea canister, the conical sugar loaf, and the sugar hammer to break up the loaf. In all Fez households this was the custom.

To Mousa's horror this cupboard had been broken open. The spot where the sugar loaf stood was empty and the blue paper in which the loaf was always wrapped lay on the floor.

"Well, Mousa," said Muhammed Ali.

Mousa looked straight up into his father's eyes. "It was not I," he said. "I have not been out of my room since I went to bed last night."

"O Mousa." His father's voice was half angry, half reproachful. "The other times I hoped so much that you were telling the truth that I believed you were. Now I know you have been lying about everything, for you are lying about this. I myself saw you this morning, when it was scarcely light, creep out of this room and up the stairs. Your stepmother was frightened because she heard a noise and asked me to go out on the balcony and look. I saw you."

"But it wasn't I. It couldn't have been I."

"It's no use, Mousa; I myself saw you. I hoped that if

I gave you this chance by showing you the cupboard you would confess. Instead you have lied again. You deserve a beating and you shall have one."

It was a cruel beating, but what hurt most was the injustice of it.

"My father is going mad," thought Mousa, choking back his tears as Muhammed Ali finally put the cane away and dismissed him.

Loualou found him behind the sacks of grain in the darkest jog of the entrance hall, crying bitterly.

"Mousa," she whispered.

There was no answer.

"Mousa, Mousa! It is I. Your Loualou. Do not be afraid."

Mousa crept out of his hiding place, smeared with dust and cobwebs. Loualou took him by the hand and led him to an even darker, more secret hiding place behind the tall wine jars, where he told her his story.

"But what if they should find us?" he whispered fearfully.

"They cannot approach without my knowing it," answered Loualou.

"How can you know?"

The old nurse took the boy's hand and laid it on the sacred lion's claw at her throat. "That is how I can tell. At the approach of the four-legged one the claw never fails to give a warning scratch across my skin. O Mousa, there is no doubt about it; Allak is One of Those, One of the Hidden Ones, One of the Eighty-seven Thousand Bodily Manifestations of Satan. In nine days he has brought nine major evils upon this house and who can count how many lesser ones? He will continue his mischief. Each day he will grow stronger and more terrible. He will end by destroying us. He *must* be stopped."

"But how? How, Loualou? Tell me what we can do." Mousa was beginning to feel brave again. Whatever it was, he would do it.

"Only one thing."

"And what is that?"

"We must gain the help of the other Hidden Ones, the Ones Who Do No Mischief, and who are, at times, even helpful to man."

Fear crept back over Mousa. He did not know himself, and he did not think Loualou knew how that could be done. These spirits were, as everyone knew, invisible in the air or wandering about in strange shapes among the dwellings of men,—gazelles, cats with slit ears, serpents, howling dogs. One never knew when one was encountering them, but to talk with them, to ask help of the friendly ones, that was indeed an awful, improbable undertaking.

"Do you know how, Loualou?"

"No, Mousa, I do not know how. If it were a jungle spirit, I might, perhaps, have some skill in summoning it, but a desert spirit, alas, no."

"Well then?"

"*You* must go to the market place, Mousa, to the *toubib*, the doctor, who sells charms and philtres against all the ills of body and spirit. You must tell him your story and ask him for the magic that will enable you to talk to the Hidden Ones. . . ."

"When?"

"At your first chance of leaving the house. You can slip past Zaid more easily than I. You must. . . ." She stopped suddenly. "Hush, *they* are coming!"

From behind the oil jars, they watched Fatma and Allak pass by. Though Allak tugged at his silken lead, and though his nostrils were pointed ominously toward the wine jars, Fatma was evidently engrossed in thoughts of her own.

As soon as they had passed out of sight, Loualou and Mousa slipped back into the courtyard and quickly separated.

4: A Whirring and a Humming

Mousa's first opportunity to leave the palace alone came one day when his stepmother was having an argument with the porter. The door stood open. Unnoticed, Mousa slipped out.

It seemed a long time since he had been on the streets of the city by himself. He would like to have lingered in the Place Nedjariine, bright with the leathers and silks of the merchants, or in the Street of Spice Sellers, fragrant from end to end, or by the Mosque of Moulai Idriss where the candle-makers sold their enormous, gaily painted candles. But he had more important work on foot and hurried up and down the steep hills till he came out through the walls of the city at the market place of the Bab Mahrouk.

Here again he was tempted to linger, to join the eager crowd that gathered round the story-tellers, and hear more about the adventures of Zama; to watch the dancing boys and their bull, decked with purple velvet and wreathed with flowers from the mountains; to lay a coin on the tongue of the black witch doctor from the Niger who pranced about in a skirt of lynx skins and a high hat of little mirrors and feathers. All these things tempted him. All these things he resisted as he made his way through the crowds, past snake-charmers, scribes, barbers and tumblers, to the spot where a *toubib*, a doctor, squatted in front of his charms and potions.

"*Eeya, eeya;* yes, yes," the *toubib* was saying sympathetically as he gravely stroked his beard and listened to the whispered appeals of his patient, a veiled woman with wide and worried eyes. While Mousa waited his turn, he examined with wonder and curiosity the hundred little saucers of powders and other cures in front of the *toubib*. "Is it with the skull of a hawk, the cast-off skin of a serpent, the tail feathers of an eagle that I will be able to call upon the good spirits for help?" he wondered. "What a wise man he must be to know the values of all these strange substances."

In the meanwhile the *toubib* had heard the last of the woman's ills and was reaching to right and left for a pinch of this and a pinch of that,—black powder, red powder, the dried hind leg of a frog, the claw of a jackal. After pounding and grinding them with pestle and mortar, he wrapped them up, handed them to the woman, accepted the copper coin she gave him and bade her go in peace. Then he lifted his piercing, deep-set eyes to Mousa.

"Peace be upon you, O *Toubib*," said Mousa.

"And upon you the peace, my son," answered the *toubib*. "You have an ailment for me to cure, if Allah is willing?"

"Not a bodily ailment, *ya Sidi*. It is your wisdom, your advice that I need."

And he told him the story of Allak and his mischief, of all that had befallen since his appearance, of his own suspicion that Allak belonged to the Hidden Ones Who Were Evil, and begged the *toubib* to teach him how to seek the aid of the Hidden Ones Who Were Good and who could perhaps offset the wicked magic of Allak.

The *toubib* stroked his beard more slowly than ever and wrinkled his forehead in deepest thought. Mousa stood before him with his knees shaking, thinking: "Perhaps he does not know. Perhaps he knows, but he will not tell me."

Finally the *toubib* spoke. "It is not often that one tells such things to children," he said, "but you are indeed in grave trouble and in need of help. Listen then carefully and forget no word of what I have to say." Mousa moved nearer as the *toubib* began in a low voice so that curious onlookers could hear nothing. His eyes opened

wider and wider as the *toubib* explained that here in the
very market place one could converse with the Unseen
Ones till the Prayer of Sundown.

"Here! In the market place!" exclaimed Mousa, astonished, "where the people gather like great herds of sheep?
One would look for them, I should have thought, I have
always been told, in lonely caves, at windy cross roads,
in an empty room where there is no light."

"Those are of course the places they prefer, the places
they inhabit, but there is a day in the week, and that day
is the fourth, the farthest removed from the Day of
Gathering when all true Believers worship Allah, when
hunger brings them to the market for bread and meat,—
for bread that has been baked without the salt that they
fear, for meat that has been killed without the pious
bismillah, in the name of Allah."

"The Ones Who Are Good as well as the Ones Who
Are Evil?" Mousa asked.

"The Ones Who Are Good as well as the Ones Who
Are Evil," repeated the *toubib*.

Mousa turned pale. "It is terror enough," he said, "to
talk to the Unseen Ones Who Are Good. O *Toubib*, what
if your magic brought me into talk with Those Who Are
Evil?"

"If you are stupid, if you are careless, if you forget what
I say," said the *toubib*, frowning, "there is that danger
and may Allah have pity on you! If you remember what
I say, there is no danger."

"By Allah and by his Prophet Muhammed," answered
Mousa, thoroughly frightened, "I will remember."

"This, then, is what you must do. At the far side of the
market place are the sellers of fish, next to them, the
butchers of cattle. Go first to the fish stalls and buy a
small fish and let him who sells it swear by Allah and by
every saint of the Mogreb that it is not a fish from the
salt waters of the ocean but a fish from the fresh waters

of mountain streams. And when you have bought the fish go to the butcher and ask for the blood of a white bullock and let the butcher swear by Muhammed and by his winged steed Al Borak upon which he ascended to Heaven that it is the blood of a white bullock and not of a black bullock, for if it should be the blood of a black bullock, then," and here the *toubib* looked with all the severity of his seventy years at Mousa, "then you will find yourself conversing with the Unseen Ones Who Are Evil, and of what would come of that, it is better not to think."

"The blood of a *white* bullock," Mousa repeated earnestly.

"Next," continued the *toubib*, "take the forefinger of your left hand, dip it in the blood and trace a serpent along your forehead from left to right; after you have done this, dip the fish in the blood and eat it in its entirety,—its body, its head and its tail."

"And then?"

"Then, if you are fortunate, you will hear a whirring and a humming. The shrill voices, the thin voices, the whistling voices of the Unseen Ones will fill the air and will talk with you and listen to your tale till the sun begins to drop and shadows lengthen and the voice of the muezzin calls the Faithful to evening prayer."

"How can I thank you," said Mousa, opening the green pouch that hung from his shoulders and taking out his only coins,—copper ones at that.

The *toubib* held up his hand and waved them away. "Save them," he said, "to buy the fish. Some day when your house is rid of evil powers, tell your father who helped you. He is an honest man and he will reward me."

Thanking him profusely, Mousa left the good *toubib* and made his way across the market place to the butchers' stalls.

"A *white* bullock," he kept repeating to himself as he

pushed impatiently through the thick crowd that had
nothing more important to do than to gossip or crowd
round story-teller and snake-charmer. "White. White.
White. White like the snow of mountain peaks; white like
the flat roofs of the city, white like the jasmine flowers
that fall into the fountain."

"A fine red mullet?" suggested the fishmonger as Mousa
stood before his wares looking them over; "a mullet fresh
and dripping from the ocean itself, or perhaps a tasty
squid or a tender sole?"

"No," said Mousa. He looked intently at the gleaming,
shimmering scales of silver and gold, till he recognized a
small heap of rainbow mullet that darted and leapt in
the mountain streams of the High Atlas. They were
among his father's favorite dishes and he had often
watched the cooks prepare them.

"One of those," he said, pointing.

"One! Ya Allah," exclaimed the fishmonger in disgust.
"They are no longer than your finger. It is madness to buy
one. It is surely one *dozen* that you mean."

"One," repeated Mousa firmly, laying down one of his
coins.

Muttering crossly, the man almost threw the little fish
at him in order to turn to a more profitable customer.

Near the butchers' stalls, he saw brown cattle, red
cattle, black cattle placidly chewing their cud among the
goats and sheep. What if there were no white bullocks!
But the first butcher he asked assured him there were.
He himself had slaughtered a fine white bullock that very
morning,—white from muzzle to tail.

"And can you swear by Muhammed and . . . . and . . . ."
To Mousa's terror his mind went suddenly blank. What
was it the butcher was to swear by? Muhammed and
. . . ? It was no good. He could not remember.

"O butcher," he said, "swear by our Prophet Muhammed, but also show me as proof the tail of your bullock."

"Alas," said the butcher, "only a few minutes ago I sold the tail to slaves from the Pasha's kitchen for a rich soup."

"He is lying," thought Mousa miserably. "It was a *black* bullock."

"But," continued the butcher, "here! Here is your proof," and he laid a white ear under Mousa's eyes.

"Allah be praised," sighed Mousa with relief.

In the milling crowd, no one noticed as Mousa traced the wavy line of a serpent from left to right across his forehead, dipped the fish in the blood and swallowed it quickly. Would the magic all go wrong because he had been unable to remember the full oath for the butcher?

Very still he stood, listening with shaking knees to the market sounds, the thudding hand-drums of the story-tellers, the shrill whine of the musician's pipes, the whin-nying of picketed horses.

Suddenly above the sound of drums and pipes, above the talk of men, he began to hear a faint whirring like the beating of birds' wings, and a humming like the noise of bees, and a whistling like the sound of wind. And as the market noises faded away altogether, this whirring, this humming, this whistling took on the sound of voices, —a chorus of thin, quavering, meagre voices all about him in the air.

"Listen! Listen, O djinns!" he heard a high voice saying. "Gather closer. Unless I am much mistaken, there is someone in the market place who wishes to talk with us."

"You speak the truth, O Baha," answered a swishing voice even closer to Mousa's ears. "He is here in our midst with the sign of the serpent across his forehead."

"If he has also swallowed the fish, then he will be able to speak to us and tell his name and what he wishes. Let him speak. Let him have no fear."

"O Spirits! O Powerful Ones!" began Mousa in a trem-bling voice, "I am Mousa, son of Muhammed Ali, and I come to you for help."

"Peace be upon you, Mousa. Speak," ordered the voices. "If it is in our power, we will help you."

"But remember," warned the voice that had spoken first, "remember not to linger too long over your tale, for at the true moment of sunset, at the moment when a white hair can no longer be distinguished from a black hair, we shall be gone."

Mousa cast a quick look at the sky. The sun hung halfway between zenith and horizon as if caught and pierced by the turquoise minaret of the Great Mosque, but shadows were beginning to lengthen, so he hurriedly began his tale, skipping some of the minor calamities like the date stones in the fountain and the cutting of lute strings. He even forgot to tell about the oranges being stolen from the trees and the departure of the doves. As it was the list was long and shocking enough.

The djinns whirred and hummed in sympathy.

"What a list of horrors," one murmured.

"Poor Mousa, you should have come to us before," said a thin voice in his left ear.

"Allak, Allak," exclaimed a whistling voice in his right ear. "Truly there is no more malefic djinn throughout the Mogreb than this Allak. One has only to look at his family to realize that. Everyone knows that his grandmother Harrar has seven heads and extinguishes fires when hungry people are trying to cook; that his grandfather Gola has the tail of a sheep and his head is in his breast. When he haunts a village the hens lay eggs of black marble. Dir, the father of Allak, has the shape of an ostrich and the skin of a leopard. How the farmers curse him, for he steals into men's gardens at night and whistles shrilly. At his whistle, every carrot, every radish, every turnip, every garden plant leaves its bed bewitched and follows this djinn out into the desert where they shrivel and die in the sun, for he calls them not from hunger but from mischief. He himself drinks the blood of new-born kids.

But wickeder than Gola, wickeder than Dir, wickedest
of them all is Waali, the mother of Allak. When men
think of her, they close their eyes and their mouths and
put their fingers in their ears so the thought cannot
escape and fly through the air doing harm. . . ."

Mousa shuddered to himself as the thin voice continued.

"Yet to look at she was often a most lovely fiend with a
great sparkling eye in the middle of her white forehead
and red hair that floated out behind her as she flew. But
as often she took the shape of an ogress with the quills
of a hedgehog instead of hair and waving cat-tails instead of fingers and toes. Then again she might appear
as a red cat or a green viper. One never knew in what
form to expect her, where to expect her or what evil to
expect from her. . . ."

"And now," asked Mousa timidly, "where is she now?
What has become of her, if one may ask?"

"One may ask," answered the whistling voice, "but
who knows the answer! The last time we saw her, a
century or so ago, she was presiding over a congress of
ogresses in the Libyan desert. Oh, but she was hideous
to look at then! After that, rumor had it that she flew to
Persia and was luring desert travelers to her cave where
the first thing they saw and smelled was their unfortunate
predecessors turning on a spit. That was when she was
said to have quarreled with her son Allak because she
did not think his magic worthy of a djinn with all his ad-
vantages. Of course she had spoiled Allak; he was the
favorite among her nine hundred and ninety-nine sons.
It was her fault and not his that he had not learned all
the magic that was expected of him."

Mousa shuddered again at the dreadful thought of
Allak being expected to know more magic than he did
already.

It also worried him to realize that while the djinn had

been talking the sun was also sinking. It had already dropped from the top of the minaret. Only its upper rim showed above the western wall of the city. Mousa looked anxiously at the black and white stripes of his burnous. The white was still white and the black was still black and now, at last, Allah be praised, the djinn who had just finished this long speech was beginning to talk of help.

"Yes," agreed the others, "it is possible that we can help you. You must excuse us while we withdraw to a short distance and discuss the matter among ourselves."

"Oh certainly. By all means," said Mousa. "And do hurry," he felt like adding (but of course did not), as the voices and words blurred again into the whirring and the humming.

Now nothing could be seen of the sun except a crimson glow along the western wall. In the market place the crowd was thinning. Mousa fastened his eyes in fear on the minaret of the Great Mosque. Any moment now the white flag might be run up that preceded the voice of the muezzin calling the Faithful.

At last! At last the whirring and the humming approached again and resolved itself into voices.

"Are you still there, Mousa?" they asked.

"Oh yes! yes!" answered Mousa eagerly.

"Well," said the voices, "we have drawn lots. One of us will come to you."

"I, Baha," said the voice which had told the tale of Allak's family, "I will come. Tomorrow I will be there. You will recognize me because...."

Here the voice was growing fainter. Mousa could hardly hear.

"I shall come in...."

It sounded as if the djinn were calling back over his shoulder.

"In the shape of...."

But the last word faded out into the thinnest and faint-

est of whistles. The white flag was flying from the minaret. In the dimming twilight the black and white stripes
of Mousa's burnous looked as grey as his father's beard.

5: *The Ear of the Fennec*

"In the shape of. . . ." what, wondered Mousa at every
step between the market and his father's house. "How
will he appear to me, this Baha who promised to help?
How shall I recognize him?" And he went over and over
in his mind all the shapes that the Hidden Ones were
known to take: dogs, generally black, but not always;
cats, generally black but not always; (was it true that
you could know them by their slit ears?) bullocks, foxes,
tortoises, snakes. The list was endless. And besides these
disguises, they were also, as everyone knew, exceedingly
fond of the shape of monsters,—Mousa's great-uncle
had once been bitten by a man with the legs of a donkey,
—though in this guise they seldom crossed the thresholds
of houses. Nor was this all, for you could not trust the
very stones in the fields. If you stumbled against one in
the dark, it was necessary to say: "Good evening to you,
O master of the Place; I meant you no harm."

Certainly there was no telling in what shape the Hidden One who called himself Baha would keep his promise.

Another thing worried Mousa as he hurried through
the twisting streets. How was he himself going to enter
the palace again without a terrible scolding, perhaps a
beating?

Luck was with him today. When he reached the door,

he found to his surprise and pleasure the farmer Brahim talking to Zaid, Brahim who managed his father's date gardens across the mountains in the oasis of Tafilalelt. He was fond of Mousa and always brought him a fine present when he came to town to present his accounts to Muhammed Ali. He would defend him from the scoldings of Zaid the porter, for Zaid had married his daughter and would not dare show disrespect to the white beard of his father-in-law.

It turned out as Mousa had hoped. Zaid scowled as he saw him but spoke respectfully enough.

"Everyone has been looking high and low for you. Hurry to your father. He is giving tea to the Pasha, the Caid Lemneffi and other notables."

Mousa hurried. Cruel as his father was to him these days, he still liked to show off his only son when his friends came to tea.

An impressive row of slippers, all of the finest goatskin, lay by the step that separated the patio from the room where his father was serving tea. Mousa added his slippers to the row and greeted his father and his father's friends.

The Pasha, with his great hooked nose, his deep-set eyes and crooked mouth, always frightened him. The famous Caid Lemneffi he had never seen before. Lemneffi, lord of one of the great mountain tribes, taller, more imperious, more eagle-like of face than the Pasha himself. Mousa felt very shy as he settled down close to his father and sipped his hot glass of mint tea. Suddenly he felt braver inside for he began to wonder if any of these grave, impressive notables had ever spent the afternoon as he, Mousa, had just done, in pleasant conversation with the Hidden Ones.

While he was finishing his second glass of tea, Brahim was ushered into the patio by Zaid. Shuffling out of his well-worn, dusty *babouches* and adding them to the row of fine goatskin ones, Brahim advanced respectfully to kiss his master's arm and wish him *"La Bas,"*—No Evil. In each hand he carried a basket.

The basket in his right hand he laid at the feet of Muhammed Ali, who motioned to Mousa to lift the lid. Mousa's eyes sparkled with pleasure at the sight of a nest of fig leaves filled with purple Tafilalelt dates, the largest, the juiciest, the most famous throughout the Mogreb. And not only Mousa's eyes sparkled; Muhammed Ali's also, for the judge was no lean, hard-riding figure like the Caid Lemneffi, but like most citizens of Fez, a barrel-shaped lover of all good things to eat, from rich pigeon stews to purple Tafilalelt dates.

And the other basket? Mousa's curiosity was aroused as he sucked the juice from the longest date. To his joy Brahim put the other basket down in front of him.

"For you, O Mousa. This my son Ahmed found in the desert outside the garden walls. He tamed it and sends it to you with wishes for your well-being and prosperity."

Very cautiously Mousa lifted the lid and peeked into the basket. Curled up in the corner was a bushy tail wrapped round the largest ears, the blackest eyes, the sharpest nose Mousa had ever seen.

"O Brahim, what is it? What is it? It isn't a dog. It isn't a jackal. It isn't a fox. It isn't anything I have ever seen."

"It *is* a fox, Mousa; not an ordinary fox, but a desert fox, a Saharan fox, what we call a fennec. No ordinary fox lets itself be tamed so easily. No ordinary fox has such enormous ears."

Mousa thrust his hand slowly and gently under the little furry body. It just fitted into his two hands. While he was running his fingers lovingly through the thick fur, he felt a soft tongue licking his wrist.

Suddenly a fearful thought came to him. Would his father let him keep this little fennec? Would he remember Fatma and her gazelle and make Brahim take it back

to the desert? He could already see doubt in his father's eyes. Muhammed Ali was about to protest.

At this point the Caid Lemneffi came to Mousa's aid.

"O Muhammed Ali, let your son Mousa keep this fennec. It is a saying current among my people: 'He who gives food and shelter to a fennec, singes the whiskers of the Powers of Evil.'"

Brahim nodded in approval. "And among us," he added, "it is said: 'Allah gave the fennec his great ears so that he could hear all the mischief plotted against mankind.'"

Mousa looked pleadingly at his father, who finally nodded his consent.

"Thank you, Brahim, thank you," said Mousa. "And my thanks to your son Ahmed. I will take good care of my pet."

Brahim acknowledged the thanks, accepted the glass of tea that Muhammed Ali poured for him, and took his place on a mattress at a respectful distance from his master and his master's guests.

In the meanwhile Mousa sat stroking his new pet, caressing the bushy tail, patting the dainty paws and feeling the softness of each huge ear, first the left ear from broad base to pointed tip, then the right ear, running his finger around the furry edge.

Suddenly his finger discovered something that forced him to exert all his self-control in order not to give a noticeable start. Near the base of the right ear, concealed by the fur, was a definite slit as long as a finger joint; a cat with slit ears was almost without doubt one of the Hidden Ones. Was this also true of a fennec?

At the same time he felt the touch of a paw on his other hand. Was it a restraining paw? Was it a warning to keep his discovery a secret? Could it be, could it possibly be, that he was caressing the ears of a djinn? Though he felt his cheeks burning at the idea, he managed to go on sipping his tea and stroking the fennec as if nothing had happened.

"Tie him to the orange tree by the fountain," ordered his father when the guests had gone, "and see that you tie him tight so that he cannot get loose and get into mischief. I do not know what your stepmother will say when she sees a fennec in the house."

Mousa hurried off with his pet and called to Loualou to find him a cord that would not cut into the little creature's neck. While he was waiting for her, holding the fennec against his cheek, he suddenly felt the little nose tickling his ear and an unmistakable whispering voice.

"It is I, Baha, who promised to come. Mousa, not a single soul inside this house or out must know who I am! It must be your secret. If you share it with anyone, my power to help you will disappear. You have heard the saying: 'Into a closed mouth no fly enters'?"

Mousa nodded. "My mouth shall remain closed," he promised. "I can't thank you enough for coming. How are you going to help me? Can I help you help? I'll do anything you say."

"Hush," whispered Baha, for Loualou was waddling across the court with a red silk cord.

"Tie it tight, Mousa," she warned in a low voice, handing it to him. "If this fennec of yours once gets loose in the palace, you will never be allowed to keep him. Upstairs your stepmother is already scolding your father for permitting it. Tell me, Mousa," she said, lowering her voice even more. "Tell me about the market place. Did you find out you-know-what from the *toubib*?"

Mousa was a truthful boy, but with the fennec's warning still in his ears, he had no choice. He shook his head sadly.

"Not a thing, Loualou. Not a thing. He would not teach me the magic because I was a child."

"Ya Allah," exclaimed Loualou, worried and disturbed. "What will become of this house!"

"Mousa," whispered the fennec as soon as she had gone, "I am sorry to be the cause of your having to lie. If all turns out well in the end, and I sincerely hope it will, I am sure that she will forgive you. Before you leave me, would you mind tieing that cord a little more loosely around my neck? I must be free to slip my head in and out at all times, but you can be sure I will be discreet about it. This evening, as soon as darkness falls, I must report to my companions on my first impressions of the situation. In the meanwhile they are scouting round to see if they can find out anything that would be of help to me. There is, for instance, a rumor that the Evil Ones are to meet somewhere soon, perhaps tonight, and an even vaguer rumor that the meeting in some way concerns Allak. Would you be good enough to be sure and feed me before I go?"

"Why of course, Baha, of course! I was just going to ask you what you liked to eat best of anything in all the world?"

"Jerboas," answered Baha without hesitation.

"Jerboas," repeated Mousa, puzzled. "O Baha, I never heard of a jerboa."

"No, I suppose not," sighed Baha. "They are the *most* delicious kind of desert mouse. Nothing tastes quite so good. But I also like locusts, quail, rabbits and grapes. Any one will do."

"Chicken?" asked Mousa hopefully.

Baha licked his lips, and Mousa hurried to the kitchen to beg Zara for a plump chicken and a bunch of Muscat grapes.

Zara scowled when she saw him standing in the doorway.

"A chicken for a fox! Ya Allah, Mousa, you are crazy! Moreover, you bring bad luck to the kitchen. Do not stand in its doorway."

Here one of the serving girls came to his rescue, not from any love of Mousa but because she was a mountain girl from the tribe of the Caid Lemneffi. She had been bringing in cakes when the Caid urged Muhammed Ali to let Mousa keep the fennec. She too had been brought up on the saying: "To give food and shelter to a fennec, is to singe the whiskers of the Powers of Evil." Not only this, but the words of the great Caid of her tribe were law to her.

"O Zara," she said, looking up from the butter she was churning. "You said yourself that the red chicken brought from the market this morning with the white ones would be too tough to serve to a beggar even if you boiled it from now till the month of Ramadan. Give it to Mousa for his fennec. And surely you can spare grapes. Three great baskets of them were sent in from the Azrou farms this morning. I myself put them in the storeroom. Moreover, O Zara, this fennec has already brought a blessing to the house, for the sweet milk has stayed sweet all day and the sour cream is turning to butter more easily than it has done in over a week."

Zara herself was a good citizen of Fez and did not hold with the superstitions of mountain folk. But the girl was not only a favorite but her best worker. She shrugged her shoulders.

"Very well," she mumbled. "Get him the chicken."

"Thank you, Mousa, it looks delicious," said Baha as Mousa set the chicken in front of him. "The chickens of Tafilalelt are not half so fat. Don't be surprised, tonight, if. . . ."

He stopped suddenly, for Muhammed Ali was coming across the court. The master of the house frowned as he saw the grapes and the chicken between Baha's dainty paws.

"It was a tough one," Mousa explained quickly. "Zara herself said so and gave it to me."

"Why are my servants not trained to be able to know tender chickens from tough ones in the market?" he muttered. "Do they think I am as rich as our Lord the Sultan (may Allah preserve him) that I can feed chickens to the wild animals of the desert? Tomorrow he shall. . . ."

At this point Zaid fortunately appeared, saying there was a messenger outside from two men who begged him to come to their house and settle a quarrel.

When his father had gone, Mousa started to ask Baha what he had been about to say, but Baha stopped him quickly.

"Your stepmother is watching us from the balcony. Come to me before you go to bed."

In spite of every effort toward the end of the evening, the patio was never empty enough for him to dare risk talking to Baha. To make matters worse, Muhammed Ali ordered the musicians to move their cushions by the fountain and orange tree for their final concert of the evening.

To Mousa, waiting impatiently, it seemed later than usual before his father ordered them to stop, before everyone went to bed, before the palace lay in darkness.

As soon as every light was out, Mousa crept down again to the court. Would Baha be gone, or would he have waited?

"Mousa!" It was Baha's voice, though Mousa could see nothing in the black shadow of the orange tree. "Mousa, listen carefully! I have two important things to say, then I must be off. First, are you always careful about turning your clothes right side out, when you undress, and folding them neatly?"

What a strange question! "Why no, Baha. I'm afraid not. Loualou is always scolding me for leaving them in a heap. Sometimes I fold them but half the time I forget."

"With such carelessness, you scarcely deserve help.

You know, of course, that by leaving them wrong side out and unfolded, Allak—any djinn—can step into them and assume your appearance."

"Oh no, Baha! I *never* knew that! So *that* explains it. Allak was wearing *my* clothes and doing the mischief!"

"Be careful from now on."

"Of course I will." Mousa's voice was full of shame.

"The second thing is what I started to say this afternoon when we were interrupted. Don't be surprised if I come to you later in the night. If I can find out where that meeting is and if it is tonight, I am planning to take you with me."

6: *The Haunted Ruins of Oulili*

Though Baha had ordered Mousa to get all the sleep he could, he was wide awake when he heard the faint click of the fennec's claws on the tiled floor. He did not move however till Baha stuck his sharp tickling nose into his ear to whisper directions. It was quite dark.

"Take hold of my tail," ordered Baha, "while I guide you up the stairs to the roof."

"The roof," thought Mousa, puzzled. "Why the roof? It must be that we are going to climb across the roof-tops of the city and gain the street through someone else's door."

Though he might have felt his way without light up the steep winding stairs, he was nevertheless glad of the feel of Baha's warm and friendly tail. Strangely enough, with each step of the stairs, the tail seemed to grow larger.

When they softly opened the door to the roof and
stepped out into the moonlight, Mousa stifled a cry of
astonishment. Baha was no longer the little fennec that
he could hold in his two hands, but had grown as large as
a great dog, though still fennec in shape, with his enormous ears, his bushy tail.

"Hush, Mousa," Baha warned him. "Do not be afraid.
I had to change my size because we must fly to the ruins
of Oulili which lie on the far side of the Mountains of the
Zerhoun, for that is where the djinns are to meet."

"Fly! But, Baha," Mousa's voice trembled with disappointment, "I can't fly. You know I can't."

"Of course you can't. That is why I have grown to this
size so I can take you on my back. Come! We must
hurry!"

Baha trotted to the edge of the roof. With pounding
heart, shaking knees, and cold hands, Mousa followed.

"Mount," ordered Baha.

Gathering up a handful of neck fur, Mousa threw his
leg over Baha's back. He was a good horseman, saddle
or no saddle, but he would have liked a bridle, especially
when the ride was to be by air and not over the good
earth.

"Ready?" asked Baha.

"Ready," answered Mousa. He could hear his own
voice squeaking with fear.

"Don't be afraid," said Baha. "You'll love it once we are
on our way."

The next thing Mousa knew they were off,—out and up
into the air. When he looked down at the white roof-tops
cut by the deep and narrow streets so far below, he did
not love it at all.

"Am I hurting you, Baha?" he asked, gripping the poor
fennec's ribs with all the strength in his knees.

"No..no," said Baha, none too convincingly. "But why
don't you relax a little? It would be more comfortable

for both of us. Try lying along my back with your arms around my neck."

No sooner had Mousa gingerly shifted to this new position, with his arms around the fennec's soft neck, his chin pillowed between his ears, than all of a sudden he did love it. He loved it so much he wanted to shout with excitement and joy. How wonderful—this rushing through the air! How wonderful to look down at the white city sliding away.

It was a brilliant night. To Mousa the moon had never seemed so immense, perhaps because he had never seemed so near it. Baha was cleaving the air in a splendid, effortless motion—not exactly a gallop, but more like the shooting forward of a strong swimmer.

Now they had passed the walls of the city. Gardens lay beneath them. In the stillness the voices of nightingales, sweeter than the music of fountains, rose up into the air. Nor were they too high to miss the fragrance of the orange and the lemon blossoms.

"Baha," asked Mousa, "did I understand you to say Oulili? Are we really going to fly the whole hundred kilometers to Oulili?"

"Yes," said Baha. "I had a most difficult time discovering their meeting place. They are, as I have told you, extremely secretive about their plans so none of us can spy on them."

"How did you find out?"

"It's rather a long story but then we have a long journey."

"Does it tire you to fly *and* talk?" asked Mousa considerately.

"Not at all."

"Then do tell me."

"The way I found out was not exactly praiseworthy but it had to be done. I bribed a little young one, one of the others. I found him wandering round sulkily in the shape of a mudpuppy, very peevish, very cross, very hurt because he had just been snubbed by a group of his elders. His vanity was in shreds. No sooner had we met than he began to wail and complain to me, talking incessantly, without even taking the trouble to find out whether I was interested or even whether I was one of his own kind.

" 'Come,' I said. 'Why don't you go to the meeting tonight and lay your troubles before the presiding spirit?'

" 'That's the whole trouble,' he whined. 'Weren't you listening to what I was telling you? Didn't you hear me say I am not *invited* to the meeting? Every important djinn of the Mogreb has been summoned except me. And just because I was trying to turn into a Persian Prince and something went wrong and I came out a mudpuppy, they are all laughing at me and saying my magic isn't good enough and I must wait another century before I can go to meetings. And for fifty years I had been looking forward to this, my first meeting,—especially because my cousin Allak, may Satan notice and punish his conceit, is to be the object of everyone's displeasure.'

" 'Where did you say the meeting was to be?' I asked artfully.

" 'I *didn't* say,' the mudpuppy said, suddenly suspicious of me. 'I don't believe you are One of Us.'

" 'It might be to your advantage,' I said, 'to tell me, because when it comes to meeting places I know a great deal. If, for instance, it were by the ruins of the Hasan Tower, I know a secret hole where one could lie hidden and though uninvited remain undiscovered; or if it were by the sulphur springs of Ain el Hamma, there is an extra thick thicket of oleander that I know; or if it were the ruins of Oulili which I, of course but not you, can remember as a fine bustling city almost twenty centuries ago when the Romans ruled this land, if by chance it *were* Oulili, there too I know a hiding place. . . .'

"Here it was easy to see by the mudpuppy's expression
that I had hit upon the right place, so I hastily added,
'and the hiding place of Oulili is the safest and best of
all hiding places.'

" 'And if it were Oulili,—mind you, I am not saying it is,'
said the mudpuppy, 'what would you suggest as a hiding
place?'

" 'Do you know Oulili well?' I asked.

" 'Not very,' he answered. 'My family sent me there to
haunt it when I was very young but it didn't appeal to
me at all. I soon ran away and haunted a very exciting
desert cross-road instead where. . . .'

" 'Never mind the desert cross-road,' I interrupted him.
Upon my word, Mousa, I have seldom encountered such
a chatter in so young a fiend. 'Let's get back to Oulili,'
I said sharply. 'Do you remember where you cross the
ford of the River of the Pharaohs and enter the city by
the ruined oil mill?'

" 'Indeed yes,' he answered. 'There was a fine old oil
jar there in which I slept during the heat of the day. One
day a serpent, a true serpent, not One of Us. . . .'

" 'Never mind about the serpent,' I said. 'From the oil
mill the road runs up into the old forum, the market
place we'd call it now, and to the temple with half-
broken columns along the steps and great blocks of
marble spilling from the walls. Do you remember?'

" 'Do I not?' said the mudpuppy. 'My great-uncle, may
our Lord Satan cherish him, carried, it is said, blocks of
this marble across the hills to Meknès-of-the-Olives for
the palace of the Sultan Ismael. He was seventeen feet
tall and he carried them on his head, one on top of the
other, and one for each of his seventeen feet. . . .'"

"I see what you mean," interrupted Mousa, "about his
being a chatterer. Didn't you lose your patience?"

"Very nearly."

"Where *was* the hiding place?" asked Mousa.

"A hole between the fountain and the Triumphal Arch. It will fit him neatly and from there he can hear and see everything that goes on. There is a tunnel that comes out at the edge of the city by the ruined aqueduct. He can enter by that unseen."

"Wouldn't it have done for us?"

"Far too small. And anyway it was only fair to reward him for disclosing the meeting place. Moreover, he may be useful to us again some time."

"Baha, shall we get there in time? When will the meeting begin?"

"Their meetings are always called for midnight. As soon as we have crossed these mountains, we shall be there."

Mousa hitched himself forward a little in order to look down between the fennec's ears.

Peaceful though the night was, the Mountains of the Zerhoun lay wild and menacing below. Though the peaks and precipices were streaked with moonlight, the gorges, the ravines, the hollows lay in the blackest darkness. They were flying low enough to hear the hooting of owls, the roaring of the cataracts. A cloud of squeaking bats circled curiously around them. Trees seemed to thrust out clutching branches.

"You're not getting tired, Baha?" Mousa asked.

"Tired!" Baha laughed. "Tired! Why this is nothing. I have flown from here to the Mountains of the Hoggar from sunset to sunrise. Very few djinns have that record! As for a camel, it would take a camel with its plodding gait three months. Not only that, but I have flown from here to Timbuctu on the Niger between one sunrise and the next. For this journey a camel would take six months."

"That is indeed wonderful," said Mousa, "but have you ever had to come down unexpectedly anywhere—in mountains like these, for instance?"

"Of course not. Unless perhaps I happened to be hungry."

"You don't happen to be hungry now, do you?"

"Not a bit."

Relieved, Mousa relaxed again. Still, he was glad to see the mountains flattening into hills, and to recognize in the moonlight a cluster of huts, with storks asleep in their roof-top nests and neat orchards of fig and walnut.

"There it is," exclaimed Baha suddenly, pointing ahead.

Mousa looked. A silver river curled around the foot of a steep hill. Ghostly grey olive trees covered the hillside except in the center. There the moonlight struck brightly over what was without doubt the tumbled marble of a ruined city.

"Are we in time?" asked Mousa anxiously.

"Half an hour to spare," answered Baha, a little proudly, as they sailed across the river, up the hillside and over the olive trees. When they came to the ruins, they circled slowly round, keeping under the shadowy fringe of trees that overhung the shattered columns and fallen stone.

Very neatly, without scratching either himself or Mousa, Baha landed on the thick horizontal branch of a carob tree.

"Here we shall be well hidden," said Baha, arranging himself into a comfortable crouching position and sticking only his nose out through the thick foliage. "None of the Others will choose trees. They will all rush for marble columns; those that are too late will crowd on arches and walls."

"Wouldn't you like me to get off your back while we are here?" asked Mousa. "I must be rather heavy."

Baha shook his head. "Stay where you are. It doesn't bother me at all. Besides, this is adventure; no adventure is without danger, and we *might* have to leave in a hurry. In that case it is better for you to be ready."

"You mean they might discover us?"

"I mean what I said. Adventure is danger. And this is adventure. Look," he whispered suddenly.

Seven monsters glowing with a green sulphurous light and mounted on baboons were streaming across the moon. Mousa shuddered and clung closer. Baha laid a comforting paw over his hand.

"The Seven Afreets of the Gorge of the Sheefa," whispered Baha. "Their magic is old and enormous."

Mousa watched fearfully as the monsters, with their fangs silhouetted in the moonlight, lit on the Triumphal Arch, dismounted and folded their legs beneath them in a glowering row, while their baboons dropped to a pile of marble below.

Now the sky began to grow shadowy with other shapes flying, leaping, gliding over the trees. Some came howling, some whistling, some screeching with thin, sharp voices. Many of them had taken the shape of animals,—hyenas, jackals, wildcats, hedgehogs, owls, but there were besides many other monstrous and indescribable shapes, half this animal, half that, to say nothing of ogres, ogresses, ghouls, werewolves and vampires.

Mousa clutched Baha's paw and buried his face in terror in the thick fur.

When he opened his eyes again, every fluted column, every crumbling wall, every pile of marble fragments had its monstrous living statue. An ill-natured whining, a high-pitched snarling, a raucous howling could be heard from every fallen stone of ruined Oulili as the djinns fought for the most advantageous places. And yet the highest spot of all, the keystone on the arch of the unfallen wall of the temple, remained unseized, unoccupied.

Suddenly the din died away. All heads turned to the eastern quarter of the sky. And now every djinn sat as immovable as if he were truly a statue. For a terrible cracking sound rent the air as a headless monster with a tail so long that three hyenas had to support it, came ramping down the sky.

"It is Gola himself," whispered Baha. Mousa had never heard his voice so full of awe. "The paternal grandfather of Allak. Without doubt it is he who is to be the presiding fiend. They have left the place of honor on the temple arch for him."

Baha was right. The headless monster flew straight to the temple wall. As soon as he alighted, the hyenas wrapped his tail seven times around his ankles. Now that he was nearer, you could see that though he wore no head upon his shoulders, a very terrible face with three eyes looked out from his breast.

These three eyes each glowed with a different colored light as he fastened them on the assembly,—the middle one with purple, the right one with orange and the left one with red. With the middle one he looked straight ahead; with the orange one he looked to the left, and with the red eye to the right. When everything was still as the moonlight itself, Gola reached with his mighty arms for one of the great blocks of marble half-falling from the arch and sent it crashing to the flagstones.

Mousa gave a start of fear.

"That is the way he always opens meetings," whispered Baha.

"Ai-yee," screamed the djinns, paying homage to their master.

"Ai-yee," screamed the Seven Afreets.

"Hail, Gola! You have summoned us," cried the leader of the Afreets, opening his fang-lined maw with a resounding bellow. "We have come to do your bidding. What is it that you wish of us?"

"Afreets, Ogres, Ghouls, Fellow Djinns," began Gola, acknowledging the homage of the assembly. "Welcome to Oulili. Yes, I have summoned you. I have a problem to put before you. I have need of your advice. It is well known that in this great and illustrious family of which I have the honor to be the head, there is one who dis-

graces our glorious reputation for evil. You will, I know, sympathize with my grief when I admit that it is my own grandson Allak. Everyone knows the trivial, the puerile, the amateurish quality of the mischief he has achieved during his nine days in a Fez household. No one has been eaten. No one has gone mad. No one has burst into flames. Ya Satan, Allak is indeed a wastrel and a dilettante. He is, however, young. Discipline, stern measures may yet save him. Afreets, fellow fiends, what is your advice?"

Silence fell after this speech of Gola's. No one presumed to advise the mightiest of djinns on how to reform his grandson.

Instead they made feeble, insincere remarks about not believing in Allak's shortcomings.

"Surely this cannot be true of any grandson of yours, O Gola," they exclaimed in smirking, flattering screeches. And one after the other rose on his column to praise Gola and his sons and his sons' sons, in long-winded, hypocritical speeches. For well they knew that the powerful ones among them like Gola, like the Seven Afreets, like some of the multiple-headed ogres, often fed on lesser djinns like themselves. It did not seem wise for an insignificant, secondary djinn in hedgehog's clothing to rise and say: "How true, O Gola, your Allak is indeed nothing but a skin stuffed with stupidity and deceit. When you are next hungry, devour him! That is our advice."

While they were thus wasting their breath, trying to ingratiate themselves with Gola, Mousa found a chance to whisper to Baha.

"How about Allak's parents, the ones you told me about, the terrible Dir, his father; the dreadful Waali, his mother? Are they here?"

"Dir! Waali! Indeed no!" answered Baha. "Didn't I tell you that Gola disinherited his son Dir when he married

Waali? He admitted of course her enchantment and her power for magic, but he recognized the giddy streak in her and foresaw rightly that she would not bring up Dir's children as an honor to the family. Having forbade the marriage, he disinherited his son and has never mentioned his name or that of his daughter-in-law since. But hush," warned Baha suddenly.

For Gola had at last tired of the flattering nonsense and was reaching for another stone from the crumbling arch. When he had sent it crashing to the marble beneath, silence reigned again. The smallest djinns cowered and shook on their pedestals. Sparks of rage,—purple, orange, red,—burst like exploding skyrockets from Gola's eyes.

He screamed, "Advice, not gibberish, is what I asked for!"

"O Gola," said a voice. It was the leader of the Seven Afreets.

"Speak, Afreet," ordered Gola in a terrible roar, "and let me at last hear some wisdom."

"It is, of course," began the Afreet, "regrettable but true that our Allak, may Satan take pity on his youth, has achieved no evil worthy of his name in his nine days in the house of Muhammed Ali. A stopped-up fountain, a stolen orange or so, a stumbling mule, a scourge of scorpions,—the merest child's play. We also know, of course, that with his inheritance he is capable of greater things. Let us warn him. Let us give him another three days in which to achieve some real and colossal mischief. If at the end of this time, he has failed again, this is what we, the Seven Afreets, advise. You have, O Gola, doubtless heard of our Uncle Taaba, uncle on our mother's side, who taught us all evil and mischief in our youth in his famous seminary in the sand dunes of Tamanrasset. Our Lord Satan has often spoken highly of his teachings.

"It is perhaps not known to you," continued the Afreet,

"that recently, urged by his admirers, he has opened a new institution in the heart of the Hoggar Mountains for difficult or, shall we say, wayward djinns. Here at Hoggar House only the strictest and most experienced fiends are in charge. Discipline is flawless. The standard of scholarship is high. All the usual subjects are not only taught, but taught with skill and a contagious enthusiasm: incendiarism, anthropophagy, malevolence, marasmus and diabolics. This then is our advice, O Gola. Give Allak one more chance. If he fails, send him to Hoggar House where he will be dealt with wisely but firmly."

He finished and dropped back on his haunches. On the tallest fluted column to the left a hesitant coughing could be heard. Gola turned his red eye in that direction. A werewolf was clearing his throat and waiting for permission to speak.

"Speak, Menlik," ordered Gola. "Is this advice good?"

"Excellent, O Gola. Perchance you remember my nephew Bunu,—Satan alone knows the full extent of his former incompetence,—Bunu, who in his youth could not scare an infant even in broad daylight, to say nothing of doing harm. We were in despair till we heard of Hoggar House and sent him there. Today you would never know him for the same werewolf. It is he who is now the terror of the Mountains of the Zerhoun. Men dare not mention his name or even think of him before they face the night. We werewolves cannot speak highly enough of Hoggar House, but we too feel that Allak should be given a warning and another chance."

Emboldened by the powerful Afreets and the werewolves, the lesser djinns one by one added their approval to this plan, even volunteering to carry the warning to Allak. It was arranged, however, that Menlik the Werewolf himself should fly to Fez before dawn and lay the ultimatum before Allak.

Just as they were in the thick of noisily discussing and

arguing about what manner of mischief Allak should accomplish, a sudden uncontrollable tickling rose in Mousa's throat. Before he knew it, he had sneezed a resounding sneeze.

Baha gave a gasp of horror and Mousa himself turned cold with fear, knowing full well that though djinns may whistle, screech and scream, roar, bellow and growl, whine, moan, sigh, even cough, never, never since the creation of Adam has a djinn been known to sneeze. Beneath Mousa Baha's muscles grew tense, ready to take off in a second in case the sneeze had betrayed their presence.

His great ears stood erect to catch every sound. Was that cluster of vampire bats squeaking ominously? Was there a louder muttering among the shapeless monsters by the fountain? Was all the whining and screeching about Allak and his mischief, or was it whispered suspicion of intruders?

"Oeeeee.... Yaaah.... Hi-eeee," suddenly screamed the djinns. "Ya Satan, someone spies upon us! Punish him! Deliver him to us!" And with a great whirring they began to rise from their columns and arches.

"We are discovered" Baha's whisper was tense. "Hold on tight! We must fly for it!"

7: *Loualou to the Rescue*

Mousa did not need Baha's warning as the fennec shot out of the branch and skimmed the olive orchard with mighty strokes. Looking back, he could see by the excited milling round of the djinns, that so far they had not spotted their enemy. Clever Baha was weaving unseen in and out of the tree tops. But when the trees stopped and they had come out into the open to cross the river, what then! At least they would have a head start!

Sure enough, as they crossed the river, a terrible united scream filled the air. All together, like an inky thunder-cloud the djinns swarmed down the hillside, Gola leading, behind him the Seven Afreets glowing most terribly.

The bright moonlight that Mousa had reveled in all night became now a menace. But what was that ahead, over the Mountains of the Zerhoun? Allah be praised, clouds or perhaps mist rising up from the ravines? At any rate a refuge from the moonlight.

Mousa marveled at Baha's strength and speed as the distance between them and their pursuers increased.

"Are we safe now?" he whispered as they finally dived into the mist over the mountains.

Baha only shook his head. Evidently he wanted to save his breath and not talk.

In the shelter of the mist, the cries and screams of the djinns sounded muffled and if possible more unearthly. All Mousa could see was the green light of the Seven Afreets. Sometimes it faded as if they might be falling behind, but sometimes it grew stronger as if they were gaining.

Fears, each one more terrible than the last, came crowding into his mind. "It is me they are after, me the human! Baha could toss me to them, save himself from being punished for bringing me!"

But Baha strained steadily ahead like the loyal, loving djinn that he was,—on through the mountain mist and out again into the moonlight, on and on, over the rolling hills and plains that lay between Zerhoun and Fez.

Now it seemed as if the djinn pack had gained on them while they had been flying blindly through the mist. Fortunately clouds began to roll across the moon. Occasional minutes of darkness confused the pursuers. But when the walls of Fez rose up white against the black night, Mousa could feel the air hot with their fiery breath and the extra rush of wind made by their wings.

Now at last the walls themselves, the roof-tops of the city, his own familiar roof-top in sight, but at the same time the djinns gaining rapidly. And now.... Oh what horror was that! His own roof-top reached but left behind!

"Mousa!" Baha's voice at last, though short and strained. "No time to open.... roof door. For you, Mosque of Moulai Idriss.... safe. For me, hole by.... fountain."

Almost as he spoke, he shot down from the roof-tops into the Place Nedjariine where fountain and Mosque faced each other. No sooner did Mousa feel the jolt of landing, than he leapt from the fennec's back to the threshold of the Mosque. Hot breath hissed behind him. A claw tore at his burnous as he reached the sacred spot, clutched at it desperately and called upon Allah for help. He was safe at last.

An angry wail of disappointment filled the air. In the whirring, screeching sky no djinn was visible, only a green light fading slowly into the darkness as the cries diminished and ceased. The good saint Moulai Idriss offered his protection and refuge from the servants of Satan.

Yes, he was safe at last. But Baha? Had he reached the hole in time? There was no way of knowing, no way of helping, nothing to do except cling to the saintly shrine till the darkness melted. Even from his own house he was shut off by the locked wooden doors that bar the main streets from midnight to dawn and prevent the circulation of robbers from one quarter of the city to the other.

Exhausted by the excitement of the night, he curled up in the corner of the threshold and slept. When he awoke,

dawn was giving color to the tiles in the fountain opposite, waterboys were filling their goatskins, and from the
minarets the muezzins were calling the Faithful to the
sunrise prayer. As he began to move, he could not imagine what had made him so stiff or why his mattress was
so hard. Gradually he remembered his extraordinary
ride and that this was not his own bed, but the stone
threshold of the Mosque.

How, oh how, was he to get into the palace without
questions impossible to answer! This time no friendly
Brahim would be chatting with Zaid at the street door.
And the door opened only with the long key belonging
to the master of the house or with the approval of Zaid
the porter.

Slowly as he crept through the empty streets, he had
thought of no scheme to outwit Zaid before his own door
came into sight. As he was standing close by but hidden
around a corner watching, waiting, hoping for something
unexpected to happen, to his surprise the door swung
slowly open. Who would come out of it? There was
only one person who would want to help him and how
could she know that he needed help? Loualou, like the
rest of the household, would not discover his absence
till breakfast time.

Yet now, O Allah be praised! There was Loualou's
black bulk waddling out through the door! And Zaid's
voice so close that Mousa could hear his words teasing
her as usual.

"Do not eat anything, not even a sesame seed, while
you are gone, O Loualou, or, by Allah, you will not be
able to squeeze through the door on your return."

Mousa could not help smiling, for Zaid was almost
right. Dressed for the street, swathed in layer upon layer
of black cotton, Loualou was a sight to make people
flatten themselves into doorways to avoid being crushed
against the walls.

"Loualou," he whispered as she passed his corner. "Loualou," he repeated, pulling at her *haik*.

As soon as she was out of sight of the palace door, she caught his hand.

"Mousa, Mousa, where have you been? You have driven me crazy with worry."

"But, Loualou, how did you know I was gone?"

"I knew you were in danger. From midnight on, I could not sleep." She put her hand against her throat where the lion-claw lay under all the cotton. "All night Master Lion clawed at my skin, warning me of danger. First he only tickled but soon he began to scratch, so I went to your room and your mattress was empty! Mousa, where were you?"

Oh, if he could only tell her!

"Where was I, Loualou? I climbed to the roof and from there across the flat roof-tops of the city till I came to a low garden wall and the river. It was a beautiful moonlight night, Loualou, and I was hot so I climbed down the wall and had a swim in the river and then I couldn't get back. Help me, dear Loualou, to get into the house unseen by Zaid."

Loualou's shrewd eyes, blacker than her black face veil, fixed him for a minute. Her hand fell on his burnous, still wet from the mist of the Mountains of the Zerhoun but she said nothing. She was thinking, and Mousa watched her eagerly as the wrinkles in her forehead deepened. Finally she pulled him farther back into the shadow of the doorway where they stood. Quickly jerking loose the lower end of her *haik*, the long cotton strip that started at her head and descended round and round till it covered even ankles and *babouches* with its loose folds, she pulled Mousa close to her and included him as she wrapped it round and round again, draping and twisting till Mousa was completely hidden from pigtail to toes.

Happy though smothered, he felt Loualou turning

back toward the palace door, heard the brass knocker falling heavily three times on the door and from within Zaid's "Who is there?" and Loualou's answer and after the drawing of the bolts, Zaid's voice again:

"Ya Allah, Loualou, you said you were going to the baths and here you are back already."

"True, O Zaid, but in the Street of the Potters a black cat crossed my path from left to right, and it was necessary to turn back. I shall go later, *inchallah*."

"You must have eaten the black cat, for you are fatter than ever," grumbled Zaid.

As soon as they had passed the jog in the vestibule, Mousa slipped out from under the *haik*.

His first act after thanking Loualou was to rush to the orange tree to see if Baha were safely back. There he was, oh praise be to Allah, curled in an innocent sleepy ball as if he had never moved farther than the length of his cord.

"How tired he must be after all that flying," thought Mousa, looking down at him, longing to hear how he managed to get back but not wanting to wake him. At that moment a fly lit on the top of the fennec's nose. Before the fly had time to catch its breath, it was snapped at, caught and swallowed. Baha was wide awake.

"O Baha, how glad I am to see you safe. Did you fly back?"

Baha yawned and stretched. "Yes, as soon as I heard the djinn pack turn away baffled, I flew out of the hole and got back here."

"Do you think they have sent Allak their decision yet?"

"Not yet. They were too confused and upset from discovering us. They will probably come tonight. I think we had better get as much sleep now as possible."

The rest of the day passed as uneventfully as if no conclave of djinns had met in the ruins of Oulili. Allak lay on his velvet mattress as indolently as ever, or frisked about chewing holes in the best leather cushions and

casting baleful glances at anyone who dared reproach
him.

When night came, and it was time for Mousa to go to
bed, he picked the fennec up in his arms and held him
close, since both his father and his stepmother were
standing within hearing, and Allak even nearer.

"Any news since I saw you last?" he whispered.

Shaking his head, Baha thrust his nose into Mousa's
ear.

"Not a thing. But don't be surprised if I come to you
with news in the night."

8: *An Ominous Visit in the Night*

Mousa awoke with a start, with Baha's warning paw
on his lips. The paw was trembling.

"Mousa, Mousa! Oh *what* I have learned! I should have
known! I should have suspected! Now I understand everything!"

"What, Baha? What have you learned?"

Baha shuddered. "It is not Allak who threatens us. No,
and it never was! It is your stepmother herself! For she
is not Fatma, a Meknès bride, but.... can you not
guess?"

"Not...." Now Mousa trembled. He did not dare say
the frightful name. "Not the mother of Allak?"

Baha nodded. "Yes, it is *She*, the terrible Waali!"

"Ya Allah!" exclaimed Mousa. "Why then were we not
destroyed nine days ago?"

"Only because even a fiend as powerful as Waali loses a third of her magic when she assumes the form of a human being, and another third if she sleeps under the roof of a human."

"Baha, how do you know it is *She?* Perhaps you are mistaken."

"Alas, no. If only I were! This is what happened in the darkest hour. I had almost gone to sleep, when I suddenly heard the unmistakable sound the paws of werewolves make as they trot instead of fly through the air, and with it the huffing sound of a werewolf. It was Menlik, come to give Allak his final warning. Landing by the fountain not a tail's length from where I lay, he stood sniffing in all directions to get his bearings. It was fortunately the blackest kind of darkness. Suddenly an idea came to me, and a very good one it turned out to be.

" 'Good evening to you, O Menlik,' I said in the shrieking voice of a jackal. As I had hoped, he gave a frightened start."

"Why?" interrupted Mousa.

"Why? Because every jackal from here to the far edges of Persia loves nothing more than to feed on the flesh of djinns. The lesser ones are devoured as a common occurrence; the powerful ones when they have done something stupid and lost their power. All djinns are polite to jackals, hoping that if some day they should lose their power, the jackal would remember and spare them. So I continued in my jackal voice: 'You are, I believe, looking for Allak, grandson of Gola, may Satan keep him in prosperity.'

" 'Why, yes,' answered the werewolf, surprised. 'As a matter of fact, I am.'

" 'O Menlik, the master of this house strews its thresholds well with salt, and in unexpected places leaves weapons of steel and ashes of rosemary,—all the substances most hateful to you. Shall I guide you through the palace to avoid their magic?'

" 'Pray do,' said the werewolf, 'and may our Lord Satan reward you for your thoughtfulness.'

"So I took the werewolf to Allak and you may be sure that after I had pretended to leave them, I crept back in time to hear Menlik say: 'Furthermore, in three days this household must be turned to stone,—cooks, kitchen maids, musicians,—but most important of all its master Muhammed Ali and his son Mousa.' "

"To stone," gasped Mousa. "But what about *Her*? Did he speak to *Her*?"

"No, after delivering his message to Allak, he trotted up the sky and disappeared while I consoled myself thinking Allak was far too stupid and indolent for any turning-to-stone magic. Just as I was trying to sleep again, an ominous whirring sound more frightful than the paws of a hundred werewolves filled the darkness. Then a whistling and the orange tree groaned and shook. This time I was frightened. Would my jackal voice save me again? There was nothing to do but try.

" 'Good evening, O Master of the Air. May Satan increase your power.'

" 'Good evening, Master Jackal,' answered a terrible voice. 'I am looking for the famous Waali and her son Allak. I was told that this was the house.'

"Waali! Well, Mousa, you can imagine my difficulty in not fainting. For a moment I thought I was going to. Instead I managed to repeat the warning about the salt and the rosemary and offered to guide him.

" 'And do you know the famous and beautiful Lalla Waali?' I asked, trying to make light conversation to hide my fear.

" 'For six hundred years, she happened to be my wife,' answered the voice grimly, as we came into the presence of Waali and Allak.

"Here again my knees knocked against each other, for now I knew it was Dir and no other, Dir whose shape was the shape of an ostrich and whose skin was the skin of a leopard. No wonder the orange tree shook and groaned at his whistle. As for the fiend Waali, she was almost as surprised and frightened as I at seeing her monster husband again, especially with two-thirds of her power gone and a guilty conscience about leaving him, though that had been five hundred and ninety years ago, and another guilty conscience for having brought Allak up so badly.

" 'Welcome. Welcome, Dir. How happy I am to see you again,' she lied. 'Do sit down. Let me look at you. Handsome as ever, I see. To think that in all these centuries you haven't changed a bit.'

" 'Well, you have,' he answered gruffly, unimpressed by her flattery. 'If you don't mind my saying so, one eye was much more becoming to you than two. I liked your hair red, and, as you may remember, I always preferred fangs to teeth. Yes, you have certainly changed, and don't expect *me* to say it is for the better. But your vanished beauty is not what I have come to discuss. Where is Allak?'

" 'Here,' said Waali, proudly thrusting the gazelle under his father's eyes. Like his father Gola, Dir himself had three eyes, though they did not glow as brightly as those of the elder demon. 'Here,' repeated Waali. 'Is he not handsome?' In answer Dir uttered a resounding snort of disdain.

" 'But, Dir, his grace! The wickedness of his nostrils! The depth of his eyes!'

" 'I have already expressed myself on the subject of eyes,' said Dir. 'Our family is noted for the odd number of its eyes. Why a son of mine should have two is something I cannot understand. And why a son of mine,' here his voice rose in anger, 'should choose the puny, futile shape of a gazelle, should acomplish nothing in the way of self-respecting mischief makes me think my father was right when he warned me against you and forbade our

marriage. Do you think I enjoy having my whole clan meet to discuss the shortcomings of my son? Do you think I shall feel proud to see him enrolled at Hoggar House with numbskulls and profligates? Does he know the turning-into-stone magic? *Do* you?' he suddenly roared, turning to Allak. Terrified, the gazelle shook his head.

" 'Do *you*?' continued Dir, addressing his wife.

" 'I used to. I used to know it very well. You have only to go to Persia and look to the south of the ruins of Susa at a circle of stones which were once young men whom I. . . .'

" 'Never mind what you used to do. You used once to be a fairly good wife. Can you do it now? Can you teach your son to do it? That is the point.'

" 'Well,' Waali hesitated. 'In this shape, under this roof, I seem to have forgotten. . . .'

" 'I thought so,' grunted Dir. 'Well, Allak, I will help you. Mind you, not because you deserve it but because the older I grow the more I realize what a remarkable, distinguished and splendid demon your grandfather Gola is and because I should like to spare him the disgrace and pain of having you, his own grandson, at Hoggar House.'

" 'Thank you, sir,' answered Allak.

"Well, Mousa, it was fortunate that I was listening, for it is not the kind of magic that our kind often practices. Oh, occasionally we petrify a robber or so but not often, and unless you are in practice you forget all the objects you have to procure. For instance I had forgotten about having to get the lock of hair, the finger-nail parings, and the bone that the victim had gnawed on. The more obvious things of course I remembered, such as a worn garment, writing charms on a peeled cooked egg and dropping a stone in every stew pot. But now I know everything we have to guard against in the next three days and I am beginning to work out a scheme."

"What about the horrible noise I heard as you woke me?"

"Oh that. Yes, a pretty sight you'll see tomorrow morning. When Dir was leaving he whistled his terrible whistle and your orange tree and your jasmine vine uprooted themselves and followed him as he flew off into the night. Who knows where they will drop to earth again? Well, goodnight, Mousa. You must refuse breakfast tomorrow. Can you pretend you are ill?"

"You mean so they won't slip any of the magic into my food? But what about my father?"

"No, it isn't exactly that. It's part of my scheme."

"You couldn't tell it to me, could you?"

"No," answered Baha, "I couldn't. Now go to sleep and don't forget about breakfast. In fact I don't want you to eat again until I give you permission,—perhaps not for three days."

"Oh, Baha!" Mousa's voice was full of reproach. "And I've hardly had any of the Tafilalelt dates."

"How much will you be able to eat if you are turned to stone?" With this parting threat, Baha pattered out of the room and Mousa went to sleep, hungry already, with nightmares about Dir and Waali alternating with dreams of almond cakes and chicken stews.

When he awoke, he rushed to the balcony to make sure that Baha's coming and his incredible story had all been a dream. The orange tree and the jasmine vine would be there to prove it. But even before he reached the balcony, he missed the fragance of the flowers and when he looked down into the patio, he saw to his horror two gaping holes between the tiles, with the earth fresh and upturned, and around these gaping holes the servants of the household muttering and looking afraid.

As soon as Mousa joined them, they turned their muttering against him. He caught his own name and that of Loualou. Someone was talking about "that black witch from the Niger." Someone else said something about bringing a fox, as unclean as any dog, into the dwellings of decent men.

When Mousa refused breakfast, they showed no sympathy. Only his stepmother, her voice turned suddenly honey-sweet as if she must be addressing not him but her gazelle, was all concern over his lack of appetite, for she came to his mattress with a bowl of hot milk and hard-boiled eggs, begging him to eat. At noon she came again. Again he refused everything. Now his father, who had appeared indifferent as to whether his son chose to eat breakfast or not, began to seem worried, and ordered Loualou to prepare the milk and raisin cousscouss that was his son's favorite dish.

How delicious Loualou's steaming cousscouss smelled as she took the pointed cover off the dish! But worse than not eating it, was having to hurt her feelings without being able to explain. Tears rolled down her black cheeks as he shook his head. Now Fatma came and brushed her roughly aside.

"O Mousa, here is chicken cooked as we cook it in Meknès with a secret recipe of herbs. It has revived many an appetite and cured many an illness. Try his tender leg."

" 'The bone he has gnawed,' " thought Mousa, remembering Baha's list of necessary charms for the turning-to-stone magic, as Fatma held out the plump leg with its crackling golden skin. Longing to seize it and gnaw off every shred of meat, he only closed his eyes and turned his head.

"Mousa, dear," he heard his stepmother say next. "How long your finger-nails have grown. Let me cut them for you. You will be much more comfortable."

Mousa clenched his fists and hid them in the folds of his burnous.

In the late afternoon, when he lay smelling the mint-tea his father was serving to friends, Loualou came to him.

"Mousa," she said in a low, worried voice, "all Fez is talking and gossiping about your father's house. In the market place, in the baths, in the coffee houses, in the Place Nedjariine, they talk of nothing else. The orange tree and the jasmine vine were found on the roof of the baths. Everyone is saying it is your fault, that your pet fennec is a desert demon and you are planning to kill your father because you are jealous of your stepmother. Mousa, you can trust me. Give me the truth."

"I know nothing, Loualou, nothing."

Twice in the night, as Mousa lay awake, sleepless from hunger, Muhammed Ali entered and laid his hand gently on his son's forehead. It consoled Mousa to discover that all the evil stirred up by the fiends who had taken possession of the house had not wholly killed his father's love.

If refusal of food on the first day was difficult, it was nothing to the ordeal it became on the second day. The fact that he was twice as hungry was the least of it. Imagine a continuous file of serving maids from the kitchen bearing platters of every dish that made the table of Muhammed Ali famous throughout the city of Fez. First appeared a flaky pie of minced pigeon sprinkled with sugar and cinnamon; next the leg of a new lamb turned on a spit over charcoal of olive wood, well basted with oil and butter; then cousscouss with almonds and olives and a golden chicken nesting in the middle; grilled mullets from the streams of the High Atlas; salads of cool lettuce and radishes sprinkled with mint; and, as if that were not enough to make the mouth water, basket upon basket of sweets,—almond cakes, "gazelle horns" of honey pastry, macaroons, Turkish paste, bowls of peeled pomegranates sweetened and iced, and pitchers of spring water flavored with orange blossoms and syrup of almonds.

The worst of it was that when he refused, they left the dishes standing there in a long double row by his bed so that it took all his will power not to reach out, lift the covers and plunge his right hand into the delicious food.

Fortunately for his self control, he felt the watchful, hopeful eyes of either Allak or his stepmother spying upon him from morning till night. What magic had they managed to slip into the pots that stood so temptingly before him, what stones with curses, what evil bits of this and that: the gizzard of a black cock, the stony eye of a serpent!

Night fell at last. One by one, at his father's orders, the dishes, the pigeon pie and the roasted lamb, the salads and the sweetmeats, were taken out of his reach, for as everyone knows, to eat in the dark is dangerous. The djinns sit at your elbow ready to bite with you into the same morsel and the next morning you find you have gone blind or lame or mad.

9: *Twin Saints of the River Zeffa*

On this, the second night of Mousa's feigned illness, his father came again to lay his hand on his son's forehead, to see whether he seemed better or worse. In the darkness, Mousa lay with half-closed eyes pretending to sleep. Suddenly the curtain was again drawn aside. Silhouetted against the starlight Mousa could see, to his surprise, the outline of his stepmother, her full, belted kaftan, her floating veil.

"O Fatma," whispered Muhammed Ali in surprise, "what has brought you here?"

"Like you, I too wanted to know how our Mousa was faring. In addition to that I awoke from a significant dream and could not rest till I told it to you, for it concerns Mousa."

"Recite your dream," ordered Muhammed Ali.

"I dreamed that I turned off the Meknès road through the ravine of the River Zeffa, and had come to the shrine of the Twin Saints Sidi Yed el Sba and Sidi Yed el Deeb. . . ."

"They are not saints of Fez," said her husband. "I have never heard of them."

"No matter," continued Fatma. "In Meknès and in the villages nearby they are well loved for the many miracles they have performed in healing the sick. It was Sidi Yed el Sba himself who appeared to me. I knew it was he by his right hand which is no hand at all but the paw of a lion as the name indicates, and it is with this miraculous paw that he heals the sick. Sid Yed el Sba said: 'It has been told to me, O Fatma, that Mousa your stepson lies ill in his father's palace at Fez. Bring him here tomorrow at midnight and I will cure him.' "

"Ya Allah!" muttered Muhammed Ali in his astonishment. "That was indeed a strange dream."

"And that is not all," continued Fatma.

"What else did he say?" asked Muhammed Ali.

"Not he, for with these words Sidi Yed el Sba disappeared, and in his place stood Sidi Yed el Deeb, and I knew it was he for his right hand was not a right hand at all but the paw of a jackal as *his* name indicates. . . ."

"And what did *he* say?" asked Muhammed Ali.

"He said: 'Start at daybreak, O Fatma, you and your stepson Mousa and his father Muhammed Ali and Mousa's nurse Loualou and your gazelle Allak and Mousa's fennec Baha, that the whole household may benefit from the *baraka*—the blessing—which Allah enables us to bestow upon man.' "

Mousa trembled with terror. "Oh, what evil is *She* plotting! The Wicked One!" he thought, longing to warn his father.

But Muhammed Ali was thanking his wife for coming and ordering her back to sleep. "For," he said, "at daybreak we start for the shrine of your Twin Saints."

"O Baha, if you were only here! If I could only tell you what I have just heard," was all Mousa could think of after they had gone. "If Baha could only manage to come before daybreak and find a way to prevent this journey."

But Baha did not come. And long before daybreak, the household had plunged into activity. Tea was being brewed, mules saddled, provisions packed, tents folded, Allak the gazelle and Baha the fennec made ready with lead and collar. And while the call of the muezzin to the prayer of daybreak was still floating through the air, the caravan of Muhammed Ali was picking its way through the western gate and joining the other travelers of the morning who turned their faces toward Meknès.

One thing only gave Mousa hope. He had managed to persuade his father that he felt strong enough to ride alone with Baha tucked between him and the bow of his saddle.

This was easier than he had hoped, for Fatma had made a most astonishing scene, absorbing all Muhammed Ali's attention. She had never come to him in the night, she protested. She had not had a single dream. She had never heard of the ravine of the River Zeffa, to say nothing of its Twin Saints. Throughout the whole Mogreb, there was no such nonsense as a saint with a lion's paw or, more ridiculous still, a saint with the paw of a jackal!

"It is you yourself who dreamed this dream and it means less than nothing. Besides, I have a headache. Go, if you like, to your ravine—I shall not go with you."

Her voice was shrill and angry and she stamped her foot so that every silver anklet jangled defiantly.

For once Muhammed Ali was firm. "Perhaps," he said, "you were walking in your sleep, but, by Allah, the dream was yours and it is a good dream and I shall obey its orders."

With these words he lifted her into the saddle with her gazelle clutched angrily in her arms, climbed to his own saddle and, with the steel corners of his stirrups, prodded his mule forward.

"How strange, how exceedingly strange," thought Mousa, puzzled and hardly able to wait till the caravan spread out a little on the Meknès road so he could tell Baha everything without danger of being overheard.

"Baha," he finally whispered, looking down at the little fennec snugly nestled in the saddle. It seemed to Mousa that Baha's eyes had an unusual sparkle, that the corners of his mouth were drawn up into something like a smile. "O Baha," he reproached him, "this is no time for smiling. This is no pleasure journey, for it is *She* who schemed it all." And he told how Fatma had come in the night with her dream.

Instead of baring his teeth in dismay at this news, Baha's smile grew longer—a veritable grin of amusement.

"So Fatma came in the darkness, did she, and recited her dream?"

"By Allah, indeed," replied Mousa. "The Infamous One herself!"

"And you are sure it was Fatma?"

"Who else?"

"You saw her face?"

"Perhaps not her face in the darkness but the velvet kaftan was hers and the wide belt embroidered in gold and the floating veil. Would I mistake her for my fat Loualou, or for the servants in their skirts of striped cotton? Who else but my wicked and beautiful stepmother?

I could even smell the jasmine perfume that is in itself proof of her presence."

"O Mousa, Mousa! It was *not* Fatma at all. It was I, Baha the fennec, who came disguised in the kaftan of purple velvet with the belt embroidered in gold, the floating veil, the jasmine perfume!"

"*You!*" Mousa exclaimed in amazement. "No, it couldn't have been you!"

"Hush. Not so loud," warned Baha. "Yes, I. I paid the Wicked One back with her own magic. Last night at last I found what I have been waiting for,—her clothes unfolded, carelessly thrown to the floor in a tumbled heap. Losing no time, I seized belt and kaftan, and stepped into them and in doing this I was of course able to assume her voice and size, just as Allak had assumed your appearance."

"But you kept paws and whiskers and tail?"

Baha nodded. "My magic was not powerful enough against her to change in anything but size and voice. I trusted to the darkness for protection and of course the tail was no problem at all, under the folds of purple velvet."

"O Baha, if I had only known! I worried so. I was positive that her Twin Saints were not saints at all but evil henchmen of Satan."

Baha chuckled. "She was right when she said throughout the Mogreb there were no such saints as Saint Lion's Paw and Saint Paw-of-the-Jackal. Certainly 'saint' is not the word for them! But you, Mousa, and your father Muhammed Ali and of course Loualou have nothing to fear. As for the Wicked One and her brittle-legged offspring! All I can say is, if my carefully planned magic fails us, may I spend the next century at Hoggar House with every other backward and fat-headed djinn of the Mogreb!"

"Oh, no, Baha," Mousa protested, shocked at the very

mention of Hoggar House for his dear and clever fennec. "It will work, your magic. . . ."

He stopped suddenly, for his father had ridden up beside him to inquire how he was standing the journey.

"I feel better already," answered Mousa.

"Allah be praised," said Muhammed Ali. "The good Saints must have sent their *baraka*—their blessing—to meet us."

During the rest of the day he rode beside Mousa, for his bride had not ceased being difficult about the journey, all the time begging him to turn back or at least to let her turn back with one of the servants. When they stopped for the midday meal, she sulked and wept and refused to eat.

The sun was setting when they reached the ford of the River Zeffa and turned in to the left to follow the ravine. Fatma was by now in such a state of fury that her mule trembled, shied and all but threw her on the narrow path cut into the rock.

At the northern end of the ravine, the river bed widened, with a sandy cove coming down to its edge. Here and there stood cairns, the piles of stones pious men erect at the shrines of saints. Half hidden by oleander bushes, one could see the mouth of a cave.

"At last, praise be to Allah!" exclaimed Muhammed Ali, giving orders for the caravan to stop and dismount.

Again Fatma refused to eat as bread, eggs and fruit were placed before her. Allak, also, refused the alfalfa that had been specially brought for him, even his favorite of all foods, a handful of tobacco, as he shrank shivering against his mistress.

By the time the servants had raised the tents and hammered in the tent pegs, the sunset sky had grown sullen and threatening. Black clouds rolled over the rocks above. Raindrops fell hissing on the hot stones. Thunder rumbled in the distance.

With every growl of the approaching thunder, Fatma's hysteria increased, reaching its climax when she could not persuade her husband to forbid Mousa to keep his fennec in the tent at night. Again Muhammed Ali dealt firmly with his bride. Mousa was ill, he explained, this was *his* journey. After the Saints had cured him of his illness, she could again have things her way. If she and her gazelle preferred, she could have one of the other tents to herself.

"How afraid she is," thought Mousa, who would have been sorry for her had she not been a fiend. "She knows something is against her. She suspects that it is Baha," and he kept turning his mind this way and that trying to imagine the nature of Baha's magic.

Baha! How innocent the little fennec looked, curled up with his nose tucked under his tail, in the crotch of Mousa's arm. Even Muhammed Ali gave the soft fur a gentle pat as he said goodnight to his son and blew out the candle.

Now wind and rain lashed against the tents, drowning the roar of the river, drowning every sound except the thunder, which grew louder with every clap. The tent pole shook. The tent ropes pulled this way and that. The tent itself swayed and flapped. There was no question of sleep.

"Ya Allah," exclaimed Muhammed Ali. "Will the Saints keep their midnight appointment in such howling weather?"

Three times he went out into the storm to his wife's tent to persuade her to join them. Three times she refused as long as the fennec Baha was allowed to remain, till he finally shrugged his shoulders and left her alone in her stubbornness.

As midnight approached, the storm increased. Mousa and his father sat side by side listening to the rain and thunder. Clasped in Muhammed Ali's right hand was the hand of his son. Clasped in his son's right hand was the paw of the fennec.

Suddenly, rising above the wind, above the rain, above the thunder, came a piercing, blood-curdling howl, a scream for help.

As Muhammed Ali jumped to his feet and dashed from the tent with Mousa behind him, a flash of lightning revealed that Fatma's tent had been caught by the wind, and, with its tent pole dislodged, lay in a floundering, billowing heap on the ground. Summoned by the cry for help, the servants had also hurried to the spot. Now in the dark and driving rain, they tried with their master to untangle the water-logged tent-cloth and rescue their mistress.

Muhammed Ali's reassuring shouts of aid had no effect on the howls and screams coming out of the darkness. At last, stumbling, tugging, master and servants pulled the tent away. Thunder! A bolt of lightning crackling across the sky revealed the cause of the screams. A jackal was attacking their mistress.

With a cry Muhammed started to seize the creature. As he did so, a figure suddenly thrust himself between him and the jackal's victim, lighted by the lightning which strangely enough continued to zigzag across the sky.

"Muhammed Ali!" The voice of the hooded figure was stern and compelling. "Your hand, Muhammed Ali."

As if bewitched, Muhammed Ali put out his hand.

"Oh," gasped Mousa, standing close enough to see that a great lion's paw closed over the right hand of his father, held it and prevented him from stirring a step to the rescue of his wife.

"Fear nothing, O Muhammed Ali. Sidi Yed el Deeb and I are saving your life. For twelve days you have been married to a djinn. Is that not twelve days too long?"

"It is not true!" cried Muhammed Ali. "Let me go! Let

me save her! It is you who are an evil demon. Help,
Mousa! Help, everybody!" he screamed, trying to break
away from the powerful paw-clasp.

No one helped. No one moved, for as he spoke a curious change was coming over the once beautiful Waali.
Not only was she shrinking rapidly in size, but her face
was growing sharp and grey and bristling. The jackal
began suddenly backing away as if his victim were a
hedgehog. And that is exactly what Waali was turning
into,—a prickly and malignant little hedgehog, every
bristle twitching with fury as she scampered out of her
scarlet silk kaftan in search of the nearest hole.

Suddenly frozen with horror, everyone looked toward
the sky. The rain had stopped, though the lightning went
on crackling. Down its zigzag path came riding a monstrous shape with three glowing lights, purple, orange,
red, followed by a hyena fully saddled and bridled. With
a swoop and a terrible roar, Gola, for it was no other,
alighted at their feet, and flashed his three eyes about
until they lit on the gazelle Allak. Then, ignoring his
squeaking, four-footed daughter-in-law, the monster
hurled his grandson into the saddle of the hyena and flew
off with him into the night.

Now at last Muhammed Ali began to understand everything. When the clasp of the lion paw finally relaxed,
the tip of his fiend-bride's tail was disappearing into a
hole in the rocks. And when he turned to thank the Saint
of the Lion's Paw, the latter had disappeared. Suddenly
the lightning stopped, and the moon broke through the
melting clouds, shining as peacefully as if no evil spirits
ever haunted the earth to plague mankind.

Hand in hand Mousa and his father returned to their
tent, where they sank to their mattresses in sound and
dreamless sleep till daybreak. The first thing that Mousa
thought of on waking, as the terrible events of the night
came back to him, was his dear fennec. Would he vanish

now that his work was done? He felt around with his hand. Allah be praised! There was the soft little fennec body nestled against his.

"Baha," he whispered. "Baha." There was no answer. "Baha, wake up," he said, carefully and gently pulling the great ears. As he did so something felt unnatural. Was it possible that the slit in the right ear had disappeared? Carefully he ran his finger along the edge. Yes, that was it. The slit was gone. Baha the fennec was no longer Baha the djinn.

"Ya Allah. Ya Allah," Muhammed Ali kept exclaiming in astonishment as Mousa, at last free to speak, told him the whole extraordinary story while they rode back along the road to Fez.

10: *The End of Mischief in Fez*

The first thing that Muhammed Ali did after the riddance of his fiend-bride, was to divorce himself. To be sure, he had seen her disappear with his own eyes, but after all she *was* a djinn and with djinns you could never be quite sure how final anything was with them, and it was better to be on the safe side and legally sunder the bonds of marriage.

Ordinarily of course one does not divorce himself, but everybody,—including the Pasha of Fez, the Caid Lemneffi, the great Shereef of the holy city of Wazzan,— agreed that this was a special case. Even the Sultan Moulai Mohand himself (may Allah keep him in prosperity) sent his vizier bearing a letter sealed with the seal of Solomon, not only permitting but ordering Muhammed Ali to divorce himself. For was he not the most powerful of all judges, and were not his decrees the most potent and lasting of all decrees?

It was Loualou who suggested the wax image of the bride, and Loualou herself who made it by melting down one of the great candles bought from the Mosque of Idriss and moulding it cunningly into shape. On the waxen face she painted two great eyes with khol and a scarlet mouth and from *haiks* and veils and head-dresses that the fiend had left behind her, she cut a smaller *haik* and veil and head-dress, and clothed her doll and brought it to Muhammed Ali.

"I divorce you. I divorce you. I divorce you," repeated Muhammed Ali three times as was the custom. The scribes recorded the divorce and Muhammed Ali sighed with relief, praising Allah for his miraculous rescue. For many are the tales of men who, like himself, had married a djinn and come to a most sudden and terrible end.

Loualou took the doll and burned it over a fire fed with tar and antimony, with rue and rosemary. And when the image was reduced to ashes, she mixed the ashes with salt and took them to the Mosque of Moulai Idriss and strewed them there at the threshold where the saint could watch over them and see that they accomplished no future mischief.

There remains only one more thing of importance to tell in the story of Mousa, though it primarily concerns Muhammed Ali.

Six weeks to the day after Mousa and Baha had rid the palace of malevolent fiends (now that we are rid of them, let us never again so much as mention their names), Muhammed Ali rode off yet again in order to bring back a bride. This time, instead of to Meknès-of-the-Olives, he journeyed to the sacred city of Wazzan where everyone is holy, where every man is a *shereeff*, every woman a *shereefa*, which means they are descended from the Saint Moulai Idriss who was himself descended from the Prophet Muhammed.

You may be sure that while he was gone, Mousa and Loualou and every servant of the palace spent the time strewing salt on the threshold, salt in the corners of the rooms, burning rue and coriander under the beds, painting with tar the mouths of the large earthenware jars and with tar the mouths of the small earthenware pots. And for extra precaution, Mousa took his father's musket and fired it off in every room of the palace, leaving the smell of powder behind, which is doubly offensive to the Hidden Ones.

Again the household of Muhammed Ali gathered at the door to greet their master and his bride.

"Allah be praised," they murmured as this time no gazelle accompanied their new mistress, but a nurse as black and fat, as old and wise as Loualou herself.

"Peace be upon you, Lalla Aziza," they cried, crowding around her and kissing her garments.

"And upon you the peace," she answered. And her voice was as gentle as her eyes.

Muhammed Ali lifted her from her saddle. With wild enthusiasm the servants of the household pressed closer, kissing her arms and her hands.

"Lalla Aziza!" Mousa pushed his way through them and stood looking up shyly at the *shereefa*.

"Mousa! Mousa! My son!" Her arm went round his shoulders and stayed there till her husband picked her up in his own arms and carried her across the salt-strewn threshold.

And from that moment on, so great was the goodness and *baraka* of Lalla Aziza that everyone in the family and household of Muhammed Ali lived happily. No evil djinn dared stick as much as his whiskers across the threshold and the fennec Baha lived longer than any fennec was known to live. In fact he is still a palace favorite.

And the good *toubib* in the market place who divulged the secret of the bullock's blood and the fish. Was he rewarded? Of course he was, for he was invited by Muhammed Ali to make the journey to Mecca, with all expenses paid, and you can see him today if you go to the market place by the Bab Mahrouk, squatting behind his charms and philtres, proudly wearing the green turban of the Mecca pilgrim.

If you liked this tale, you will also enjoy two other good stories by Eleanor Hoffmann, Four Friends, *published by Macmillan, and* White Mare of the Black Tents, *published by Dodd, Mead.*

The King of the Golden River

BY JOHN RUSKIN

Illustrations by Fritz Kredel

> When John Ruskin, the well-known English author and art critic, turned his hand to the writing of a fairy tale for boys and girls, it is not surprising that he produced a gripping and highly dramatic story which has remained a favorite for over a hundred years.

1

How the Agricultural System of the Black Brothers Was Interfered With by South-West Wind, Esquire

IN a secluded and mountainous part of Stiria there was, in old time, a valley of the most surprising and luxuriant fertility. It was surrounded, on all sides, by steep and rocky mountains, rising into peaks, which were always covered with snow, and from which a number of torrents descended in constant cataracts. One of these fell westward, over the face of a crag so high, that, when the sun had set to everything else, and all below was darkness, his beams still shone full upon this waterfall, so that it looked like a shower of gold. It was, therefore, called by the people of the neighborhood the Golden River. It was strange that none of these streams fell into the valley itself. They all descended on the other side of the mountains, and wound away through broad plains and by populous cities. But the clouds were drawn so constantly to the snowy hills, and rested so softly in the circular hollow,

that in time of drought and heat, when all the country round was burnt up, there was still rain in the little valley; and its crops were so heavy, and its hay so high, and its apples so red, and its grapes so blue, and its wine so rich, and its honey so sweet, that it was a marvel to everyone who beheld it, and was commonly called the Treasure Valley.

The whole of this little valley belonged to three brothers, called Schwartz, Hans, and Gluck. Schwartz and Hans, the two elder brothers, were very ugly men, with overhanging eyebrows and small dull eyes, which were always half shut, so that you couldn't see into *them*, and always fancied they saw far into *you.* They lived by farming the Treasure Valley, and very good farmers they were. They killed everything that did not pay for its eating. They shot the blackbirds, because they pecked the fruit; and killed the hedge-hogs, lest they should suck the cows; they poisoned the crickets for eating the crumbs in the kitchen; and smothered the cicadas, which used to sing all summer in the lime trees. They worked their servants without any wages, till they would not work any more, and then quarreled with them, and turned them out of doors without paying them. It would have been very odd, if with such a farm, and such a system of farming, they hadn't got very rich; and very rich they *did* get. They generally contrived to keep their corn by them till it was very dear, and then sell it for twice its value; they had heaps of gold lying about on their floors, yet it was never known that they had given so much as a penny or a crust in charity; they never went to Mass; grumbled perpetually at paying tithes; and were, in a word, of so cruel and grinding a temper, as to receive from all those with whom they had any dealings, the nickname of the "Black Brothers."

The youngest brother, Gluck, was as completely opposed, in both appearance and character, to his seniors as could possibly be imagined or desired. He was not above twelve years old, fair, blue-eyed, and kind in temper to every living thing. He did not, of course, agree particularly well with his brothers, or rather, they did not agree with *him*. He was usually appointed to the honorable office of turnspit, when there was anything to roast, which was not often; for, to do the brothers justice, they were hardly less sparing upon themselves than upon other people. At other times he used to clean the shoes, floors, and sometimes the plates, occasionally getting what was left on them, by way of encouragement, and a wholesome quantity of dry blows, by way of education.

Things went on in this manner for a long time. At last came a very wet summer, and everything went wrong in the country around. The hay had hardly been got in, when the haystacks were floated bodily down to the sea by an inundation; the vines were cut to pieces with the hail; the corn was all killed by a black blight; only in the Treasure Valley, as usual, all was safe. As it had rain when there was rain nowhere else, so it had sun when there was sun nowhere else. Everybody came to buy corn at the farm, and went away pouring maledictions on the Black Brothers. They asked what they liked, and got it, except from the poor people, who could only beg, and several of whom were starved at their very door, without the slightest regard or notice.

It was drawing toward winter, and very cold weather, when one day the two elder brothers had gone out, with their usual warning to little Gluck, who was left to mind the roast, that he was to let nobody in, and give nothing out. Gluck sat down quite close to the fire, for it was raining very hard, and the kitchen walls were by no means dry or comfortable looking. He turned and turned, and the roast got nice and brown. "What a pity," thought Gluck, "my brothers never ask anybody to dinner. I'm sure, when they've got such a nice piece of mutton as this, and nobody else has got so much as a piece of dry bread, it would do their hearts good to have somebody to eat it with them."

Just as he spoke, there came a double knock at the house door, yet heavy and dull, as though the knocker had been tied up—more like a puff than a knock.

"It must be the wind," said Gluck; "nobody else would venture to knock double knocks at our door."

No; it wasn't the wind: there it came again very hard, and what was particularly astounding, the knocker seemed to be in a hurry, and not to be in the least afraid of the consequences. Gluck went to the window, opened it, and put his head out to see who it was.

It was the most extraordinary-looking little gentleman he had ever seen in his life. He had a very large nose, slightly brass-colored; his cheeks were very round, and very red, and might have warranted a supposition that he had been blowing a refractory fire for the last eight-and-forty hours; his eyes twinkled merrily through long silky eyelashes, his mustaches curled twice round like a corkscrew on each side of his mouth, and his hair, of a curious mixed pepper-and-salt color, descended far over his shoulders. He was about four feet six in height, and wore a conical pointed cap of nearly the same altitude, decorated with a black feather some three feet long. His doublet was prolonged behind into something resembling a violent exaggeration of what is now termed a "swallow tail," but was much obscured by the swelling folds of an enormous black, glossy-looking cloak, which must have been very much too long in calm weather, as the wind, whistling round the old house, carried it clear out from the wearer's shoulders to about four times his own length.

Gluck was so perfectly paralyzed by the singular appearance of his visitor, that he remained fixed without uttering a word, until the old gentleman, having performed another, and a more energetic concerto on the knocker, turned round to look after his fly-away cloak. In so doing he caught sight of Gluck's little yellow head jammed in the window, with its mouth and eyes very wide open indeed.

"Hullo!" said the little gentleman, "that's not the way to answer the door: I'm wet, let me in."

To do the little gentleman justice, he *was* wet. His feather hung down between his legs like a beaten puppy's tail, dripping like an umbrella; and from the ends of his mustaches the water was running into his waistcoat pockets, and out again like a mill stream.

"I beg pardon, sir," said Gluck, "I'm very sorry, but I really can't."

"Can't what!" said the old gentleman.

"I can't let you in, sir—I can't, indeed; my brothers would beat me to death, sir, if I thought of such a thing. What do you want, sir?"

"Want?" said the old gentleman, petulantly. "I want fire, and shelter; and there's your great fire there blazing, crackling, and dancing on the walls, with nobody to feel it. Let me in, I say; I only want to warm myself."

Gluck had had his head, by this time, so long out of the window, that he began to feel it was really unpleas-

antly cold, and when he turned, and saw the beautiful
fire rustling and roaring, and throwing long bright
tongues up the chimney, as if it were licking its chops at
the savory smell of the leg of mutton, his heart melted
within him that it should be burning away for nothing.
"He does look *very* wet," said little Gluck; "I'll just let
him in for a quarter of an hour." Round he went to the
door, and opened it; and as the little gentleman walked
in, there came a gust of wind through the house that
made the old chimneys totter.

"That's a good boy," said the little gentleman. "Never
mind your brothers. I'll talk to them."

"Pray, sir, don't do any such thing," said Gluck. "I can't
let you stay till they come; they'd be the death of me."

"Dear me," said the old gentleman. "I'm very sorry to
hear that. How long may I stay?"

"Only till the mutton's done, sir," replied Gluck, "and
it's very brown."

Then the old gentleman walked into the kitchen, and
sat himself down on the hob, with the top of his cap
accommodated up the chimney, for it was a great deal
too high for the roof.

"You'll soon dry there, sir," said Gluck, and sat down
again to turn the mutton. But the old gentleman did not
dry there, but went on drip, drip, dripping among the
cinders, and the fire fizzed, and sputtered, and began
to look very black, and uncomfortable: never was such
a cloak; every fold in it ran like a gutter.

"I beg pardon, sir," said Gluck at length, after watching
the water spreading in long quicksilver-like streams over
the floor for a quarter of an hour; "mayn't I take your
cloak?"

"No, thank you," said the old gentleman.

"Your cap, sir?"

"I am all right, thank you," said the old gentleman
rather gruffly.

"But—sir—I'm very sorry," said Gluck, hesitatingly; "but —really, sir—you're—putting the fire out."

"It'll take longer to do the mutton, then," replied his visitor dryly.

Gluck was very much puzzled by the behavior of his guest; it was such a strange mixture of coolness and humility.

He turned away at the string meditatively for another five minutes.

"That mutton looks very nice," said the old gentleman at length. "Can't you give me a little bit?"

"Impossible, sir," said Gluck.

"I'm very hungry," continued the old gentleman: "I've had nothing to eat yesterday, nor today. They surely couldn't miss a bit from the knuckle!"

He spoke in so very melancholy a tone, that it quite melted Gluck's heart. "They promised me one slice today, sir," said he; "I can give you that, but not a bit more."

"That's a good boy," said the old gentleman again.

Then Gluck warmed a plate, and sharpened a knife. "I don't care if I do get beaten for it," thought he. Just as he had cut a large slice out of the mutton, there came a tremendous rap at the door. The old gentleman jumped off the hob, as if it had suddenly become inconveniently warm. Gluck fitted the slice into the mutton again, with desperate efforts at exactitude, and ran to open the door.

"What did you keep us waiting in the rain for?" said Schwartz, as he walked in, throwing his umbrella in Gluck's face. "Ay! what for, indeed, you little vagabond?" said Hans, administering an educational box on the ear, as he followed his brother into the kitchen.

"Bless my soul!" said Schwartz when he opened the door.

"Amen," said the little gentleman, who had taken his cap off, and was standing in the middle of the kitchen, bowing with the utmost possible velocity.

"Who's that?" said Schwartz, catching up a rolling-pin, and turning to Gluck with a fierce frown.

"I don't know, indeed, brother," said Gluck in great terror.

"How did he get in?" roared Schwartz.

"My dear brother," said Gluck, deprecatingly, "he was so *very* wet!"

The rolling-pin was descending on Gluck's head; but, at the instant, the old gentleman interposed his conical cap, on which it crashed with a shock that shook the water out of it all over the room. What was very odd, the rolling-pin no sooner touched the cap, than it flew out of Schwartz's hand, spinning like a straw in a high wind, and fell into the corner at the further end of the room.

"Who are you, sir?" demanded Schwartz, turning upon him.

"What's your business?" snarled Hans.

"I'm a poor old man, sir," the little gentleman began very modestly, "and I saw your fire through the window, and begged shelter for a quarter of an hour."

"Have the goodness to walk out again, then," said Schwartz. "We've quite enough water in our kitchen, without making it a drying house."

"It is a cold day to turn an old man out in, sir; look at my gray hairs." They hung down to his shoulders, as I told you before.

"Ay!" said Hans, "there are enough of them to keep you warm. Walk!"

"I'm very, very hungry, sir; couldn't you spare me a bit of bread before I go?"

"Bread, indeed!" said Schwartz; "do you suppose we've nothing to do with our bread, but to give it to such red-nosed fellows as you?"

"Why don't you sell your feather?" said Hans, sneeringly. "Out with you."

"A little bit," said the old gentleman.

"Be off!" said Schwartz.

"Pray, gentlemen——"

"Off and be hanged!" cried Hans, seizing him by the collar. But he had no sooner touched the old gentleman's collar, than away he went after the rolling-pin, spinning round and round, till he fell into the corner on top of it.

Then Schwartz was very angry, and ran at the old gentleman to turn him out; but he also had hardly touched him, when away he went after Hans and the rolling-pin, and hit his head against the wall as he tumbled into the corner.

And so there they lay, all three.

Then the old gentleman spun himself round with velocity in the opposite direction; continued to spin until his long cloak was all wound neatly about him; clapped his cap on his head, very much on one side (for it could not stand upright without going through the ceiling), gave an additional twist to his corkscrew mustaches, and replied with perfect coolness: "Gentlemen, I wish you a very good morning. At twelve o'clock tonight I'll call again; after such a refusal of hospitality as I have just experienced, you will not be surprised if that visit is the last I ever pay you."

"If ever I catch you here again," muttered Schwartz, coming, half frightened, out of the corner—but, before he could finish his sentence, the old gentleman had shut the house door behind him with a great bang: and there drove past the window, at the same instant, a wreath of ragged cloud, that whirled and rolled away down the valley in all manner of shapes; turning over and over in the air; and melting away at last in a gush of rain.

"A very pretty business, indeed, Mr. Gluck!" said Schwartz. "Dish the mutton, sir. If ever I catch you at such a trick again—bless me, why, the mutton's been cut!"

"You promised me one slice, brother, you know," said Gluck.

"Oh, and you were cutting it hot, I suppose, and going to catch all the gravy. It'll be long before I promise you such a thing again. Leave the room, sir; and have the kindness to wait in the coal-cellar till I call you."

Gluck left the room melancholy enough. The brothers ate as much mutton as they could, locked the rest in the

cupboard, and proceded to get very drunk after dinner.

Such a night as it was! Howling wind, and rushing rain, without intermission. The brothers had just sense enough left to put up all the shutters, and double bar the door, before they went to bed. They usually slept in the same room. As the clock struck twelve, they were both awakened by a tremendous crash. Their door burst open with a violence that shook the house from top to bottom.

"What's that?" cried Schwartz, starting up in his bed.

"Only I," said the little gentleman.

The two brothers sat up on their bolster, and stared into the darkness. The room was full of water, and by a misty moonbeam, which found its way through a hole in the shutter, they could see in the midst of it an enormous foam globe, spinning round, and bobbing up and down like a cork, on which, as on a most luxurious cushion, reclined the little old gentleman, cap and all. There was plenty of room for it now, for the roof was off.

"Sorry to incommode you," said their visitor ironically. "I'm afraid your beds are dampish; perhaps you had better go to your brother's room: I've left the ceiling on there."

They required no second admonition, but rushed into Gluck's room, wet through, and in an agony of terror.

"You'll find my card on the kitchen table," the old gentleman called after them. "Remember, the *last* visit."

"Pray Heaven it may!" said Schwartz, shuddering. And the foam globe disappeared.

Dawn came at last, and the two brothers looked out of Gluck's little window in the morning. The Treasure Valley was one mass of ruin and desolation. The inundation had swept away trees, crops, and cattle, and left in their stead a waste of red sand and gray mud. The two brothers crept shivering and horror-struck into the kitchen. The water had gutted the whole first floor; corn, money, almost every movable thing had been swept away, and there was left only a small white card on the kitchen table. On it, in large, breezy, long-legged letters, were engraved the words:

2

Of the Proceedings of the Three Brothers after
the Visit of South-West Wind, Esquire; and
How Little Gluck Had an Interview with
the King of the Golden River

South-West Wind, Esquire, was as good as his word. After the momentous visit above related, he entered the Treasure Valley no more; and, what was worse, he had so much influence with his relations, the West Winds in general, and used it so effectually, that they all adopted a similar line of conduct. So no rain fell in the valley from one year's end to another. Though everything remained green and flourished in the plains below, the inheritance of the three brothers was a desert. What had once been the richest soil in the kingdom, became a shifting heap of red sand; and the brothers, unable longer to contend with the adverse skies, abandoned their valueless patrimony in despair, to seek some means of gaining a livelihood among the cities and people of the plains.

All their money was gone, and they had nothing left but some curious old-fashioned pieces of gold plate, the last remnants of their ill-gotten wealth.

"Suppose we turn goldsmiths?" said Schwartz to Hans, as they entered the large city. "It is a good knave's trade; we can put a great deal of copper into the gold, without anyone's finding it out."

The thought was agreed to be a very good one; they hired a furnace, and turned goldsmiths. But two slight circumstances affected their trade: the first, that people did not approve of the coppered gold; the second, that the two elder brothers, whenever they had sold anything, used to leave little Gluck to mind the furnace, and go and drink out the money in the ale-house next door. So

they melted all their gold, without making money enough
to buy more, and were at last reduced to one large drinking mug, which an uncle of his had given to little Gluck,
and which he was very fond of, and would not have
parted with for the world; though he never drank anything out of it but milk and water. The mug was a very
odd mug to look at. The handle was formed of two
wreaths of flowering golden hair, so finely spun that it
looked more like silk than metal, and these wreaths descended into, and mixed with, a beard and whiskers of
the same exquisite workmanship, which surrounded and
decorated a very fierce little face, of the reddest gold
imaginable, right in the front of the mug, with a pair of
eyes in it which seemed to command its whole circum-
ference. It was impossible to drink out of the mug without being subjected to a intense gaze out of the side of
these eyes; and Schwartz positively averred, that once,
after emptying it, full of Rhenish, seventeen times, he had
seen them wink! When it came to the mug's turn to be
made into spoons, it half broke poor little Gluck's heart;
but the brothers only laughed at him, tossed the mug
into the melting-pot, and staggered out to the ale-house:
leaving him, as usual, to pour the gold into bars, when
it was all ready.

When they were gone, Gluck took a farewell look at
his old friend in the melting-pot. The flowing hair was
all gone; nothing remained but the red nose, and the
sparkling eyes, which looked more malicious than ever.
"And no wonder," thought Gluck, "after being treated
in that way." He sauntered disconsolately to the window,
and sat himself down to catch the fresh evening air, and
escape the hot breath of the furnace. Now this window
commanded a direct view of the range of mountains,
which, as I told you before, overhung the Treasure Valley, and more especially of the peak from which fell the
Golden River. It was just at the close of the day, and,

when Gluck sat down at the window, he saw the rocks of
the mountain tops, all crimson and purple with the sunset; and there were bright tongues of fiery cloud burning
and quivering about them; and the river, brighter than
all, fell, in a waving column of pure gold, from precipice to precipice, with the double arch of a broad purple
rainbow stretched across it, flushing and fading alternately in the wreaths of spray.

"Ah!" said Gluck aloud, after he had looked at it for a
while, "if that river were really all gold, what a nice thing
it would be."

"No, it wouldn't, Gluck," said a clear, metallic voice,
close at his ear.

"Bless me, what's that?" exclaimed Gluck, jumping up.
There was nobody there. He looked round the room, and
under the table, and a great many times behind him, but
there was certainly nobody there, and he sat down again
at the window.

This time he didn't speak, but he couldn't help thinking again that it would be very convenient if the river
were really all gold.

"Not at all, my boy," said the same voice, louder than before.

"Bless me!" said Gluck again, "what *is* that?" He looked again into all the corners and cupboards, and then began turning round and round as fast as he could in the middle of the room, thinking there was somebody behind him, when the same voice struck again on his ear. It was singing now, very merrily, "Lala-lira-la"; no words, only a soft running effervescent melody, something like that of a kettle on the boil. Gluck looked out of the window. No, it was certainly in the house. Upstairs, and downstairs. No, it was certainly in that very room, coming in quicker time and clearer notes every moment. "Lala-lira-la." All at once it struck Gluck that it sounded louder near the furnace. He ran to the opening and looked in; yes, he saw right, it seemed to be coming, not only out of the furnace, but out of the pot. He uncovered it, and ran back in a great fright, for the pot was certainly singing! He stood in the farthest corner of the room, with his hands up and his mouth open, for a minute or two, when the singing stopped, and the voice became clear and pronunciative.

"Hullo!" said the voice.

Gluck made no answer.

"Hullo! Gluck, my boy," said the pot again.

Gluck summoned all his energies, walked straight up to the crucible, drew it out of the furnace, and looked in. The gold was all melted, and its surface as smooth and polished as a river; but instead of reflecting little Gluck's head, as he looked in, he saw meeting his glance from beneath the gold, the red nose and sharp eyes of his old friend of the mug, a thousand times redder and sharper than ever he had seen them in his life.

"Come, Gluck, my boy," said the voice out of the pot again, "I'm all right; pour me out."

But Gluck was too much astonished to do anything of the kind.

"Pour me out, I say," said the voice, rather gruffly. Still Gluck couldn't move.

"*Will* you pour me out?" said the voice, passionately. "I'm too hot."

By a violent effort, Gluck recovered the use of his limbs, took hold of the crucible and sloped it, so as to pour out the gold. But, instead of a liquid stream, there came out, first a pair of pretty little yellow legs, then some coat tails, then a pair of arms stuck a-kimbo, and finally the well-known head of his friend the mug; all which articles, uniting as they rolled out, stood up energetically on the floor, in the shape of a little golden dwarf, about a foot and a half high.

"That's right!" said the dwarf, stretching out first his legs, and then his arms, and then shaking his head up and down, and as far round as it would go, for five minutes without stopping, apparently with the view of ascertaining if he were quite correctly put together, while Gluck stood contemplating him in speechless amazement. He was dressed in a slashed doublet of spun gold, so fine in its texture, that the prismatic colors gleamed over it as if on a surface of mother of pearl; and, over this brilliant doublet, his hair and beard fell full half way to the ground in waving curls, so exquisitely delicate, that Gluck could hardly tell where they ended; they seemed to melt into air. The features of the face, however, were by no means finished with the same delicacy; they were rather coarse, slightly inclining to coppery in complexion, and indicative, in expression, of a very pertinacious and intractable disposition in their small proprietor. When the dwarf had finished his self-examination, he turned his small sharp eyes full on Gluck, and stared at him deliberately for a minute or two. "No, it wouldn't, Gluck, my boy," said the little man.

This was certainly rather an abrupt and unconnected mode of commencing conversation. It might indeed be supposed to refer to the course of Gluck's thoughts, which had first produced the dwarf's observations out of the pot; but whatever it referred to, Gluck had no inclination to dispute the dictum.

"Wouldn't it, sir?" said Gluck, very mildly and submissively indeed.

"No," said the dwarf, conclusively, "no, it wouldn't." And with that the dwarf pulled his cap hard over his brows, and took two turns, of three feet long, up and down the room, lifting his legs up very high, and setting them down very hard. This pause gave time for Gluck to collect his thoughts a little, and, seeing no great reason to view his diminutive visitor with dread, and feeling his curiosity overcome his amazement, he ventured on a question of peculiar delicacy.

"Pray, sir," said Gluck, rather hesitatingly, "were you my mug?"

On which the little man turned sharp round, walked straight up to Gluck, and drew himself up to his full height. "I," said the little man, "am the King of the Golden River." Whereupon he turned about again, and took two more turns, some six feet long, in order to allow time for the consternation which this announcement produced in his auditor to evaporate.

After which, he again walked up to Gluck and stood still, as if expecting some comment on his communication.

Gluck determined to say something at all events. "I hope your Majesty is very well," said Gluck.

"Listen!" said the little man, deigning no reply to this polite inquiry. "I am the King of what you mortals call the Golden River. The shape you saw me in, was owing to the malice of a stronger king, from whose enchantments you have this instant freed me. What I have seen of you, and your conduct to your wicked brothers, renders me willing to serve you; therefore, attend to what I tell you. Whoever shall climb to the top of that mountain from which you see the Golden River issue, and shall cast into the stream at its source, three drops of holy water, for him, and for him only, the river shall turn to gold. But no one failing in his first, can succeed in a second attempt; and if any one shall cast unholy water into the river, it will overwhelm him, and he will become a black stone." So saying, the King of the Golden River turned away and deliberately walked into the center of the hottest flame of the furnace. His figure became red, white, transparent, dazzling—a blaze of intense light—rose, trembled, and disappeared. The King of the Golden River had evaporated.

"Oh!" cried poor Gluck, running to look up the chimney after him; "Oh, dear, dear, dear me! My mug! my mug! my mug!"

3

How Mr. Hans Set Off
on an Expedition to the Golden River,
and How He Prospered Therein

The King of the Golden River had hardly made the extraordinary exit related in the last chapter, before Hans and Schwartz came roaring into the house, very savagely drunk. The discovery of the total loss of their last piece of plate had the effect of sobering them just enough to enable them to stand over Gluck, beating him very steadily for a quarter of an hour; at the expiration of which period they dropped into a couple of chairs, and requested to know what he had got to say for himself.

Gluck told them his story, of which, of course, they did not believe a word. They beat him again, till their arms were tired, and staggered to bed. In the morning, however, the steadiness with which he adhered to his story obtained him some degree of credence; the immediate consequence of which was, that the two brothers, after wrangling a long time on the knotty question, which of them should try his fortune first, drew their swords and began fighting. The noise of the fray alarmed the neighbors, who, finding they could not pacify the combatants, sent for the constable.

Hans, on hearing this, contrived to escape, and hid himself; but Schwartz was taken before the magistrate, fined for breaking the peace, and, having drunk out his last penny the evening before, was thrown into prison till he should pay.

When Hans heard this, he was much delighted, and determined to set out immediately for the Golden River. How to get the holy water, was the question. He went to the priest, but the priest could not give any holy water to so abandoned a character. So Hans went to vespers in the evening for the first time in his life, and, under pretense of crossing himself, stole a cupful, and returned home in triumph.

Next morning he got up before the sun rose, put the holy water into a strong flask, and two bottles of wine and some meat in a basket, slung them over his back, took his alpine staff in his hand, and set off for the mountains.

On his way out of the town he had to pass the prison, and as he looked in at the windows, whom should he see but Schwartz himself peeping out of the bars, and looking very disconsolate.

"Good morning, brother," said Hans; "have you any message for the King of the Golden River?"

Schwartz gnashed his teeth with rage, and shook the bars with all his strength; but Hans only laughed at him, and advising him to make himself comfortable till he came back again, shouldered his basket, shook the bottle of holy water in Schwartz's face till it frothed again, and marched off in the highest spirits in the world.

It was, indeed, a morning that might have made any one happy, even with no Golden River to seek for. Level lines of dewy mist lay stretched along the valley, out of which rose the massy mountains—their lower cliffs in pale gray shadow, hardly distinguishable from the floating vapor, but gradually ascending till they caught the sunlight, which ran in sharp touches of ruddy color, along the angular crags, and pierced, in long level rays, through their fringes of spear-like pine. Far above, shot up red splintered masses of castellated rock, jagged and shivered into myriads of fantastic forms, with here and there a streak of sunlit snow, traced down their chasms like a line of forked lightning; and, far beyond, and far above all these, fainter than the morning clouds, but purer and changeless, slept, in the blue sky, the utmost peaks of the eternal snow.

The Golden River, which sprang from one of the lower and snowless elevations, was now nearly in shadow; all but the uppermost jets of spray, which rose like slow smoke above the undulating line of the cataract, and floated away in feeble wreaths upon the morning wind.

On this object, and on this alone, Hans's eyes and thoughts were fixed; forgetting the distance he had to traverse, he set off at an imprudent rate of walking, which greatly exhausted him before he had scaled the first range of the green and low hills. He was, moreover, surprised, on surmounting them, to find that a large glacier, of whose existence, notwithstanding his previous knowledge of the mountains, he had been absolutely ignorant, lay between him and the source of the Golden River. He entered on it with the boldness of a practised mountaineer; yet he thought he had never traversed so strange or so dangerous a glacier in his life. The ice was excessively slippery, and out of all of its chasms came wild sounds of gushing water; not monotonous or low, but changeful and loud, rising occasionally into drifting passages of wild melody, then breaking off into short melancholy tones, or sudden shrieks, resembling those of human voices in distress or pain. The ice was broken into thousands of confused shapes, but none, Hans thought, like the ordinary forms of splintered ice. There seemed a curious *expression* about all their outlines—a perpetual

resemblance to living features, distorted and scornful. Myriads of deceitful shadows, and lurid lights, played and floated about and through the pale blue pinnacles, dazzling and confusing the sight of the traveler; while his ears grew dull and his head giddy with the constant gush and roar of the concealed waters. These painful circumstances increased upon him as he advanced; the ice crashed and yawned into fresh chasms at his feet, tottering spires nodded around him, and fell thundering across his path; and though he had repeatedly faced these dangers on the most terrific glaciers, and in the wildest weather, it was with a new and oppressive feeling of panic terror that he leaped the last chasm, and flung himself, exhausted and shuddering, on the firm turf of the mountain.

He had been compelled to abandon his basket of food,

which became a perilous incumbrance on the glacier, and had now no means of refreshing himself but by breaking off and eating some of the pieces of ice. This, however, relieved his thirst; an hour's repose recruited his hardy frame, and with the indomitable spirit of avarice, he resumed his laborious journey.

His way now lay straight up a ridge of bare red rocks, without a blade of grass to ease the foot, or a projecting angle to afford an inch of shade from the south sun. It was past noon, and the rays beat intensely upon the steep path, while the whole atmosphere was motionless, and penetrated with heat. Intense thirst was soon added to the bodily fatigue with which Hans was now afflicted; glance after glance he cast on the flask of water which hung at his belt. "Three drops are enough," at last thought he; "I may, at least, cool my lips with it."

He opened the flask, and was raising it to his lips, when his eye fell on an object lying on the rock beside him; he thought it moved. It was a small dog, apparently in the last agony of death from thirst. Its tongue was out, its jaws dry, its limbs extended lifelessly, and a swarm of black ants were crawling about its lips and throat. Its eye moved to the bottle which Hans held in his hand. He raised it, drank, spurned the animal with his foot, and passed on. And he did not know how it was, but he thought that a strange shadow had suddenly come across the blue sky.

The path became steeper and more rugged every moment; and the high hill air, instead of refreshing him, seemed to throw his blood into a fever. The noise of the hill cataracts sounded like mockery in his ears; they were all distant, and his thirst increased every moment. Another hour passed, and he again looked down to the flask at his side; it was half empty; but there was much more than three drops in it. He stopped to open it, and again, as he did so, something moved in the path above him.

It was a fair child, stretched nearly lifeless on the rock, its breast heaving with thirst, its eyes closed, and its lips parched and burning. Hans eyed it deliberately, drank, and passed on. And a dark gray cloud came over the sun, and long, snake-like shadows crept up along the mountain-sides. Hans struggled on. The sun was sinking, but its descent seemed to bring no coolness; the leaden weight of the dead air pressed upon his brow and heart, but the goal was near. He saw the cataract of the Golden River springing from the hillside, scarcely five hundred feet above him. He paused for a moment to breathe, and sprang on to complete his task.

At this instant a faint cry fell on his ear. He turned and saw a gray-haired old man extended on the rocks. His eyes were sunk, his features deadly pale, and gathered into an expression of despair. "Water!" he stretched his arms to Hans, and cried feebly. "Water! I am dying."

"I have none," replied Hans; "thou hast had thy share of life." He strode over the prostrate body, and darted on. And a flash of blue lightning rose out of the East, shaped like a sword; it shook thrice over the whole heaven, and left it dark with one heavy impenetrable shade. The sun was setting; it plunged toward the horizon like a red-hot ball.

The roar of the Golden River rose on Hans's ear. He stood at the brink of the chasm through which it ran. Its waves were filled with the red glory of the sunset; they shook their crests like tongues of fire, and flashes of bloody light gleamed along their foam. Their sound came mightier and mightier on his senses; his brain grew giddy with the prolonged thunder. Shuddering he drew the flask from his girdle, and hurled it into the center of the torrent. As he did so, an icy chill shot through his limbs; he staggered, shrieked, and fell. The waters closed over his cry. And the moaning of the river rose wildly into the night, as it gushed over THE BLACK STONE.

4

*How Mr. Schwartz Set Off
on an Expedition to the Golden River,
and How He Prospered Therein*

Poor little Gluck waited very anxiously alone in the house, for Hans's return. Finding he did not come back, he was terribly frightened, and went and told Schwartz in the prison, all that had happened. Then Schwartz was very much pleased, and said that Hans must certainly have been turned into a black stone, and he should have all the gold to himself. But Gluck was very sorry, and cried all night. When he got up in the morning, there was no bread in the house, nor any money; so Gluck went and hired himself to another goldsmith, and he worked so hard, and so neatly, and so long every day, that he soon got money enough together to pay his brother's fine; and he went, and gave it all to Schwartz, and Schwartz got out of prison. Then Schwartz was quite pleased, and said he should have some of the gold of the river. But Gluck only begged he would go and see what had become of Hans.

Now when Schwartz had heard that Hans had stolen the holy water, he thought to himself that such a proceeding might not be considered altogether correct by the King of the Golden River, and determined to manage matters better. So he took some more of Gluck's money, and went to a bad man, who gave him some holy water very readily for it. Then Schwartz was sure it was all quite right. So Schwartz got up early in the morning before the sun rose, and took some bread and wine, in a basket, and put his holy water in a flask, and set off for the mountains. Like his brother he was much surprised at the sight of the glacier, and had great difficulty in crossing it, even after leaving his basket behind him. The

day was cloudless, but not bright: there was a heavy
purple haze hanging over the sky, and the hills looked
lowering and gloomy. And as Schwartz climbed the steep
rock path, the thirst came upon him, as it had upon his
brother, until he lifted his flask to his lips to drink. Then
he saw the fair child lying near him on the rocks, and it
cried to him, and moaned for water.

"Water, indeed," said Schwartz; "I haven't half enough
for myself," and passed on. And as he went he thought the
sunbeams grew more dim, and he saw a low bank of black
cloud rising out of the West; and, when he had climbed
for another hour, the thirst overcame him again, and he
would have drunk. Then he saw the old man lying before
him on the path, and heard him cry out for water. "Water,
indeed," said Schwartz, "I haven't half enough for myself," and on he went.

Then again the light seemed to fade from before his eyes, and he looked up, and, behold, a mist, of the color of blood, had come over the sun; and the bank of black cloud had risen very high, and its edges were tossing and tumbling like the waves of the angry sea. And they cast long shadows, which flickered over Schwartz's path.

Then Schwartz climbed for another hour, and again his thirst returned; and as he lifted his flask to his lips, he thought he saw his brother Hans lying exhausted on the path before him, and, as he gazed, the figure stretched its arms to him, and cried for water. "Ha, ha," laughed Schwartz, "are you there? Remember the prison bars, my boy. Water, indeed! Do you suppose I carried it all the way up here for *you*?" And he strode over the figure; yet, as he passed, he thought he saw a strange expression of mockery about its lips. And, when he had gone a few yards farther, he looked back; but the figure was not there.

And a sudden horror came over Schwartz, he knew not why; but the thirst for gold prevailed over his fear, and he rushed on. And the bank of black cloud rose to the zenith, and out of it came bursts of spiry lightning, and waves of darkness seemed to heave and float between their flashes, over the whole heavens. And the sky where the sun was setting was all level, and like a lake of blood; and a strong wind came out of that sky, tearing its crimson clouds into fragments, and scattering them far into the darkness. And when Schwartz stood by the brink of the Golden River, its wares were black, like thunder clouds, but their foam was like fire; and the roar of the waters below, and the thunder above met, as he cast the flask into the stream.

And, as he did so, the lightning glared in his eyes, and the earth gave way beneath him, and the waters closed over his cry. And the moaning of the river rose wildly into the night, as it gushed over the Two Black Stones.

5

How Little Gluck Set Off
on an Expedition to the Golden River,
and How He Prospered Therein;
with Other Matters of Interest

When Gluck found that Schwartz did not come back, he was very sorry, and did not know what to do. He had no money, and was obliged to go and hire himself again to the goldsmith, who worked him very hard, and gave him very little money. So, after a month or two Gluck grew tired, and made up his mind to go and try his fortune with the Golden River. "The little king looked very kind," thought he. "I don't think he will turn me into a black stone." So he went to the priest, and the priest gave him some holy water as soon as he asked for it. Then Gluck took some bread in his basket, and the bottle of water, and set off very early for the mountains.

If the glacier had occasioned a great deal of fatigue to his brothers, it was twenty times worse for him, who was neither so strong nor so practised on the mountains. He had several very bad falls, lost his basket and bread, and was very much frightened at the strange noises under the ice. He lay a long time to rest on the grass, after he had got over, and began to climb the hill just in the hottest part of the day. When he had climbed for an hour, he got dreadfully thirsty, and was going to drink like his brothers, when he saw an old man coming down the path above him, looking very feeble, and leaning on a staff. "My son," said the old man, "I am faint with thirst; give me some of that water." Then Gluck looked at him, and when he saw that he was pale and weary, he gave him the water. "Only pray don't drink it all," said Gluck. But the old man drank a great deal, and gave him back the bottle two-thirds empty. Then he bade him good speed, and Gluck went on again merrily. And the path became easier to his feet, and two or three blades of grass appeared on it, and some grasshoppers began singing on the bank beside it; and Gluck thought he had never heard such merry singing.

Then he went on for another hour, and the thirst increased on him so that he thought he should be forced to drink. But, as he raised the flask, he saw a little child lying panting by the road-side, and it cried out piteously for water. Then Gluck struggled with himself, and determined to bear the thirst a little longer; and he put the bottle to the child's lips, and it drank it all but a few drops.

Then it smiled on him, and got up, and ran down the hill; and Gluck looked after it, till it became as small as a little star, and then turned and began climbing again. And then there were all kinds of sweet flowers growing on the rocks, bright green moss, with pale pink starry flowers, and soft belled gentians, more blue than the sky at its deepest, and pure white transparent lilies. And crimson and purple butterflies darted hither and thither, and the sky sent down such pure light that Gluck had never felt so happy in his life.

Yet, when he had climbed for another hour, his thirst became intolerable again; and, when he looked at his bottle, he saw that there were only five or six drops left in it, and he could not venture to drink. And, as he was hanging the flask to his belt again, he saw a little dog lying on the rocks, gasping for breath—just as Hans had seen it on the day of his ascent. And Gluck stopped and looked at it, and then at the Golden River, not five hundred yards above him; and he thought of the dwarf's words, "that no one could succeed, except in his first attempt"; and he tried to pass the dog, but it whined piteously, and Gluck stopped again. "Poor beastie," said Gluck, "it'll be dead when I come down again if I don't help it." Then he looked closer and closer at it, and its eye turned on him so mournfully, that he could not stand it. "Confound the king and his gold, too," said Gluck; and he opened the flask, and poured all the water into the dog's mouth.

The dog sprang up and stood on its hind legs. Its tail disappeared, its ears became long, longer, silky, golden; its nose became very red, its eyes became very twinkling; in three seconds the dog was gone, and before Gluck stood his old acquaintance, the King of the Golden River.

"Thank you," said the monarch; "but don't be frightened, it's all right"; for Gluck showed manifest symptoms of consternation at this unlooked-for reply to his last observation. "Why didn't you come before," continued the dwarf, "instead of sending me those rascally brothers of yours, for me to have the trouble of turning into stones? Very hard stones they make, too."

"Oh, dear me!" said Gluck, "have you really been so cruel?"

"Cruel!" said the dwarf, "they poured unholy water into my stream: do you suppose I'm going to allow that?"

"Why," said Gluck, "I am sure, sir—your Majesty, I mean—they got the water out of the church font."

"Very probably," replied the dwarf; "but," and his countenance grew stern as he spoke, "the water which has been refused to the cry of the weary and the dying, is unholy, though it had been blessed by every saint in heaven; and the water which is found in the vessel of mercy is holy, though it had been defiled with corpses."

So saying the dwarf stooped and plucked a lily that grew at his feet. On its white leaves there hung three drops of clear dew. And the dwarf shook them into the flask which Gluck held in his hand. "Cast these into the river," he said, "and descend on the other side of the mountains into the Treasure Valley. And so good speed."

As he spoke the figure of the dwarf became indistinct.

The playing colors of his robe formed themselves into a prismatic mist of dewy light: he stood for an instant veiled with them as with the belt of a broad rainbow. The colors grew faint, the mist rose into the air; the monarch had evaporated.

And Gluck climbed to the brink of the Golden River, and its waves were as clear as crystal, and as brilliant as the sun. And, when he cast the three drops of dew into the stream, there opened where they fell, a small circular whirlpool, into which the waters descended with a musical noise.

Gluck stood watching it for some time, very much disappointed, because not only the river was not turned into gold, but its waters seemed much diminished in quantity. Yet he obeyed his friend the dwarf, and descended the other side of the mountains toward the Treasure Valley; and, as he went, he thought he heard the noise of water working its way under the ground. And, when he came in sight of the Treasure Valley, behold, a river, like the Golden River, was springing from a new cleft of the rocks above it, and was flowing in innumerable streams among the dry heaps of red sand.

And as Gluck gazed, fresh grass sprang beside the new streams, and creeping plants grew, and climbed among the moistening soil. Young flowers opened suddenly along the river sides, as stars leap out when twilight is deepening, and thickets of myrtle, and tendrils of vine, cast lengthening shadows over the valley as they grew. And thus the Treasure Valley became a garden again, and the inheritance, which had been lost by cruelty, was regained by love.

And Gluck went and dwelt in the valley, and the poor were never driven from his door: so that his barns became full of corn, and his house of treasure. And, for him, the river had, according to the dwarf's promise, become a River of Gold.

And, to this day, the inhabitants of the valley point out

the place where the three drops of holy dew were cast into the stream, and trace the course of the Golden River under the ground, until it emerges in the Treasure Valley. And at the top of the cataract of the Golden River, are still to be seen TWO BLACK STONES, round which the waters howl mournfully every day at sunset; and these stones are still called by the people of the valley

THE BLACK BROTHERS.

John Ruskin wrote The King of the Golden River; *or* The Black Brothers *in 1841 when he was only twenty-two years old. Attractive editions are published today by Macmillan (Little Library), illustrated by Mary L. Seaman; and by World (Rainbow Classics), illustrated by Fritz Kredel.*

Mr. Toad

BY KENNETH GRAHAME

Illustrations by Ernest H. Shepard

Toad is one of the most lovable and at the same time most exasperating of all story-book characters. He is crafty, conceited, and boastful—and he always wants his own way. What a trial to his friends—kind old Water Rat, gentle Badger, and peace-loving Mole! These little animals are as real as your friends next door and once their acquaintance has been made it is impossible to forget them.

IT was a bright morning in the early part of summer; the river had resumed its wonted banks and its accustomed pace, and a hot sun seemed to be pulling everything green and bushy and spiky up out of the earth towards him, as if by strings. The Mole and the Water Rat had been up since dawn very busy on matters connected with boats and the opening of the boating season; painting and varnishing, mending paddles, repairing cushions, hunting for missing boathooks, and so on; and were finishing breakfast in their little parlour and eagerly discussing their plans for the day, when a heavy knock sounded at the door.

"Bother!" said the Rat, all over egg. "See who it is, Mole, like a good chap, since you've finished."

The Mole went to attend the summons, and the Rat heard him utter a cry of surprise. Then he flung the parlour door open, and announced with much importance, "Mr. Badger!"

This was a wonderful thing, indeed, that the Badger should pay a formal call on them, or indeed on anybody. He generally had to be caught, if you wanted him badly, as he slipped quietly along a hedgerow of an early morning or a late evening, or else hunted up in his own house in the middle of the wood, which was a serious undertaking.

The Badger strode heavily into the room, and stood looking at the two animals with an expression full of seriousness. The Rat let his egg-spoon fall on the table-cloth, and sat open-mouthed.

"The hour has come!" said the Badger at last with great solemnity.

"What hour?" asked the Rat uneasily, glancing at the clock on the mantelpiece.

"*Whose* hour, you should rather say," replied the Badger. "Why, Toad's hour! The hour of Toad! I said I would take him in hand as soon as the winter was well over, and I'm going to take him in hand today!"

"Toad's hour, of course!" cried the Mole delightedly. "Hooray! I remember now! *We'll* teach him to be a sensible Toad!"

"This very morning," continued the Badger, taking an armchair, "as I learnt last night from a trustworthy source, another new and exceptionally powerful motor-car will arrive at Toad Hall on approval or return. At this very moment, perhaps, Toad is busy arraying himself in those singularly hideous habiliments so dear to him, which transform him from a (comparatively) good-looking Toad into an Object which throws any decent-minded animal that comes across it into a violent fit. We must be up and doing, ere it is too late. You two animals will accompany me instantly to Toad Hall, and the work of rescue shall be accomplished."

"Right you are!" cried the Rat, starting up. "We'll rescue the poor unhappy animal! We'll convert him!

He'll be the most converted Toad that ever was before
we've done with him!"

They set off up the road on their mission of mercy,
Badger leading the way. Animals when in company
walk in a proper and sensible manner, in single file,
instead of sprawling all across the road and being of
no use or support to each other in case of sudden
trouble or danger.

They reached the carriage-drive of Toad Hall to find,
as the Badger had anticipated, a shiny new motor-car,
of great size, painted a bright red (Toad's favourite
colour), standing in front of the house. As they neared
the door it was flung open, and Mr. Toad, arrayed in
goggles, cap, gaiters, and enormous overcoat, came
swaggering down the steps, drawing on his gauntleted
gloves.

"Hullo! come on, you fellows!" he cried cheerfully on catching sight of them. "You're just in time to come with me for a jolly—to come for a jolly—for a—er—jolly——"

His hearty accents faltered and fell away as he noticed the stern unbending look on the countenances of his silent friends, and his invitation remained unfinished.

The Badger strode up the steps. "Take him inside," he said sternly to his companions. Then, as Toad was hustled through the door, struggling and protesting, he turned to the chauffeur in charge of the new motor-car.

"I'm afraid you won't be wanted today," he said. "Mr. Toad has changed his mind. He will not require the car. Please understand that this is final. You needn't wait." Then he followed the others inside and shut the door.

"Now, then!" he said to the Toad, when the four of them stood together in the hall, "first of all, take those ridiculous things off!"

"Shan't!" replied Toad, with great spirit. "What is the meaning of this gross outrage? I demand an instant explanation."

"Take them off him, then, you two," ordered the Badger briefly.

They had to lay Toad out on the floor, kicking and calling all sorts of names, before they could get to work properly. Then the Rat sat on him, and the Mole got his motor-clothes off him bit by bit, and they stood him up on his legs again. A good deal of his blustering spirit seemed to have evaporated with the removal of his fine panoply. Now that he was merely Toad, and no longer the Terror of the Highway, he giggled feebly and looked from one to the other appealingly, seeming quite to understand the situation.

"You knew it must come to this, sooner or later, Toad," the Badger explained severely. "You've disre-

garded all the warnings we've given you, you've gone
on squandering the money your father left you, and
you're getting us animals a bad name in the district
by your furious driving and your smashes and your
rows with the police. Independence is all very well,
but we animals never allow our friends to make fools
of themselves beyond a certain limit; and that limit
you've reached. Now, you're a good fellow in many
respects, and I don't want to be too hard on you. I'll
make one more effort to bring you to reason. You will
come with me into the smoking-room, and there you
will hear some facts about yourself; and we'll see
whether you come out of that room the same Toad
that you went in."

He took Toad firmly by the arm, led him into the
smoking-room, and closed the door behind them.

"*That's* no good!" said the Rat contemptuously. "*Talking* to Toad'll never cure him. He'll *say* anything."

They made themselves comfortable in armchairs and
waited patiently. Through the closed door they could
just hear the long continuous drone of the Badger's
voice, rising and falling in waves of oratory; and
presently they noticed that the sermon began to be
punctuated at intervals by long-drawn sobs, evidently
proceeding from the bosom of Toad, who was a soft-
hearted and affectionate fellow, very easily converted
—for the time being—to any point of view.

After some three-quarters of an hour the door opened,
and the Badger reappeared, solemnly leading by the
paw a very limp and dejected Toad. His skin hung
baggily about him, his legs wobbled, and his cheeks
were furrowed by the tears so plentifully called forth
by the Badger's moving discourse.

"Sit down there, Toad," said the Badger kindly, pointing to a chair. "My friends," he went on, "I am pleased
to inform you that Toad has at last seen the error of

his ways. He is truly sorry for his misguided conduct
in the past, and he has undertaken to give up motor-
cars entirely and for ever. I have his solemn promise
to that effect."

"That is very good news," said the Mole gravely.

"Very good news indeed," observed the Rat dubiously,
"if only—*if* only—"

He was looking very hard at Toad as he said this,
and could not help thinking he perceived something
vaguely resembling a twinkle in that animal's sorrowful eye.

"There's only one thing more to be done," continued
the gratified Badger. "Toad, I want you solemnly to
repeat, before your friends here, what you fully admitted to me in the smoking-room just now. First, you
are sorry for what you've done, and you see the folly
of it all?"

There was a long, long pause. Toad looked desperately this way and that, while the other animals waited
in grave silence. At last he spoke.

"No!" he said a little sullenly, but stoutly. "I'm *not*
sorry. And it wasn't folly at all! It was simply glorious!"

"What?" cried the Badger, greatly scandalized. "You
backsliding animal, didn't you tell me just now, in
there——"

"O, yes, yes, in *there*," said Toad impatiently. "I'd
have said anything in *there*. You're so eloquent, dear
Badger, and so moving, and so convincing, and put
all your points so frightfully well—you can do what you
like with me in *there*, and you know it. But I've been
searching my mind since, and going over things in it,
and I find that I'm not a bit sorry or repentant really,
so it's no earthly good saying I am; now, is it?"

"Then you don't promise," said the Badger, "never to
touch a motor-car again?"

"Certainly not!" replied Toad emphatically. "On the

contrary, I faithfully promise that the very first motor-car I see, poop-poop! off I go in it!"

"Told you so, didn't I?" observed the Rat to the Mole.

"Very well, then," said the Badger firmly, rising to his feet. "Since you won't yield to persuasion, we'll try what force can do. I feared it would come to this all along. You've often asked us three to come and stay with you, Toad, in this handsome house of yours; well, now we're going to. When we've converted you to a proper point of view we may quit, but not before. Take him upstairs, you two, and lock him up in his bedroom, while we arrange matters between ourselves."

"It's for your own good, Toady, you know," said the Rat kindly, as Toad, kicking and struggling, was hauled up the stairs by his two faithful friends. "Think what fun we shall all have together, just as we used to, when you've quite got over this—this painful attack of yours!"

"We'll take great care of everything for you till you're well, Toad," said the Mole; "and we'll see your money isn't wasted, as it has been."

"No more of those regrettable incidents with the police, Toad," said the Rat, as they thrust him into his bedroom.

"And no more weeks in hospital, being ordered about by female nurses, Toad," added the Mole, turning the key on him.

They descended the stair, Toad shouting abuse at them through the keyhole; and the three friends then met in conference on the situation.

"It's going to be a tedious business," said the Badger, sighing. "I've never seen Toad so determined. However, we will see it out. He must never be left an instant unguarded. We shall have to take it in turns to be with him, till the poison has worked itself out of his system."

They arranged watches accordingly. Each animal

took it in turns to sleep in Toad's room at night, and they divided the day up between them. At first Toad was undoubtedly very trying to his careful guardians. When his violent paroxysms possessed him he would arrange bedroom chairs in rude resemblance of a motor-car and would crouch on the foremost of them, bent forward and staring fixedly ahead, making uncouth and ghastly noises, till the climax was reached, when, turning a complete somersault, he would lie prostrate amidst the ruins of the chairs, apparently completely satisfied for the moment. As time passed, however, these painful seizures grew gradually less frequent, and his friends strove to divert his mind into fresh channels. But his interest in other matters did not seem to revive, and he grew apparently languid and depressed.

One fine morning the Rat, whose turn it was to go on duty, went upstairs to relieve Badger, whom he found fidgeting to be off and stretch his legs in a long ramble round his wood and down his earths and burrows. "Toad's still in bed," he told the Rat, outside the door. "Can't get much out of him, except, O, leave him alone, he wants nothing, perhaps he'll be better presently, it may pass off in time, don't be unduly anxious, and so on. Now, you look out, Rat! When Toad's quiet and submissive, and playing at being the hero of a Sunday-school prize, then he's at his artfullest. There's sure to be something up. I know him. Well, now I must be off."

"How are you today, old chap?" inquired the Rat cheerfully, as he approached Toad's bedside.

He had to wait some minutes for an answer. At last a feeble voice replied, "Thank you so much, dear Ratty! So good of you to inquire! But first tell me how you are yourself, and the excellent Mole?"

"O, *we're* all right," replied the Rat. "Mole," he added incautiously, "is going out for a run round with Badger.

They'll be out till luncheon-time, so you and I will spend a pleasant morning together, and I'll do my best to amuse you. Now jump up, there's a good fellow, and don't lie moping there on a fine morning like this!"

"Dear, kind Rat," murmured Toad, "how little you realize my condition, and how very far I am from 'jumping up' now—if ever! But do not trouble about me. I hate being a burden to my friends, and I do not expect to be one much longer. Indeed, I almost hope not."

"Well, I hope not, too," said the Rat heartily. "You've been a fine bother to us all this time, and I'm glad to hear it's going to stop. And in weather like this, and the boating season just beginning! It's too bad of you, Toad! It isn't the trouble we mind, but you're making us miss such an awful lot."

"I'm afraid it *is* the trouble you mind, though," replied the Toad languidly. "I can quite understand it. It's natural enough. You're tired of bothering about me. I mustn't ask you to do anything further. I'm a nuisance, I know."

"You are, indeed," said the Rat. "But I tell you, I'd take any trouble on earth for you, if only you'd be a sensible animal."

"If I thought that, Ratty," murmured Toad, more feebly than ever, "then I would beg you—for the last time, probably—to step around to the village as quickly as possible—even now it may be too late—and fetch the doctor. But don't you bother. It's only a trouble, and perhaps we may as well let things take their course."

"Why, what do you want a doctor for?" inquired the Rat, coming closer and examining him. He certainly lay very still and flat, and his voice was weaker and his manner much changed.

"Surely you have noticed of late——" murmured Toad.

"But no—why should you? Noticing things is only a trouble. Tomorrow, indeed, you may be saying to yourself, 'Oh, if only I had noticed sooner! If only I had done something!' But no; it's a trouble. Never mind— forget that I asked."

"Look here, old man," said the Rat, beginning to get rather alarmed, "of course I'll fetch a doctor for you, if you really think you want him. But you can hardly be bad enough for that yet. Let's talk about something else."

"I fear, dear friend," said Toad, with a sad smile, "that 'talk' can do little in a case like this—or doctors either, for that matter; still, one must grasp at the slightest straw. And, by the way—while you are about it—I *hate* to give you additional trouble, but I happen to remember that you will pass the door—would you mind at the same time asking the lawyer to step up? It would be a convenience to me, and there are moments—perhaps I should say there is *a* moment—when one must face disagreeable tasks, at whatever cost to exhausted nature!"

"A lawyer! O, he must be really bad!" the affrighted Rat said to himself, as he hurried from the room, not forgetting, however, to lock the door carefully behind him.

Outside, he stopped to consider. The other two were far away, and he had no one to consult.

"It's best to be on the safe side," he said, on reflection. "I've known Toad fancy himself frightfully bad before, without the slightest reason; but I've never heard him ask for a lawyer! If there's nothing really the matter, the doctor will tell him he's an old ass, and cheer him up; and that will be something gained. I'd better humour him and go; it won't take very long." So he ran off to the village on his errand of mercy.

The Toad, who had hopped lightly out of bed as soon

as he heard the key turned in the lock, watched him eagerly from the window till he disappeared down the carriage-drive. Then, laughing heartily, he dressed as quickly as possible in the smartest suit he could lay hands on at the moment, filled his pockets with cash which he took from a small drawer in the dressing-table, and next, knotting the sheets from his bed together and tying one end of the improvised rope round the central mullion of the handsome Tudor window which formed such a feature of his bedroom, he scrambled out, slid lightly to the ground, and, taking the opposite direction to the Rat, marched off light-heartedly, whistling a merry tune.

It was a gloomy luncheon for Rat when the Badger and the Mole at length returned, and he had to face them at table with his pitiful and unconvincing story. The Badger's caustic, not to say brutal, remarks may be imagined, and therefore passed over; but it was painful to the Rat that even the Mole, though he took his friend's side as far as possible, could not help saying, "You've been a bit of a duffer this time, Ratty! Toad, too, of all animals!"

"He did it awfully well," said the crestfallen Rat.

"He did *you* awfully well!" rejoined the Badger hotly. "However, talking won't mend matters. He's got clear away for the time, that's certain; and the worst of it is, he'll be so conceited with what he'll think is his cleverness that he may commit any folly. One comfort is, we're free now, and needn't waste any more of our precious time doing sentry-go. But we'd better continue to sleep at Toad Hall for a while longer. Toad may be brought back at any moment—on a stretcher, or between two policemen."

So spoke the Badger, not knowing what the future held in store, or how much water, and of how turbid a character, was to run under bridges before Toad should sit at ease again in his ancestral Hall.

Meanwhile, Toad, gay and irresponsible, was walking
briskly along the high road, some miles from home. At
first he had taken bypaths, and crossed many fields, and
changed his course several times, in case of pursuit; but
now, feeling by this time safe from recapture, and the
sun smiling brightly on him, and all Nature joining in a
chorus of approval to the song of self-praise that his own
heart was singing to him, he almost danced along the
road in his satisfaction and conceit.

"Smart piece of work that!" he remarked to himself,
chuckling. "Brain against brute force—and brain came
out on the top—as it's bound to do. Poor old Ratty! My!
won't he catch it when the Badger gets back! A worthy
fellow, Ratty, with many good qualities, but very little
intelligence and absolutely no education. I must take
him in hand some day, and see if I can make something
of him."

Filled full of conceited thoughts such as these he
strode along, his head in the air, till he reached a little
town, where the sign of "The Red Lion," swinging across
the road half-way down the main street, reminded him
that he had not breakfasted that day, and that he was
exceedingly hungry after his long walk. He marched into
the inn, ordered the best luncheon that could be pro-
vided at so short a notice, and sat down to eat it in the
coffee-room.

He was about half-way through his meal when an only
too familiar sound, approaching down the street, made
him start and fall a-trembling all over. The poop-poop!
drew nearer and nearer, the car could be heard to turn
into the inn-yard and come to a stop, and Toad had to
hold on to the leg of the table to conceal his overmaster-
ing emotion. Presently the party entered the coffee-room,
hungry, talkative, and gay, voluble on their experiences
of the morning and the merits of the chariot that had
brought them along so well. Toad listened eagerly, all

ears, for a time; at last he could stand it no longer. He slipped out of the room quietly, paid his bill at the bar, and as soon as he got outside sauntered round quietly to the inn-yard. "There cannot be any harm," he said to himself, "in my only just *looking* at it!"

The car stood in the middle of the yard, quite unattended, the stable-helps and other hangers-on being all at their dinner. Toad walked slowly round it, inspecting, criticizing, musing deeply.

"I wonder," he said to himself presently, "I wonder if this sort of car *starts* easily?"

Next moment, hardly knowing how it came about, he found he had hold of the handle and was turning it. As the familiar sound broke forth, the old passion seized on Toad and completely mastered him, body and soul. As if in a dream he found himself, somehow, seated in the driver's seat; as if in a dream, he pulled the lever and swung the car round the yard and out through the archway; and, as if in a dream, all sense of right and wrong, all fear of obvious consequences, seemed temporarily suspended. He increased his pace, and as the car devoured the street and leapt forth on the high road through the open country, he was only conscious that he was Toad once more, Toad at his best and highest, Toad the terror, the traffic-queller, the Lord of the lone trail, before whom all must give way or be smitten into nothingness and everlasting night. He chanted as he flew, and the car responded with sonorous drone; the miles were eaten up under him as he sped he knew not whither, fulfilling his instincts, living his hour, reckless of what might come to him.

The Wind in the Willows *was first published in 1908. Attractive editions are now published by Charles Scribner's Sons, illustrated by Ernest H. Shepard; and by The Heritage Press, illustrated by Arthur Rackham.*

The Mermaids' Lagoon

BY J. M. BARRIE

Illustrations by Cliff Condak

Wendy, John, and Michael Darling have flown away with Peter Pan to Neverland, where Wendy has agreed to be a mother to all the boys. And quite a responsibility it is, too—with constant danger from jealous fairies, fierce redskins, the terrible Captain Hook, and all his bloodthirsty pirates.

IF you shut your eyes and are a lucky one, you may see at times a shapeless pool of lovely pale colours suspended in the darkness; then if you squeeze your eyes tighter, the pool begins to take shape, and the colours become so vivid that with another squeeze they must go on fire. But just before they go on fire you see the lagoon. This is the nearest you ever get to it on the mainland, just one heavenly moment; if there could be two moments you might see the surf and hear the mermaids singing.

The children often spent long summer days on this lagoon, swimming or floating most of the time, playing the mermaid games in the water, and so forth. You must not think from this that the mermaids were on friendly terms with them; on the contrary, it was among Wendy's lasting regrets that all the time she was on the island she never had a civil word from one of them. When she stole softly to the edge of the lagoon she might see them by the score, especially on Marooners' Rock, where they loved to bask, combing out their hair in a lazy way that

quite irritated her; or she might even swim, on tiptoe as
it were, to within a yard of them, but then they saw her
and dived, probably splashing her with their tails, not by
accident, but intentionally.

They treated all the boys in the same way, except of
course Peter, who chatted with them on Marooners' Rock
by the hour, and sat on their tails when they got cheeky.
He gave Wendy one of their combs.

The most haunting time at which to see them is at the
turn of the moon, when they utter strange wailing cries;
but the lagoon is dangerous for mortals then, and until
the evening of which we have now to tell, Wendy had
never seen the lagoon by moonlight, less from fear, for
of course Peter would have accompanied her, than because she had strict rules about every one being in bed
by seven. She was often at the lagoon, however, on
sunny days after rain, when the mermaids come up in
extraordinary numbers to play with their bubbles. The
bubbles of many colours made in rainbow water they
treat as balls, hitting them gaily from one to another
with their tails, and trying to keep them in the rainbow
till they burst. The goals are at each end of the rainbow,
and the keepers only are allowed to use their hands.
Sometimes hundreds of mermaids will be playing in the
lagoon at a time, and it is quite a pretty sight.

But the moment the children tried to join in they had
to play by themselves, for the mermaids immediately
disappeared. Nevertheless we have proof that they secretly watched the interlopers, and were not above taking an idea from them; for John introduced a new way
of hitting the bubble, with the head instead of the hand,
and the mermaid goal-keepers adopted it. This is the one
mark that John has left on the Neverland.

It must also have been rather pretty to see the children
resting on a rock for half an hour after their midday
meal. Wendy insisted on their doing this, and it had to be

a real rest even though the meal was make-believe. So they lay there in the sun, and their bodies glistened in it, while she sat beside them and looked important.

It was one such day, and they were all on Marooners' Rock. The rock was not much larger than their great bed, but of course they all knew how not to take up much room, and they were dozing, or at least lying with their eyes shut, and pinching occasionally when they thought Wendy was not looking. She was very busy, stitching.

While she stitched a change came to the lagoon. Little shivers ran over it, and the sun went away and shadows stole across the water, turning it cold. Wendy could no longer see to thread her needle, and when she looked up, the lagoon that had always hitherto been such a laughing place seemed formidable and unfriendly.

It was not, she knew, that night had come, but something as dark as night had come. No, worse than that. It had not come, but it had sent that shiver through the sea to say that it was coming. What was it?

There crowded upon her all the stories she had been told of Marooners' Rock, so called because evil captains put sailors on it and leave them there to drown. They drown when the tide rises, for then it is submerged.

Of course she should have roused the children at once; not merely because of the unknown that was stalking toward them, but because it was no longer good for them to sleep on a rock grown chilly. But she was a young mother and she did not know this; she thought you simply must stick to your rule about half an hour after the midday meal. So, though fear was upon her, and she longed to hear male voices, she would not waken them. Even when she heard the sound of muffled oars, though her heart was in her mouth, she did not waken them. She stood over them to let them have their sleep out. Was it not brave of Wendy?

It was well for those boys then that there was one among them who could sniff danger even in his sleep. Peter sprang erect, as wide awake at once as a dog, and with one warning cry he roused the others.

He stood motionless, one hand to his ear.

"Pirates!" he cried. The others came closer to him. A strange smile was playing about his face, and Wendy saw it and shuddered. While that smile was on his face no one dared address him; all they could do was to stand ready to obey. The order came sharp and incisive.

"Dive!"

There was a gleam of legs, and instantly the lagoon seemed deserted. Marooners' Rock stood alone in the forbidding waters, as if it were itself marooned.

The boat drew nearer. It was the pirate dinghy, with three figures in her, Smee and Starkey, and the third a captive, no other than Tiger Lily. Her hands and ankles were tied, and she knew what was to be her fate. She was to be left on the rock to perish, an end to one of her race more terrible than death by fire or torture, for is it not written in the book of the tribe that there is no path through water to the happy hunting-ground? Yet her face was impassive; she was the daughter of a chief, she must die as a chief's daughter, it is enough.

They had caught her boarding the pirate ship with a knife in her mouth. No watch was kept on the ship, it being Hook's boast that the wind of his name guarded the ship for a mile around. Now her fate would help to guard it also. One more wail would go the round in that wind by night.

In the gloom that they brought with them the two pirates did not see the rock till they crashed into it.

"Luff, you lubber," cried an Irish voice that was Smee's; "here's the rock. Now, then, what we have to do is to hoist the redskin on to it and leave her there to drown."

It was the work of one brutal moment to land the

beautiful girl on the rock; she was too proud to offer a vain resistance.

Quite near the rock, but out of sight, two heads were bobbing up and down, Peter's and Wendy's. Wendy was crying, for it was the first tragedy she had seen. Peter had seen many tragedies, but he had forgotten them all. He was less sorry than Wendy for Tiger Lily: it was two against one that angered him, and he meant to save her. An easy way would have been to wait until the pirates had gone, but he was never one to choose the easy way.

There was almost nothing he could not do, and he now imitated the voice of Hook.

"Ahoy there, you lubbers," he called. It was a marvellous imitation.

"The captain," said the pirates, staring at each other in surprise.

"He must be swimming out to us," Starkey said, when they had looked for him in vain.

"We are putting the redskin on the rock," Smee called out.

"Set her free," came the astonishing answer.

"Free?"

"Yes, cut her bonds and let her go."

"But, captain——"

"At once, d'ye hear," cried Peter, "or I'll plunge my hook in you."

"This is queer," Smee gasped.

"Better do what the captain orders," said Starkey nervously.

"Ay, ay," Smee said, and he cut Tiger Lily's cords. At once like an eel she slid between Starkey's legs into the water.

Of course Wendy was very elated over Peter's cleverness; but she knew that he would be elated also and very likely to crow and thus betray himself, so at once her hand went out to cover his mouth. But it was stayed even in the act, for "Boat ahoy!" rang over the lagoon in Hook's voice, and this time it was not Peter who had spoken.

Peter may have been about to crow, but his face puckered in a whistle of surprise instead.

"Boat ahoy!" again came the cry.

Now Wendy understood. The real Hook was also in the water.

He was swimming to the boat, and as his men showed a light to guide him he had soon reached them. In the light of the lantern Wendy saw his hook grip the boat's side; she saw his evil swarthy face as he rose dripping from the water, and, quaking, she would have liked to swim away, but Peter would not budge. He was tingling with life and also top-heavy with conceit. "Am I not a wonder, oh, I am a wonder!" he whispered to her; and though she thought so also, she was really glad for the sake of his reputation that no one heard him except herself.

He signed to her to listen.

The two pirates were very curious to know what had brought their captain to them, but he sat with his head on his hook in a position of profound melancholy.

"Captain, is all well?" they asked timidly, but he answered with a hollow moan.

"He sighs," said Smee.

"He sighs again," said Starkey.

"And yet a third time he sighs," said Smee.

"What's up, captain?"

Then at last he spoke passionately.

"The game's up," he cried, "those boys have found a mother."

Affrighted though she was, Wendy swelled with pride.

"O evil day," cried Starkey.

"What's a mother?" asked the ignorant Smee.

Wendy was so shocked that she exclaimed. "He doesn't

know!" and always after this she felt that if you could have a pet pirate Smee would be her one.

Peter pulled her beneath the water, for Hook had started up, crying, "What was that?"

"I heard nothing," said Starkey, raising the lantern over the waters, and as the pirates looked they saw a strange sight. It was the nest I have told you of, floating on the lagoon, and the Never bird was sitting on it.

"See," said Hook in answer to Smee's question, "that is a mother. What a lesson. The nest must have fallen into the water, but would the mother desert her eggs? No."

There was a break in his voice, as if for a moment he recalled innocent days when—but he brushed away this weakness with his hook. ·

Smee, much impressed, gazed at the bird as the nest was borne past, but the more suspicious Starkey said, "If she is a mother, perhaps she is hanging about here to help Peter."

Hook winced. "Ay," he said, "that is the fear that haunts me."

He was roused from this dejection by Smee's eager voice.

"Captain," said Smee, "could we not kidnap these boys' mother and make her our mother?"

"It is a princely scheme," cried Hook, and at once it took practical shape in his great brain. "We will seize the children and carry them to the boat: the boys we will make walk the plank, and Wendy shall be our mother."

Again Wendy forgot herself.

"Never!" she cried, and bobbed.

"What was that?"

But they could see nothing. They thought it must have been a leaf in the wind. "Do you agree, my bullies?" asked Hook.

"There is my hand on it," they both said.

"And there is my hook. Swear."

They all swore. By this time they were on the rock, and suddenly Hook remembered Tiger Lily.

"Where is the redskin?" he demanded abruptly.

He had a playful humour at moments, and they thought this was one of the moments.

"That is all right, captain," Smee answered complacently; "we let her go."

"Let her go?" cried Hook.

"'Twas your own orders," the bo'sun faltered.

"You called over the water to us to let her go," said Starkey.

"Brimstone and gall," thundered Hook, "what cozening is here?" His face had gone black with rage, but he saw that they believed their words, and he was startled. "Lads," he said, shaking a little, "I gave no such order."

"It is passing queer," Smee said, and they all fidgeted uncomfortably. Hook raised his voice, but there was a quiver in it.

"Spirit that haunts this dark lagoon to-night," he cried, "dost hear me?"

Of course Peter should have kept quiet, but of course he did not. He immediately answered in Hook's voice:

"Odds, bobs, hammer and tongs, I hear you."

In that supreme moment Hook did not blanch, even at the gills, but Smee and Starkey clung to each other in terror.

"Who are you, stranger, speak?" Hook demanded.

"I am James Hook," replied the voice, "captain of the *Jolly Roger*."

"You are not; you are not," Hook cried hoarsely.

"Brimstone and gall," the voice retorted, "say that again, and I'll cast anchor in you."

Hook tried a more ingratiating manner. "If you are Hook," he said almost humbly, "come tell me, who am I?"

"A codfish," replied the voice, "only a codfish."

"A codfish!" Hook echoed blankly; and it was then, but

not till then, that his proud spirit broke. He saw his men
draw back from him.

"Have we been captained all this time by a codfish?"
they muttered. "It is lowering to our pride."

They were his dogs snapping at him, but, tragic figure
though he had become, he scarcely heeded them. Against
such fearful evidence it was not their belief in him that
he needed, it was his own. He felt his ego slipping from
him. "Don't desert me, bully," he whispered hoarsely
to it.

In his dark nature there was a touch of the feminine,
as in all the great pirates, and it sometimes gave him
intuitions. Suddenly he tried the guessing game.

"Hook," he called, "have you another voice?"

Now Peter could never resist a game, and he answered
blithely in his own voice, "I have."

"And another name?"

"Ay, ay."

"Vegetable?" asked Hook.

"No."

"Mineral?"

"No."

"Animal?"

"Yes."

"Man?"

"No!" This answer rang out scornfully.

"Boy?"

"Yes."

"Ordinary boy?"

"No."

"Wonderful boy?"

To Wendy's pain the answer that rang out this time
was "Yes."

"Are you in England?"

"No."

"Are you here?"

"Yes."

Hook was completely puzzled. "You ask him some questions," he said to the others, wiping his damp brow.

Smee reflected. "I can't think of a thing," he said regretfully.

"Can't guess, can't guess," crowed Peter. "Do you give it up?"

Of course in his pride he was carrying the game too far, and the miscreants saw their chance.

"Yes, yes," they answered eagerly.

"Well, then," he cried, "I am Peter Pan."

Pan!

In a moment Hook was himself again, and Smee and Starkey were his faithful henchmen.

"Now we have him," Hook shouted. "Into the water, Smee. Starkey, mind the boat. Take him dead or alive."

He leaped as he spoke, and simultaneously came the gay voice of Peter.

"Are you ready, boys?"

"Ay, ay," from various parts of the lagoon.

"Then lam into the pirates."

The fight was short and sharp. First to draw blood was John, who gallantly climbed into the boat and held Starkey. There was a fierce struggle, in which the cutlass was torn from the pirate's grasp. He wriggled overboard and John leapt after him. The dinghy drifted away.

Here and there a head bobbed up in the water, and there was a flash of steel followed by a cry or a whoop. In the confusion some struck at their own side. The corkscrew of Smee got Tootles in the fourth rib, but he was himself pinked in turn by Curly. Farther from the rock Starkey was pressing Slightly and the Twins hard.

Where all this time was Peter? He was seeking bigger game.

The others were all brave boys, and they must not be blamed for backing from the pirate captain. His iron claw made a circle of dead water round him, from which they fled like affrighted fishes.

But there was one who did not fear him: there was one prepared to enter that circle.

Strangely, it was not in the water that they met. Hook rose to the rock to breathe, and at the same moment Peter scaled it on the opposite side. The rock was slippery as a ball, and they had to crawl rather than climb. Neither knew that the other was coming. Each feeling for a grip met the other's arm: in surprise they raised their heads; their faces were almost touching; so they met.

Some of the greatest heroes have confessed that just before they fell to they had a sinking. Had it been so with Peter at that moment I would admit it. After all, this was the only man that the Sea-Cook had feared. But Peter had no sinking, he had one feeling only, gladness; and he gnashed his pretty teeth with joy. Quick as thought he snatched a knife from Hook's belt and was about to drive it home, when he saw that he was higher up the rock than his foe. It would not have been fighting fair. He gave the pirate a hand to help him up.

It was then that Hook bit him.

Not the pain of this but its unfairness was what dazed Peter. It made him quite helpless. He could only stare, horrified. Every child is affected thus the first time he is treated unfairly. All he thinks he has a right to when he comes to you to be yours is fairness. After you have been unfair to him he will love you again, but will never afterwards be quite the same boy. No one ever gets over the first unfairness; no one except Peter. He often met it, but he always forgot it. I suppose that was the real difference between him and all the rest.

So when he met it now it was like the first time; and he could just stare, helpless. Twice the iron hand clawed him.

A few minutes afterwards the other boys saw Hook in the water striking wildly for the ship; no elation on his pestilent face now, only white fear, for the crocodile was in dogged pursuit of him. On ordinary occasions the boys would have swum alongside cheering; but now they were uneasy, for they had lost both Peter and Wendy and were scouring the lagoon for them, calling them by name. They found the dinghy and went home in it, shouting "Peter, Wendy" as they went, but no answer came save mocking laughter from the mermaids. "They must be swimming back or flying," the boys concluded. They were not very anxious, they had such faith in Peter. They chuckled, boylike, because they would be late for bed; and it was all mother Wendy's fault!

When their voices died away there came cold silence over the lagoon, and then a feeble cry.

"Help, help!"

Two small figures were beating against the rock; the girl had fainted and lay on the boy's arm. With a last effort Peter pulled her up the rock and then lay down beside her. Even as he also fainted he saw that the water was rising. He knew that they would soon be drowned, but he could do no more.

As they lay side by side a mermaid caught Wendy by the feet, and began pulling her softly into the water. Peter, feeling her slip from him, woke with a start, and was just in time to draw her back. But he had to tell her the truth.

"We are on the rock, Wendy," he said, "but it is growing smaller. Soon the water will be over it."

She did not understand even now.

"We must go," she said, almost brightly.

"Yes," he answered faintly.

"Shall we swim or fly, Peter?"

He had to tell her.

"Do you think you could swim or fly as far as the island, Wendy, without my help?"

She had to admit that she was too tired.

He moaned.

"What is it?" she asked, anxious about him at once.

"I can't help you, Wendy. Hook wounded me. I can neither fly nor swim."

"Do you mean we shall both be drowned?"

"Look how the water is rising."

They put their hands over their eyes to shut out the sight. They thought they would soon be no more. As they sat thus something brushed against Peter as light as a kiss, and stayed there, as if saying timidly, "Can I be of any use?"

It was the tail of a kite, which Michael had made some days before. It had torn itself out of his hand and floated away.

"Michael's kite," Peter said without interest, but next moment he had seized the tail, and was pulling the kite toward him.

"It lifted Michael off the ground," he cried; "why should it not carry you?"

"Both of us!"

"It can't lift two; Michael and Curly tried."

"Let us draw lots," Wendy said bravely.

"And you a lady; never." Already he had tied the tail around her. She clung to him; she refused to go without him; but with a "Good-bye, Wendy," he pushed her from the rock; and in a few minutes she was borne out of his sight. Peter was alone on the lagoon.

The rock was very small now; soon it would be submerged. Pale rays of light tiptoed across the waters; and by and by there was to be heard a sound at once the most musical and the most melancholy in the world: the mermaids calling to the moon.

Peter was not quite like other boys; but he was afraid

at last. A tremour ran through him, like a shudder passing over the sea; but on the sea one shudder follows
another till there are hundreds of them, and Peter felt
just the one. Next moment he was standing erect on
the rock again, with that smile on his face and a drum
beating within him. It was saying, "To die will be an
awfully big adventure."

The last sounds Peter heard before he was quite alone
were the mermaids retiring one by one to their bed-
chambers under the sea. He was too far away to hear
their doors shut; but every door in the coral caves where
they live rings a tiny bell when it opens or closes (as
in all the nicest houses on the mainland), and he heard
the bells.

Steadily the waters rose till they were nibbling at his
feet; and to pass the time until they made their final
gulp, he watched the only thing moving on the lagoon.
He thought it was a piece of floating paper, perhaps
part of the kite, and wondered idly how long it would
take to drift ashore.

Presently he noticed as an odd thing that it was
undoubtedly out upon the lagoon with some definite
purpose, for it was fighting the tide, and sometimes
winning; and when it won, Peter, always sympathetic
to the weaker side, could not help clapping; it was such
a gallant piece of paper.

It was not really a piece of paper; it was the Never
bird, making desperate efforts to reach Peter on her
nest. By working her wings, in a way she had learned
since the nest fell into the water, she was able to some
extent to guide her strange craft, but by the time Peter
recognised her she was very exhausted. She had come
to save him, to give him her nest, though there were
eggs in it. I rather wonder at the bird, for though he
had been nice to her, he had also sometimes tormented
her. I can suppose only that, like Mrs. Darling and the

rest of them, she was melted because he had all his first teeth.

She called out to him what she had come for, and he called out to her what was she doing there; but of course neither of them understood the other's language. In fanciful stories people can talk to the birds freely, and I wish for the moment I could pretend that this was such a story, and say that Peter replied intelligently to the Never bird; but truth is best, and I want to tell only what really happened. Well, not only could they not understand each other, but they forgot their manners.

"I—want—you—to—get—into—the—nest," the bird called, speaking as slowly and distinctly as possible, "and—then—you—can—drift—ashore, but—I—am—too—tired—to—bring—it—any—nearer—so—you—must—try—to—swim—to—it."

"What are you quacking about?" Peter answered. "Why don't you let the nest drift as usual?"

"I—want—you—" the bird said, and repeated it all over.

Then Peter tried slow and distinct.

"What—are—you—quacking—about?" and so on.

The Never bird became irritated; they have very short tempers.

"You dunderheaded little jay," she screamed, "why don't you do as I tell you?"

Peter felt that she was calling him names, and at a venture he retorted hotly:

"So are you!"

Then rather curiously they both snapped out the same remark:

"Shut up!"

"Shut up!"

Nevertheless the bird was determined to save him if she could, and by one last mighty effort she propelled the nest against the rock. Then up she flew; deserting her eggs, so as to make her meaning clear.

Then at last he understood, and clutched the nest and waved his thanks to the bird as she fluttered overhead. It was not to receive his thanks, however, that she hung there in the sky; it was not even to watch him get into the nest; it was to see what he did with her eggs.

There were two large white eggs, and Peter lifted them up and reflected. The bird covered her face with her wings, so as not to see the last of her eggs; but she could not help peeping between the feathers.

I forget whether I have told you that there was a stave on the rock, driven into it by some buccaneers of long ago to mark the site of buried treasure. The children had discovered the glittering hoard, and when in mischievous mood used to fling showers of moidores, diamonds, pearls and pieces of eight to the gulls, who pounced upon them for food, and then flew away, raging at the scurvy trick that had been played upon them. The stave was still there, and on it Starkey had hung his hat, a deep tarpaulin, watertight, with a broad brim. Peter put the eggs into this hat and set it on the lagoon. It floated beautifully.

The Never bird saw at once what he was up to, and screamed her admiration of him; and, alas, Peter crowed his agreement with her. Then he got into the nest, reared the stave in it as a mast, and hung up his shirt for a sail. At the same moment the bird fluttered down upon the hat and once more sat snugly on her eggs. She drifted in one direction, and he was borne off in another, both cheering.

Of course when Peter landed he beached his barque in a place where the bird would easily find it; but the hat was such a great success that she abandoned the nest. It drifted about till it went to pieces, and often Starkey came to the shore of the lagoon, and with many bitter feelings watched the bird sitting on his hat. As we shall not see her again, it may be worth mentioning here that all Never birds now build in that shape of nest, with a broad brim on which the youngsters take an airing.

Great were the rejoicings when Peter reached the home under the ground almost as soon as Wendy, who had been carried hither and thither by the kite. Every boy had adventures to tell; but perhaps the biggest adventure of all was that they were several hours late for bed. This so inflated them that they did various dodgy things to get staying up still longer, such as demanding bandages; but Wendy, though glorying in having them all home again safe and sound, was scandalised by the lateness of the hour, and cried, "To bed, to bed," in a voice that had to be obeyed. Next day, however, she was awfully tender, and gave out bandages to every one; and they played till bed-time at limping about and carrying their arms in slings.

Peter Pan *was first published in 1911 under the name* Peter and Wendy. *One of the most distinguished modern editions is published by Charles Scribner's Sons, with illustrations by Nora S. Unwin.* Peter Pan in Kensington Gardens, *also published by Charles Scribner's Sons, illustrated by Arthur Rackham, tells of Peter's adventures after lockout time in the famous London park.*

Twenty-One Balloons

BY WILLIAM PENE du BOIS

Illustrations by the author

At the age of sixty-six, Professor William
Waterman Sherman decided he needed a
rest from teaching arithmetic. So he built
himself a huge balloon and set off on a trip,
leaving his destination to the winds. Naturally, he ran into trouble right away.

WHEN released, my balloon instantly and gracefully rose to a height of sixteen hundred feet, and kept this altitude as a swift wind carried me out over San Francisco and over the Pacific Ocean. Before taking off, I had lain down on my balloon mattress on the floor of my basket house and held tightly to two handles attached to the floor to bolster myself against the shock of a quick ascension. The first jolt was quite a large one, but as soon as the *Globe* reached its cruising altitude, which seemed to take only a minute or two, my flying basket house was as calm and easy to move around in as if it were on the ground. I swallowed several times to clear my ears because they felt stuffed up while the balloon was climbing fast. I got up off my mattress, straightened some books which had fallen from their shelves, and walked out on my porch to have a last look at San Francisco. It was a clear sunny afternoon, and I must say the city beneath me looked most beautiful. I noticed quite a few people looking up at me. Evidently the actual sight of my giant balloon and basket house was considerably more excit-

ing to see than pictured in the newspaper stories. I even noticed crowds of people running down the streets in the same direction that I was flying, so absorbed at looking up at me that they kept bumping into other people at street intersections. There was considerable confusion and even what appeared to me to be a street fight. This was most flattering.

In less than ten minutes, I was out over water and watching the coastline disappear from view. Several sea gulls were following the *Globe* as it flew off over the Pacific. Some of them rested occasionally on the balustrade around my porch, making my balloon descend a

little; some of them rested on the silken surfaces of the balloon itself, which gave me some cause to worry. I knew the cloth, which was specially prepared and made to withstand tremendous punishment of all kinds, wouldn't be damaged by the gulls. But the sight of the birds, their sharp claws extended, coming in for a fast landing on my huge balloon, scared me to death.

Mariners have often told me that they consider sea gulls to be good luck and always feed them by throwing garbage overboard. I didn't have any garbage at that early stage of my trip and couldn't afford to spare any of my precious food for feeding birds so I had to risk misfortune and let the gulls go hungry.

My balloon house was nice to travel in, for except at
noontime, when the sun was directly overhead, there was
always one side of the porch where I could sit in the
warm sun. I did a great deal of reading. Seated in a comfortable chair, my feet propped up on the balustrade—
this was a truly enjoyable mode of life.

I saved all of my garbage for the first three days,
storing it up front where the wind would carry its odor
off ahead of the balloon. On the morning of the fourth
day, I must say the odor from this garbage was becoming
quite unbearable. The wind, of course, is always behind
you when you fly a balloon; and since the wind travels
faster than the balloon, due to the friction present when
such a massive body moves through the atmosphere, it
carries all odors forward. However, the odors from my
garbage had become so persistent by the fourth day, that
I was finding myself to be constantly flying through my
own smells, as it were—a most disagreeable state of
affairs. But then something truly wonderful happened.
Rain clouds formed directly above me, that morning of
the fourth day, and it began to rain and the wind blew
the rain against my wicker house making things generally
unpleasant. This was excuse enough to unload my food

ballast. Holding my nose with one hand, I walked up front and dumped all of the garbage over the side. The *Globe* instantly bounded up through the rain clouds, into the sun again, and I continued on in fresh air and sunshine. As I looked down at the rain clouds and took deep breaths of fresh air, I felt that I had indeed mastered the elements to a most satisfactory degree.

Night time in my balloon house was particularly enjoyable. The gentle motion of the balloon and my soft inflated mattress made a combination for perfect sleeping. I spent the early evening on my porch in solitary contentment, studying the stars. I think I can honestly say that my few days flying over the Pacific in the *Globe* were the happiest days of my life.

Everything worked pretty much as planned on the first few days of my trip. Doing my laundry and washing my dishes by dunking them at the end of my fishing line was fairly satisfactory. Reeling in a wet suit was quite tiresome, but I was invariably pleased to find my suit nearly dry by the time I had pulled it in. Fishing was poor from such a height. To reel in a fish at the end of a fourteen-hundred-foot line was too tricky for a fisherman of my caliber, and I dropped many of them long before I could even distinguish what kind of a fish I had hooked. I exercised by walking around the porch of my house— that is, I exercised my legs in this manner. My arms got plenty of exercise reeling in the laundry and dishes.

I sighted a small fishing boat in the afternoon of the fifth day. This was the first sign of life I had seen since leaving San Francisco. I soon noticed that I was going to fly directly over it, so I decided to try and signal it. I knew a little Morse code, so I took a mirror and flashed the message, "I am Professor Sherman of San Francisco and all is well." The fishing boat, manned evidently by a Japanese crew, slowly flashed back the simple message, "No speak English." This to me was just right. I wanted to be alone, out of touch with the world. This was the first sign of life I had seen in five days and it couldn't possibly contact me. All was indeed well.

The sixth day was perfect: calm and uneventful. My garbage was again beginning to make its presence felt, but it wasn't too bad.

The seventh day, Ladies and Gentlemen, was catastrophic!

I shall never forget the seventh day of this voyage of mine for as long as I live. Just about everything went wrong, and my dreams of spending a year in a balloon were shattered. The first thing I noticed on the morning of that fateful day was a small speck far off on the horizon which couldn't possibly be anything else but land. Land on my seventh day out—I had flown straight across the Pacific Ocean at a fabulous rate of speed! I had originally hoped that the winds would blow me first in one direction and then in another and that I would spend at least a month without seeing any land whether it be on the Asiatic side of the ocean or back on the American side. But there in the distance before me was a small speck which was slowly taking on the shape of a little volcanic island, most of it mountain, with a column of smoke slowly rising from it into the blue sky.

Then, seemingly from out of nowhere, appeared sea gulls—the same sort of birds that had seen me off from San Francisco now forming a welcoming committee for an island I hadn't the slightest desire to visit.

At the sight of the gulls, I instantly dumped my garbage overboard. This I thought to be a fine idea. I was not only feeding the gulls but also rising up high enough to clear the island by a wide margin, to get away as far as possible from this unwelcome sight of land. However, it didn't work out quite the way I had hoped. The gulls plunged avidly into the water after my food. One of them grabbed the remains of a carcass of smoked turkey I had

been living on for most of the week, took it onto the very
top of my balloon, and settled down to devour it in comfort. The other gulls, after having dived for all of the
smaller pieces of food in the ocean, flew back up to where
I was and noticed their comrade comfortably feasting on
cold turkey on the top of my balloon. This instantly set
off a loud symphony of cawing, and a big fight over the
carcass started to shape up at once. This was all out of
my reach and all I could do was pace around my small
porch, praying that nothing would happen to my balloon.
I leaned over the balustrade, looked up, and saw one lone
sea gull gliding very slowly over the *Globe*, his head
hanging down with that frightening look of a hawk
studying his prey. This was horrible. I hadn't thought of
bringing a gun with me. The gull circled slowly around
the balloon once, then dove. He plummeted straight for
the turkey carcass. Whether he got it or not, I'll never
know. There was loud and confused sea gull action on
top of my balloon. It seemed to me they all flew away at
once—and then I heard something ghastly: the sound
of a sea gull beating his wings and cawing for breath
in the rarefied atmosphere inside the silken bag of my
balloon.

On this seventh day of my trip, which was supposed to
last a year, I found myself with a hole in my balloon the
size of a sea gull.

I was heartbroken. It was impossible for me to get at
the hole in order to attempt to mend it. The *Globe* had
already begun to lose altitude. I had only one choice: to
try to land on the island. I saw immediately that at the
rate I was descending I would be in the ocean long before
I reached the island. I started throwing things overboard
to make my basket house lighter so that I would fly above
water longer. I had no idea of the nature of the island I
was approaching, so at first I decided to save all of my
food in case I needed it to live on when I landed. I threw

chairs, table, books, water-distilling apparatus, water
cans, dishes, garbage containers, cups, saucers, charts,
globes, coat hangers, clothes—everything noneatable.
Clocks, scissors, towels, combs, brushes, soaps, everything I could lay my hands on I threw out through the
doors, off the porch, out of the windows, the fastest possible way I could rid myself of anything which weighed
anything. The *Globe* continued to descend at a speed
which was far too great if I were to make the island. I
had to throw away my food. I threw all of the heavier
canned goods first. This wasn't good enough. I threw
the fruits, vegetables, smoked meats, everything in my
house. I looked overboard. I was but a few hundred
feet above water and the island was still over a mile off.
Then I discovered something new and worse in the way
of horrors. A school of sharks was following me in the
water beneath and swallowing the food I threw as soon
as it hit the water. This meant that I had to make the
island or fall among the sharks. I was desperate.

There was nothing left in the house to throw overboard. I emptied my pockets, saving only my pocket
knife. I threw the clothes I was wearing next, all of them
except my right shoe. I walked around the porch and,
clinging to the window sills with my arms, I kicked the
balustrade and uprights off the porch with my right foot.
The balloon still had a half mile to go. There was only
one thing left to do. I climbed up on the roof of my basket house, pulled the ladder up and threw that overboard. With my pocket knife, I cut four of the ropes
which attached the house to the balloon—one from each
corner—and tied them securely together. I looped my left
arm through these ropes. I then grabbed my knife and
slashed all of the other ropes supporting my house. My
basket house fell and splashed among the sharks and the
Globe gave a small leap upward. I dropped my pocket
knife, kicked off my right shoe, and prayed.

A minute or two later, I felt my toes hit the water and I shut my eyes, afraid to look and see if any sharks were about. But my toes only skipped once or twice on the water's surface when I found myself being dragged across the beach of the island and the giant deflated bag of the *Globe* came to rest on top of a tall palm tree.

I was exhausted, burned by the sand, and too weak to crawl out of the sun into the shade. I must have gone to sleep on this beach.

After having slept for what must have been four or five hours, I found myself being gently awakened. I opened my eyes. My body was bright red from sun and sandburn. I looked up at what I thought was a man kneeling over me, shaking my shoulder and saying in perfect English, "Wake up, man, you've got to get some things on and get out of the sun, wake up, wake up." I thought that this must be part of some delirious dream. The idea of a man who spoke English on a small volcanic island in the Pacific seemed so odd. I shut my eyes again. But as soon as I did this, I felt my shoulder again being shaken and heard this same voice which kept saying, "Wake up, wake up; you've got to get in the shade!"

I shook my head and opened my eyes again. There was a man kneeling over me. As I sat up he stood up. He was handing me some clothes, and he was dressed in a most unusual manner. This man wasn't a native, and didn't suggest an explorer or a traveler. He looked like an over-dressed aristocrat, sort of a misplaced boulevardier, lost on this seemingly desolate volcanic island. He was wearing a correctly tailored white morning suit—if you can imagine such a suit—with pin-stripe pants, white ascot tie, and a white cork bowler. The suit he was urging me to put on was just the same as the one he had on, only in my size.

"Am I dead?" I asked. "Is this Heaven?"

"No, my good man," he answered, "this isn't Heaven. This is the Pacific Island of Krakatoa."

"But I always thought Krakatoa was uninhabited," I told the gentleman in the white morning suit as I started painfully to put on the clothes he was handing me. "I always heard that the volcanic mountain made living on the Island impossible."

"This is Krakatoa, all right," he said. "And we who live here are most pleased that the rest of the world is still convinced that Krakatoa is uninhabited. Hurry up, put on your clothes."

I had put on the white pin-stripe trousers and the

shirt as the gentleman handed them to me. The shirt had starched cuffs, a small white starched dickey, and a detachable wing collar. I didn't bother putting on the collar, and started rolling up my sleeves. "Let's go, lead on," I said.

"Come, come," said the gentleman from Krakatoa. "You can't come and visit us like that. Is that the way you would call on respectable people in San Francisco, New York, London, or Paris? Roll down those sleeves. Put on this collar, vest, and coat." As he was saying this he was smiling warmly to show that he meant no ill feeling but was merely setting me straight on Krakatoa style and manners. "I'll admit," he continued, "that on other islands in the Pacific it is considered quite the thing to give up shaving, forego haircuts, and wear whatever battered white ducks and soft shirts are available. Here, we prefer a more elegant mode of life. You, sir," he said, "are our first visitor. I am quite certain that you will be rather impressed with the way we live and with the various aspects of our Island. I hope you will be impressed anyhow, for since we believe in keeping this place absolutely secret, I believe you will be finding yourself spending the rest of your life as our guest."

While he was talking, I had obediently rolled down my sleeves. He handed me a pair of cuff links made simply of four diamonds the size of lima beans. He handed me diamond studs with which to do up my shirt front. I attached my wing collar. He held a small mirror so that I might more easily tie my white ascot. As I donned my white bowler I was filled with many emotions. I thought that this was without doubt the most extravagantly absurd situation in which I had ever found myself. I was also giving a large amount of thought to that remark of his about being a guest of the people of Krakatoa for life. It was with deep, mixed feelings that I assured the gentleman that I was already quite impressed.

"Well, come then," he said. "First I'll show you our mountain."

He led me through a small forest of palm trees. The underbrush was thick and wild, quite similar to the untouched jungle life found on any Pacific island. My host walked through this in a most peculiar way. He was holding up his pantlegs and gingerly picking the right spots on which to rest his feet so as not to disturb the creases in his suit. My suit being a borrowed one, I felt that I had to treat it with equal care. We must have made a funny sight: two gentlemen in white suits and white bowlers tiptoeing through the jungle.

Suddenly a remarkable change took place in our surroundings. As we neared the mountain, the underbrush in the jungle became less and less bothersome and then ceased to exist altogether. Instead of thick wild roots, giant ferns, banyan trees, and the usual webs of jungle vegetation, I found myself walking on soft green grass which smelled and looked as though it had just been mowed. It had evidently been given all of the care of a lawn on an English estate. It was like a tropical garden in the zoo of some great Capital. I was quite astounded by this and remarked about it to my host. He explained that the underbrush had been cleared everywhere except for a fringe of jungle all the way around the Island. This made the Island seem uninhabited to passing ships.

When we were about a hundred yards from the foot of the mountain we stopped and sat on a bench. I took the opportunity to introduce myself. "My name is Professor William Waterman Sherman," I said, extending my hand. He shook hands with me and said, "I am Mr. F."

"Mr. F. what?" I asked.

"Simply Mr. F.," he said. "I shall have to explain about that later. The reason I suggested that we sit down on this bench is that we are quite close to the mountain. The mountain has been quiet all morning. This is rare. It is seldom quiet for more than an hour at a time. When the mountain starts rumbling, you will feel the whole island move violently beneath you. You will find this to be quite frightening and disagreeable at first. We all did. It will take you some time to get what we call 'mountain legs.' 'Mountain legs' are to us what 'sea legs' are to sailors.

Many of us were sick, in the same manner as a passenger gets seasick on a rough voyage, when the mountain used to rumble before we got our 'mountain legs.' I am just warning you of this phenomenon so that you won't be scared. The land is roughest near the mountain."

As if this explanation had been a cue for the mountain to perform, we had no sooner left the bench and continued on than we heard a noise like muffled thunder coming seemingly from underfoot. This noise became louder and louder, and the surface of the earth started to shake and roll. I ran back to the bench, lay on it, and clung to it with all my might. I looked at Mr. F. He was watching me, smiling amiably, and was calmly moving up and down with the surface of the earth like a bottle in rough water. The earth didn't crack or split beneath us at all. I thought at the time that being in Krakatoa was like riding on the back of some giant prehistoric animal. The noise could be compared to great abdominal rumblings. The surface of the earth was like some huge bit of hide, stretching and buckling over monstrous muscles and bones.

Mr. F. waved to me to come on. He was standing in a very casual way as if on firm ground except, of course, that he was moving up and down. I felt positively drunk. I fell down four times between the bench and Mr. F. To my complete shame and disgust, I became violently ill while attempting to rejoin my companion. Mr. F. helped me off the ground. He grabbed me by the arm with a firm grip as though he were escorting some drunk away from a lawn party.

"You can see now why Krakatoa was always considered unfit to live on," said Mr. F.

"I couldn't be more completely convinced," I groaned.

"That's the peculiar thing about nature," explained Mr. F., "it guards its rarest treasures with greatest care. Every year on other Pacific islands hundreds of natives lose their lives trying to bring up pearls from the floor of the sea. Man pays nature dearly for pearls. This noisy volcano on Krakatoa has frightened men away from the island for centuries. This fickle, dangerous, and fearful mountain has a mine at its feet. I am now leading you to this mine."

With considerable difficulty, due altogether to my stupid inability to walk as easily as Mr. F., we reached the foot of the mountain. We were suddenly standing on a piece of ground which didn't move at all. I can assure you that I was considerably relieved. There was another bench on this motionless piece of earth and I ran to it and sat down. I looked out over the quivering landscape and listened to the thunderous rumblings. I found I couldn't stand even to look at it for any length of time, for just the sight of this billowing lawn and the bending and bobbing palm trees almost made me ill again. Mr. F. sat beside me for a while and then suggested that we move on. He took me to a wall of the mountain behind this second bench. There appeared to be an entrance in this wall, an entrance covered up by an old wooden door from a ship. Mr. F. reached in his pocket and took out two pairs of glasses with dark lenses. "You'll need these," he explained, "and whatever you do, do not remove them while in the mines." I put them on. Mr. F. moved the old door to one side and asked me to follow him. I obeyed.

As soon as I entered the mines I understood why the ground above, where I had just been, didn't move. I understood why the walls about me didn't move, why the ceiling and ground beneath me didn't budge, and why this was a peaceful retreat in a rumbling, throbbing landscape.

Ladies and gentlemen, the walls, the floor, the ceiling of this mine were hewn out of the hardest of all of nature's minerals: pure, clear, dazzling diamond. I was up

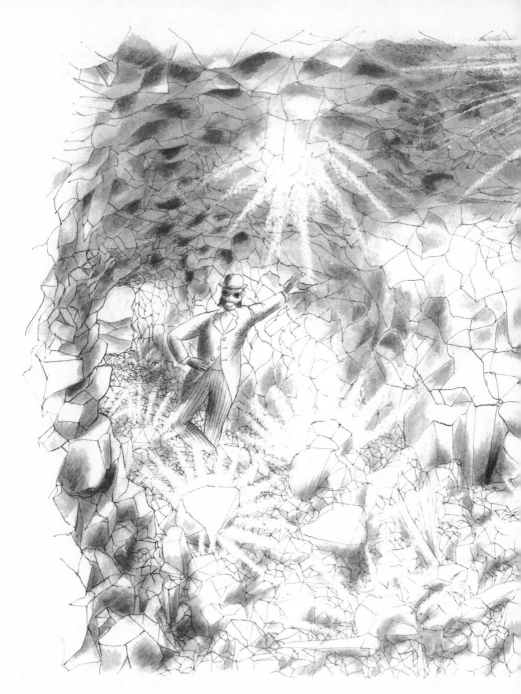

to my ankles in diamond pebbles. The floor was covered
with diamond boulders and diamonds as big as cobble-
stones. If the famous Jonkers' diamond had been tossed
on the brilliant floor of the Krakatoa diamond mines, it
would have been as impossible to find as a grain of salt in

a bag of sugar. This was diamond in its cleanest state,
ready to be cut; pure crystallized carbon unblemished by
any form of dirt or impurities.

I was naturally dumbfounded. I had read about and
seen pictures of the famous salt mines of Poland, the

crystal caves of Bermuda. Here was a sight a thousand times more blinding, infinitely more awe inspiring; a sight to make reality of the most imaginative fairy tale.

I waded around in the diamonds, picked up great handfuls of the jewels letting the smaller ones slip through my fingers. I juggled with two heavy diamonds the size of baseballs. I suddenly felt like a small child let loose in a candy shop.

"May I have some of these?" I asked. My voice was trembling.

"Sure," he said, "fill your pockets if you wish. But come outside with me for a moment."

I eagerly stuffed my pockets and followed him out of the mine. The light in the sun outside seemed dark in comparison with the sparkling, blazing, spangled brightness inside the mine. Even without our dark glasses it seemed as though the blue sky had suddenly turned gray. It was hard at first to distinguish any color in the tropical landscape. But then our eyes became used to the comparative darkness of sunlight and the grass again became green, the sky blue, and my companion's complexion took on a healthier glow.

"Sit down," he said, pointing to the bench nearest the mine. "I have quite a bit to tell you. You may think that your landing on this island was all by accident. The only accident is that the wind blew you exactly in the direction of Krakatoa. The fact that a hungry sea gull dove into your balloon, forcing you to land here, might be termed an accident; but if that hadn't happened, I would have made several holes in your balloon with this pistol. So in any case you would have landed here, sooner or later, unless a shift in the wind had suddenly blown you off in a different direction. If you had flown over Krakatoa, you would have been the first outsider ever to do so; you would have seen that there are houses on the island, you would have seen our buildings, parks, and playgrounds. You would have told the rest of the world that there are people on Krakatoa. We wouldn't have liked that at all. A young boy, the son of Mr. B., sighted you early this morning; and I was sent to the beach with a pistol to make sure that you landed here. I was chosen because I am one of the better hunters on the island. You have seen our diamond mines, that is, you have seen one of them; there are many other unexplored plots of ground around the base of the mountain where the earth doesn't ever move. Do you understand now why you will have to remain our permanent guest?"

"I do indeed," I assured him.

"Later on, after you have had time to think this all over carefully, I am convinced that you won't have any desire to leave Krakatoa at all. There is fabulous wealth and power attached to owning a share in the mines. You do own a share now, because the ownership of the mines is divided equally among all who know that they exist. We might have killed you when you landed here, and kept the secret from you in that violent way. We are fortunate here in that there are no murderers amongst us.

"So now that you are here, you are automatically a citizen of Krakatoa. You own a share of the mines. If you could possibly spend the amount of money you are worth at the present cost of diamonds in other countries, you would have to spend a billion dollars a day for the rest of your life. But if you took your share of diamonds, loaded them in a freighter, and carried them with you to another country you would be making a horrible mistake. Diamonds are priced as high as they are because they are extremely rare jewels in other countries. Unloading a boatload of diamonds in any other port of the world would cause the diamond market to crash; the price of diamonds would drop to next to nothing; and your cargo would scarcely be worth more than a shipload of broken glass.

"Every year, the men of Krakatoa take trips to some foreign country in the world, a different country every time. I shall tell you about these trips in detail later. We buy our supplies for the year and return to Krakatoa. We each take with us one fairly small diamond which we sell to different brokers in different big cities of the country we visit. At first we thought it necessary to solemnly swear that we wouldn't tell anybody of the whereabouts of Krakatoa, the secrets of our diamond mines. But this wasn't at all necessary. You will find that out as soon as you go to a different country. You'll start thinking of the fabulous wealth in diamonds you have back in Krakatoa, realize the power of diamonds in other countries, and remember that telling of Krakatoa would destroy the diamond market. You will find out that you will avoid even mention of the Pacific Ocean. Your only fear will be that you will talk in your sleep.

"You asked me a short while ago if you might have a few diamonds. Help yourself. It is only natural to want to carry some around your first few days here. We are so used to them that we just leave them in the mines. They are worthless to us here. We each own a fortune about one hundred times as big as the Treasury of the United States, but there is no place here to spend money, so we leave them where they are."

This talk made me feel rather silly. I sheepishly walked to the mines and tossed back the paltry half-million dollars' worth of stones I had picked up. My mind was in a turmoil. The excitement of my crash, the rolling of the ground, these unbelievable mines had completely exhausted me physically.

The earth had stopped rolling by this time for one of its few brief daily pauses. Mr. F. pointed to an extraordinary group of houses in the distance. "That is our village," he explained. "We are headed that way."

Fearing that the earth would again start to pitch and roll, I ran to the village from bench to bench. I was followed closely by Mr. F., who seemed to take great enjoyment in my fear of the volcanic action of the earth. When we at last stopped in front of Mr. F.'s house, I was completely worn out.

"Will you lead me directly to my room?" I asked him. "I feel I have had quite enough excitement for today. After a good night's sleep, I know that I shall be in far better condition to cope with the novelty of this fabulous Island."

Mr. F. kindly showed me to a room, gave me some pajamas, brought me a meal, and said, "Good night."

I thanked him, ate the meal in bed, and shortly afterward dropped off into heavy slumber.

The Twenty-One Balloons was awarded the Newbery Medal in 1948. The author-artist has given us another story of an amusing elderly scientist in Peter Graves *(Viking). In* The Giant *(Viking), he tells of a boy who stood seven stories high and had a hard time making friends.*

The Old Lady's Bedroom

BY GEORGE MacDONALD

Illustrations by Nora S. Unwin

*A princess may have wonderful toys to play
with and beautiful clothes to wear, but she
can be a very lonely little girl for all that,
Of course, if she has a fairy godmother, the
loneliness is almost certain to go away.*

THE Princess Irene was about eight years old when
my story begins. And this is how it begins.

One very wet day, when the mountain was covered
with mist which was constantly gathering itself together
into rain-drops and pouring down on the roofs of the
great old house, whence it fell in a fringe of water from
the eaves all round about it, the princess could not of
course go out. She got very tired, so tired that even her
toys could no longer amuse her. You would wonder at
that if I had time to describe to you one half of the toys
she had. But then you wouldn't have the toys themselves, and that makes all the difference: you can't get
tired of a thing before you have it. It was a picture,
though, worth seeing—the princess sitting in the nursery
with the sky-ceiling over her head, at a great table
covered with her toys. If the artist would like to draw
this, I should advise him not to meddle with the toys.
I am afraid of attempting to describe them, and I think
he had better not try to draw them. He had better not.
He can do a thousand things I can't, but I don't think

he could draw those toys. No man could better make the princess herself than he could, though—leaning with her back bowed into the back of the chair, her head hanging down, and her hands in her lap, very miserable as she would say herself, not even knowing what she would like, except to go out and get very wet, catch a particularly nice cold, and have to go to bed and take gruel. The next moment after you see her sitting there, her nurse goes out of the room.

Even that is a change, and the princess wakes up a little, and looks about her. Then she tumbles off her chair, and runs out of the door, not the same door the nurse went out of, but one which opened at the foot of a curious old stair of worm-eaten oak, which looked as if never anyone had set foot upon it. She had once before been up six steps, and that was sufficient reason, in such a day, for trying to find out what was at the top of it.

Up and up she ran—such a long way it seemed to her —till she came to the top of the third flight. There she found the landing was the end of a long passage. Into this she ran. It was full of doors on each side. There were so many that she did not care to open any, but ran on to the end, where she turned into another passage, also full of doors. When she had turned twice more, and still saw doors and only doors about her, she began to get frightened. It was so silent! And all those doors must hide rooms with nobody in them! That was dreadful. Also the rain made a great trampling noise on the roof. She turned and started at full speed, her little footsteps echoing through the sounds of the rain—back for the stairs and her safe nursery. So she thought, but she had lost herself long ago. It doesn't follow that she *was* lost though, because she had lost herself.

She ran for some distance, turned several times, and then began to be afraid. Very soon she was sure that

she had lost the way back. Rooms everywhere, and no
stair! Her little heart beat as fast as her little feet ran,
and a lump of tears was growing in her throat. But she
was too eager and perhaps too frightened to cry for
some time. At last her hope failed her. Nothing but
passages and doors everywhere! She threw herself on
the floor, and began to wail and cry.

She did not cry long, however, for she was as brave
as could be expected of a princess of her age. After a
good cry, she got up, and brushed the dust from her
frock. Oh, what old dust it was! Then she wiped her
eyes with her hands, for princesses don't always have
their handkerchiefs in their pockets, any more than
some other little girls I know of. Next, like a true princess, she resolved on going wisely to work to find her
way back: she would walk through the passages, and
look in every direction for the stairs. This she did, but
without success. She went over the same ground again
and again without knowing it, for the passages and
doors were all alike. At last, in a corner, through a half-
open door, she did see a stair. But alas! It went the
wrong way: instead of going down, it went up. Frightened as she was, however, she could not help wishing
to see where yet farther the stair could lead. It was very
narrow, and so steep that she went up like a four-legged
creature on her hands and feet.

When she came to the top, she found herself in a
little square place with three doors, two opposite each
other, and one opposite the top of the stair. She stood
for a moment without an idea in her little head what
to do next. But as she stood, she began to hear a curious
humming sound. Could it be the rain? No. It was much
more gentle, and even monotonous, than the sound of
the rain, which now she scarcely heard. The low sweet
humming sound went on, sometimes stopping for a little
while and then beginning again. It was more like the

hum of a very happy bee that had found a rich well of honey in some globular flower, than anything else I can think of at this moment. Where could it come from? She laid her ear first to one of the doors to hearken if it was there—then to another. When she laid her ear against the third door, there could be no doubt where it came from: it must be from something in that room. What could it be? She was rather afraid, but her curiosity was stronger than her fear, and she opened the door very gently and peeped in. What do you think she saw? A very old lady who sat spinning.

"Oh, Mr. Editor! I know the story you are going to tell: it's The Sleeping Beauty; only you're spinning too, and making it longer."

"No, indeed, it is not that story. Why should I tell one that every properly educated child knows already? More old ladies than one have sat spinning in a garret. Besides, the old lady in that story was only spinning with a spindle, and this one was spinning with a spinning-wheel, else how could the princess have heard the sweet noise through the door? Do you know the difference? Did you ever see a spindle or a spinning-wheel? I daresay you never did. Well, ask your mamma to explain to you the difference. Between ourselves, however, I shouldn't wonder if she didn't know much better than you. Another thing is, that this is not a fairy story, but a goblin story. And one thing more, this old lady spinning was not an old nurse—but—you shall see who. I think I have now made it quite plain that this is not that lovely story of The Sleeping Beauty. It is quite a new one, I assure you, and I will try to tell it as prettily as I can."

Perhaps you will wonder how the princess could tell that the old lady was an old lady, when I inform you

that not only was she beautiful, but her skin was smooth and white. I will tell you more. Her hair was combed back from her forehead and face, and hung loose far down and all over her back. That is not much like an old lady—is it? Ah! But it was white almost as snow. And although her face was so smooth, her eyes looked so wise that you could not have helped seeing she must be old. The princess, though she could not have told you why, did think her very old indeed—quite fifty—she said to herself. But she was rather older than that, as you shall hear.

While the princess stared bewildered, with her head just inside the door, the old lady lifted hers, and said in a sweet, but old and rather shaky voice, which mingled very pleasantly with the continued hum of her wheel:

"Come in, my dear; come in. I am glad to see you."

That the princess was a real princess, you might see now quite plainly; for she didn't hang onto the handle of the door, and stare without moving, as I have known some do who ought to have been princesses, but were only rather vulgar little girls. She did as she was told, stepped inside the door at once, and shut it gently behind her. "Come to me, my dear," said the old lady.

And again the princess did as she was told. She approached the old lady—rather slowly, I confess, but did not stop until she stood by her side, and looked up in her face with her blue eyes and the two melted stars in them.

"Why, what have you been doing with your eyes, child?" asked the old lady.

"Crying," answered the princess.

"Why, child?"

"Because I couldn't find my way down again."

"But you could find your way up."

"Not at first—not for a long time."

"But your face is streaked like the back of a zebra. Hadn't you a handkerchief to wipe your eyes with?"

"No."

"Then why didn't you come to me to wipe them for you?"

"Please, I didn't know you were here. I will next time."

"There's a good child!" said the old lady.

Then she stopped her wheel, and rose, and, going out of the room, returned with a little silver basin and a soft white towel, with which she washed and wiped the bright little face. And the princess thought her hands were so smooth and nice!

When she carried away the basin and towel, the little princess wondered to see how straight and tall she was, for, although she was so old, she didn't stoop a bit. She was dressed in black velvet with thick, white, heavy-looking lace about it; and on the black dress her hair shone like silver. There was hardly any more furniture in the room than there might have been in that of the poorest old woman who made her bread by her spinning. There was no carpet on the floor—no table anywhere—nothing but the spinning-wheel and the chair beside it. When she came back, she sat down again, and without a word began her spinning once more, while Irene, who had never seen a spinning-wheel, stood by her side and looked on. When the old lady had succeeded in getting her thread fairly in operation again, she said to the princess, but without looking at her:

"Do you know my name, child?"

"No, I don't know it," answered the princess.

"My name is Irene."

"That's *my* name!" cried the princess.

"I know that. I let you have mine. I haven't got your name. You've got mine."

"How can that be?" asked the princess, bewildered. "I've always had my name."

"Your papa, the king, asked me if I had any objection to your having it; and of course I hadn't. I let you have it with pleasure."

"It was very kind of you to give me your name—and such a pretty one," said the princess.

"Oh, not so *very* kind!" said the old lady. "A name is one of those things one can give away and keep all the same. I have a good many such things. Wouldn't you like to know who I am, child?"

"Yes, that I should—very much."

"I'm your great-great-grandmother," said the lady.

"What's that?" asked the princess.

"I'm your father's mother's father's mother."

"Oh, dear! I can't understand that," said the princess.

"I daresay not. I didn't expect you would. But that's no reason why I shouldn't say it."

"Oh, no!" answered the princess.

"I will explain it all to you when you are older," the lady went on. "But you will be able to understand this much now: I came here to take care of you."

"Is it long since you came? Was it yesterday? Or was it to-day, because it was so wet that I couldn't get out?"

"I've been here ever since you came yourself."

"What a long time!" said the princess. "I don't remember it at all."

"No. I suppose not."

"But I never saw you before."

"No. But you shall see me again."

"Do you live in this room always?"

"I don't sleep in it. I sleep on the opposite side of the landing. I sit here most of the day."

"I shouldn't like it. My nursery is much prettier. You must be a queen too, if you are my great big grandmother."

"Yes, I am a queen."

"Where is your crown then?"

"In my bedroom."

"I *should* like to see it."

"You shall some day—not to-day."

"I wonder why nursie never told me."

"Nursie doesn't know. She never saw me."

"But somebody knows that you are in the house?"

"No; nobody."

"How do you get your dinner then?"

"I keep poultry—of a sort."

"Where do you keep them?"

"I will show you."

"And who makes the chicken broth for you?"

"I never kill any of my chickens."

"Then I can't understand."

"What did you have for breakfast this morning?"

"Oh! I had bread and milk and an egg—I daresay you eat their eggs."

"Yes, that's it. I eat their eggs."

"Is that what makes your hair so white?"

"No, my dear. It's old age. I am very old."

"I thought so. Are you fifty?"

"Yes—more than that."

"Are you a hundred?"

"Yes—more than that. I am too old for you to guess. Come and see my chickens."

Again she stopped her spinning. She rose, took the princess by the hand, led her out of the room, and opened the door opposite the stair. The princess expected to see a lot of hens and chickens, but instead of that, she saw the blue sky first, and then the roofs of the house, with a multitude of the loveliest pigeons, mostly white, but of all colors, walking about making bows to each other and talking a language she could not understand. She clapped her hands with delight, and up rose such a flapping of wings that she in her turn was startled.

"You've frightened my poultry," said the old lady, smiling.

"And they've frightened me," said the princess, smiling too. "But what very nice poultry! Are the eggs nice?"

"Yes, very nice."

"What a small egg-spoon you must have! Wouldn't it be better to keep hens and get bigger eggs?"

"How should I feed them, though?"

"I see," said the princess. "The pigeons feed themselves. They've got wings."

"Just so. If they couldn't fly, I couldn't eat their eggs."

"But how do you get at the eggs? Where are their nests?"

The lady took hold of a little loop of string in the wall at the side of the door, and lifting a shutter showed a great many pigeon-holes with nests, some with young ones and some with eggs in them. The birds came in at the other side, and she took out the eggs on this side. She closed it again quickly, lest the young ones should be frightened.

"Oh, what a nice way!" cried the princess. "Will you give me an egg to eat? I'm rather hungry."

"I will some day, but now you must go back, or nursie will be miserable about you. I daresay she's looking for you everywhere."

"Except here," answered the princess. "Oh, how surprised she *will* be when I tell her about my great big grand-grandmother!"

"Yes, that she will!" said the old lady with a curious smile. "Mind you tell her all about it exactly."

"That I will. Please will you take me back to her?"

"I can't go all the way, but I will take you to the top of the stair, and then you must run down quite fast into your own room."

The little princess put her hand in the old lady's, who, looking this way and that, brought her to the top of the first stair, and thence to the bottom of the second, and did not leave her till she saw her halfway down the third. When she heard the cry of her nurse's pleasure at finding her, she turned and walked up the stairs again, very fast indeed for such a very great grandmother, and sat down to her spinning with another strange smile on her sweet old face.

Nothing more happened worth telling for some time. The autumn came and went by. There were no more

flowers in the garden. The winds blew strong, and
howled among the rocks. The rain fell, and drenched
the few yellow and red leaves that could not get off
the bare branches. Again and again there would be a
glorious morning followed by a pouring afternoon, and
sometimes, for a week together, there would be rain,
nothing but rain all day, and then the most lovely cloudless night, with the sky all out in full-blown stars—not
one missing. But the princess could not see much of
them, for she went to bed early. The winter drew on,
and she found things growing dreary. When it was too
stormy to go out, and she had got tired of her toys,
Lootie would take her about the house, sometimes to
the housekeeper's room, where the housekeeper, who
was a good, kind, old woman, made much of her—sometimes to the servants' hall or the kitchen, where she was
not princess merely, but absolute queen, and ran a great
risk of being spoiled. Sometimes she would run of herself to the room where the men-at-arms, whom the king
had left, sat, and they showed her their arms and ac-
coutrements, and did what they could to amuse her.
Still at times she found it very dreary, and often and
often wished that her huge great-grandmother had not
been a dream.

One morning the nurse left her with the housekeeper
for a while. To amuse her, she turned out the contents
of an old cabinet upon the table. The little princess
found her treasures, queer ancient ornaments and many
things the uses of which she could not imagine, far more
interesting than her own toys, and sat playing with them
for two hours or more. But at length, in handling a
curious old-fashioned brooch, she ran the pin of it into
her thumb, and gave a little scream with the sharpness
of the pain, but would have thought little more of it,
had not the pain increased and her thumb begun to
swell. This alarmed the housekeeper greatly. The nurse

was fetched; the doctor was sent for; her hand was poulticed, and long before her usual time she was put to bed. The pain still continued, and although she fell asleep and dreamed a good many dreams, there was the pain always in every dream. At last it woke her up.

The moon was shining brightly into the room. The poultice had fallen off her hand, and it was burning hot.

She fancied if she could hold it into the moonlight, that would cool it. So she got out of bed, without waking the nurse, who lay at the other end of the room, and went to the window. When she looked out, she saw one of the men-at-arms walking in the garden with the moonlight glancing on his armor. She was just going to tap on the window and call him, for she wanted to tell him all about it, when she bethought herself that that might wake Lootie, and she would put her into bed again. So she resolved to go to the window of another room, and call him from there. It was so much nicer to have somebody to talk to than to lie awake in bed with the burning pain in her hand. She opened the door very gently and went through the nursery, which did not look into the garden, to go to the other window. But when she came to the foot of the old staircase, there was the moon shining down from some window high

up, and making the worm-eaten oak look very strange
and delicate and lovely. In a moment she was putting
her little feet, one after the other, in the silvery path up
the stair, looking behind as she went, to see the shadow
they made in the middle of the silver. Some little girls
would have been afraid to find themselves thus alone
in the middle of the night, but Irene was a princess.

As she went slowly up the stairs, not quite sure that
she was not dreaming, suddenly a great longing woke
up in her heart to try once more whether she could not
find the old, old lady with the silvery hair.

"If she is a dream," she said to herself, "then I am the
likelier to find her, if I am dreaming."

So up and up she went, stair after stair, until she came
to the many rooms—all just as she had seen them before.
Through passage after passage she softly sped, comforting herself that if she should lose her way it would not
matter much, because when she woke she would find
herself in her own bed, with Lootie not far off. But as
if she had known every step of the way, she walked
straight to the door at the foot of the narrow stair that
led to the tower.

"What if I should realliality-really find my beautiful
old grandmother up there!" she said to herself, as she
crept up the steep steps.

When she reached the top, she stood a moment listening in the dark, for there was no moon there. Yes, it was!
It was the hum of the spinning-wheel! What a diligent
grandmother to work both day and night!

She tapped gently at the door.

"Come in, Irene," said the sweet voice.

The princess opened the door, and entered. There was
the moonlight streaming in at the window, and in the
middle of the moonlight sat the old lady in her black
dress with the white lace, and her silvery hair mingling
with the moonlight, so that you could not have distinguished one from the other.

"Come in, Irene," she said again. "Can you tell me what I am spinning?"

"She speaks," thought Irene, "just as if she had seen me five minutes ago, or yesterday at the farthest. —No," she answered; "I don't know what you are spinning. Please, I thought you were a dream. Why couldn't I find you before, great-great-grandmother?"

"That you are hardly old enough to understand. But you would have found me sooner if you hadn't come to think I was a dream. I will give you one reason, though, why you couldn't find me. I didn't want you to find me."

"Why, please?"

"Because I did not want Lootie to know I was here."

"But you told me to tell Lootie."

"Yes. But I knew Lootie would not believe you. If she were to see me sitting spinning here, she wouldn't believe me either."

"Why?"

"Because she couldn't. She would rub her eyes, and go away and say she felt queer, and forget half of it and more, and then say it had been all a dream."

"Just like me," said Irene, feeling very much ashamed of herself.

"Yes, a good deal like you, but not just like you; for you've come again; and Lootie wouldn't have come again. She would have said, no, no—she had had enough of such nonsense."

"Is it naughty of Lootie then?"

"It would be naughty of you. I've never done anything for Lootie."

"And you did wash my face and hands for me," said Irene, beginning to cry.

The old lady smiled a sweet smile and said: "I'm not vexed with you, my child—nor with Lootie either. But I don't want you to say anything more to Lootie about me. If she should ask you, you must just be silent. But I do not think she will ask you."

All the time they talked, the old lady kept on spinning. "You haven't told me yet what I am spinning," she said.

"Because I don't know. It's very pretty stuff."

It was indeed very pretty stuff. There was a good bunch of it on the distaff attached to the spinning-wheel, and in the moonlight it shone like—what shall I say it was like? It was not white enough for silver—yes, it was like silver, but shone gray rather than white, and glittered only a little. And the thread the old lady drew out from it was so fine that Irene could hardly see it.

"I am spinning this for you, my child."

"For me! What am I to do with it, please?"

"I will tell you by-and-by. But first I will tell you what it is. It is spider-webs—of a particular kind. My pigeons bring it to me from over the sea. There is only one forest where the spiders live who make this particular kind—the finest and strongest of any. I have nearly finished my present job. What is on the rack now will be quite sufficient. I have a week's work there yet, though," she added, looking at the bunch.

"Do you work all day and night too, great-great-great-great grandmother?" said the princess, thinking to be very polite with so many *greats*.

"I am not quite so great as all that," she answered, smiling almost merrily. "If you call me grandmother, that will do. —No, I don't work every night—only moonlit nights, and then no longer than the moon shines upon my wheel. I shan't work much longer to-night."

"And what will you do next, grandmother?"

"Go to bed. Would you like to see my bedroom?"

"Yes, that I should."

"Then I think I won't work any longer to-night. I shall be in good time."

The old lady rose, and left her wheel standing just as it was. You see there was no good in putting it away, for where there was not any furniture, there was no danger of being untidy.

Then she took Irene by the hand, but it was her bad hand, and Irene gave a little cry of pain.

"My child!" said her grandmother, "what is the matter?"

Irene held her hand into the moonlight, that the old lady might see it, and told her all about it, at which she looked grave. But she only said—"Give me your other hand"; and, having led her out upon the little dark landing, opened the door on the opposite side of it. What was Irene's surprise to see the loveliest room she had ever seen in her life! It was large and lofty and dome-shaped. From the center hung a lamp as round as a ball, shining as if with the brightest moonlight, which made everything visible in the room, though not so clearly that the princess could tell what many of the things were. A large oval bed stood in the middle, with a coverlid of rose-color, and velvet curtains all around it of a lovely pale blue. The walls were also blue—spangled all over with what looked like stars of silver.

The old lady left her, and going to a strange-looking cabinet, opened it and took out a curious silver casket. Then she sat down on a low chair, and, calling Irene, made her kneel before her, while she looked at her hand. Having examined it, she opened the casket, and took from it a little ointment. The sweetest odor filled the room—like that of roses and lilies—as she rubbed the ointment gently all over the hot swollen hand. Her touch was so pleasant and cool, that it seemed to drive away the pain and heat wherever it came.

"Oh, grandmother! It is *so* nice!" said Irene. "Thank you; thank you."

Then the old lady went to a chest of drawers, and took out a large handkerchief of gossamer-like cambric, which she tied around her hand.

"I don't think that I can let you go away to-night," she said. "Do you think you would like to sleep with me?"

"Oh, yes, yes, dear grandmother!" said Irene, and would have clapped her hands, forgetting that she could not.

"You won't be afraid then to go to bed with such an old woman?"

"No. You are so beautiful, grandmother."

"But I am *very* old."

"And I suppose I am very young. You won't mind sleeping with such a *very* young woman, grandmother?"

"You sweet little pertness!" said the old lady, and drew her toward her, and kissed her on the forehead and the cheek and the mouth.

Then she got a large silver basin, and having poured some water into it, made Irene sit on the chair, and washed her feet. This done, she was ready for bed. And, oh, what a delicious bed it was into which her grandmother laid her! She hardly could have told she was lying upon anything: she felt nothing but the softness. The old lady having undressed herself, lay down beside her.

"Why don't you put out your moon?" asked the princess.

"That never goes out, night or day," she answered. "In the darkest night, if any of my pigeons are out on a message, they always see my moon, and know where to fly to."

"But if somebody besides the pigeons were to see it— somebody about the house, I mean—they would come to look what it was, and find you."

"The better for them then," said the old lady. "But it does not happen above five times in a hundred years that anyone does see it. The greater part of those who do, take it for a meteor, wink their eyes, and forget it again. Besides, nobody could find the room except I pleased. Besides again—I will tell you a secret—if that light were to go out, you would fancy yourself lying in a bare garret, on a heap of old straw, and would not see one of the pleasant things round about you all the time."

"I hope it will never go out," said the princess.

"I hope not. But it is time we both went to sleep. Shall I take you in my arms?"

The little princess nestled close up to the old lady, who took her in both her arms, and held her close to her bosom.

"Oh, dear, this is so nice!" said the princess. "I didn't

know anything in the whole world could be so comfortable. I should like to lie here forever."

"You may if you will," said the old lady. "But I must put you to one trial—not a very hard one, I hope. This night week you must come back to me. If you don't, I do not know when you may find me again, and you will soon want me very much."

"Oh, please, don't let me forget."

"You shall not forget. The only question is whether you will believe I am anywhere—whether you will believe I am anything but a dream. You may be sure I will do all I can to help you to come. But it will rest with yourself, after all. On the night of next Friday, you must come to me. Mind now."

"I will try," said the princess.

"Then good-night," said the old lady, and kissed the forehead which lay in her bosom.

In a moment more the little princess was dreaming in the midst of the loveliest dreams—of summer seas and moonlight and mossy springs and great murmuring trees and beds of wild flowers with such odors as she had never smelled before. But after all, no dream could be more lovely than what she had left behind when she fell asleep.

In the morning she found herself in her own bed. There was no handkerchief or anything else on her hand, only a sweet odor lingering about it. The swelling had all gone down; the prick of the brooch had vanished— in fact her hand was perfectly well.

With the thread that she has been spinning, the old lady makes a magic ball for Irene. "If you find yourself in danger, follow the thread where it leads you," she tells the little princess. You can read about more of Irene's adventures in The Princess and Curdie, *published by The Macmillan Company.*

INDEX of Authors and Titles

ACKNOWLEDGMENTS

The publishers wish to express their appreciation to the following publishers, agents, authors, and artists who have granted permission to use material appearing in this book. Any errors or omissions are unintentional and will be corrected in future printings if notice is sent to The Crowell-Collier Publishing Company.

E. P. DUTTON & CO. "Winnie-the-Pooh," from *Winnie-the-Pooh,* by A. A. Milne, illustrated by E. H. Shepard, copyright 1926 by E. P. Dutton & Co.; 1954 by A. A. Milne; reprinted by permission of the publishers.

HARCOURT, BRACE & WORLD, INC. "The Borrowers," from *The Borrowers,* by Mary Norton, illustrated by Beth and Joe Krush, copyright 1952, 1953 by Mary Norton; used by permission of Harcourt, Brace & World, Inc.

HOLIDAY HOUSE, INC. *Mischief in Fez,* by Eleanor Hoffmann, illustrated by Fritz Eichenberg, copyright by Eleanor Hoffman, is reprinted by special arrangement with the original publisher, Holiday House, Inc.

ALFRED A. KNOPF, INC. "A Crime Wave in the Barnyard," reprinted from *Freddy the Detective,* by Walter R. Brooks, illustrated by Kurt Wiese, copyright 1932 by Walter R. Brooks; by permission of Alfred A. Knopf, Inc.

J. B. LIPPINCOTT COMPANY Illustrations by Anne Heyneman from *Pinocchio,* by Carlo Collodi, copyright 1945 by J. B. Lippincott Company; by permission of J. B. Lippincott Company.

THE MACMILLAN COMPANY OF CANADA, AND MACMILLAN COMPANY, LTD. Illustrations by Sir John Tenniel from *Alice in Wonderland,* reproduced in Canada by permission of Macmillan and Company, Ltd., and The Macmillan Company of Canada.

THE MACMILLAN COMPANY "The Old Lady's Bedroom," from *The Princess and the Goblin* by George MacDonald, illustrated by Nora S. Unwin, copyright 1951 by The Macmillan Company; used by permission of The Macmillan Company.

CHARLES SCRIBNER'S SONS "The Mermaid's Lagoon," from *Peter Pan,* by James M. Barrie, copyright 1911, 1921, 1939, 1949 by Lady Cynthia Asquith and Peter L. Davies; "Mr. Toad," text reprinted from and illustrations reproduced from *The Wind in the Willows* by Kenneth Grahame, illustrated by E. H. Shepard, copyright 1908, 1933, 1953 by Charles Scribner's Sons; used by permission of Charles Scribner's Sons.

THE VIKING PRESS, INC. "Miss Hickory," from *Miss Hickory,* by Carolyn Sherwin Bailey, illustrated by Ruth Gannett, copyright 1946 by Carolyn Sherwin Bailey; "Twenty-One Balloons," from *The Twenty-One Balloons,* written and illustrated by William Pene du Bois, copyright 1947 by William Pene du Bois; reprinted by permission of The Viking Press, Inc.

THE WORLD PUBLISHING COMPANY Illustrations by Fritz Kredel from *The King of the Golden River,* by John Ruskin (Rainbow Classics Series), reproduced by permission of The World Publishing Company, Cleveland and New York.